# APPROACHING THE SWINGULARITY

TALES OF
SWINGING & POLYAMORY
IN PARADISE

COOPER S. BECKETT

HUMP &
CIRCUM
STANCE

Cover Illustration by Corbett Vanoni

Published Internationally by Hump and Circumstance Printed in the United States

ISBN: 978-1-946876-00-3

BISAC: Fiction / Literary

Hump & Circumstance Press Chicago, Illinois

CooperSBeckett.com

*For a place that still amazes me*
*And the people who make it home*

# PART I

*Old Friends*

# 1

## RYAN

Foam gushes forth from the two-foot-wide nozzle on the end of the pipe and slams into Ryan Lambert. The surprising weight of the white suds shoves him under, forcing him to confront his notions of how smart this idea was. Bobbing like an astronaut below the surface of the pool, he centers himself and looks out on a vast showcase of legs, genitalia, and the lower crescents of breasts. He closes his eyes and tries to focus on the fact that he's trying new things and isn't that wonderful? He manages a moment unbroken, mere seconds, with a smile on his face. This serenity begins to erode as the single breath he's holding nears its end, reminding him of the inevitable: He'll have to return to the surface soon, to be surrounded by foam once again.

His throat tightens.

He considers that entering directly below the spout of the machine creating the foam may not have been the ideal way for him to "hold his breath and jump," his go-to mantra for trying new things. Could've waded in from the shallows and still considered it trying new things. The jump need not have been literal.

His breath spent, Ryan stands and breaks the surface of the water with a gasp. Tiny bubbles fill his mouth and throat, their oxygen delivery method decidedly unhelpful. Ryan hacks, and the panic begins to rise. He reaches straight up and cannot feel a ceiling to the foam. His mind races, catching itself on a thought of the swim goggles sitting atop the bathing suit he reasoned he wouldn't need at a "clothing optional" resort, left behind in the middle drawer of his dresser at home.

To quell the rising panic, he tries to be in the moment again. To revel. He hears the steady rumble of the machine, accompanied by the giggles and gasps of nude revelers around him, and the *umph-umph-umph-umph* of the nondescript background music pumping out of speakers throughout the resort. The vast weighty white that fills his vision and has wormed its way into his ears muffles all of these sounds. His cough clears out a small spherical margin between him and the foam, and he can breathe in shallow and short breaths for the moment.

Progress. His breathing eases.

He brings his hands up and clears foam from his face, then carves away some in front of him, increasing his margin and lessening the feeling of being smothered. As his sphere expands, he breathes easier, feeling a flush of pride at his decision to brave the spout.

He almost didn't go in at all, preferring to watch from his pool chair as staff rushed around the rumbling red machine with *¡Fiesta de la Espuma!* in sharp yellow letters on the side. Disconcerting power cables and extension cords ran along the edge of the pool to the machine. The man in the red *¡Fiesta de la Espuma!* T-shirt required the assistance of several resort staff members to get it running in the first place, and after twenty minutes of wispy foam dribbling out and floating away, a belch of suds finally indicated that *la fiesta de la espuma* was imminent.

He watched from his pool chair as the foam flowed, hitting the blue surface of the deep end and spreading toward the revelers waiting by the submerged bar in the shallows. As they sipped their last-call pre-foam drinks, they threw furtive glances between the bar and the foam. Ryan knew that once the foam blanketed the pool, it would be oppressive, claustrophobic.

His wife Jenn's exuberant laugh when she saw the rising foam meant he didn't need to ask, "What do you think?" She would go in with or without him. He kept his apprehension about claustrophobia to a mere mention. Moments later she went, her naked body vanishing into the pool and the foam and the revelry. To be as free as his Jenn, well, he had to take chances and risks, didn't he? Risks greater than simply being out in the sun, fully exposed here for the first time this week without scrim or umbrella or grassy roof to protect his pallid body. He wasn't certain how much he trusted the SPF 60 either. Not with the bits that had so rarely seen the sun, anyway. The glistening of the sun off his cock, which he'd slathered in sunscreen, conjured a psychosomatic sizzle.

Facing the weenie roast on the pool deck, or the undulating white unknown of *la fiesta de la espuma,* he wandered the resort to clear his head, or to find courage, or to find other firsts, before returning to the pool and dropping directly into the foam deluge.

Now he seems to be the only person in the pool, despite the din of people and music and machine thrumming. Auditory illusions, maybe. How would he know otherwise? He drops below the water again to reassure himself and opens his eyes, wincing at the chlorine. Damned worthless middle-drawer goggles. Sure enough, there are people all around. Some close enough to touch. But he mustn't do that, of course.

Without swimsuits to jog his memory like they were name tags, the sea of pale and tan and brown and freckled and sunburnt flesh does little to let him know where he should head. For a moment, he vainly tries to pick out someone he knows based on pubic hair alone. He's certain he's seen that little bushy heart before, but uncertain on whom. He doesn't see Jenn's landing strip, or Paige's red patch, proclaimed "Firebush" at the welcome festivities two days prior. Maybe he could find a signpost uncircumcised cock? But then what? Shake it hello?

Nope.

Ryan breaches the surface again with no idea what to do beyond stand still in this netherworld of foam. He's uncertain quite how to reach *la fiesta* portion of this *fiesta de la espuma.* His tiny oasis has vanished during his submersion, and he chokes on another inhalation of foam.

Hands appear on his shoulders then move down his back. Jenn emerges from the white, sliding her arm around him. His wife wears a broad smile. The water plasters her short chestnut hair to her cheeks. Her perky pink nipples bob just above the waterline.

As quickly as she's appeared, the foam has filled her entrance. They stand beneath a dome of white as though they are the only two people in the world. She brings her face close to his, and he sees that the combination of foam and chlorine has stripped her light makeup, yet she glows even more than she had last night, done-up to-the-nines with fake lashes and red lipstick. A lock of her hair hangs over her right eye, the pink lock, dyed at two in the morning before their 9:00 AM flight to Cancún.

He loves it.

He loves her.

"Breathe," she tells him. "Just not too deep. Shallow breaths don't draw in the bubbles."

He nods again.

"How's the claustrophobia?"

How *is* the claustrophobia? Well, he's impressed that, despite the mild panic of the bubble inhalation, he hasn't spiraled off screaming "I'm done! Get me out of here!" Though maybe that isn't the most ringing endorsement. Instead, he tells her, "Not bad."

"See, I told you it'd be fun."

He can't say it's been "fun" thus far. Interesting. Not dull. *Oh, don't be* that *guy,* he tells himself.

Jenn scoops a handful of foam and blows it toward the apex of their dome. She giggles as the foam separates into dozens of tiny bubbles. He wishes he could be so enthusiastic and open. He wishes instead that he didn't see the fact that their dome is shrinking. The foam pushes against the back of his neck and ears. Soon it'll spill over and block his hearing, and as it crawls around his temples to his eyes, the panic will return. Then he'll start—

Her hand finds his cheek, giving him a gentle caress. She tucks the pink lock of hair behind her ear and purses her lips, kissing him gently on the nose, then lips. The kiss deepens, and he feels her other hand slide down his stomach, through his patch of pubic hair, and encircle his hardening cock. Her right moves from his cheek to the back of his head, fingers spreading and grasping at his hair.

Ryan takes a deep breath through his nose. No foam drifts in as Jenn's increasingly powerful strokes have caused their dome to expand. At once she stops, her hazel eyes glistening, her grin broad.

Ryan stares at her, noticing how vivid the flecks of brown in her eyes appear. Beyond that he sees intensity, hunger. "What?" he asks.

"Let's do the thing," she says. Her strokes resume, now slow and deep.

"What thing?" Ryan realizes the answer to his question as he asks it.

Bareback.

Fluid bonding.

The conversation came up at dinner the night before, at La Grande Fête, the fanciest of restaurants on the resort. "Do you have any concerns about ditching condoms?" she asked.

Ryan quickly swallowed a mouthful of lobster ravioli and coughed.

"Sorry," she said. "Out of left field, I know."

He gulped some wine to quell the coughing. When he regained his composure, he asked, "For us, or..."

"For us. I'm not asking if you have philosophical concerns." She put her napkin on the table and folded her hands in front of her. "I've got the Mirena now, and that's pretty much foolproof. And we're both STD free. Is it just inertia at this point?"

Ryan considered the question. Early in their relationship, he'd been so paranoid about the minuscule failure rate of hormonal birth control that he'd continued to use condoms while she used the pill. After that, well, it become how they rolled, hadn't it? The Lamberts used condoms. Paige had raved about her IUD and the magical elimination of periods, so Jenn had one put in late last year. Extra foolproof, now, and mitigated pregnancy risk in case of condom breakage with Jenn's other male partners. But to the question at hand, in their time together, "I'll grab the condoms," had just been their rote response to "Let's have sex."

"I can't think of any argument for keeping condoms that doesn't sound dramatically paranoid," he said. "Even more paranoid than usual for me."

The conversation paused due to the dramatic entrance of Kendra and Vince de Martolos, Kendra wearing a dress cut down to her navel that displayed her ample cleavage in spectacular fashion. Both Ryan and Jenn stopped, losing the thread of their bareback discussion.

Under the dome of foam, Ryan smiles and pulls his wife to him. The words don't need to be repeated, as their reasons for extra-cautious sex feel so unnecessary now. She moves her hands to his shoulders, and hops, wrapping her legs around his hips.

"You sure?" she asks.

"I'm sure," he replies.

This is their week of adventure, after all; adventure and trying their best to avoid roadblocks. Her roadblock involves work, and they're doing their best not to let it follow them here. His roadblock looks like anxiety and paranoia, and there's no leaving that at home for Ryan Lambert. He can try to follow the example Jenn has set since they first decided to open their relationship nearly two years ago, to change their lives, to hold hands and jump into the deep end. Because they'd been no longer content to "just live."

"Rory kissed me," he says. "Thought you should know."

Jenn coughs and laughs. "Would you like to elaborate?"

"Not at the moment," he says. "There are more pressing matters."

Here in this deep end, surrounded by foam, he addresses a more pressing issue. He slides his cock inside her, making a point to feel every sensation he's never felt sans condom, to let them register on a deeper level. Her warmth. Her wetness. The soft texture of her body. The faint throb of her heartbeat. How slippery it all is. "You're really wet," he says, with a wink.

She scrunches her nose at him. "Paige told me to always put some silicone lube inside before you get into the pool."

"That's a good life hack," he says with a gasp as Jenn tightens her legs around him, arches her back, and gloriously fucks him. The Lamberts share their first condomless sex surrounded by foam, in the deep end of the pool that sits at the center of the one hundred and eleven rooms that make up Aphrodite's Resort and Spa on the Riviera Maya in Cancún, Mexico.

She slides her nails across his shoulder blades. She tilts her head back, and that lock of pink slips from behind her ear as her eyelids flutter. He puts his hands on her thighs, helping her grind, moving her body against his, with his. He feels the nearing orgasm, brought on far more quickly than usual. For a moment, his mind starts to tick through the reasons he'll be coming so quickly. *First time without condoms. New sensations. I just can't—*

"You gonna come?" she asks, eyes locked onto his. Her pelvis grinds against him in that wonderfully painful way. He realizes he can feel her G-spot's textured surface rubbing against the top of his cock, bumping against the ridge of his head as he slides in and out.

Unable to speak, especially after that exquisite new sensation, always muted before by latex or polyisoprene, he flings his head in an enthusiastic and erratic nod.

"You should do it then." She grins. "Come inside me."

Come inside. The recognition of the moment hits him. What it is, what it means. He's about to mention how momentous it— "God," he says, elongating the o into an exultation. He thrusts involuntarily as the sublime spasms rock through him.

His wife clamps her legs tighter, eyes widening. "I can feel it!" she exclaims and giggles. "Inside!"

As he comes, his orgasm lasting longer than usual, his brain disconnects. He can see it all at once. The first time he ever had sex with her, short and sweet, and surprisingly romantic so long ago. This moment melds and merges with everything they've done in the last two years, all the exploration and adventure, all bringing them closer, building on the connections, and now, finally, with no more barriers between them. As the flashings quicken and he spasms the last time, he sees them three days prior, at the moment of their arrival at the resort, the start of this adventure, when Marisol handed them a flute of champagne and said, "Welcome home." He snickered then at the flowery sentiment, but gets it here and now.

He is home.

Tears of joy flow down his face.

Some may also be due to ocular irritation from the foam.

# 2

# BRUCE

The cell phone rests in Bruce Shepard's lap.

"She is not your— *our* responsibility," Paige tells him. She stands in the open doorway for a moment, waiting, the sounds of the evening on the resort drifting past. He looks at his wife and finds himself unable to respond with anything more substantial than a sigh. The powerful phone vibration draws his attention back down. The screen flashes a notification displaying her name. **Emily**. The door clicks shut, and he knows without looking up that Paige has left him here. Here with the phone. Here with Emily.

He should get up. Right now. Put his phone back in the safe. Throw on his blazer. Go to dinner. Eat sushi with that sexy couple they met earlier today. Alexis and, shit, what was his name? Bruce hates that. He had an entire conversation with Alexis's husband, but can't quite remember the gentleman's name. Paige knows, of course; she always does, whether interested in the person or not. But to get that information he'll have to ask, and the mood she's in...That's not fair. Paige isn't "in a mood," she is justifiably upset with him. For sitting here in their suite instead of walking arm-in-arm with her to dinner. Sitting here holding his goddamned phone.

As if on cue, the vibrations begin anew, and **Emily-Cell** comes up. Another call, not a text message. This intrusion includes a picture of Emily Laurel, forty now, ages from the girl they met once upon a time, from that firecracker twenty-four-year-old who changed everything. His reconnection with her after so long began less than a week before their trip, when she sent him the photo that now appears on the screen. In the photo, Emily's raven-black hair hangs around her face, literal feet shorter than it had been when last Bruce saw it in person. The signs of age are nearly invisible on her, with none of the culture-shock-momentary-dysphoria that can accompany seeing someone again after such a long time gap.

Bruce hits the red phone icon, and Emily's picture vanishes as the screen goes dark. The silence is loud in the room, the undertone of the air conditioner. He should put his phone in the safe, right now. That's the right way to play it.

The walk to Rakuen, the resort's sushi restaurant, is short enough that Paige has undoubtedly already arrived. He can see her, standing there in that backless dress, explaining to Alexis and... *C'mon, man.* Alexis and...

"Fuck." He throws his phone onto the bed behind him, narrowly missing the towel-art erection the maid left while they were at hot-tub-happy-hour. "Malcolm," he says under his breath, then nods. "Alexis and Malcolm." Explaining to Alexis and Malcolm that he is staying in the room and will be missing their reservation because he is too busy talking to an old—

He pauses. That's an excellent question. What is Emily? An old girlfriend? A former lover? Their triad completion? Once, maybe. What is she now, though? This new Emily Laurel who spent a decade as Emily Fitzgibbons in Green Bay, Wisconsin, and insists that name is not long for this world. This new Emily Laurel in crisis. Though when has Emily not come accompanied by crisis?

He glances at the phone, precariously perched on the edge of the mattress. He lifts it and stares into the black mirror.

*Dinner*, he reminds himself. *Dinner then dancing.* And if Alexis looks half as good in the disco as she did on the beach this morning, strolling in the sunshine, he'll...well, he'll enjoy himself thoroughly. That is, if the trio taking their seats for dinner hasn't written him off. Malcolm is probably thanking Aphrodite herself that he doesn't have to share these two stunning women with another man tonight. Because that other man now sits on the edge of the bed in his suite, khakis on, belt not even buckled.

All preparation for dinner stopped, earlier, when the phone began to buzz. Paige grabbed it out of the safe.

"The kids?" he asked, drying his freshly shaven cheeks.

"Now she's calling you," Paige said, her voice flat. She didn't offer the phone to him.

He threw his towel over his shoulder and waited, holding his wife's sharp stare. After a moment, he reached out. The buzz of the phone vibration overpowered the sound of the air conditioner. When Paige still didn't hand over the phone, he shook his hand in her direction. She slapped the phone into his palm hard enough to make him wince.

"I don't like this," she said.

*I know,* he thought, but said nothing.

Now he sits in the empty room and stares at the dark phone. He and Paige have prided themselves on being the very definition of disconnecting vacationers. The phone is only left on for the boys. Hunter has the house to himself this week, and Bruce doesn't trust that Adam's offer to check in on him would lead to anything other than a hot tub party. This would be okay, of course, but there must be a lifeline if the boys need Mom and Dad.

Day one the disconnect had worked. Day two the first text had appeared. A barely heard *bloop* while grabbing the room key.

**I know you're away and you said not to,** texted Emily. **Mike emptied our account. I just need...someone.**

"Someone," emphasized Paige, after reading it. "Does that make you feel important?"

"Hey," said Bruce, holding up his hands in a defensive pose.

"She'll vanish again. You watch."

Emily's texts continued through dinner that night. Would he ruin another dinner for Emily, tonight? Would he let her ruin another?

"That's it," he says, standing. He has already let this go on for far too long, let it become too much. He throws the towel into the bathroom and goes to the closet. He runs his fingers along the hanging shirts, selecting a pale blue bamboo-cotton button down. With the shirt on, his belt buckled, shoes in hand, Bruce puts the phone back into the safe and closes its door. He manages to hit the one and seven, the first half of their go-to room safe code, before the vibration begins anew. He pauses and sighs. Again. Again. Again.

Bruce opens the safe and takes the phone out. She'll keep calling. Keep calling until he answers or until the phone's battery dies. Bruce doesn't think he can outlast it.

"I really can't do this right now, Emily."

He hears her breath catch, sure she hadn't expected him to actually answer. "Bruce!" she exclaims. That voice saying his name raises goosebumps on his arms. Her voice. Her voice in panic and crisis. He can't remember the last time he spoke to her. Their communication in this cycle has all been digital. He sighs.

"I'm sorry. I know. I'm sorry. But I don't have anybody else."

Her voice takes him back to the kitchen table of their first house, almost sixteen years ago, when Emily said, with similar urgency, "I don't know what it would mean, but I want to have a relationship with you both. Like, more than friends."

Paige flopped onto the chair next to Emily, as that revelation, that idea, was the very thing she'd been talking about with him, but had no clue how to approach the conversation with Emily. Emily, her assistant. Emily, their nanny. Uncertain what to say himself in response to the revelation, Bruce was thankful when Adam, then two, blasted his way through the kitchen, holding two toy trucks over his head. Always grateful for a distraction to give him time to think.

He has no such distraction now, at Aphrodite's Resort and Spa in Cancún. No way out, save ending this conversation. Doing what he ought to and severing this connection. "Emily, I have to go," he says.

"Wait!"

"I'm on vacation, and you've upset Paige—"

"I never want to upset her, I just—"

"I know you don't. But right now, me being on the phone with you isn't making it better." Bruce runs his hand down his face and waits for a response.

She takes a while before saying, "I know."

"I have to go. And you need to stop contacting us for now. At least until we're back in the States."

Silence on the line. Maybe she too is hoping for a distraction.

"I need to know you hear me, Emily."

He hears a sniffle in reply. Then the muffled and choked sound of a sob.

His heart lurches. Always the crying, and he'll always be the sucker. She knows. She must know. What this does to him. How to melt him. How to make him drop his guard. How to make him say, "Shh, it's alright. Don't cry." He says it before he realizes that he's doing it. He plays right in. He falls for it. "I need to—" he starts, but she cuts him off.

"You were the only ones who were ever good to me," she says, in-between deep sniffles. "When we were together. When we were whole."

Bruce feels heat in his throat, the beginnings of anger. For her to use that phrase, now. Whole. That phrase they'd used during the good times. Back then he and Paige had been waiting for the final pieces without knowing how it might look. Emily completed the puzzle. Such tripe in retrospect, such squishy poly fairytale nonsense.

"Nope," he says, slapping his other hand down onto his knee. "Not going to have this conversation with you, Emily. Not going to. You're upset, and for that I'm sorry. I empathize with what you're going through. But as I am in another country, with my wife, with our friends, there is nothing I can do for you at this moment." He pauses, unsure what response from her would satisfy him. Thankfully Emily remains silent. "So, while I will be happy to communicate with you in the future via the occasional text, not here. And I need to ask you to respect that you cannot call us any—"

"You were the only ones I loved."

There it was. Emily had saved it. Just a little longer. Just until it would knock him on his ass. His mouth hangs, with the second half of his word waiting to be said. He feels the door inside him, the one he's been trying to shut, slide back open. Someone has jammed her scuffed red Chuck Taylor All-Star into the doorway.

"Fuck," he says, dropping the phone from his face.

"Bruce?" comes her quiet voice from the speaker.

He moves his thumb up and presses the red phone, ending the call.

## 3

# PAIGE

Emily knows what she's doing, Paige Shepard is confident of that. Just as she has known in the past. One doesn't simply wander in like a cyclone and then back out again without having some idea of the destruction she leaves in her wake. Such consistent a pattern over the years. Over the many years. Seventeen now.

Or is it possible she doesn't know?

*Focus, Paige!* Yes, she really should, shouldn't she? After all, there are only so many multis she can task. Emily shouldn't be allowed to be one of them. Not here at Aphrodite's. Not almost fifteen hundred miles away. Not after what she did last year. Not after the way she—

Paige's eyes roll up, and she bites her lip. A gentle nibble, of course, one wouldn't want to draw blood, certainly not when one is in such a delicate position. Her hand finds Malcolm's smooth pate, feels the beginnings of stubble across his dome. She holds him against her. He intensifies his tongue movements in response. She feels the tickle of wispy black curls on the tip of her nose and nuzzles forward.

She made clear to Emily last year, as clear as one can make things via text, that this last time was, well, the last time. **I don't want you to come back. For real. Not ever.** Sure, a little like the old "you can't break up with me, I'm breaking up with you" trick, but Paige had to say something. After the bad influence comment. After the slut comment. That one still pings her if she's not careful, if she can't block it.

(slut)

*Fuck, he's good at this*, she thinks, pulling herself back, away from the memory and the unwelcome ping, and grips his head with fingers splayed. She realizes that Alexis is unlikely to think the same of her if she doesn't focus.

Emily is still mucking up the place, isn't she? Even thousands of miles away, even without direct contact, she's getting in the way. She's just wedging herself between Paige and Bruce; between Paige and playmates, lovers, friends. Emily. Always Emily. She's a window Paige can look through at the rest of the world. But she's always there, always between. Like distorted glass.

Paige resolves to do better here in the present, here with this lovely woman, as another shudder rocks through her body. She slides her tongue along the entire beautiful length of Alexis's brown labia. The thighs on either side of her face tremble, and Alexis's fingers twist a length of Paige's curly hair. There we go. Better now. More of that. More of that and Alexis will come. More of that and the focus can drift, can shift away.

Away from Emily. Emily who isn't here, after all. Emily who's set her shingle back out in their minds. Emily who has no business, no right. Not after last time. Or the time before.

Paige's tongue slides along Alexis's vulva, hitting every fold, *majora*, *minora*. Circling the clit, darting under the hood. There we go. Tremors building for both of them. Another spasm rocks through Paige and her hand clenches on Malcolm's bald head, shoving him closer. His tongue dances in and out of her own *majora* and *minora*, faster and faster. His thumb presses against her—

Boom!

The orgasmic surge shudders through Paige's body. She wraps her legs around Malcolm, realizing that she never removed her shoes. She tries to adjust so she doesn't drag these spiky heels down Malcolm's back. He takes her shudder as confirmation and tightens the hold of his left arm around her thigh, going deeper. She feels his nose pressing against her pubic bone. That can't be comfortable for—

Boom!

The second surge makes her wobbly, and she presses her forehead just below Alexis's belly button to recompose. Malcolm has slid his thumb inside her ass, and the third surge to hit causes her to push it deep. For a moment, she feels him touch his thumb with his tongue through the wall. Through her wall. Then a fourth surge. She squeezes her eyes shut and uses the momentum of this surge to redouble her efforts on Alexis. She reaches up and runs her nails down this woman's beautiful back. Alexis's fingers slide over Paige's scalp, through her hair, and she shudders from that alone.

No easy task, being the center. People talk about how hard focus can be when you're sixty-nining, but they don't speak of being the center of the threesome, giving and receiving. So many people to please. Over the years, she's gotten better at the dual foci. To allow yourself to feel pleasure and give it, to be present. That's it, isn't it? Presence. If you allow yourself to drift too far, someone's liable to come out disappointed. If you allow yourself memories.

Memories of that time.

With that girl.

Her assistant.

Their nanny.

With Emily.

Fuck.

They lived at the small house, then. The box with five rooms. Cozy, though. So much to love, in fact. Their first house. But with Hunter due soon, so damned soon after they had Adam, it'd be way too small. They never intended two kids so quickly, just the one. Then, maybe someday. And Emily wanted to help. To help her. More than just coordinating at the office. More than just managing her planner. *We fucked the babysitter, the secretary. We ran the fantasy board, didn't we?*

*Stoppit!*

Alexis's thighs clench and squeeze. Her ears blocked, Paige loses contact with the outside world. She feels the disorienting sensation of floating away. She wishes she could embrace that drift, become nothing but an umbilicus between Alexis and Malcolm. Send and receive pleasure. Without a care, without a sound, without

(Emily)

needing to spend so much time in her head.

She closes her eyes and feels everything in a moment. The

smoothness of Alexis's labia on her tongue. The wispy pubic hair against her nose. How soft Alexis's thighs are. The evening shadow stubble on Malcolm's cheeks. The much finer evening shadow on his head. His thumb deep inside her ass, sliding against her inside. His tongue going deeper than she feels is rightly possible. Dexterously flicking. Such sensation. Such—

Boom!

*Thank Christ!* The fifth surge takes her the rest of the way, bringing with it the buildup, the sensation of the dam about to break. She taps Malcolm's head in warning. *We've gotta squall comin' in!* He doesn't relent. She wonders if Alexis can feel her smile. There's nothing so blackboard-clearing, nothing so mind-scrambling as her gushing orgasms. If only she could—

She'd never seen a woman ejaculate before Emily did it. Emily said it all came down to the G-spot, then slid her finger inside and pressed against the top of Paige's vaginal canal.

"Can you feel it?"

Paige felt pressure. Wasn't sure exactly what specifically she should be feeling. Not that night, of course. Not that month, either. But when the dam broke, she'd been with Emily. She soaked clean through to the mattress. And the blackboard cleared. Because Emily had helped, hadn't she? She came into their lives and made things better. She was a nexus, a point on which they could rely. The center of new and different things for her and Bruce. Swinging was a sport, a hobby, after all. Something they did on weekends.

*What'd you do last weekend, Rick?*

*Played thirty-six holes, you?*

*Orgy.*

But Emily. Well, they didn't know what to call that new thing with Emily. When they were whole. They just knew what to call it when it ended. A genuine breakup. Not just the fade-away or the "we got busy" they'd experienced in swinging. But a breakup that hurt like a motherfucker. That made them all—

*You're not fucking going to cry while a lovely man is eating your pussy and his lovely wife is riding your face, do you hear me?* She squeezes her eyes shut to hold back the tears. Tears for Emily. *Fuck that!*

Paige Shepard wraps her arms around Alexis's thighs and dives deep. She squeezes her own on either side of Malcolm's head, sending the message down through the neural network,

"Let's fucking do this!" She feels him nod against her and bring his other hand up. Now there are fingers inside her, both sides. The new fingers rub that spot, the one that Emily helped her discover. As Paige helped Jenn.

But Emily isn't here now. Malcolm and Alexis are. And they're going to push her over. And the dam will break. And the blackboard will clear. Will clear off that one thing. That one word. That one name. Emily.

The surge reaches its apex, and Paige lets go. The ping from the past diminishes and fades, barely a word now. The name and face go too, and all that's left are these three, this connection of circuits from Malcolm's toes to the top of Alexis's head, and here, in the middle, is Paige.

The three fall apart to the bed, breathing heavily, smiles on their faces.

Lying here, head finally clear, Paige hopes that Bruce also found whatever he needed to clear his own head.

## 4

# JENN

Jennifer Lambert, lately Jenn, feels as though she's come unstuck in time. She feels relief at that rather than panic, and while the looming specter of her job and all that accompanies it isn't gone, it's more muted than it has been all week. She sees her hair hanging above her head, above as she hangs down, upside down. Her hair, shorter than she's ever worn it as an adult, doesn't quite touch the floor below her. The lock of Manic Panic Hot Hot Pink is vivid even in the dim light of the playroom. Bare legs, feet, inches from her, inches from that lock of Hot Hot Pink. Right there. All right there.

*Today is Tuesday, isn't it?* She doesn't know the answer to the question that her mind seems to have asked itself. She's also unsure if she could reconstruct anything resembling a timeline of the last few days since they arrived here and were welcomed home. If today is indeed Tuesday, then this is day four of the trip. Half-way. But everything that has come so far feels shuffled and re-dealt. Everything shadows, hazy. She wishes she'd had the foresight to write everything down.

She wonders why she doesn't journal anymore, why she's so in her head? The job thing, sure, but—

A gasp escapes her lips, and she follows it with a low moan. Her eyes roll up as she leaves her head, and her body if one believes in such things. By and large, Jenn doesn't, but here, at this moment, in this place, well, one would be foolish to rule out concepts like transcendence. The woman between her legs continues a spectacular showy act of enthusiastic cunnilingus as Jenn hangs in the sex swing with her head down low.

She sees feet turn toward her. An audience of feet standing on the ceiling. Her companion's munching and her liquid enjoyment of that munching seems to have become a show for other playroom denizens. For those who've finished their part in the orgy, those yet to begin, and those for whom voyeurism is their chosen form of participation. She wonders if her enthusiasm is too showy, but as she grabs a clump of Zoë's springy hair, she discards the notion with *So what?* Zoë's vigor intensifies, spurred by the grab, and her tongue goes deep.

This time Jenn's moan isn't quiet and includes that rare religious proclamation, "Yes, God!" Whatever that means. Jenn brings her other hand to her forehead, then presses it against the floor in nearly a headstand as her back arches further. Arms encircle her thighs as Zoë reclaims the dominant role in this interaction. Jenn feels the early indicators deep inside, the wave growing, the intensification.

"I'm a squirter," she told Zoë during their pre-cunnilingus negotiation.

"Excellent," said Zoë with a grin. She grabbed an extra towel, throwing it over her shoulders and around her neck like a boxer after a bout. "Let's do this."

Perception tends to get a bit wibbly-wobbly when Jenn nears squirting. When compounded with the cumulative effect of these four days on the resort so far, the unsticking in time and the missing moments seem just right.

Paige proclaimed it sex brain when Jenn mentioned it to her. "I think when we find ourselves going outside the margins of experience, we go into another space."

Jenn scoffed. "Since when are you woo-woo."

"Not woo-woo," Paige insisted, "just acknowledging that it's possible for something to happen that's so awesome it knocks you out of the world a little. Into someplace other." She grinned and continued. "Fully inside your head, here, darling. Like when you were little, and vacation moved so fast, but the last day of school moved so slow. Our brains oversee our perceptions of time."

Jenn's perception is indeed a moving target right now. To realize that she and Ryan are here, at Aphrodite's Resort and

Spa, a place often spoken of in hushed tones as "that resort," less than two years since they first discovered the big scary hedonistic world of swinging, is quite overwhelming. Especially hanging in a sex swing in the resort playroom, surrounded by fellow orgy participants, beds full of undulating revelers around her, those toes and feet and legs of people standing at attention around her and her playmate, watching her get off. Watching Zoë work her, waiting for the promised explosive finale, for the watershed.

Unstuck in time seems like the bare minimum of feels appropriate for this act of carnality that honors its location. In-between swells, the rising of her wave, the impending finale, she wonders how Ryan's evening has gone and sighs, thinking about reconnecting over an espresso martini or two with him later. He's off with Lydia, a woman he actually pursued despite his deep-rooted anxiety. Pursued the way Zoë went after her.

"I've been watching you," Zoë told her, in the courtyard. Had it been yesterday? Today? Time's relentless refusal to align itself suggests that it could've been decades ago. Then, it seemed, embarrassment hit Zoë, and she clarified. "I mean, not in a creepy way. Just..." she sighed. "It's hard to talk to girls."

Jenn agreed. Luckily most women in her life have approached her initially. Had Paige not made her interest clear, well, things might have been entirely different.

"I just meant that I noticed you, and wanted to come and tell you I wanted to talk to you. And maybe we could do that, sometime. You know, talk."

"I noticed you too," Jenn replied with a smile. Zoë had been hard to miss, since the welcome on day one, glasses, freckles, with curls of chestnut brown hair down to her shoulder blades. Jenn had taken note. "And I'd also like to talk. And other stuff."

Zoë beamed, her face radiating relief and barely masked sexual hunger. They talked, and flirted, and nuzzled, and kissed, and now here they are, together at the mid-week orgy. When all of time refuses to align, Jenn can at least be assured that in this moment, she is about to explode. This moment at least is now.

Zoë changes up her technique yet again and dives back in with a new ferocity. The wave breaks and Jenn gushes, sending her orgasmic wave cascading across Zoë's face and over her shoulders, dripping down onto the towel that Jenn spread on the floor in eager anticipation.

Even unstuck in time, Jenn tries to be a prepared and polite guest.

After the rolling waves go on and on for minutes maybe hours, Jenn feels the moment where she must stop, or else become dehydrated. Between ecstatic shudders, she pushes against the floor with one hand and reaches up with the other in a fluid motion that impresses her probably more than anyone watching. The gushing is usually more than enough to astonish onlookers. She catches the straps of the swing and takes herself back to a sitting position, looking down between her legs at Zoë.

A surprised laugh bursts from Jenn's mouth when she sees that at some point, unbeknownst to her, Zoë had put on the massive purple-lensed steam-punk goggles she brought for yesterday's foam party. She makes a show of pulling the sopping wet towel off her shoulders and wiping down each goggle-eye, then stands and embraces Jenn. Their tongues mingle, and Jenn can taste herself.

Not long ago, that very idea would've appalled her, to taste herself from "down there." But in that same "not so long ago" time, letting someone new get so up close and personal with her, to put their face between her legs, would've also been unthinkable. And a *girl* at that! So much has changed, after all. She and Ryan are very different people now than the couple they'd been with their status quo marriage and sex life. Such emotional children they'd been when they wandered into a Christmas party and accidentally met a couple of swingers who changed their lives. And less than two years later they've arrived here. This nexus point in the world, where hedonists come to meet others like them. A place where they can all be themselves. Where she can be Jenn, this new version of herself, this authentic version, birthed from the crucible of intensity that defined those first couple months as swingers. She can be Jenn without fear of further shaming, further remuneration. Without fear of morality clauses.

Jenn shed the pupa and soared.

"Thank you," says Zoë, when their kiss breaks. "That was incredible."

"That. Yes. Amazing." Jenn nods. "I words good, sometimes. There will be...others in the future."

"I would enjoy more than words." Zoë kisses her once more and stands.

"Can I," Jenn begins, "More than words? Anything? You?"

Zoë laughs. "I'd like to check in with my husband in that pile over there. And being able to do that was thanks enough."

Jenn assures her that in the portion of the week remaining, that at once seems vast and almost non-existent, there will be more time. She wonders as she leaves the playroom through the disco, which of them will wear the harness, wield the cock. Winding through dancing people, grinding well beyond the limits of "real world" public decorum, Jenn notes the discordance of Beyoncé singing about single ladies on the sound system. The warmth and humidity of the resort at night hits Jenn as she emerges into the courtyard, and there finds Ryan having a quiet drink at the bar. She watches from afar for signs of isolation or loneliness and sees none of that. He is watching a music video on the flat screen above the bar, smiling into his drink. Her husband is taking a beat.

"Hello, beautiful," he says, handing her an espresso martini. "Enjoy yourself?"

"I had a fabulous time, you?"

"Unique," he says.

"Not unique bad, I hope," she replies.

"Not unique bad at all. New, different."

She sits next to him and rests her head on his shoulder. They clink their martinis together, raining bits of chocolate and sugar onto the glass bar-top.

"*¡Buenas noches, Señorita!*" offers Miguel as he scoops up two empty glasses near them.

"*¡Buenas noches, Miguel!*" Jenn returns with a content smile.

"*¿Cómo estás?*"

"*Muy bien,*" she says. "*Muy muy bien.*"

*Muy bien* indeed. Both Lamberts lift their glasses toward Miguel, who tilts his own back then slides down to the far end of the bar. She looks into the swirl of chocolate and coffee and cream in her martini glass.

"What're you thinking about?" asks Ryan,

"How lucky we are," she replies.

"I agree," says Ryan. "Was it something specific?"

"All of it. Lucky we're here, lucky that we met, that we met Bruce and Paige, that we endured and persevered."

Ryan nods. "I love you, *Señora* Lambert."

"I love you, *Señor* Lambert."

"Hot tub o'clock?"

"Why yes, I think it may well be. I want to hear all about your night."

"I'd love to hear about yours. Come, madam, let's away," he offers his hand, and she takes it, giggling at the bit of Shakespeare, which had been the direction of her college dreams and ambitions. To once have thought that her future lay on the scholarship of the Bard. Then to social work. Then to business management at parental insistence. How quickly our dreams of beauty can become those of function. How strange that a place like this, a place of and for beauty, could exist in this world. The same world of morality clauses and backstabbing lovers. The same world of uptight opinions about those desires we all share.

Jenn shakes her head. They are here because they choose to live in that world as little as possible, aren't they? This world is better, safer. Here, where she and her husband can explore the boundaries of themselves, their relationship, and their own edges. She nestles herself beneath his arm as they walk into the night. Time begins to reassemble itself into something approaching chronology, and the days fall back away.

Back to the beginning. Day one. Saturday.

# PART II

*Saturday*

# 5

# RAYMOND

"Welcome home," says Marisol, flashing her practiced smile. Despite the no doubt rote nature of the welcome and the smile, practiced many times per day on everyone to come through this lobby, the smile is one of the warmest Raymond Horne has ever seen. Or maybe it just feels that way, today. Today brings him here, to Aphrodite's. Today returns him home. He feels the emotions well up inside him. This reaction isn't unexpected. This isn't the first time he's cried being welcomed home to Aphrodite's, after all. Not the first time, no. But maybe the time he's needed the welcome most.

"Welcome home," Marisol hasn't said it again, but Raymond hears it again.

He squeezes Mia's hand without looking in her direction and wipes at the light tears that have yet to fall. *"Muchas gracias,"* he tells Marisol, then repeats his thanks once again for good measure.

*"De nada,"* she replies. "Champagne?" She waves a hand up and her hair bounces in silky black waves. Behind her stands a gentleman in pale maroon, holding a tray with two champagne flutes gleaming in the center. Just two. Two for them alone.

He shivers. The air conditioning always seems to bring this lobby down to refrigerator temperatures. Though it could be just the contrast with the Mexican heat. The temperature outside is ninety-three and on the rinse cycle, as his mother used to say. He takes a flute from the tray and hands it to Mia, then another for himself. The gentleman in maroon disappears behind the wall.

Raymond loses himself in the champagne flute, watching the bubbles march and pop. Marisol talks to Mia, who is visibly excited about her first time at Aphrodite's. His distraction must be transparent to her. *You need to get it together, here, Ray.* He nods to placate himself. Get it together, indeed. With one hundred and ten couples arriving today. The couples of Xanadu X, his tenth trip to this resort. He can't be this morose mope, this mess of a man. *Get it together for them! Fake it, Ray. Do that thing you do.*

He's spent the last two decades of his life helping people to fake their confidence until they have confidence. It's not lying, it's conjuring. He needs to conjure some confidence of his own right now, some semblance of leadership. *O captain, my captain.* Otherwise, the comment cards for Xanadu X may be right shit.

*The Xanadu trips were great until Raymond Horne had a nervous breakdown on the takeover. Should've stayed small.*

He needs to banish those words, doesn't he? Nervous breakdown. If he's thinking them, someone might say them. Out loud. Out there. He's had a breakup, that's all. Universally understandable. A recent breakup, not even a month old, would distract anyone.

Even their fearless leader. Even Raymond Horne.

Because breakups still hurt like a motherfucker, don't they? Compassionate or not. Whether you believe in impermanence or not. Whether you want to release your paramours to the proverbial wind to explore who they want to be, or not. Hurt like a motherfucker.

Colleen was compassionate. As compassionate as one could be while still standing firm. "I'm moving out," she told him. She held his hands as she said it, but it felt more for her benefit than his. Textbook Raymond Horne, in fact. *Video 121: Breaking Up Is Hard on Both Sides.* How could he be upset when she followed the script?

He supposed it wasn't a surprise, though he still felt the shock wash over him. He'd kicked her suitcase when he got home, hadn't he? When he went to put his keys in the key tray.

"Are you listening to me?" she asked, then shook his hands for good measure. He nodded slowly, taking in the weight of what she said, what she meant. "You need to get back to who you were, and I feel like I'm rewarding your stasis by staying."

"Who was I?" he asked.

Colleen dropped his hands and folded her arms. She cocked her jaw to one side in a smirk that asked *are you fucking kidding me?*

He still couldn't answer that question when she left and isn't confident he has any idea now who he was or is. Just that here is home. Has to be. Same as it ever was. The ritual, welcoming home, overwhelmed him on his first return trip, when Luis welcomed him home by name. Emotions overcame him that time as well, but for different reasons, and latched onto Luis in a bear hug.

Today he wonders where his old friend is. Luis moved from bag-man to greeter to floor manager, now to general manager of the whole place. Luis will know who Raymond is. Because Luis very clearly knows who *he* is.

Raymond spares a glance for Mia, filling out her welcome paperwork between deep sips from her champagne flute, a broad smile on her face. Mia, who leaped at the opportunity to join him. Mia, who reminded him that she'd be going as his friend for a well-deserved vacation, not to work, or—

"I don't expect you to fuck me," he told her.

"Good, 'cuz I won't." She smiled and hugged him. "But that doesn't mean I don't love you, or that I don't appreciate this trip."

"I know," he told her.

Mexico suits Mia, who wears an enormous floppy-brimmed off-white straw hat. Her bug-eyed round sunglasses sit on the brim, making the whole thing look like a character in an old cartoon. Beneath, her face already deeply tanned from two decades of Georgia sun, devoid of makeup, the way she rolled.

To think, if he hadn't been such an asshole once upon a time, she might be here *with* him. More than friends. But thirty-year-old Ray Horowitz had been a right shit. Especially to twenty-year-old girls. Back then, his friends had called him Bike, and he'd been a fool to think it had to do with his occasional bicycle trips.

"Bike," he asked Reid, his closest friend at the time.

"Because everybody gets to ride," said Reid.

Back then, there wasn't much differentiation between taken

women and single women. Not once-upon-a-time, not twenty-one years gone, not when he was Ray Horowitz. He'd chided Mia for not understanding, then, and being uptight, and not— blah blah blah.

Fifty-one-year-old Raymond Horne is trying. Trying to be better. He's been trying long enough that he thought he was succeeding. Until Colleen packed a bag before talking with him. Before giving him an opportunity to—

*To what? Defend your stasis? To—*

"*Señor* Raymond!" The voice is warm, immediately familiar. Raymond snaps away from his past and turns to see Luis striding across the marble lobby toward him. Luis's vestments indeed seem to indicate a change in stature, an elevation. When the man is close enough to Raymond, the confirmation on his name badge is very clear. **Luis Ochoa - General Manager** / *Gerente General.*

Luis's large hand envelops Raymond's, then he pulls him in for a semi-hug with back slapping. The final slap holds, and Raymond feels that this is where you can tell there's genuine affection. "Welcome home," says Luis. "We have missed you."

The tears well again. Raymond brushes at his face to quell them and momentarily seems to succeed. He gestures toward Mia. "Luis, I want to introduce you to Mia Benjamin, one of the best sex educators I know."

*El Gerente General* takes Mia's small hand in two of his and plants a kiss on the back. Mia laughs at the gesture. "Pleasure to meet you, Luis. You know, you're all Raymond could talk about on the way here!"

"This guy," says Luis, ribbing Raymond with his elbow.

"This guy," Mia repeats, staring into Raymond's eyes.

He feels a quick flush of embarrassment. If Luis might know who he was, back then, before whatever stasis Colleen saw, then Mia surely can see who he *is* in the here and now. Can see into him, through him. Perhaps that's why they won't be having sex this week. Perhaps that's why—

"Mia has had a rough year," he finds himself rambling, noting Mia's narrowed brow. "I told her that this is the place to escape it."

"*Sí,*" says Luis, his face showing concern. "Rejuvenation. Something in the water! You must drink deep." He laughs.

Raymond appreciates the quick-change emotional range that

people in the service industry need to perfect. Good ones can mirror emotions. The best, well, the best actually feel them. There's no doubt in Raymond's mind that he's looking at the best. He pours his guts out.

"Tell you the truth, Luis," he begins, "I'm also having a rough year. Colleen. Left." He stumbles.

Like a priest, Luis holds a solemn gaze for confession.

"Trying to keep together for the trip. Brought my wonderful friend and educator Mia." He feels a fool and looks away. Noticing the champagne flute on the desk, he lifts it.

"*Señor* Raymond," says Luis, again taking his hand, then Mia's. "This week will wash away your sadness. Your friends have begun to arrive. They look forward to meeting you." That knowing look again. "All will be well. Please, no sorrow here." And now the smile. The beam.

Raymond feels the weight in his chest lessen, if only a touch.

Marisol comes around the desk with two small bracelets.

"Please, let me," Luis tells her, taking them from her.

Functionally, the bracelets are identifiers that you are a guest of Aphrodite's Resort and Spa. In the beginning, on Raymond's early trips, they were just a step up from carnival or bar plastic wristbands. Snapped on and snipped off upon your farewells. This year, the resort has spared no expense. Now a brown faux wooden version of the Aphrodite's logo, the word and an impression of the goddess herself rendered in vague swoops, is strung on a black nylon band between two pearlescent beads. As Luis ties it around Raymond's wrist, then clamps a metal band around the tie, he feels it take on a talismanic quality. He chides himself that this year he's liable to feel myriad amplified emotions. A smart leader would take each hill on that roller coaster with healthy skepticism. A leader not stuck in stasis.

Raymond smiles at Mia as Luis finishes attaching her bracelet, and she smiles back at him. In her face, he sees that she, at the very least, understands him at a surface level. He's had a hard couple of weeks. Mia's year has been a nightmare. Together, they may unwind the tangle of the year.

"You're all set, *mi amigo, mi amiga,*" says Luis, putting his hands on each of their shoulders. "Why don't you go to the bar and I will personally take your bags to your room." He gestures out, through the sliding glass doors, where Aphrodite's main courtyard awaits.

Raymond nods. A drink would do nicely. Before he must put on the costume. Go the full Horne. Lead. He shudders. That's hours on, still. Not yet. Not yet. They thank Luis and walk toward the resort. To the sliding glass doors that serve as the gateway. Raymond takes a deep breath as the glass doors slide open and the sounds of Aphrodite's tumble in. Bird calls, whispers of wind through palm fronds, the faint thrum of a driving beat over the speakers. Behind it, the pool's party captain asks folks to "join the *limbooooooo*!"

They step through.

His eyes adjust to the brightness of the mid-morning sun, and he takes in the courtyard. He allows himself a moment of very simple recognition. He may not understand who he is at this very moment, but without question, he knows where he is. The centerpiece to the courtyard is an eight-foot sculpture of goddess Aphrodite in abstract and somehow sensual swoops. The statue rests on a half shell in the center of a fountain.

Raymond holds his wrist up, and looks from the sculpture to the impression of her on his bracelet, takes in all that's around him and understands something deeper about what he wears. This bracelet may have started as a simple indicator that you're allowed to stroll the meandering paths of this singular place.

In its current form, however, this bracelet doesn't just remind Raymond that he is a guest of Aphrodite's. It reminds him that he belongs there.

## 6

# CRISTA

Crista clings to room 2402's door handle. She can't adequately explain why she won't let the door close, especially not to Allie. She's never been naked outside. Not in thirty-nine years of life. "It feels," she gropes for the words, "wrong!"

Allie, already naked outside, with her hands on her gorgeous hips, purses her lips and nods. She looks completely at home. As Crista holds the door handle, Allie leans against the balcony rail and crosses her ankles. The move flexes the muscles in her thighs and seems to, for a distracting moment, emphasize Allie's sex.

A smirk rises on Allie's face. "If you want more of that, you'll have to come outside."

Crista sighs, giving a forlorn look through the open door, toward the safety and modesty their room offers. The balmy wind blows across her nipples and vulva, causing sudden goose-flesh down her shoulders and back. "I want to. But I feel all exposed."

"You do realize that you're already naked outside, yes?" her wife points out, moving toward her. "You just need to break the conduit to the room."

"If I do that, it'll be real."

"It is real."

She feels Allie's lips below her ear, her hot breath. On her shoulder, her arm. Then Allie stands in front of her and kisses each of Crista's nipples.

"That's not helping," says Crista, looking down at her newly perky nipples on her small breasts. Even the lazy nipple is wide awake. "Now I'm naked and look turned on."

"You're naked and look gorgeous," says Allie. "Come, *mi amor,* let's go to the cocktail party!" She grabs Crista's hand and gives a little yank. Not a *do it now* yank, but a *you can do it, I promise* yank. It's gentle, and so is the look on Allie's face, in her eyes. She tucks her hair behind her ears and smiles. "Would you feel better in a sarong?"

Crista's heart sinks. She thinks she can hear the twinge of disappointment in her wife's voice, but maybe she's just projecting. This isn't going how they planned after all.

"We'll stride down to their party, two gorgeous naked lesbians, like we own the motherfucking place!" Allie assured her on the plane. "No one will question if we belong here. The lesbians. We're going to plant our flag. With two crossed dildos on it. Double dildos."

Crista laughed and gave her wife a reluctant nod.

"And you," Allie whispered into her ear, hot breath causing shivers, "you are going to get so much ass."

So much ass. Is that even what she wants? Crista doesn't know anymore. When they first started planning this trip, when it was still six months, eight months off, it had been easy to fantasize about crashing the hetero party. Coming in here, planting the flag that said lesbian and acting as though they owned the place. As the probable future became the actual present, standing naked on the patio outside their room, naked outside with the ocean breeze running places and the sun hitting places it has never seen before... "It's just all very real."

Allie kneels in front of her, taking her hands. For one terrifying moment, Crista thinks her wife is going to bury her face between her legs. That'd be too much. *Too damned much!* Instead their eyes connect. "If you don't want to go naked to the party, you don't go naked to the party. If you'd rather I put something on so we show up topless, or looking stunning in our evening wear, that's what we do."

Crista looks away, face hot.

"All that matters is that you're there with me. That we're

holding hands. That we meet this world together. All that matters is you, *mi amor*."

Crista looks back to her wife, kneeling nude before her, eyes wide, face so open. Gone is the hard-ass MSNBC anchor, replaced by the vulnerable truth of Alejandra Vargas. The person on the inside that only Crista ever gets to connect with, to see, to feel. Her Allie. "Maybe just for...the bottom," she says. "Maybe sarongs."

Allie nods. "Color?"

"Red."

When the door to the room does close, maroon sarongs surround Allie and Crista's waists, breasts bare to the resort. Crista's comfort level has increased thanks to the cover-up, but the breeze on her nipples still makes her self-conscious. They walk from their rattan-roofed building toward the courtyard outside the lobby, the central hub of the resort. As they near, the sound of the cocktail party grows, voices blending into a blanket of sound, a driving beat below rises and falls. They pass the bungalow rooms, closer to the hub. Crista feels the anxiety rising again.

Allie squeezes her hand and leans in to her ear. "You've been to the Gaza Strip, downtown Baghdad, Tehran. You are brave, you are strong, you are gorgeous." A pause, and a smile filled with hunger. "You are mine."

Crista stops walking as she sees a couple not much younger than she and her wife join the path up ahead. The woman is slender, also with small breasts, Crista notes with some relief. Her imagined version of Aphrodite's was full of women stacked like her wife, whose buxom physiques existed only to make her feel more like a boy. Nice to see an ordinary woman, a woman like her. The woman's hair is short and brown, with a streak of hot pink.

"I'd bet dollars to donuts that's Manic Panic Hot Hot Pink," says Allie in a stage whisper.

Crista shushes her, mortified.

"Oh, she can't hear us," Allie waves away the concern. "Besides, it looks good on her."

Crista concedes the point with a nod, then whispers, "She's kinda cute."

Allie smiles and kisses her. "So are you."

Moments later, they emerge from the paths shaded by palm

trees into the central courtyard surrounding the odd sculpture fountain that seems to have reduced the goddess of love to a series of bulging crescents. People pack the courtyard, many in pairs, the couples, but some have begun to mingle, some have formed even larger clusters. Crista thinks, absurdly, of the formation of the solar system. First, there was chaos, and from chaos slowly developed order. She laughs.

"What?" asks Allie, handing her a champagne flute snatched from a passing waiter.

"Nothing," says Crista.

She looks around the crowd, observing the way she used to, the way she did in Kabul, in Jerusalem. An elderly couple, probably mid-seventies, stand off to the side. Both show their age, him more than her, but stand confidently nude with big smiles on their faces as they interact with a much younger couple. The foursome clink their glasses. The younger woman holds a massive hurricane glass. The glass and the blue hurricane inside it makes Crista yearn for one of her own. "Bar, then people watch?" she asks Allie out of the side of her mouth.

"Anything you want, *mi amor*."

The bar is long and crowded, but they easily slide in and sit. Here the nondescript beat thrums out of a speaker set high in the bar's vaulted roof. Two bartenders avoid each other as they rush from customer to customer. Crista notes that they do seem to favor the ones with tits, and of those, the bigger tend to get priority.

*I'm similar in that respect*, thinks Crista with a snicker.

A sign on the bar top confirms that the huge glass does contain the drink of the day, Hurricane Aphrodite, bright blue, with a huge chunk of pineapple stuck on the rim. She points at the sign and says, "*Un*, um, hurricane, *por favor*."

Allie smiles and holds up two fingers. "*Dos*."

Leaning against the bar with hurricanes in hand, blood alcohol level on the rise, Crista surveys the growing throng of guests in the courtyard and feels more at home. After a decade of journalism, of watching people, if Crista can just see this all as one big research excursion, hold onto that feeling of observation, maybe the anxiety will subside. She's here to observe and report, to study the erotic rites of swingers in their natural habitat. She smiles at that. There's the woman with the Manic Panic in her hair, grinning, champagne in hand, who has apparently lost her bikini top somewhere. Her companion on the path stands next to her, glancing around, maybe nervous, maybe overwhelmed. Crista gets that. His tropical print shorts barely contain his obvious erection, and she feels happy that she doesn't have as obvious an arousal tell.

"Shall we type?"

Crista smiles and nods, not taking her eyes off the crowd. She's no longer just observing, now she has a goal, find Allie's type. Not Manic Panic, she's a touch too high-school-rebellion for Allie. Though maybe that's not fair. Oh, but what's this? Manic Panic and her man with the sandy brown hair, are joined by a woman who's older than them, with long curly strawberry-blonde hair unfurled down to her shoulder blades. Crista loses herself for a moment in the curve of her back, just down to that peach of an ass.

"You and your strawberry-blondes! I win!" says Allie.

"I thought I got to go first."

"In everything, darling."

Crista kisses Allie and resumes her perusal, taking another long drink-in of the ass on that strawberry-blonde. She scrunches her lips and realizes that Allie had her number in a second, without even trying. Strawberry-Blonde is definitely her type: Curvy, older, confident enough to stand in a crowd wearing nothing but sunglasses, a necklace, and a visor that says Xanadu. As Strawberry-Blonde turns, Crista catches a glimpse of a vivid red patch of hair between her legs.

"Yeah," Crista concedes, "you've got me. Strawberry-Blonde is gorgeous."

"Now do me!" says Allie.

"'Do me,' eh?" Crista snickers.

"You're seriously a teenager, you know that?"

"I thought that's why you like me."

"Shut up and type me!"

Crista throws another glance at Strawberry-Blonde, wondering what it'd be like to kiss her. The woman's confidence would make her difficult to approach. Maybe another Hurricane Aphrodite would do it. Maybe not today. Approaching has always made Crista anxious. Allie hadn't been easy either. Well, she'd been easy, but not easy to walk up to at that awards banquet, even though Crista had just received the obnoxious orange resin monstrosity that the Chicago Journalists Association called the Courage in Journalism Award. She might have had courage in journalism, but not in asking Alejandra fucking Vargas from MSNB fucking C to come up to her hotel room. Somehow, though, she asked. She did it.

A man with a mustache joins the threesome of Manic Panic, Sandy-Hair, and Strawberry-Blonde. He bears more than a striking resemblance to Burt Reynolds in his heyday. Maybe Tom Selleck. His chest is hairy, his balls are hairy. She snickers again.

Enough distraction, back into the crowd now to find Allie's type. Not the pale freckled beanpole in the teal sarong staring at the sculpture as though she's trying to resolve it into something resembling a person. Not the dark haired and shockingly dark lipped nudist-cum-goth with the magenta mohawk on the swinging bed across the way. Nor the boyish blonde who looks like she climbed directly out of a hot spring in some Nordic country.

Unlike Crista's type, which Allie nailed without a second thought, Allie's type is more nebulous, a moving target. Crista herself doesn't fit into the classification with her flat mousy brown hair, pale blue eyes, small breasts, and limited curves. Sometimes she's amazed she got anywhere at all at that conference when she crossed the room, holding her damned award, and stood in front of Alejandra Vargas. The Alejandra Vargas whose Pulitzer made the Flamey McFlame award Crista held not just irrelevant, but—

Alejandra winked at her. Not just met eyes, but actually winked. Winked from within her conversation; polite, friendly, engaged, but not *too* engaged. Don't want to give those journalist boys a foothold, after all. She was, without a doubt, the most gorgeous woman with whom Crista had ever been in the same room. Her curly locks shone as though lit from within. Alejandra begged off from her conversation, giving the cursory pats and encouragement and winks, then pointed to the flame.

"You probably don't have to carry that around. I don't think anyone will steal it," Alejandra said. "It does have your name on it and everything, Miss Norris."

A flush rose in Crista's cheeks as she looked down at the award. Why *was* she carrying it? She took a deep breath, conjured the courage riding on the backs of a glass and a half of merlot and two flutes of champagne. "Well, it might get tossed by the clean-up crew if I leave the room with someone interesting and don't return until after this whole reception is over." The words came out of Crista as though someone else had said them. Just to make her come-on clear, she added, "Leave the room with that interesting person to show her my hotel room."

Alejandra stared at her for a moment, took a sip of her drink, then smiled. "Well alright."

"Her," Crista says, tipping her hurricane toward a woman in the Aphrodite's courtyard who is unquestionably to Allie's taste. "Berkley."

Allie gives a shrug that becomes a smile that becomes a reluctant nod. While her tastes and whims may change, in any party, at any bar, at the clubs, the granola girls are always the dark horse favorite. The one Crista pointed to has a leather lace around her neck and wrist, fabric band in her hair, dangly earrings, and large circular sunglasses. Crista knows that if this woman had clothes on, they'd be a billowy skirt and a blouse that'd be right at home on a pot farm. She feels a momentary pang of guilt at the stereotyping nature of their little game. When all is said and done, humans are incredibly predictable. The things they like and don't, the things they want and don't.

Her apprehension falls away, though, when Allie leans to her ear and whispers, "What do you say to you, me, Berkley, and Strawberry-Blonde finding out how each other taste?" The suggestion makes Crista tingle, like Allie just strummed the bass string of her clitoris. But behind the tingle, there's apprehension, wonder, the fear of being last to this particular party.

Crista nods to her. "Maybe you could do the asking."

"Anything for you, *mi amor.*"

Crista grins and scrunches her nose. She takes another glance out over the courtyard. Opposite the bar is a small store, its windows lined with mannequins in lingerie flanked by a line of dildos in the bottom of the window. Beside the store is a row of wooden strut structures with beds dangling on swings beneath them. Next to those, a stage.

Her eyes reach the stage just in time to see a man climb onto it wearing a large white toga and a wreath of leaves and grapes atop his head. She knows Raymond Horne's face from his emails and videos, though she only watched half of one before stopping, having found it rather hetero/mono-normative, and something she could get to...well...when she got to it. That said, she liked the personality that shone through their email exchanges leading up to the trip, and now she digs his willingness to look silly. The courtyard erupts in applause.

As the applause subsides, he raises a glass of wine to toast all of them. "Behold! Bacchus blesses this occasion, bidding you all to eat!" A roar from the crowd. "Drink!" A heartier roar. "Fuck!" The word is accompanied by a Groucho eyebrow waggle and the heartiest roar yet. "And be merry!" He tips his glass toward them, then pours the red down his gullet, dribbling a healthy amount down his cheeks and the front of his toga. He looks down at it. "Well, typical." He reaches down and yanks off his toga in a single pull. Considering it falls away so easily, Crista is rather impressed it managed to stay on while he climbed the stage. "You know," he says, "I still feel overdressed!" It's a show, to be sure, but it's a good show, and Raymond Horne clearly knows that as he yanks down his gold Speedo and tosses it into the audience with the cheesy flourish of a Chippendale's dancer. "Much better!"

The audience roars in tipsy appreciation as he strikes a Superman pose. She's impressed by the confidence on display here. Especially since that Speedo had apparently held him tight, his dick turtled in on itself, surrounded by manicured gray-blond curls. He holds that pose and takes it further, thrusts out his jaw and basks in the admiration and amusement. Stripping himself bare save his laurels, for his guests; that's certainly some kind of confidence.

At once, the red sarong around her waist feels unnecessary. She rubs her hand across it, spreading it apart. As she slowly exposes herself, she sees Allie looking intently.

"Peek-a-boo," says her wife, her lover, her longest relationship, the most beautiful woman in this courtyard.

And that's enough, Crista yanks the sarong away with a nod and slaps it on the bar. It's real now. No door handle to ground her. She's outside naked.

"I could just eat you up," says Allie, and bites Crista's earlobe.

The shudder begins there and travels all the way through her, as that bass string thrums again. "Oh," says Crista, wishing she could give herself over to that. There are others in the courtyard whose fingers and tongues are already wandering. The barest prospect of that here, now, for her, makes Crista's face hot with embarrassment.

She gives her wife a quick kiss on the nose.

## 7

---

## JENN

The man on stage wearing the toga, with the light scruff of blond beard, raises his over-sized and over-full glass of red wine toward them, and Jenn Lambert raises hers in reply.

"Behold! Bacchus blesses this occasion, bidding you all to eat!"

She cheers.

"Drink!"

Ryan roars at that, holding his hurricane to the sky.

"Fuck!"

"That's my favorite," Paige whispers in her ear, sending tingles down Jenn's spine.

"Mine too," she whispers back. Isn't that a marvel? Not so long ago, that wouldn't have been the case. Food and drink, food and wine, mainly, still occasionally take priority spots on Jenn's list. This time two years ago, fucking would've been hard pressed to crack the top five, in fact. Quite the change. Here stands Jennifer Lambert, she of the late bloom, of the once-prudish nature. She'd never gone skinny dipping, or visited a nude beach, or even gotten terribly frisky in the back seat of a car. Now she stands topless. Topless in a crowd. Sure, she's flanked by the people she loves most in the world, but that's no reason to discount the moment, the growth. The growth that has transformed her from Jennifer to Jenn.

The man on stage has lost his toga, showing a shiny golden Speedo that makes her think of Rocky Horror. Specifically, Ryan, nude save for a very similar Speedo this past Halloween, at Chicago's Music Box Theater for the annual screening of *The Rocky Horror Picture Show*. She was Janet and Paige was Magenta, and the audience went wild when they made out during the costume contest. That clinched it. *Tell us about it, Janet.*

The man seems to throw her a wink, then drops the Speedo to the stage. He stands in his glory, as the cheers from her and all around her crescendo. He spins the Speedo above his head and shoots it into the audience, following it with a set of finger guns. *Bang!*

"Raymond's showmanship is…" says Bruce, searching for just the right word to describe what they're seeing.

"Goofy," offers Ryan.

Bruce laughs. "Yes, indeed, goofy."

Ryan winks at her, and she plants a kiss on his cheek. "Happy we're here?" he whispers.

She is happy, of course, to be here in paradise, to be here for Bruce and Paige's anniversary. She's lucky. But when she nods, throwing him a smile that would be convincing to others, but not to him, he knows. She sees in his eyes. She also knows that her clock is ticking. The minor reprieve between arriving at something fun, something exciting, and the moment when the weight returns to her. The embarrassment. The stammering. The straight up shame of having lost her job.

"What's up?" she asked Lenny Dohlen, her manager, in the room behind the front desk of the Westin. "I'm on my way down to maintenance with the reports."

Lenny's face was empty. His eyes were pointed in her direction but didn't really see her. The face of the human resources woman with him was not so empty. Her face held judgment.

The silence lingered as Jenn, still Jennifer according to her name tag, shuffled the stack of reports growing heavier by the moment, from the crook of her right arm to its mirror in her left. She smiled and gave a laugh that approximated "Heh," before trying to get someone to talk with, "I was summoned?"

"Yes, Je— Mrs. Lambert," began Lenny, then he stopped.

*La-di-dah, Missus Lambert. Shit. Must be serious.* She looked from Lenny's face, sweat on his exceedingly broad brow, droopy cheeks, to HR incarnate standing next to him in her blouse buttoned to her throat, lips pressed together hard enough to be turning white.

After a pause so pregnant it could be having triplets, Lenny swiveled his chair ninety degrees and looked directly up at HR. "Grace?"

Jenn felt her head nod in recognition of Grace even as embarrassment burned within her. Whatever was about to happen wasn't good, there was no mistaking that. She ran through her mental catalog of transgressions. She'd sent the room reports to the wrong email address the week prior. She'd complained that upper management got Labor Day off, but they didn't. Neither of those things would warrant a visit from HR, though. Johnny from the valet service had come on to her, not the other way around, though his twenty-two-year-old chiseled jaw had sent quivers all through her, she'd turned down his offer of a drink and then masturbated furiously when she'd returned home that night.

*Squeaky clean, jelly bean,* her mind insisted.

Grace puffed a breath out, apparently put out by being asked to lead this meeting. "Are you familiar with a website called *In the Lifestyle?*"

Jenn heard her mind say *Oh,* so clearly that she was sure she'd said it aloud. The warm unpleasantness in her stomach crept north, and her chest got tight. *In the Lifestyle?* She sure as shit did know *In the Lifestyle.* She and Ryan had connected profiles on that particular site. The kind of profiles where you specify what kind of fun you're looking for tonight, where you specify how likely your evening *rendezvous* is to end in fucking. Not even just sex, fucking. Jenn hoped her face wasn't betraying her, as she still felt she might be able to get away with, "No, what's that?" as she ran through the photo galleries on her profile, on his, in her mind. Never face and genitals, right? Faces always behind a gateway, password protection, passwords they only shared with those select few. Those *rendezvous* users where the fucking approached levels of *Very Likely.*

A tickle nagged, but Jenn couldn't remain silent longer without saying anything. "Is that the diet website that Rina used last month?"

They stared at her. She stared back, inwardly congratulating herself on the quick cover, on not answering their question.

Then she resumed cataloging and tried to chase down the source of that tickle.

"We received an email, Mrs. Lambert," Grace intoned, in that ominous fashion that only someone who enjoys swinging the ax can use.

Jenn could feel the noose tightening and couldn't uncover the tickle. What had it been, what had she forgotten?

The sheet of paper hit the desk between them, a photo printed on it by an ink jet printer, horizontal lines of discoloration interrupting the image. Somehow that made it seemlier. A post-it covered her nudity, sure, but that face was without a doubt Jennifer Lambert of the Westin. Without a doubt, Jennifer Lambert bent over in front of a young woman with a rainbow cock poking out from between her legs. Without a doubt, Jennifer Lambert, mouth in the O of ecstasy from that young woman yanking the cock out of her and unleashing the flood of orgasm. Without a doubt.

"The email said this photo came off a site called *In the Lifestyle*, and if we looked, we could find profiles for our desk manager Jennifer Lambert and her husband on it." Grace spoke in such a clipped fashion each word felt like a lash.

Jenn opened her mouth but said nothing.

"Are you aware that the Westin has a morality clause in its employment contracts?" asked Lenny. He put a blank sheet of paper on the desk, covering the inkjet printout. No more Sapphic debauchery on display, no Jennifer Lambert. His face wasn't blank so much as...sorry? She couldn't tell.

She shook her head. No, she was not aware of that.

The tickle resolved. The young woman. Rebecca. Beck, she'd wanted to be called. The twenty-year-old who, in the span of two days, had worked her way from meeting them at a bar to asking if she could stay at their house for a while because her boyfriend was, what had she said? A real cunt-nugget. When told no, they didn't think that'd work for them, Beck had broken the two front windows on their first floor. On that gloriously raunchy first night, though, Beck had asked Ryan to document the moment she pulled out on her phone. Beck, who'd said that she knew they didn't like identifiable nudes out "in the world," but just couldn't bring herself to delete such a beautiful sight.

"Besides, I'm naked in it too, right? Mutually assured

destruction!" Then she'd dropped to her knees and put Ryan's cock in her mouth.

Paige had called it a swinging rite of passage. The loony. Bruce called them Alexes, after Glenn Close's character in *Fatal Attraction*. Or had it been after the psychotic and perverse lead of *A Clockwork Orange*? Maybe both. She couldn't remember. Regardless, they would not be ignored.

"Did you read your contract before you signed it?" asked Grace, folding her arms, bunching up the garishly patterned blouse that covered her unmentionables.

Jenn pursed her lips but said nothing.

"It stipulates that all Westin employees keep a standard of professionalism and decorum. Naked pictures on a swinging website." Grace stopped short of actually saying, "For shame," and shook her head slowly. She removed the sheet of paper Lenny had laid atop the image of Beck and Jenn *in flagrante delicto* then threw Jenn a look that said, *so there*.

Jenn traded her stack of reports for a cardboard box containing her money plant, a picture of Ryan, and her word-of-the-day calendar.

"Grounds for immediate termination." Those words ring in her ears all the way down here in Mexico. She's roused from her shame by the sensation of both Ryan and Paige's hands on the small of her back, the combined support of the both of them. In the nearly two years they've known the Shepards, this gesture has emerged as one of the most comforting bits of affection she's ever felt. Their combined love and touch draws her back, severing the tendrils of connection to the stress and shame at home. The tendrils aren't gone by any means, not even truly hiding. They have just afforded her a wide enough berth to be here in this moment, with the goofy naked host wearing the leafy headdress, with her wonderful husband and girlfriend, with the people they're closest to, with a throng of revelers who may well be able to start a bonfire right here in the center of Aphrodite's Resort and Spa just from the heat of their collective passions.

She hopes she can leave that shame for just a little while. Hasn't she earned a reprieve?

## 8

### RYAN

Ryan holds his wife's hand as they climb the stairs up to Aphrodite's rooftop hot tub. The chill of evening blows in on the breezes, more as they get closer to the top. Both he and Jenn wear plush brown robes with the Aphrodite's name and swoop logo stitched into the breasts. He sees her pull hers closed as they get higher on the staircase

"Man, this is like the stairs in *The Exorcist*!" says Ryan.

Jenn smiles.

"Look out Damien Karras!"

Jenn squints.

"Too much," Ryan nods. He'd thought it might be as he said it.

They reach the roof and behold the hot tub, sprawling atop the tallest building on the resort, albeit only three stories. "It looks like a pool!" says Ryan, gaping at the enormous tub overflowing with people. The hot tub is shaped like a bean and backs up to another rattan roofed bar at one end, complete with in-tub-seating. On the deck to the left is a line of pool lounge chairs, to the right, a row of outdoor beds held up by massive wooden struts and surrounded by billowy curtains that, Ryan supposes, could be used for privacy if one were so inclined. The various bodies rolling and fucking on the beds don't seem to have privacy on their minds, as the curtains are all tied to the struts.

His focus and attention narrow to a pair of women on the last bed. The curvy one is on her back with her legs spread, a freckled redhead with round firm breasts kneels before her, sliding a glinting piece of stainless steel inside her. The vastness of the item awes Ryan. *It's like a club!* he thinks.

"Would you like to go *in* the hot tub?" asks his wife, amusement in her voice.

Ryan nods, turning away from the women on the bed. "There's a lot of visual input here."

Jenn laughs. "There is indeed." She gives his hand a squeeze. "You okay?"

"Do I not look okay?" he asks.

Jenn shrugs. "You look worried." She takes off the robe, slings it over her arm. She smiles, standing naked in flip-flops.

Is he okay? He thinks so. There's a lot here. Like, a *lot* a lot. But nothing seems insurmountable. "I'm good," he says. Her eyes are wide and shiny, but not worried. She looks hopeful. He nods. "How are you?"

"I want to go hang out with that sexy group right there." She extends her finger toward the bar end of the hot tub bean, where Bruce and Paige hold court.

"Let's do that," he says. She didn't answer his question, and during the welcome in the courtyard she seemed to drift. He knows what that means; he knows where she went. He can't blame her, focusing on the job she lost, the circumstances surrounding it. As the time kept marching on, from losing the job to now, without new employment, he felt the pressure as well. They talked about canceling the trip, as their savings grew smaller each week.

"Canceling so close to the trip, though," he reasoned, "we couldn't get our flights refunded, we'd lose the deposit. We'd get some of the money back, sure, but..."

"I don't want to cancel," she said. "I really want this." He did too.

So here they are, in sunny Cancún, the Riviera Maya, at Aphrodite's Resort and Spa. It's a place of reverence for those who've been, infamy for those who've heard, and curiosity for those who know only that there's a "Sandals for swingers" resort on this strip of beach. Those who are curious wander up and down the long public beach, hoping that around each berm they'll see the **Clothing Optional** sign and they can look, despite the anger in their partner's eyes. Ryan laughs at such a particular vision.

They walk to the edge of the hot tub, the center of the bean, and a group sitting just below the waterline parts to bid them enter. Ryan holds Jenn's hand as she steps down onto the seat just inside, and a man with a Yankees cap and a tribal tattoo takes her other hand and helps to ferry her safely into the throng of people that fills almost every available space. Ryan follows, without Tribal Tattoo's help (or offer of) and they slide through a sea of naked revelers, dropping *excuse me*'s and *thank you*'s all the way.

"Welcome, Lamberts!" shouts Bruce, raising his drink to them. The cluster of people around him all applaud, making Ryan laugh. "I've been singing your praises."

"Well, thank you!" says Ryan.

Bruce pokes two fingers at them. "Espresso martinis?"

"That's a thing?" asks Ryan, while Jenn's neck can barely support the strength of her affirmative nod.

"Oh, my, yes, Ryan, it is quite a thing."

"How do you think anyone can maintain the energy for a week here?" asks Paige, sliding in behind them with two ridiculously large martini glasses. Chocolate syrup coats the interior of each, and they're rimmed with large sugar crystals.

Jenn's eyes widen further.

"Yes," says Ryan, "We should get two of those."

"Oh, these *are* yours," says Paige, handing over the two glasses.

To confirm, Bruce holds his own up and points at it. "Dark chocolate syrup, Bailey's, vodka, Kahlua, and a shot of espresso."

"That sounds heavenly," says Jenn.

"They are," assures Paige, wrapping her arms around Jenn from behind, resting her head on Jenn's shoulder.

"So!" exclaims Bruce. He points at Ryan and Jenn, "Ryan and Jenn," then points around his circle of friends. "Here we have Rory, Terrence, and Marley, a triad." The two men and a woman are younger than Ryan and Jenn; all three look athletic. Rory's attention seems to be elsewhere and he offers basic pleasantries; Terrence and Marley give warm smiles.

"I think we may be the token triad on the resort this trip," says Marley.

Terrence nods. "Last year there were two."

Bruce continues, "James and Debra."

The couple in their seventies, she with short white hair, a ring of white fluff around his bald dome, reach out their hands. Their smiles are warm, their hellos and handshakes friendly.

"They've been on every Xanadu trip but the first."

"Indeed! And if we could go back in time, we'd go on that one!" James laughs heartily and turns to Debra. "And start this whole thing earlier?"

"A couple decades earlier, I think," suggests Debra. "Though if we'd known then what we know now, you might still be with your first wife!"

"Perish the thought!"

"Clark would've still been Clark."

"Will and..." Bruce continues his introduction, squinting for a moment, "Madison!"

Will, formerly Tribal Tattoo to Ryan, is tall, with a small belly, probably early to mid-forties, and Madison, next to him, can't be five feet. She looks seventeen to Ryan, but he's confident that the resort has a twenty-one and over policy. Young, though. Damn young.

Ryan waves a hi to the group. "Is it anyone else's first time here?" he asks, following it with a chuckle.

"Mine!" exclaims Madison. The sheer amount of enthusiasm that explodes from her tiny frame in that single word nearly knocks Ryan back. He smiles and tries to wipe away his premature judgment of her.

"It's our first," he says, looking to Jenn for, what? Confirmation? Jenn is busy and focused, though, face between Paige's breasts, as Paige pours a slow trickle of espresso martini down. Well then. "Some of us are adapting nicely," he says with a chuckle, turning back to the group.

The hot tub must have been at peak popularity when they arrived; as the hot red sun drifts down behind the beds on the deck, it begins to thin out. People break off for dinner, for *rendezvous* both in those beds and in their rooms. Though not all of them feel the compulsion to leave for their fun, as Ryan notes a cluster of women on the outside rim of the hot tub, with one lucky man moving from lap to lap enjoying a cunnilingus sampler.

Ryan notices his tension subsiding as the hot tub grows

sparser. He's no longer knocking into people at every turn, and now there are seats available at the bar. He takes one next to Bruce, the one that Jenn held until Paige whispered in his ear, "I'm going to borrow her," and the two women lit off for a bed. He throws a casual glance now and then, not because he feels the need to check up on Jenn, but so he knows what's what. In the time since that party they'd gone to, where they hadn't checked in with each other, both of them always made sure to give the other a heads-up before a venue change.

Bruce throws an arm around his shoulders. "What do you think of the place?"

"It's," Ryan begins, then cannot fathom how to follow that up.

"It *is*, isn't it?" says Bruce after some time has passed. "There is no place on Earth I'd rather be." He grins. "Don't tell the boys."

Ryan smiles and nods.

"She doing okay?" Bruce asks, gesturing toward the bed with his drink.

"I think the job thing and the morality clause thing are holding major space in her brain, and I've noticed her drift over into what I've called 'Jenn's Pensive Mode.'"

"Like at the welcome," says Bruce.

"Like at the welcome," repeats Ryan.

"That happens. Not just to you. Everybody here has something that won't stay at home. Insists on coming 'on resort.'" He wipes his hand down over his face and takes the final sip of his espresso martini. "Paige has convinced herself that this will be our last trip here."

"Do you think it will be?"

"I hope not. I don't believe so." Bruce shrugs, flagging down the bartender whose name Ryan hadn't noticed. "Do you want another?" he asks, pointing to Ryan's almost finished drink. "One more before dinner?"

Ryan looks down at it, then to the beds. All are empty except for the one occupied by Jenn and Paige. The boiling sun has vanished behind the balcony edge behind the beds. The entire hot tub platform exists in shadowy twilight. He smiles, nowhere to drive after all. "Why not, one for the road?"

"I'll probably leave the orchestra if things don't turn around.

Paige doesn't want me to. And things aren't dire yet, and may not become so. But..." Bruce shrugs again, this time his face more somber. "Is what it is, I suppose."

"Isn't it always?" the voice comes from down the bar. A voice Ryan knows but cannot place.

Bruce looks up. "Hmm?"

"Sorry, looks like the conversation was more serious than I supposed. Just joshing you."

Ryan really does know that voice. He turns and gives the man down the bar a nice long look. The man's hair is curly, his face coated with a conscious choice of three to five-day scruff.

"Not a problem," says Bruce, then points to himself. "Bruce," then to Ryan, "Ryan."

The young man slides closer. "Eric," he says. "However, if it so happens that either of you are consumers of podcasts, you may know me by a different name."

*Podcasts,* Ryan thinks. *Yes, maybe that's where—*

Before he can follow his train of thought into the station, Eric turns to show them his shoulder where a tattoo declares in bright red letters, **SWINGERQATSI**.

"Swinger—" Bruce stops. "You're missing a U there."

*"Qatsi.* Like cot." Eric grins.

*Swingerqatsi, right,* thinks Ryan. He listened to that podcast way back, once they got their heads on straight as swingers, when he started consuming all the media he could on the subject. He'd stopped listening shortly after, though, and can't remember why. "I've heard it," he says, hoping there isn't a question of what he's heard.

"Pleasure to count you as one of our gaggle of listeners." Eric's grin is broad. He looks to Bruce. "*Swingerqatsi* is a story-telling podcast that I run with my lover, Lena." He points. A vivid red pixie-cut is visible, but little else, obscured by a man and a woman alternating between sucking on Lena's nipples and kissing up and down her body. Her eyes are closed, her mouth agape in pleasure. "They're fans," says Eric.

"Clearly," says Bruce, amusement in his voice.

Ryan recognizes the red-head. "Wasn't she just fisting someone?"

"Probably," says Eric with a laugh. "Anyway. She and I go on sexy adventures and then talk about them on the show."

"Aha," says Bruce.

Ryan recalls now why he'd stopped listening. A conflict had broken out on the show, where both hosts remembered some indiscretion differently, and rather than stop the recording and work it out, they'd gone on for almost the entire hour about not who was right, but who was definitely wrong.

"And as you astutely noticed, the Q has no U after it," says Eric.

Ryan notices Bruce's jaw muscles clench at being called *astute*.

"It's because we take our title from a series of experimental films by Godfrey Reggio. Spent several years training to be a monk, in fact. His films are about life and the imbalance of it. Qatsi means life. From the Hopi Indians. So *Swingerqatsi,* to us, means either," he looks up and touches his finger to his lips, taking what seems to Ryan an exceedingly long time for something he so clearly has said more than once already today, "swinging life, or a way of life that calls for swinging."

"Wonderful," says Bruce. He hands Ryan the newly ordered espresso martini. "Eric," he begins.

"You can call me Strom if you want, that's my name on the show."

Bruce pauses.

"Hers is Kitten."

*Yes,* Ryan thinks, *that's it! The fucking Strom and Kitten shit-show.*

"Well, Eric, my friend and I have dinner reservations shortly. Pleasure to meet you." Bruce gestures with the new martinis toward the beds. Ryan notes that Paige and Jenn seem to have emerged into the afterglow.

"The pleasure was mine!" Eric presses his hands together and gives them a nod that makes Ryan wonder how the *namaste* gesture could possibly look so sarcastic. But if anyone can wring the sarcasm out, it has to be Strom.

They climb from the hot tub and lift their matching robes over their shoulders. As they walk to Jenn and Paige, Bruce flicks a thumb behind him. "That guy's a douchebag," he says out of the corner of his mouth.

"Oh," says Ryan, "You have no idea. Thanks for the exit."

"Ladies," says Bruce when they arrive at the bed.

Paige sits cross-legged. "Hello, *men,*" she says with a smile.

Jenn lies with her head in Paige's lap. "What are you two up to?"

"Evasive maneuvers," says Ryan.

Bruce laughs. "Well done," he says and claps Ryan on the back. "Our reservations are nigh. La Grande Fête at eight."

"I can't wait," says Jennifer, a blissed-out smile crossing her lips.

# 9

# BRUCE

"You're sure," says Ryan. "I mean—"

Bruce smiles at his friend and puts a hand on his shoulder, hoping to ease the worry. "The de Martolos are great people; we're both looking forward to getting to know them more."

Ryan nods, still looking tense.

"Chill, my friend. You're in paradise. Look around!" The two men stand in front of La Grande Fête, the fanciest of the three restaurants at Aphrodite's Resort and Spa. Bruce raises his hands, gesturing first up at the large script lettering on the side of the white stucco building, then toward the pool, glistening in the dark with the final waning bit of moon barely shining off its surface. The deck is full of empty chairs. The palm trees surrounding it are lousy with twinkle lights.

Ryan nods again. "I just don't want to upset the balance if you two wanted a...foursome date."

"Oh, well," Bruce waves that away, "we can always do that at home."

"True."

"Aphrodite's is a place to fuck new people, after all." Bruce laughs.

No laughter comes from Ryan.

Bruce smiles at his young friend, recognizing that the ribbing had pushed past where Ryan would still find it funny. Past where he would be able to count it as a joke. Into that difficult gray area where, if allowed to dangle, it would begin to nibble away at him. "Oh, c'mon. Paige has already fucked Jenn here once after all! We're not discarding you two." Bruce slings his arm around Ryan's shoulders, momentarily noting that Ryan must have splashed out on the stylish Tommy Bahama shirt he wears. To impress the de Martoloses? *To impress the resort, more like,* thinks Bruce.

"I know," says Ryan. "Thanks."

"And speaking of..." Bruce raises his hand down the low-lit path where Paige and Jenn walk, arm in arm. As the shadows of night fall back to reveal his wife and her girlfriend, he feels that bit of giddy thrill.

Paige's cleavage runs deep, her curls fall like flames, her eyes sparkle something fierce, even from this distance and in this dim light. The dress could be sued for copyright infringement by the Slinky corporation. The thought makes Bruce snort, as he realizes he's running the inner monologue of a 1930s dime-store knockoff hard-boiled detective.

The girl, no, woman, on her arm looks stunning as well, hopefully having left some of her stressors, if not back at home, then at least in the safe in the room. As he'd tried to. So hard not to think of her as a girl in need of help.

"She's a grown-assed-woman," Paige said when he'd fretted about Jenn's lost job. "It'll be hard, but this is what makes us. It's terrible, but this is how we flourish." After a while, she added, "Don't try to fix it. It'll come across as terribly paternal. And I imagine you'd still like her to be interested in the wonders that your cock brings to the, erm, table."

Noting this very real concern, instead of rushing in, with, "How can I fix this?" when he first saw Jenn after she lost her job, he gave her a long hug, making sure she knew that he'd be there if she needed him, and left it at that.

The "grown-assed-woman" phrase came back earlier today as well, as did the recognition that sliding into that paternal role seems to be something he does. When the *bloop* in the safe stopped him while grabbing their room key.

He and Paige held eye contact.

"Could be the boys," she said.

He nodded and went back, typed in his code, and opened the safe. He looked at the phone.

**I know you're away and you said not to. Mike emptied our account. I just need...someone,** texted Emily.

He sighed.

Paige peered over his shoulder. "I thought you told her—"

"I did." She shouldn't be texting. They talked about this. Certainly not now. Not until they returned home. And even then... Bruce held the phone, not returning it. The screen timer activated and darkened.

"Shall we?" asked Paige, the tinge of annoyance in her voice pronounced. Not annoyance, though, was it? Not jealousy either. Something deeper. Ache.

"She just needs—"

"She's a grown-assed-woman," said Paige. "One who doesn't understand boundaries. She just needs," she paused dramatically and then overemphasized, "*someone.*"

Bruce put the phone back into the safe and said nothing.

"Someone," Paige said. "Does that make you feel important?"

"Hey," said Bruce holding up his hands.

"She's just going to vanish again. You watch."

In front of La Grande Fête, Paige and Jenn are all smiles as they walk up. Paige in black and white, Jenn in a blue so deep Bruce feels he might fall in.

*Put your feet up on the desk, Sam Spade, this dame is trouble!* thinks Bruce. Of course, she's not trouble. Not in the least. Only a bit, back at the beginning. But she and Ryan had been fresh and new then, babes in the woods. And if it's trouble he seeks, well, she's right there in his pocket, isn't she? Hopefully set to vibrate.

He hasn't returned Emily's text, or the follow up that he saw on his solo walk to La Grande Fête. **I can't help but think of you.** Without context, he could take that to mean whatever his ego needed, couldn't he? How calculated are these messages? Are they merely emotional outbursts? Or is she using him? There was a time when he wouldn't have believed Emily Laurel capable of such things. When that woman they were with seemed to be the very nature of giving. When they were whole. The years had been unkind. The plot had thickened, as it were.

After they're all seated in the darkened restaurant, he watches Jenn read the menu, her eyes wide at all the options. She is indeed a grown-assed-woman. A sexy as hell grown-assed-woman, sitting next to him. Paige, across the table, quietly flirts with Ryan. A grown-assed-man. Certainly not the wide-eyed and perhaps naïve couple they'd met once upon a time. The last year and change have been very kind to them on that front. They'd settled into non-monogamy like they were born to play the game. Thankfully, the initial upsets hadn't scared them away. Thankfully, they were all sitting here together now.

Between Ryan and Jenn, at the back side of their square table, are two empty chairs for The Lamberts' friends. Bruce looks forward to learning more about them. He's seen Kendra and Vince de Martolos around, at house parties, but never fully engaged. Not for any reason he could think of, just never did.

He watches his wife flirt, pressing her shoulder against Ryan's, laughing heartily and leaving the briefest of lingering touches on his wrist, his arm, his shoulder. Sharing a whispered joke. She catches Bruce watching and gives him a wink. He beams back at her.

"I can't decide! It's so amazing!"

"Well," Bruce tells Jenn, "the big secret is that you don't have to."

She blinks at him, clearly not comprehending what that could mean.

"It's all inclusive, my dear. If you want the steak *and* the scampi, you get both."

Her already wide eyes go wider. "They have steak?"

Ryan takes her menu and flips the page, then points to the steak section.

"*Señor* Ryan," says Tomás he approaches the table, trailed by Ryan and Jenn's friends Vince and Kendra. Both still wear their Chicago clothes and look harried, yet thrilled to be here. Vince is lanky and has leaned into his receding hairline by cropping it very close. His blonde wife could be the definition of Rubenesque, even in jeans and an AC/DC shirt.

The four at the table rise and share hugs and kisses hello, a show of unspoken camaraderie that Bruce has always loved about the swing community, where friends of friends are treated as friends prime.

"*Buen provecho,*" says Tomás, giving a little bow and a wave. Before he leaves, he translates, "Enjoy your dinner."

"He insisted that we come here immediately," says Vince.

"That may be my fault," says Ryan. "I did tell him to bring

you directly here. My two espresso martinis before telling him that may have caused extra emphasis on the *directly* part."

"I don't mind," says Kendra, who shares a kiss with Ryan, then sits. "Though, as I'm uninterested in talking about the bullshit day we've had, I'll just say the George Bush International Airport is a shit-show, and I'm going to do my best to change our return flights to direct."

"We had a return through Bush a couple of years ago," says Bruce. "Booked too late for direct. Missed the second leg."

"Never again!" exclaims Kendra.

Bruce concurs. "Never again."

*bloop!*

A flush of embarrassment hits Bruce. *Fuck!*

Paige discontinues her flirty cleavage bearing lean and sits up straight, fixing him with a hardline look that asks him what the hell he's doing, that wonders why on Earth his phone is in his pocket and not in the safe three buildings down and up a flight of stairs. His look back isn't sufficient. She doesn't acknowledge the ocular apology, just turns back to Ryan and the new guests. She sits perpendicular to him now, her shoulder pointing, accusing. He fumbles under the table, trying to make his glance down only momentary. Just long enough to go from *bloop!* to silent.

Just long enough to see: **New Message, Emily Laurel**.

When the first course comes, the mood has lightened. Paige has turned slightly more toward him now. *The old three-quarters pose*, he thinks. She's not let it go, certainly, but wants to keep up appearances for the rest of their dinner companions.

Watching Ryan talk with Kendra distracts Bruce. Ryan leans toward her and whispers. At the same time, Bruce notes, he keeps returning to Paige. Back and forth. He's got this whole non-monogamy thing down. Doesn't let anyone feel left out. Not for too long, anyway. Jenn, on the other hand, has been presented with both lobster ravioli and a medium rare *filet mignon* and seems perfectly content to focus all her attention toward them. The conversation has certainly quieted since the food arrived.

"Ryan and Jenn tell me you play in the symphony," says Vince.

"Civic Orchestra," says Bruce. *But for how long?* "It's like grad school, while the Chicago Symphony Orchestra is, well, *the* show. I play the cello."

"I played violin throughout college. Still have some of the callouses." Vince laughs and holds up his hand.

"Means we have excellent digital stamina," says Bruce with a grin, showing his hands.

"Oh, yes," Kendra says, "I took for granted how dexterous one must be to play a stringed instrument."

The other two ladies at the table, who've both felt at least fifty percent of the string players' fingers, offer nods of approval.

"I played piano," says Ryan, before undercutting himself with, "but only for two years."

"Flute," says Jenn, without looking up from her ravioli. Then she reddens as a snicker works its way across the table.

"Strings aren't the only instruments that enhance sexual prowess," offers Paige. "I didn't play anything. But I did have a lot of sex, so..." She holds up her hands as though weighing scales. "Six of one?"

*Brzzzzzzzzzzzt.*

Paige's eyes dart to him. He felt the vibration, he heard it, so did she. No one else at the table seems to have noticed. She holds his gaze as the conversation shifts around him. Her face is a puzzle. Frustration is a large piece, anger another. Not necessarily anger at him, he thinks, not initially. The anger stems from Emily; he's just getting it all over his hands. If he were smart, he'd take the phone out of his pocket, turn it off, and give it to his wife. Not because he owes it to her, or because she would ever ask for it, but because then it'd be out of his hands. He would be unable to fall into the web. The spider has always started with, **Hey, handsome.** He wonders if that's how tonight's series begins.

He finds it hard to read malicious intent into Emily's flitting conversations. They've been the scattered neurons of a former relationship, firing back to life, but not all together, not all at once. Nowhere near the strength. Nowhere near the import. All must be weighed against Paige's feelings, of course. He sighs, looking at her shoulder again, back to perpendicular. She stays that way for much of dinner, focusing her attention on the four people at the table who aren't currently communicating with their ex...ex what? She's been girlfriend, lover, paramour, partner, for the briefest of moments, almost wife, not legally no, but still.

What Emily is for him, though is far different than for Paige. After the events last year, it's a wonder that his wife hasn't asked that Emily be excluded from their lives forever. But she won't request that. Probably not, at least. Regardless, he shouldn't have his phone here. Paige doesn't deserve the reminder, not now, not here, not after all the stress.

"What if this is the last one?" Paige asked him as they packed for the trip, sitting on their bed amid the piles of dresses and shoes that were in the "possibly" category.

"It won't be," he assured her. The business was hurting, yes, but they've been through hardships before. "We can weather this. Norton's weathered worse."

Before Paige had taken over the family business, in fact, it had endured the steepest drop in the company history. She hadn't saved it, only stepped in when her brother Corbin stepped out.

"And I," he began, knowing that he ought to address the elephant in the room, his career, and the dramatic lack of money it offered, "I can always leave the or—"

"Stop," she said. "No. That's everything."

"It's *not* everything," he sat next to her, putting his arm around her shoulders. "It's *a* thing, yes. *You* are everything."

She looked at him, tears forming. She sniffed them back. "All I'm saying is, let's enjoy ourselves," she said, jumping up to resume her packing. "Let's enjoy as though it *is* the last trip."

He agreed.

Enjoying themselves like this visit to Aphrodite's Resort and Spa would be their last does not include dodging texts from an ex-something while still carrying the phone around in his pocket and steadily upsetting his magnificent wife further and further. He ought to throw it into the ocean.

Paige had the right idea. She didn't charge her phone the night before the trip. On their arrival at the airport yesterday morning, the battery was at twenty-two percent. Before takeoff, sixteen. At the Cancún airport, the phone warned **Less than 10% Battery Remains! Power Saver Mode Enabled!** She brazenly flipped Power Saver Mode back off, despite the dying phone's pleas. On the shuttle to the resort, she streamed a music video where P!NK extolled the virtues of being dirty little freaks and asked them both to raise their glasses until the phone finally gave up.

"Shepard, out!" she said, dropping the phone into his lap.

He needs to do something about this, here, with Emily, put a stop to it in a meaningful way. Could let the phone drain, sure, the boys could always reach them at the resort's family friendly number after all. But that's addressing the problem without addressing the source.

His dinner companions make short work of their various desserts. Bruce notes that Jenn has heeded his advice and there are parfaits, and creme brulee, and brownies, and something that looks like a giant brown marble with a sparkler sticking out of it, all lining the table in front of her and the rest.

He excuses himself from the table, vaguely and politely referencing the restroom, located outside the restaurant itself. He steps out into the evening and breathes the sea air. The resort is quiet except for the distant sound of tonight's festivities beginning and waves lapping at the shore.

He pulls his phone from his pocket and unlocks the screen.

**hey, handsome :)**
**hows paradise?**

"I shouldn't be surprised," says Paige. She chews the inside of her cheek and fixes him with a look that reveals more sadness than anger.

Bruce doesn't try to hide the phone. He's been caught. He looks down at it. So does Paige.

"She's not even trying to keep a cohesive narrative together. First woe is me, now flirty. It'll be woe is me again later if you don't tell her to stop." Paige sighs and rests her head on his shoulder. "Then it'll be," she waves her hands in front of her face, like a magician performing a trick, "she's gone."

"I came out here to tell her," says Bruce.

"Good, because while Vince and Kendra are ready to crash out from the day's travel, Ryan and Jenn are especially frisky, and I'd like to see what I can do about that." She steps back in front of him and fixes her eyes to his. "You interested?"

He nods.

"Then will you tell Emily, for me, to pretty-please fuck off and let's go have some fun?"

He nods again, a weary smile on his face.

She gives him a kiss, then puts her fingers on his chin, holding his gaze. "I love you," she tells him. Her wide eyes always signify special import. They suggest he needs to *believe it right now*.

"I love you," he returns. "So very much!"

She disappears in the direction of the rising sounds of a party.

He looks at his phone. **hey, handsome :) hows paradise?**

"Paradise needs one less Emily Laurel," he says with a sigh, then texts back, **Please respect that we are on vacation and stop texting me.**

He hits send.

# 10

# ALEJANDRA

"Look, it's schoolgirl night, *mi amor*," whispers Alejandra to her wife, imbuing the words with as sensuous a spin as she can muster without snickering. "Did you bring your cliché?"

Crista hides her laugh at the framed poster on the side of the lobby announcing tonight's theme. A man brandishing a ruler, who looks as though he's wandered right off a surfboard and into a graduation cap and gown swats at a schoolgirl, all eyes and tits and plaid skirt, bending over before him. Her hand hovers in front of her yawning O of a mouth, beneath the words **Tonight's Theme: Schoolgirls & Headmasters! Contest! Prizes!**

"Well, Allie, how can you have any pudding if you don't eat your meat?" Her wife grins and scrunches her nose.

Alejandra loves that, loves her. She pulls her close and kisses her. "Shall we go to the bar and make sidelong snarky comments while we find out what 'Contest! Prizes!' means?"

Crista nods and takes her hand.

The courtyard has been transformed. The seating around the sculpture and fountain has given way to two long runway platforms. Colored uplighting points everywhere, to the trees, to the rattan roofs, to the sky. Whereas earlier the crowd had yet to congeal into the beginnings of trysts, now the clumping is quite apparent. Foursomes, sixsomes, scattered nervous twosomes. The very occasional single.

"It is quite a thing to observe swingers in the wild," whispers Alejandra, affecting an approximation of David Attenborough, filtered through the traces of her Latin heritage. Approximation or not, though, Crista laughs, and this urges Alejandra on. "Witness a pack of wild swingers descend on a unicorn." Alejandra points from the hip – one mustn't be observed observing, after all.

"How old do you think she is?" Crista asks in a whisper.

"Twenty-one, maybe. I mean, *look at her*."

The unicorn stands alone near the stage, swaying to the warm-up music, hair in pigtails, and wearing a Halloween costume school-girl outfit. The kind you'd find at one of those pop-up stores that are always long gone by November 3rd, in a section marked Adult Costumes. Probably with the word *sexy* haphazardly added to its description. Come to think of it, Alejandra has seen that specific outfit before.

"Is her skirt made of vinyl?"

"It is," confirms Alejandra, "vinyl skirt, quarter of a button-down shirt, that silly plaid tie—"

"Shouldn't the tie match the skirt?"

"Right?" Alejandra waves Miguel the bartender over, orders a pair of dirty vodka martinis, then leans back to Crista. "You have to provide your own cotton panties. They don't come in the bag."

As if on cue, the unicorn turns to talk to the couple that has descended upon her, revealing a tiny ass on display beneath the skimpiest of cotton panties. Alejandra allows herself to stare as the unicorn bends over and proffers that ass to the couple. The man gives her a playful and polite slap. The woman affects a "let me show you how this is done" demeanor, and her slap echoes through the courtyard.

"Oof! Too much," says Crista.

"Yeah, not going to like that," replies Alejandra.

The unicorn's face advertises pain as she reaches back and rubs her ass. It quickens into pleasure, though, and she bites her lip. She gives the woman a quick kiss, then the man. Then she scampers off. The couple watches after the unicorn, broad smiles on their faces. He whispers something to her. She nods and frowns.

"Do you think he's telling her not to hit so hard in the future? Or..."

Alejandra tracks the unicorn through the crowd, bobbing in and out of clusters of couples, nearly all of whom try to draw her into their orbit. She reaches her destination just down the bar, where a man in his forties, wearing a purple button-down and black slacks, sips something brown without ice.

"Daddy, can I go out and play?" Alejandra asks, now trying on the voice of a six-year-old.

Crista laughs and swats at her shoulder. "Stop, she's right there!"

Alejandra drops her voice. "Only if you're back in time for bed! And save a little sugar for Daddy."

Crista shakes her head.

"Too much?" asks Alejandra.

"Squicked," says Crista.

The unicorn bounds back off into the crowd toward the couple, who now seem to be deeper in negotiation. Daddy at the bar knocks back his drink and waves Miguel down toward him.

"What would you like to do tonight, *mi amor*?" Alejandra slides her arm around Crista and pulls her closer. She sees uncertainty in her wife's face, the way she glances around, the way she watches the women pass.

Crista shrugs.

"Something's bothering you," says Alejandra.

Crista shrugs again.

"C'mon. What is it?"

The look on Crista's face slides from mild uncertainty to something deeper, and she scrunches her mouth to one side.

*Fig. 1. Portrait of a young woman with crippling self-doubt.*

"Them," she says after a while. "The women. They're all so..." She looks away. "Perfect."

Alejandra looks around at the crowd. The women out there are either dressed as glam as can be in slinky cocktail dresses, the kind that grownups don't wear out on the town, the kind reserved for bar-crawling bridal parties, and a smattering of schoolgirls, whose numbers will undoubtedly increase as the evening marches on.

"I see beauty, to be sure," offers Alejandra.

"Like her," says Crista, indicating the unicorn with her head.

"The unicorn? Perfect?"

Crista nods.

"*Mi amor*, don't forget that youth is a ticking clock." She presses her elbow into Crista's side, but not hard.

"So, you don't like her more than me?" Those wide Crista eyes blink at her.

"Oh, honey," laughs Alejandra. She stops laughing when Crista's face falters again. She takes her wife's hands and looks deep into her eyes. "No. Not more than you. Perfection, though? Look around this courtyard, *mi amor*. There's fat and skinny and old and young and huge boobs and no boobs. All these prom dresses? These are people glamming it up because it's fun. Nothing more. Not perfection. Not better than—"

"Hi." The man in purple inserts himself into the conversation, bringing his crotch far too close to their legs. "How are you gorgeous girls tonight?"

Alejandra smiles. "Well, we're not girls, we're fantastic, and we're set—" But before she can unspool her usual "move along, my friend" spiel, he sets his drink, now three fingers full, on the bar between them.

"The two of you are together," he says.

"Are you asking?" asks Alejandra.

"I noticed." He winks.

"Yes, we're together," says Crista, leaning closer to Alejandra and caressing her upper arm in a surprisingly possessive fashion.

"And how do you two play?"

Alejandra has a feeling that the man in purple, with his strong chin and those crystal blue eyes, doesn't get turned down very often. Her first urge is to snap, "Well, we're lesbians, so..." and leave it at that. But the fact is, as the only lesbians here, they'll have to explain their play style a lot on this resort. May as well give it a go.

"Well," she begins with a deep breath, "we tend to play with married couples and unicorns. We'll play with the wife while the husband watches. Then he's welcome to join and—"

"Sounds like fun," he lifts his drink again, sips it, and puts it back on the bar between the two of them.

"And play with his partner," finishes Alejandra, pointedly.

The man's grin falters a touch, and he stares at her.

"I'm Alejandra, by the way," she says, offering her hand, defiance on her face.

"I know who you are." He drops his voice and leans in closer wafting the scent that's surely made by Axe toward Alejandra. "Don't worry. I won't tell."

"And I'm Crista." Her wife sticks her hand out toward them.

"Will," he says, not taking her hand. His eyes narrow, not with menace, or anger, just a note of confusion. "And my wi—" He stumbles. "Girl. Person." He points to the schoolgirl unicorn chatting up the couple across the courtyard. "She's Madison."

After a moment of waiting, Crista pats his shoulder, leans in, and tells him, "I don't think we're what you're looking for, Will. We *only* play with women."

Once more, he flashes his smile. "Only?"

Alejandra leans forward and tells him, with unmistakable resolve, "*Only.* Unequivocally."

Again, Will's eyes narrow just the tiniest of bits. "But—"

*Enough,* thinks Alejandra. "Do tell Madison, though, that Crista and Alejandra say hello."

He looks back and forth between them, and Alejandra sees in the way he looks at them, a man sizing them up, looking for his angle, for the right thing to say, the best weakness to exploit. He's about to go there. Here it comes. Instead, he gives an aggressively nonchalant shrug, takes another sip and steps off without a goodbye.

Having tired of the preamble to the promised fashion show, the women quit the courtyard for a walk on the beach.

"Were we too intense?" asks Crista as they walk.

"With that guy?" Alejandra asks. "No. If the door's open a crack, he'll jam his foot in it and wiggle. In the end, he was about to ask us to reconsider. His dangling 'but' spoke volumes."

Crista considers.

Alejandra lifts her hand and kisses it. The damp sand feels so good between her toes, and she's soothed by the gentle *shuuush* of the waves. "Look where we are."

"It's wonderful," says Crista. "Truly."

"I'm so happy that we're here." Alejandra stops and turns to her wife. "You and me."

Crista takes a breath and looks away. "You really want to be here with me?"

"I don't want to be here with anyone but you."

They kiss.

"I'll bet the unicorn munches like a champ," says Crista.

Alejandra snorts a laugh. "What makes you think that?"

"Youthful enthusiasm? Still having something to prove? Hell, maybe even that 'I've never done this before, so I don't know if I'm any good.'" Crista always looks away when she's snarky. Alejandra wonders if it's so she won't have to see the judgment if she crosses a line. Though of the two of them, Alejandra tends to be the one who travels right over the line into sarcastic dyke territory.

She grins at her wife, at that comment. The memory is so strong, so vivid. The irony. Oh, the delicious irony. "You mean something like 'I've never just approached a woman before, and here with my award, I thought...'"

"Shut up," says Crista, trading looking away for looking at her feet, shuffling through the sand.

Alejandra stops walking and tips Crista's face up to hers. "*Mi amor*, you approaching me at that banquet was the best thing that ever happened to me. Truly."

"You wouldn't rather have your pussy munched by the unicorn?"

"Rather? No," Alejandra says, then smiles. "Though if she ate me out while you sat on my face?"

Crista laughs nervously, then wrinkles her nose and kisses Alejandra.

The line of beds along the beach are empty, stripped of their linens to discourage night time beach sex. Alejandra notices a sign proclaiming ***¡Cuidado con los Cocodrilos!*** - **Watch Out for Crocodiles!** as they step onto the beach from the patio. She leads Crista to the bed.

"What?"

Alejandra sits on the edge of the nearest beach bed; the cold vinyl cover of the mattress makes her tingle. "I want you to sit on my face."

Crista laughs again, the nervousness more apparent.

"Now?"

Alejandra nods.

"Here?"

Alejandra nods.

"What if someone—"

"No one's coming out here," says Alejandra, "and if they do, it's for the same reason we did."

"I thought we just came out here to walk," says Crista. "And it's chilly!"

"I can keep you warm."

The playful, the hard to get, that adorable quality in her wife, drifts away. "Couldn't we just...later?"

Alejandra stares at her. This woman who had, in fact, sat on her face less than forty-five minutes after the first words they'd exchanged. The one who said that very thing, "I've never done this before," when she asked her to strap it on.

Crista holds her gaze for a moment, then looks away.

*Well, how did we get here?* Alejandra stands, takes Crista's hand, and continues their walk along the beach, unconcerned about *los cocodrilos.*

The sand becomes rocky and unkempt as they reach the end of Aphrodite's beach. The dark resort next door appears to exist in a quantum state of neither being built nor demolished, with its stretch of beach overgrown and covered with rocks and seaweed. They stop and Alejandra scans the horizon, seeing the distant lights of downtown Cancún.

"I love you," Crista says, still looking down, barely audible.

"Yeah," says Alejandra, "I love you, too."

They head back toward resort center.

After a twist in the path between buildings, she sees Strawberry-Blonde and Manic Panic making out in the dark, hands exploring each other's backs and asses. *Looks like they're still hot for each other,* thinks Alejandra. She considers skirting around the building next to them, so as not to interrupt, but then wonders why she should be so polite. They are, after all, sucking tongues on the public walk. Crista seems to have noticed them too, but Alejandra doesn't look directly at her to know.

As they approach, Strawberry-Blonde makes eye contact over the shoulder of Manic Panic. She laughs, a sheepish and melodic sound, then wipes her mouth with the back of her hand.

"Hi," says Strawberry-Blonde.

Manic Panic also looks sheepish, embarrassed, and throws them a wave. "What, um, what're you two up to?"

"Just wandering," says Alejandra. "You?"

"Until we got distracted," says Strawberry-Blonde, "we were on our way back to our suite for an orgy." The two women look at each other, then back at Crista and Alejandra. "Want to wander to our suite with us?"

As soon as the offer is out, that's *all* Alejandra wants to do.

# 11

# PAIGE

As they walk, Paige wraps her arms around Jenn from behind. Jenn's hands find Paige's wrists and squeeze.

"You know it's all going to be okay, right?" says Paige.

Despite a lip bite that indicates she doesn't *entirely* believe that, Jenn nods.

"I've noticed you," Paige tries to find the right way to put this, the way that won't make Jenn self-conscious, "go off, now and then."

Jenn stops on the path.

There's quiet but not silence, In the distance an announcer's muffled, echoing voice calls for applause. The crowd obliges. "It's not obvious, is it?"

"That you're in a rough place?"

Jenn nods.

"No, not obvious. Well, maybe obvious to people who love you." Paige turns her around to look at her. This woman who dove into the deep end of swinging, displaying such bravery and determination. This woman standing before her with her sheath of a dress clinging to her body. This amazing woman who feels at times a sister, a lover, a best friend, a confidant, a playmate. "People like me."

The blush hits Jenn's cheeks, visible even in the darkness along the path between La Grande Fête and their suite.

"Other people will just say, 'Look at that smart, sexy woman! She's deep in thought.'"

The burst of laughter that comes forth from Jenn startles some small woodland creature that darts through the underbrush. "Is that good? 'She's deep in thought?'"

"Works for me," says Paige. She brings her fingers up to the two points at the front of Jenn's dress and traces circles around her nipples.

"But what *doesn't* work for—" Jenn's eyelids flutter. "Mmm."

"Now, now, not everybody gets the direct channel to my brain and bits like you."

"I'm a lucky girl," says Jenn with a grin.

"We both are!"

They wrap their arms around each other's necks and get close, to that sublime point where Jenn's face goes out of focus and Paige can feel her hot breath. Their lips meet.

Paige hears footsteps in the darkness and opens her eyes. Over Jenn's shoulder, she sees two women come up the walk. She's caught a glimpse of them around the resort today, but never this close. They're both younger than her, but not by much. One keeps glancing at the ground as though she'd like to disappear into the underbrush with that woodland creature. Her hair is simple and straight. The same lovely simplicity as her beloved Jenn, in fact. The other, with hair curly and long, and a dress that showcases her cleavage, seems the opposite, someone who would like to be noticed.

*And now they've noticed us!* Paige stops her kiss and wipes at her lips, still tasting of Jenn, with her hand. "Hi," she says.

Jenn presses her head into Paige's shoulder for a moment, then spins to face the couple and waves. "What, um, what're you two up to?"

"Just wandering," says the one who wants to be noticed. Paige realizes that she recognizes her. Not just from earlier today, but from beyond these walls. She's not certain how, or from where, but there's something. "You?"

What *are* they up to, her and Jenn? Just now? Right here? Making out on the path because they couldn't be bothered to get all the way to the suite? Not that they needed a reason to play outside. The warm night breeze coming off the water is plenty. "Until we got distracted," Paige offers with a laugh, "we were on our way back to our suite for an orgy."

*An orgy of four,* Paige thinks. *I thought our orgy definition was five or better.*

She looks at Jenn, a quick flick of her eyebrow in the direction of the two women. *Read my mind, Jenn! Let's see what these two have!* As if the synapses had fired directly between them, a small smile reaches Jenn's lips, and she winks.

Paige turns back to the women on the path. "Want to wander to our suite with us?"

One of the women looks game, if surprised, the other seems hesitant. Paige thinks she ought to change tactics. "How about we start with niceties! I'm Paige."

"Jennifer – Jenn!"

"I'm Alejandra, and this is my wife, Crista."

"It's a delight to meet you both," Paige smiles. "We have some men joining us shortly."

"They went to the courtyard to buy cigars from the roller," says Jenn.

"Oh, we don't—" begins Crista.

Paige waves this off, this confirmation of what she suspected. "Not a problem, they're very caring gentlemen who'd never complain about being left out, or push boundaries they've not been asked to push."

"We're not interested in crashing your party," says Alejandra.

"If you weren't crashing?" offers Jenn.

"Fully invited?" adds Paige. "I think Robert's Rules should suffice. I move that we add our new friends Crista and Alejandra to the orgy guest list, posthaste."

"Seconded," says Jenn.

"All in favor?"

Crista and Alejandra look at each other. The question passes between them, in their eyes, in the little gestures, shoulder tics, head tilts, an almost imperceptible nod. They each tentatively raise their hands. "Aye?" they ask in unison.

Jenn laughs. "Opposed?"

Only the sound of the waves.

"Well, I'd say that's unanimous. Hugs?"

A cheer rises from the courtyard in the distance.

The women laugh and come in for a hug, the four of them. Paige's arms slide around Jenn and Alejandra, Jenn has hers around Crista. They lean their heads in, an impromptu football huddle. Paige is uncertain when it started, but suddenly, there's kissing. Light at first, between her and Jenn, between Alejandra and Crista, but then kisses go the other way, Jenn and Crista, Paige and Alejandra. They smile at each other.

"I've wanted to kiss you since the welcome festivities," Crista blurts, so quickly and without clearly identifying anyone that Paige isn't certain who she's talking to or about. Silence follows, and Crista seems to slump. She pokes her finger in Paige's direction and quietly adds, "You."

"Well, come here," says Paige with a smile.

Crista leans across their huddle and places a soft and gentle kiss on Paige's lips, then a second, then things intensify.

"Look what happens when we leave them alone for a second. A *second,* Ryan!"

"I can't blame them."

"Such kissability."

Paige separates from Crista and looks around the small huddle. "To be continued *very* shortly," she whispers. She takes Jenn's hand again, turning to face Bruce and Ryan coming up the walk. "We've met these two lovely women, Alejandra and Crista. And through Robert's Rules, the ayes had it, and they'll be joining us upstairs."

"Wonderful!" says Bruce. "As it happens, I asked Tomás to send up a cheese plate and some champagne."

"Excellent. Shall we?" Paige leads the way, down the path, up the stairs to their suite, to debauchery.

## 12

### JENN

Sitting at the courtyard bar at just after three in the morning, hours since the orgy, Jenn can still feel the exquisite touch of six separate hands guiding her toward orgasm after orgasm after orgasm. Waves breaking, towel soaking. She sighs and closes her eyes, re-experiencing the lingering phantom sensations, and a tingle runs through her.

Her husband sits next to her, chatting with a gentleman whose name she's sure she heard when they sat down, but doesn't remember. She's blissed out, as Paige has often described it, eased on down the yellow brick road to the merry old land of come-drunk. She leans her head back and looks to the sky beyond the bristles of rattan hanging off the roof of the bar. The stars flicker like twinkle lights as wispy clouds blow across them.

Behind the bar, Gabriela prepares and delivers hot pizzas to a smattering of night owls, and Miguel tries to keep up with drinks. The music in the courtyard is quiet, almost only thrumming bass, and it allows the distant waves and the crackle of the wind through the rattan.

With their pepperoni pizza due to take *quince minutos*, and the hum of the blender down the bar indicating drinks on their way, Jenn allows herself to reflect on her evening. She drifts backward, starting with her final stolen kiss from Alejandra at the threshold of their room, all the way back to the four women, sitting on the bed in Bruce and Paige's sprawling suite while the men milled about.

"Champagne?" asked Bruce, holding the bottle out toward them, white linen napkin over his forearm and everything.

Meanwhile, Ryan dimmed the track lighting over the sectional couch, adjusted the air conditioner, and unzipped their bag of tricks. Eying their bag, Jenn felt a long way from Jennifer Straub on her youthful Pocket Rocket adventures. In their toy bag were dildos and harnesses; vibrators; and not one, but two, of the grand standard, the jackhammer of sex toys, the Hitachi Magic Wand. Ryan lifted out the smaller black leather bag, home to their safer sex supplies, condoms, lube, gloves, dental dams, setting it on the tile step near the mirror-walled hot tub.

"Just to confirm, we are off-limits," said Alejandra to the men.

"Alejandra, nothing would make me happier than waiting on the four of you while you enjoy yourselves," said Bruce as he filled a champagne flute Paige held then passed to Crista.

"We're okay with you joining, too," said Crista. "Just not with us. We don't really..." She seemed to lose her train of thought.

"Crista's trying to say we just don't go in for dick."

"Absolutely." Bruce smiled. "Thank you for taking care of yourselves."

Jenn sought eye contact with Ryan, who was nibbling on some cheese from the platter before him, sitting on the sectional couch. He smiled at her, and in that she read quite clearly, *I'm alright, you have fun.*

"I can't believe your room," Ryan said, an understatement indeed. The suite, more than double the size of their own meager room, sprawled like an L. In the center stood the mirrored walls and hot tub, flanked by white columns; to the left, a sectional couch and sliding glass balcony door; to the right, a riser, and the king-sized bed where the women sat, still not discussing tonight's agenda.

Jenn felt an urge to kiss, well, she couldn't decide who should be first. Paige, sure, the attraction was obvious, always had been. Paige was a self-possessed sexual being, and they had nearly two years of history and love. That said, Jenn had a fleeting thought that one doesn't fly to France to eat New York style pizza. The idea struck her as funny, and she narrowly missed holding back the giggle-snort. The coughing fit that followed wasn't as funny, but she waved off concern from all in the room.

"Before Jenn dies, we should offer our preamble. And I feel comfortable speaking for her because we use the same precautions," said Paige.

Jenn nodded and coughed a weak, "Yes."

"We test every six months, Jenn and Ryan tested last month, negative on everything."

"Cold sores," croaked Jenn.

"Yes, right," said Paige. "Me too on that. I've had HPV, high-risk strain, but it is no longer detectable. Anything I need to add?"

Finally feeling her voice return, Jenn added. "Condoms on toys, gloves if there's going to be body switching."

"Like *Freaky Friday*," offered Ryan.

"Who brought this guy?" Bruce asked. Jenn looked over with a smirk to see Bruce smack Ryan on the back.

"How about you both?"

"HPV about a decade ago," said Crista.

"A cold sore maybe once every year or so," said Alejandra.

"We got tested a couple of weeks ago," continued Crista, "negative everything else."

"Now that we've gotten the housekeeping out of the way," said Jenn, "we want you to know that we find you interesting regardless. We have a whole week here in paradise."

Paige nodded.

"Do we want to fuck you?" asked Jenn. "Yes. Do we want to be your friends even if we don't get to fuck you?"

Paige beamed at her. Despite her love's smile, Jenn felt self-conscious about having lifted the Shepards' signature line. They were Ryan and her swinging sires, after all. The ones who inducted them into this world of delights and terrors, where everything, emotions, desires, stresses, find themselves magnified.

"Yes," confirmed Paige.

With a smile, Jenn asked that ever-important question, another one she learned from the Shepards: "So, what do you want to do tonight?"

"Jenn." Ryan brings her back to the courtyard bar with her name and a touch on her wrist. A lime green drink in a plastic tumbler sits in front of her, another in front of him, both flanking a pepperoni pizza, still sizzling.

"Lost in the memories," she says.

"It was," he laughs, "something else."

"You had fun, right?" she asks. "Just watching."

"I had fun."

"And you're not upset we invited Alejandra and Crista?"

"Not in the least."

"Maybe I'll give you a blowjob later?"

"I'll enjoy that thoroughly." He points at her drink. "Try your melon ball."

She sips the icy drink slowly through the straw. It hits her tongue, sweet and tart and heavenly cold. "Excellent choice," she tells him.

"I thought so." He nods, staring at the slice of pizza on his plate, untouched, cooling.

"You somewhere else too?" she asks.

"I'm thinking about your sexuality," he says.

She blinks at him. "My sexuality."

"Not in a creepy way."

"I didn't think it was creepy."

He holds her gaze for a moment, trying to read deeper than the surface, perhaps. "It's a huge part of your identity, now," he says.

She nods. "It has become that, I think."

"I mean, Paige is your girlfriend, you've talked about bisexuality on social media, you've come out to so many friends and family members."

"It's more than a hobby, you mean."

"Yeah," he says. "A far cry from just swinging for the sex or the hedonism or the wild abandon."

"Though there's still that," she says with a smirk, recalling with a full body tremor the moment Crista's hand slid inside her.

"I've watched you discover things," he says. "Like doors to new rooms inside you. An expanding web."

"Things about myself?" she asks to confirm. "New facets?"

"Yeah." He looks back down at his pizza. "I don't think I've left myself as open to that as you have."

She considers. In their nearly two years of swinging, they've explored many different facets of sexuality. For a while, they had a membership at a BDSM club in downtown Chicago, before deciding it ultimately wasn't their speed. They explored the boundary between swinging and developing longer-term relationships with people, both her with Paige, and for the couple months that Ryan dated Kendra.

"I don't think you're giving yourself enough credit," said Jenn. "You've come a hell of a long way from the Ryan Lambert I married. You push your boundaries."

"Only just," says Ryan. "But not really outside the box."

"This is pretty boundary pushing," she said. "Being here. Going outside naked!"

"Absolutely!"

Her husband has something he wants to say, but she can see him holding it back. "Are there specific boundaries you'd like to push this week?" she asks, having some idea of his mind.

"I think. I should try. Something," he says, then takes a long sip of his Melon Ball. "With a guy. Maybe."

*Bingo.*

She's noticed that Ryan's curiosity piques around certain men. Certainly times around Bruce, where they found themselves exceptionally close together. The odd shared blowjob, here or there. Jenn smiles and drifts for a moment, spinning up the projector in her mind, seeing Ryan and Bruce next to each other. The image is low because she's kneeling. Their cocks meet before her face, and she takes them both in hand, then in her mouth. Then they're kissing each other. Then they're stroking each other. Then they're—

"Jenn?"

"Sorry," she says, snapping back to the bar.

"Sorta worried about your reaction to it all."

"What?" She throws herself into encouraging voice. "No! I mean." She takes a moment to center herself and slide the new image away, of Ryan getting down on his knees next to her to take Bruce's cock into his mouth. "I mean I support you one hundred percent." She puts her hand on his knee. "This is a week of exploration and the new. We've cast off the shackles of life and lit out for paradise!" She kisses him. "If you want to get some hands-on penis time, I support you. Fully. And, for the record, would love like hell to see it."

Ryan laughs, visible relief washing over him. "Good. Thank you."

"Now this pizza looks great, and I am famished!"

"You did have quite a lot of exercise tonight," he laughs.
"I did indeed!"
She lifts a steaming slice of pizza and devours it.

# 13

# RYAN

"You did have quite a lot of exercise tonight." Ryan laughs.

"I did indeed!" Jenn devours a slice of pizza with the ravenous hunger that she only seems to exhibit after particularly intense play sessions. So often his wife picks at her food, as though it's only a necessary evil getting in the way of her contemplation.

He smiles and lifts a slice of stunningly hot pepperoni pizza.

If he were to explore, Aphrodite's would be the place to do so, wouldn't it? Surrounded by people that he's never met before, save five. A crowd theoretically more open than the rest of the world. At home, his only rare glimpses of guy-on-guy activity have been at private parties, and even then, in a corner somewhere, or behind an almost-closed door. Not out in the open like the women. Watching tonight floored him. The fluidity with which that foursome writhed on the bed in Bruce and Paige's suite. Watching Jenn ebb and flow through it. He's seen her with numerous women at this point, in so many different configurations. Tonight struck him as different, though. New.

In the past, he's seen Jenn with Paige, Jenn with the female half of another couple, Jenn with a unicorn, with that horrible girl Beck. He shudders even to think of Beck. Playing with women has so often been a prelude, though. Then the men come in, and the splits happen. Jenn goes to Bruce; he goes to Paige.

Jenn and Vince, him and Kendra. He and Jenn play with the unicorn. This rote progression is probably why Jenn treasures her one-on-one time with Paige so very much.

Tonight's grouping in Bruce and Paige's suite on the ocean, this configuration was new.

From his vantage point on the sectional sofa near the sliding glass doors, he saw the gravitational pull of Paige. Both Alejandra and Crista moved toward her almost immediately. He felt anxiety creeping up in his chest, extending its claws, digging in. For Jenn on the outside edge, left behind. Because things were so fragile, now, weren't they? With the emotional beating and bruising she took. On a trip they most certainly could not afford. To be passed over, slid out of priority, to be...ignored?

He saw the flash of it in her eyes. The momentary, "Oh, alright guys, I'll just be over here..." that turned her right back into Jennifer, rolling back the confidence, rolling back the change, rolling back the years. After such a strong beginning, too, tossing off the Shepards' signature line without a second thought. Owning the room. Then to have these women, these lesbians, confident in what they wanted, slide across the huge king bed into almost another continent, slide away from her into another play space.

The anxiety whispered to him, projecting film of what it'll be like to leave this suite later. He'll console her. He'll remind her that she's beautiful and sexy, and that any woman would be—

Jenn lunged to whisper something into Alejandra's ear. Alejandra halted her nibbling on Paige's shoulder, and a grin spread across her face. She nodded. Jenn smiled back and moved from the bed to their toy bag, pulling her dress over her head as she went.

"Why waste time with undies here, right?" Crista asked and laughed, watching Jenn cross the floor, nude.

That'd been all she needed. That momentary appreciation. Jenn putting her desires into the world, pouring them into Alejandra's ear, and then getting up to own them. Her ability to take the momentary discomfort and twist it.

A wave of jealousy surprised him.

Not jealousy, though. That would be reading the parchment wrong. What had Bruce told him? He glanced at the man he wanted most to be like, bending before the cadre of women with a bottle of lube and a box of rubber gloves.

"Envy is the word you're looking for," repeated Bruce in Ryan's head, the memory so vivid he thought the words had been spoken aloud. The inflection was that of three-drinks-Bruce, pontificating Bruce, Professor Bruce. Ryan loved that Bruce. "Jealousy means you don't want her to have it. Envy means you would like it as well."

That made sense. He envied his wife's ability to switch from the wide-eyed hurt of being momentarily excluded to controlling the situation. He watched her tighten the straps on a black leather harness covered with a vivid red-stitched spider-web pattern. Jenn took her favorite dildo, hot pink at the base, mellowing to a frosty white, and slid it through the harness ring above her pubic bone.

*The dildo matches that lock of her hair!* realized Ryan.

She stood at the side of the bed, reaching up to finger the billowy curtains attached to the ceiling, waiting, having her moment, demanding acknowledgment and appreciation, her rigid pink cock pointing toward them. The three women on the bed crawled toward her, like the brides to Jonathan Harker. As fascinated by what would happen below his wife's waist as he was, he couldn't help but watch her face. Her hazel eyes showed everything, widening as the women moved toward her. Her eyebrows momentarily flicked upward as contact was made. The flutter of her eyelids as one of them, Ryan couldn't even be sure which, took Jenn's hot pink dong into her mouth. The impassioned closing of her eyes and opening of her mouth to expel a short gasp. Ryan knew that another of the three just inserted her fingers into his wife.

The game was afoot, and Jenn Lambert was winning.

"Now I think it's you that's drifting," says Jenn at the bar, sucking the last icy droplets of melon-ball through her straw.

"You're different," he tells her after a moment, still thoughtful. He notices her expression change, from content to worry, and rushes to correct the injustice. "No, no!" he tells her. "Not different bad."

"Different how?"

"Jenn versus Jennifer different."

"Oh," she says, concern lingering in her voice.

He takes a bite of the cooling pizza, using the time to consider what to say. "You were worried they didn't like you," he tells her with a mouthful, then swallows.

"Alejandra and Crista?"

"Yeah."

"I was," she confirms with a nod.

"But then it changed."

"They really wanted Paige," says Jenn.

Ryan moves to defend her, if even from herself. "No, I think—"

She shakes her head at him. The pink lock of hair drops into her eyes. She blows it away. "No need, hon. They really wanted Paige. Trust me, I could tell. I was there at the beginning, but as an afterthought, for them." She takes a moment, looking down, sliding her palm along the glass bar top. Without looking up she says, "So I made myself essential." After saying it, she raises her eyes to him, and it's almost as if the revelation happens to her just now before him.

She walked away from a cluster of women that left her out, put her sexy on, and came right back. Confident, cool, collected. "Who wants to ride me," she asked after the women gave her a thorough three-way blowjob. She had multiple volunteers.

"What would you have done if they weren't interested?" he asks her, feeling the anxiety in his stomach.

She shrugs. "I didn't think about it." Her eyes meet his, considering him. She smiles. "You felt the nerves more than I did, I think."

He nods. "So it would seem."

"I decided to enjoy myself, so I enjoyed myself." She waves to Miguel, pointing at her empty tumbler. He nods and waves back, then heads to the blender.

She grins. "If they hadn't gone for it, maybe I would've just jerked off for a while, 'cuz that's fun."

The enjoyment and pride in herself looked exceptionally good on his wife as both Crista and Paige took turns riding her. Then the foursome slid into pairings. He watched Crista and Jenn whispering back and forth, negotiating something. He felt such curiosity, needing to know, but hadn't want to mess with the mood by asking.

Bruce knelt at the edge of the bed, running his fingers through Paige's hair as orgasms courtesy of Alejandra's tongue rolled through her. After a while, Paige pulled on Alejandra's shoulders, and the woman walked on her knees over Paige's entire body before stopping with knees and shins on either side of Paige's head. Paige wrapped her arms around Alejandra's hips and plunged her face into the glistening brown vulva beneath the light wisps of an almost entirely shorn mound.

His wife's negotiation seemed to have reached an accord, as Crista pulled on two purple rubber gloves and knelt between Jenn's legs. Jenn turned her head to look at him with her wide-eyed, "Is this really happening?" silent question and a grin.

He nodded and watched Crista work her hand deftly between Jenn's legs. At three fingers, his wife moaned, and her eyelids fluttered, at four she gripped Crista's shoulder, and her moans became more emphatic, and at five the moans became calls, nearly screams, of, "Yes," and, "Oh, God."

Paige and Alejandra stopped to watch.

"She's good at fisting," said Alejandra.

"Looks it," said Paige.

When Crista's entire hand disappeared, Jenn's eyes rolled. Her mouth became an elongated O but produced no sound as she jittered and shook her way through orgasm after orgasm after orgasm.

Ryan saw a point where he could help and leaped to it. He lifted a plush white towel off a stack near the bed and moved around to the side.

Jenn continued to shake and spasm, wave after wave.

He silently moved next to Crista, and they made eye contact. She grinned as he held up the towel, nodded, and moved to the side, allowing him to spread the towel under her arm, between his wife's legs. Jenn lifted her ass ever so slightly, so he could slide it under her.

"You must be a squirter," said Crista, intensely.

Still no sound came from Jenn, but she threw her head in a spastic nod.

"Well, shall we pull the cork?"

"I'm..." she gasped. "Afr— Afraid. Don't. Soak. You."

"Soak me, sexy," said Crista.

It appeared to happen in slow motion. Crista's hand slid out of Jenn, who sucked in a dramatic breath. The spasms that rocked through her were more intense than he'd ever seen, the whole room stopping to watch. The arc of fluid that poured forth from between her legs looked like the blast from a fire hose. Ryan's towel preparation felt woefully inadequate.

Cheers and applause followed the squirting.

Crista did, indeed, get soaked, laughing as she wiped at her face, clearly very proud of herself.

"Quite a day," says Ryan, tipping his quarter of a melon-ball to his wife's new one, already a third gone.

"Quite a day," she repeats and sighs a profoundly contented sigh. "Now, I think I'd really like to go back to our room and have you fuck me."

"Then blowjob," Ryan reminds.

"First blowjob, after blowjob, fucking." She giggles and bites her lip at him.

Ryan nods. "*¡Buenas noches*, Miguel!"

"*¡Buenas noches, Señorita y Señor!*"

As they hurry to the room, it occurs to Ryan that less than twenty-four hours before, they'd been just getting up to go to the airport. It seems impossible that so much could happen in the space of a day.

He wonders if maybe time has elongated, somehow.

# PART III

*Sunday*

## 14

## RAYMOND

The blinding rising sun bleeds along the water's surface at the horizon. Waves lap lazily onto the shore. Passing into the fire, Raymond Horne sees the silhouette of a small sail boat. He sits with his laptop open in front of him atop white linens on a beach bed. He hasn't looked at his computer since he opened it, instead focusing all his attention on the sand, on the water, on the sights and sounds of early morning at Aphrodite's Resort and Spa. The line of twenty or so beach beds to his right are empty save one way down at the end, bare feet hanging over the edge.

To his right, Celia, a sturdy dark-haired woman wearing an Aphrodite's visor, mills about the wooden tiki bar, complete with long tree stump stools and a gloriously full palm thatch roof. She spins up the blender and smiles when she notices him looking at her. Raymond raises his hand in a lazy wave.

"¡Buenos días, Señor Raymond!"

"Buenos días, Celia. ¿Cómo estás?"

"¿Bien, y tú?"

Raymond tries to find the word for tired in Spanish but knows that Celia will have no problem understanding his English. "Tired," he tells her.

"Cansado," says Celia with a nod.

Raymond smiles and nods back. That's it, tired. "Cansado."

"Bloody Maria?" she asks.

"That would be perfection," says Raymond.

Celia turns her attention from him to his drink.

Beyond the bar, a family strolls down Cancún's endless public beach. Like many families who deign to wander past the **Warning: Clothing Optional Beach Ahead (*Advertencia: Playa Nudista Adelante*)** sign, the mister's eyes roll in his head like a spooked horse's, the missus looks grumpy, and the child oblivious.

Raymond slides his laptop between himself and the lost pilgrims. No family should have to see his balls before breakfast. He looks down at his half-written morning email that begins, "Good morning, campers!" His heart isn't in the playfulness now. The man-child persona that people have flocked to over the last decade, despite its growing irrelevance, has not joined him on the resort this year. The Bacchus simulacrum yesterday was all he'd been able to muster, a fiction made manifest with a bed sheet and leafy garland purchased at Michael's craft store for seven dollars.

He not sure if he knows quite how to do this, this year. To *do* Aphrodite's. To *do* Xanadu.

"You should name it Xanadu." Colleen suggested one sunny morning six years and change ago.

He laughed and kissed her nipple. "What am I naming after an Olivia Newton John movie?"

She looked at him with that look, her look. The one that saw the child in him above the manchild persona. "Oh, you sad man. 'In Xanadu did Kubla Khan a stately pleasure dome decree.'"

He continued to smile, waiting.

"It's a poem," she said, then shook her head. Her endless blonde hair drifted over her breasts. "And you're decreeing a stately pleasure dome at Aphrodite's, aren't you?"

"Ah, we're talking about naming my Aphrodite's trip after an Olivia Newton-John movie."

"Asshole," she said and bent to kiss the tip of his cock.

"Will you be there with me, eternally?" he asked her, Shatner style.

"I cannot believe that you know that *terrible* song, but not the Kubla Khan poem." She folded her arms. "It was in *Citizen Kane*!"

"Of course I know the Coleridge poem, give me some credit."

"Asshole," she said again. Sometimes he thought it her true pet name for him.

"And will you help me run my Xanadu?"

"It would be *my* pleasure."

"A stately pleasure dome indeed," Raymond says, scanning the ocean from the last bed of the resort on his right to the first on his left, a full one-eighty of sand and water and beauty. Paradise.

This morning's quiet, as usual, runs inversely proportionate to the bacchanalia of last night. He was there. He saw. His tenth stately pleasure dome. In the hot tub, he'd watched his flock enjoy themselves thoroughly, taking pleasure in the new dynamics at play. Not only had he fought to get Aphrodite's to allow a lesbian couple to attend, but an incredible triad, a gay man, a bi man, and a straight woman as well. He laughs. "What a relationship sampler pack," he says aloud, before reminding himself silently that his victory for acceptance shouldn't come at the expense of tokenizing those being accepted. The voice that reminds him belongs to Colleen.

On one of the beds near the hot tub, he watched Terrence lie down, Rory slide down onto his cock, and Marley sit on his face. She rode that face as hard as Rory rode that cock. In the end, after the triad collapsed into a puddle, Raymond managed a moment of eye contact with Terrence. They exchanged nods and grins. He wondered if Terrence knew that he may well have been the first man to ever penetrate another man in public at this resort. In years past, before the takeover, the unspoken rule had been guy-on-guy stuff should be kept in-room. Unspoken, of course, because Aphrodite's didn't want to appear discriminatory. But the resort policy still followed the winds of the greater swinger community, and as those winds blew, male contact was still woefully rare.

"And how do you feel this morning," asks Mia. Her hat shades her face, her breasts already glisten from suntan lotion and the heat. He wonders if she can see his stiffening cock behind the laptop.

"Eh," he tells her, after wondering if he should make something up or answer honestly. No need to put on airs with her.

"This is quite a group you've cultivated," she tells him. "May I join you?"

"Please," he says, gesturing to the mattress.

Mia steps up and removes her turquoise sarong. She does it in that effortless fashion of someone who's spent far more time naked in public than most. Without a thought to modesty, shame. His cock stiffens further. *Put that away, Ray,* he thinks, *it's not sex o'clock!* He throws a towel over his personal sundial gnomon and sets his laptop atop his lap. She lies next to him and stares silently out at the water. The large round lenses of her sunglasses reflect the horizon with startling clarity.

"*Señor* Raymond," says Celia, out from behind her bar and next to their bed, offering up his tumbler, replete with an enormous celery stalk and a plastic stirrer shaped like a pinup lady. "Good morning!" she says to Mia.

"*Muchas gracias,*" Raymond says, taking the drink. "Mia, this is Celia. She's been here for almost ten years."

"*Doce años,*" says Celia.

"Twelve!" replies Mia. "You must love it!"

Celia grins, takes a moment of reflection, then nods. "*Sí, Señorita.* Would you like a drink?"

"Do you have mango?"

"*Sí.*"

"Something with mango."

"I'll surprise you."

As the resort begins to awaken around them, more and more people drift slowly onto the beach.

"These mornings at Aphrodite's can be like watching the aftermath of a most glorious hangover," Raymond tells Mia.

"I was impressed by the number of people at the gym," she says with a smile.

"Morning people," Raymond says, affecting a shudder.

"Says the man who was up before me."

"Couldn't sleep," says Raymond.

Last night, after enjoying the triad's show, he wandered down to the mostly empty courtyard bar. He arrived in the nether-time between the evening's planned festivities in the courtyard and late-night pizza and sandwiches at the bar. Most hedonists had found their way to their rooms to fuck, to the disco to dance (and then to the connected playroom, likely), or back up to the hot tub.

Melancholy took him at the bar when he mistakenly ordered "*Dos* espresso martinis," before correcting himself with, "*uno.*"

One. Solo. Single. On day one of his vacation. Day one of Xanadu.

In the morning, a flash of bright red hair flickers across the beach.

"I think you should give your guests more credit," says Mia, putting her hand on his knee.

A few moments ago, he would've had to re-adjust his towel thanks to this contact, but the red hair is enough of a distraction. He growls, "Kitten."

"Excuse me?"

"Oh, Kitten!" he calls out.

The young woman with the bright red hair in a pixie cut stops her jog and looks back at them. She waves. Raymond beckons to her, girding himself. One must be polite after all. Kitten – real name Lena, he recalls, but doesn't care – makes a showy jog over, her full breasts bouncing as she runs. She steps up to the bed, folding her arms on its ledge. "Hey!" she says. "Good morning!"

Raymond frowns. *What's the plan here?* he asks himself. *Gonna yell? It may be too early for that. Too early in the morning, too early on the trip.*

*Or perhaps you just shouldn't fucking yell at your guests*, suggests Colleen.

"I listened to your show this morning," says Raymond through a tense smile.

"Oh, yeah?"

Can she not sense the tension? Does she not understand that he might be miffed?

"You have a show?" asks Mia.

"Yeah, my boyf—"

"I think," Raymond says, measured but still tense, "that you both were perhaps a touch unfair."

Surprised to see a new episode of *Swingerqatsi* on his phone after he retired last evening, he thought he'd download and enjoy the first missive from paradise. As much as he didn't particularly like Strom and Kitten's brand of podcasting, a couple just unspooling their adventures without reflection or irony, he found it enjoyable that they'd be sharing this trip. This takeover.

"You called me a poser," snarls Raymond at Kitten. He folds his arms, then recognizing that he must look like that very child Colleen always saw throwing a tantrum, unfolds them again.

"Well, I didn't," says Kitten, emphasizing the *I* with caution on her face. Her demeanor turns bubbly again. "I thought you were fun."

He stammers. This shouldn't bother him. He shouldn't care what these two people, maybe as little as half his age, think of him, of this trip, should he? Of course not. But first thing in the morning, on the first full day of Xanadu X, he wants to be defended.

"Why didn't you say that on the show?" he asks.

Kitten shrugs. "Eric likes us to be more unified." She smiles and turns to Mia. "I'm Lena. But you can call me Kitten if you want."

"Hi, Kitten," says Mia, amusement in her voice, extending her long fingers to shake Kitten's hand.

Raymond shakes his head and notices the other half of the *Swingerqatsi* podcast slide up to the bar, making flirty small talk with Celia. For no particular reason, Strom's oversized plaid swim trunks make him angry. "Strom!" he bellows.

"There you are!" says Strom to Kitten. He slips back off the stool and comes over to the bed. Raymond thinks, for a moment, he may be subtly flexing his pecs.

Strom puts his arm around Kitten, who introduces him to Mia as, "my boyfriend, Eric."

"So, you two do a show?" asks Mia.

"A podcast, yes," says Strom. "We take our title, *Swingerqatsi*, from a series of experimental films by Godfrey Reggio."

"I know *Koyaanisqatsi* well," says Mia. "Used to teach it in my storytelling class."

"Wonderful film. Life changing."

Raymond gulps his Bloody Maria.

"The other two in the trilogy are rather good as well," says Mia.

Strom blinks at her for a moment, his face blank. Then he flashes perfect teeth. "So, to us, *Swingerqatsi* means either," he pauses a moment and puts his finger to his lips, "swinging life, or a way of life that calls for swinging."

"Clever." Mia smirks.

"I'm not a poser," says Raymond, unable to let this continue.

Strom blinks at him, his smile never wavering.

"I just call it as I see it, man," he says. "Our listeners expect brutal honesty. It'd be unethical for me to soften my opinions or tone."

Before Raymond can respond to the absurdity that *Swingerqatsi* has some bastardized form of journalistic ethics, Strom has turned his body toward Kitten almost entirely, showing Raymond his shoulder. "Still want breakfast?"

"I do!"

"Pleasure to meet you, Mia" says Strom. He turns back to Raymond, that annoying smirk still on his face. "Dude, don't let it bug you. That was just one moment. We've got a whole week."

Without waiting for a reply, Strom and Kitten walk down the beach, arm in obnoxious arm.

Raymond scowls.

# 15

## PAIGE

"I'll race you," says Paige, as her toes hit the sand.

Bruce grins.

The Shepards take off down the beach, past several beds, empty this early in the morning. Bruce runs hard; he's a fierce competitor. But Paige fiercer. She overtakes him by a couple inches, then loses that lead. That just kicks her competition up higher, though. She winks at him and pulls ahead again, just enough to turn right sharply in front of him, and put her hands on the beach bar.

"*Buenos días*, Celia," she says.

"*Buenos días, Señora* Paige."

"You didn't say we were racing to the bar," Bruce says, stopping, his hands on his thighs.

"Where did you think we were headed?" Paige asks him.

"Well, the bed, probably." He throws a weary finger in the direction of their bed down the row.

Paige weighs this. "Logical, but wrong. Bloody Mary?" she asks him.

He nods.

"You're more out of breath than usual," she says.

He looks at her with an incredulous smile. "We did just come from the gym, you know."

The ribbing is playful, but she senses she might be in imminent danger of pushing it too far. She smiles back and pats the stool next to her.

He sits with a nod and confirms "Bloody Mary for me, too," to Celia.

"I bring them," says Celia, shooing her and Bruce in the direction of their bed.

"*Muchas gracias*," says Paige. She takes Bruce's hand.

Walking toward the bed, she sees their host, Raymond, working on his laptop. Next to him is a woman Paige doesn't recognize, but who certainly isn't Colleen, his usual companion.

"Do you know what happened to Colleen?" she whispers to Bruce. She notices Raymond look up and wave. "Good morning!" she calls.

"Good morning!" he calls back, then returns to his laptop.

"I've been told that he had a bit of a tail-spin this past year. Colleen left."

"Oh, sad," says Paige. "I liked her."

"Me too," says Bruce.

They arrive at their beach bed, directly in front of their balcony. It's more secluded than some, since it isn't beach center. Paige drops her sarong and pulls off her sports bra. She walks to the waterline, and giggles as the first wave slides over her toes. The water is chilly, to be expected for November, but so lovely. The sky is clear. Another day in paradise. She stretches her arms over her head and looks up, squinting at the heavens.

"Do you want sunscreen?"

"Just dipping my toes." She stands in the water for a moment, feeling it lap against her ankles. The morning sun beats down on her chest, shoulders, and face. She breathes, centering herself here, reminding herself to be mindful, be in the moment.

When Paige returns to the bed, Bruce has laid two towels down and drawn the linen side curtains closed. He lies, nude, fingers intertwined over his chest, sunglasses on.

"Not asleep already, are you?" she asks.

"Oh, no."

She climbs onto the bed and lies on her side next to him, running fingernails through his bushy chest hair, down to his stomach, dipping below the line usually covered by shorts or swim trunks.

"Something on your mind, angel?"

She focuses on her fingers as they drift back up to his chest.

Of course there's something on her mind. The same something that's been on her mind for weeks. The same something that'll be on her mind until it all—

*Stop,* she tells herself.

He hesitates. "It's not about her, is it?"

Her. Emily. "No. Not her. It's that which should not be named or discussed."

"Well," says Bruce. "If you're cycling on it, it might be helpful—"

"I know." She sighs, then says, "If they try to reach me, they can't."

"No, they can't. But what could they need?"

Bruce is right. Her company, Norton Fixtures, would be fine for the week. "They'll be okay," she assures herself, then laughs. "But I suppose 'okay' is relative."

"The bottom line is, it'll still be there when you get home."

"True. They can't declare bankruptcy without me."

"It's not that dire."

"No," she agrees. "It's not." She reaches over and takes his hand. He holds hers to his chest. The movement of his breathing, the feel of his chest hair, is comfort incarnate.

He takes his sunglasses off and fixes her with a firm stare. "You know if we need extra money, I can go back to—"

She shakes her head. "I couldn't bear to steal you from the boys, or the orchestra."

"It's an option," he says.

"Fine," she agrees, clipped, wishing she'd brought down her own sunglasses. But they're just in the room behind her, just up that flight of stairs. He'd get them for her if she'd only ask.

If she'd only ask.

He'd leave the orchestra, too. Put the suit back on. Get on the next plane and consult. Like the old days, when he traveled. "I don't want that for you. The planes. The...away."

"You are not responsible for us, angel." He squeezes her hand. "Say it."

She squints at him.

"Please?"

She closes her eyes, nodding, and tells him something she'll never be able to bring herself to quite believe. "I am not responsible for us." She may not be, but she wants to be.

"*We,*" he emphasizes, "we are responsible for us."

Paige nods and looks away from his face again. Back to her fingers in his chest hair. She plays with it, wistfully, before running her purple nail down what she likes to call his center seam, where the hair changes direction in a vertical line between his pecs and down his stomach. She traces a circle around his navel and then finds the black thatch of his pubic hair. His flaccid penis lies on its side, facing away from her. When she touches just above it, it twitches. She flicks her eyes back up at his face.

Bruce looks down at her, with a half squinting, bemused expression on his face.

Paige doesn't look away as she slides her finger down further, along the length of his shaft to the folds of skin covering the mushroom cap ridge of his head. As she slides her finger back up toward his navel, she notes that the trip, among other things, has grown longer. She curls her fingers around his stiffening cock and sees the folds pull back, tighten, as his head pops out and flushes a deeper pink than the skin around it. He fills her hand, strains against her fingers. She opens her mouth and takes him in, feeling him stiffening further. She sucks gently until he reaches his full hardness, then more vigorously.

Their bodies move and adjust. Now side by side, yin and yang. His lips find her thigh, and she spreads her legs to accommodate him. His mustache and two-days growth of bristles tickle her. As she imagines him tasting her, before his tongue even reaches her, the floodgates open.

She's uncertain how long they'll stay like this, this twisted sixty-nine. It's long enough for her to feel both her own juices and Bruce's saliva slide down her thighs to the towel beneath her. It's long enough for her to feel the pulsing in her mouth that lets her know an eruption may be imminent.

She encircles his balls with her left hand, holding them gently but firmly. The pulsing grows stronger, and she feels him pull his face away from her pussy, resting on her inner thigh. He exhales a happy sigh.

A flash of shade makes her open her eyes.

Celia, in the middle of setting the second Bloody Mary on the ledge surrounding the beach bed, freezes as they make eye contact.

Paige's head jerks back, and Bruce's penis slides out of her mouth with a slurpy *pop!* that Paige is confident the entire resort must've heard.

"So, sorry!" says Celia. "I'm leaving drinks!"

Paige laughs.

"No, Celia, we're sorry," says Bruce, his head now resting on her leg.

"I'm leaving, you continue. Drinks are here!" She points to the two Bloody Marys, puts her hands together as if in prayer, and kisses her index fingers. "You continue!" She smiles, the smile of someone who's seen more than her fair share of fucking happening on this beach in her time here.

"Sorry, Celia!" Paige calls after her, to emphasize, as Celia rushes back toward the bar. She looks back to Bruce, his cock already back to its flaccid state. "We need to tip her again."

"And again, and again," says Bruce, laughing.

Paige begins to laugh as well.

"I hope you don't mind that we watched," comes a voice from above.

Paige looks up to the walkway behind the beds and sees a beautiful black couple, arm in arm, looking down at them. The woman's eyes shine a rich brown, her hair tight black curls radiating from her head. Her body toned, breasts round and long, with tell-tale breastfeeding nipples. She wears blinding white bikini bottoms.

"Don't mind at all," says Paige.

"We were on our way to our bed," says the man, bald and clean shaven, with a bright smile. He's bare-chested, pecs and abs glistening, and wears white linen pants that nearly glow in the sunlight. He extends a finger toward the one next to them. "It's just there. But we became..."

"Distracted," she says.

"Enchanted." They come around to the next bed, their bed. He offers his hand. "Malcolm. My wife is Alexis."

"Pleasure," says Bruce.

"Is ours," Alexis tells them.

"I must confess," says Malcolm. "This is not exactly happenstance."

Paige smiles at his infectious grin.

"This is our second Xanadu trip," says Alexis. "We've noticed you two."

"And may have asked for the bed next to you," says Malcolm. "Might force us to talk to you this time. Not like last time."

Paige looks to her husband, who seems similarly enchanted by the compliment. "Sneaky," she says.

"Well, then," begins Bruce. "Now that your hand has been forced, what shall we talk about?"

# 16

# JENN

All at once, Jenn wishes she'd never looked at her phone. She sets it on the table beside the bed. Face down. It can't hurt her any further that way. It can't tell her more frustrating news.

Ryan exits the bathroom, wiping his freshly shaved face with a towel. Jenn tries to hide her panic, but can't, so she just stares at him, eyes wide.

"What?" he asks, face going pale.

After just a momentary glance to the side, her eyes flick toward her phone.

"What now?" is his next question. For the last couple months, it's always been "what now?"

"What," she struggles. "Fresh. Hell?" She picks up the phone and tosses it to the other side of the bed without turning it back on. She doesn't need to see it again. There's nothing new it can tell her, nothing good. "Denied." The word itself is putrid, dripping, oozing toxicity.

"For unemployment?" he asks. Of course, he knows.

Everything about the past seven weeks, since she was terminated for violating the morality clause of her contract, has been a shit show.

"Why did they need to string me along like that? If they knew they were going to deny it, why ask for everything? Then why ask again? Why the constant check-ups? 'Please resubmit your IDs, Mrs. Lambert.' Why—" She feels her adrenaline rising. Her hands flail, not grasping for anything. She sees blotchy purple spots in the edges of her field of view.

Then Ryan is there. He kneels before her, taking her hands, sitting her back down on the bed. She hadn't even realized she'd stood up.

She takes a deep breath but doesn't release it.

Ryan is saying something, but Jenn can't hear him. The blotches grow, and there's a high pitched— What? What is—

He snaps his finger in front of her face, and her attention turns back to him. She's about to tell him not to do that, that she hates that, when he kisses her. The kiss is gentle but assertive. He holds their faces together with his hands.

Jenn lets her eyes close. In the dark, she can still see the purple blotches firing, like dim fireworks on the midnight sky in her mind. His voice pops in and out. Pieces of words, pieces that don't make much sense. She doesn't know if she's creating the purple blotches out of her imagination now, or if they're still happening. She feels his hands on her cheeks.

*Open your eyes, Jennifer.*

Of course, she'll have to.

They still have six days.

Jenn Lambert inhales a long slow breath, then opens her eyes. She's pleased that the purple splotches are gone.

Ryan is wide eyed. His face has lost its color and his mouth is tight, tense.

"I'm so embarrassed," she tells him.

"Why?"

"Because I fucked up so—"

"You didn't fuck up," he assures her. He shakes his head to reinforce it.

"How can I go out there—"

"They won't know. How would they know? Why?"

"I—" she says, but doesn't know how to finish.

"Besides," he breaks eye contact, but only for a second. "I think you'd be hard pressed to find a group of people more on your side in this situation than everyone at this resort. What swinger hasn't worried about the possibility of being outed and losing a job?"

She hadn't considered this. She looks down at her lap and tugs absently on the fringe at the edge of the sarong.

"Yeah?"

"So, tell them," he says. "Or don't."

"Do you hate me? Because now I not only don't have a job but no unem—"

"I could never hate you." His smile is weak but genuine.

She trusts it.

"You know what we're going to do?" he asks.

Jenn shakes her head.

"We're going to go out there," he points to the door. "We're going to meet some sexy people. We're going to fuck some sexy people. We're going to eat some great food. We're going to fuck some more sexy people. We're going to drink some great drinks."

She realizes that she's laughing.

"We're going to fuck some more sexy people. We're going to fuck each other so much you're going to get sick of me."

"I could never get sick of you." She laughs.

"But we're not going to worry at all about the job. Or the money."

Her laugh dies in her throat and she glances at her phone without intending to. The Job. The Money. They're very real. How can she—

"Stay with me," he says.

She looks back to him.

"The Lamberts of the Future are going to have to deal with some things."

A laugh that's barely a laugh escapes her.

"But the Lamberts of the Present?"

She gives him a real smile. "It sounds like they're going to fuck a lot of people."

"You bet your sweet ass, they are!" Ryan stands quickly, the towel around his waist falling off. He stands naked before her, cock pointing out at a forty-five-degree angle.

"You've thought this through," she asks, and means it as a plea that he isn't just trying to cheer her up now so he can get his cock (its angle rapidly becoming less acute as she watches) sucked. Placate the girl now, deal with the fallout later.

"No," he says. "But I do know there's absolutely nothing we can do from here to improve the situation at home, right?"

She frowns.

The Lamberts have been lucky, thus far, she considers. They've never really had any huge money problems. No more than anyone else in the mid-middle class. That's a sort of privilege they've had. Wandering into the often-opulent world of swinging had been an awakening, sure, that there were people who'd never had to compare prices on grocery store shelves. But since they'd moved in together, since they had first left their parents' houses, the Lamberts had always had the privilege of having two incomes. The privilege of being able to come to a place like this at all. To be able to scrape together the four grand and change. To put the rest on their ample credit. To waste it would be a sin, wouldn't it? A slap in the face to their friends who could never even have considered a trip like this. With six days remaining, she cannot in good conscience let *denied* or *morality clause* beat her.

"Right," she decides. "We should go out and have fun."

"Yes. Are you ready to meet a whole lot of people?"

She frowns. "Not really. Why?"

"Speed dating."

*Oh, fuck,* thinks Jenn. *Speed dating.* The welcome document they received before the trip had claimed that Speed Dating would be the single easiest way to meet fellow travelers (they were called "campers" in the document) on this trip. The other email on her phone was a reminder that today would include Speed Dating. It promised over half of the couples on resort had signed up.

Over half.

"Are *you* ready to meet fifty-ish couples?" she asks as Ryan pulls on a pair of shorts.

He looks back at her. "No?"

"But you want to."

He answers with the same lack of confidence. "Yes?"

She laughs, this time a real laugh, a loving laugh. Her husband, of the, "I guess so," response to, "Are you ready to rock?"

"We can leave it at home," she says, more to herself than to him.

He nods.

"It will be waiting."

"Absolutely."

"Clothes?" asks Jenn, pointing to his khaki shorts.

He looks down at the shirt in his hands, then at his shorts, then back up at her. He shrugs. "No clothes?"

Jenn looks down at herself, nude with her sarong in her lap. She looks back up to her husband as he pulls his T-shirt over his head, then shrugs back.

"Is it bad form to meet people naked?" he asks.

"I'm not sure Emily Post made a ruling on that." She smiles. "We've met people naked before."

"True." He gives it a long think. "Well, Speed Dating is in the buffet restaurant."

"Yes," she says.

"And clothes are required in the restaurant."

"Yes."

"Ergo," he says with a laugh.

She can't help but smile again. For all her husband's talk of being out of his element, she believes his humor will out. "Ergo," she agrees, and takes the necessary measures.

"Let's go meet sexy people."

They take each other's hands, and the door snaps shut behind them. As they hit the beach, they see that all the beds have filled up, either with people or towels or bags. Ryan signs up on the bed request list for tomorrow and then strolls with her down the beach. They walk just along the waterline, each lap of the waves covering their bare feet with cool water, then leaving in their wake the thirsty sand. Jenn notes her husband's antsiness, he's tugging at his shirt, as though it's been forever since he's worn one. He keeps glancing at her sarong and bikini.

"See," he says, pointing at her, "you could be naked at any moment."

"Did you put on underwear?" she asks him.

He shakes his head.

"Oh, was that a bridge too far?" she ribs him. "Then you have fewer articles on than me, paranoia boy."

Her heartbeat quickens as she sees Paige, naked but for sunglasses, on a lounge chair in front of one of the beds. On the bed lies Bruce, a straw fedora over his face. Like iron to a magnet, the Lamberts' path skews, and they wind up before the Shepards. Their couple.

Paige smiles, breaking the illusion that she is asleep beneath her sunglasses. "And where are you two sexy people off to?"

"Speed dating," says Jenn.

Paige sits up on her elbows and removes her sunglasses. She fixes her striking blue eyes on Jenn. There's a quality in Paige's look. One Jenn can't quite place, but one that feels very much akin to what she'd experienced in the room. Paige pats the lounge chair next to her.

Jenn sits. Paige smiles at her and leans her head forward. Jenn joins her, pressing her forehead to Paige's. Her eyes can't quite focus on the woman before her, but she looks deep into her all the same. Jenn feels a tugging, as though Paige is pulling at the feelings inside her, drawing them out, taking them on. She can tell there's something there for Paige too. She supposes they both have a good idea of what's wrong, between Paige's company's woes, and Jenn's unemployment. The similarity isn't lost on either of them. Another commonality. Another shared experience. All of it is for Future Them. It needn't be discussed, not now.

Jenn feels a tear drip down her cheek, and she laughs. Paige kisses her, and in that kiss, she can taste the saltiness of this woman she loves' own tears. They kiss again and lean back, hands grasping each other's. Jenn isn't sure when they'd done that.

"I think," says Paige, making a production out of the sentence, "that Bruce and I are going to spend the afternoon out here."

"Not interested in Speed Dating?" asks Ryan.

"Not so much," says Paige. "But!" she adds, stabbing the air with her finger, "It'll be perfect for you two."

One more kiss feels necessary to Jenn, essential even. She kisses Paige again, then stands. "Maybe we can hang out after?"

"We'll be here," says Paige.

She holds Paige's hand until the last moment, then Jenn and Ryan walk toward their appointment with Speed Dating.

# 17

# RYAN

As he watches Jenn and Paige's hands pull apart, Ryan feels a momentary urge to retract the Speed Dating decision, to instead stay there in the relative safety of Bruce and Paige and their quiet stretch of beach. To lose the clothing that's making him reflexively self-conscious and return to the safety of nudity. He laughs at this absurdity, and lifts Jenn's hand to his mouth, kissing it.

"What's funny?" she asks.

"This place is weird."

She nods.

La Fiesta, the low-key restaurant, is just off the pool, between La Grande Fête and the fancy sushi restaurant Rakuen. Ryan is overwhelmed by the sheer size of the place when they enter. Where La Grande Fête and Rakuen are clearly designed to foster a feeling of intimacy, La Fiesta seems to have aimed for the multitudes.

"Welcome to Jurassic Park," says Ryan, observing the similarity between this place and the film's visitor's center with its exposed rattan roof and rounded, sweeping atrium.

"I was thinking that, too," says Jenn with a laugh.

La Fiesta's atrium has been cleared, with all the tables pushed to the sides and chairs stacked up, leaving a vast open expanse of polished concrete floor. Milling about in the center, Ryan sees what must be more than fifty couples. He finds the variety of their dress fascinating, swimsuits, sarongs, a smattering full nudity. Ryan's favorite is a threesome (two men, and a woman) wearing nothing but socks and matching blue Chuck Taylor All-Stars. Their host, Raymond Horne, in khaki shorts and black T-shirt with the trip's Xanadu X logo, stands on a small riser toward the back.

"I know that's supposed to be Xanadu Ten," Ryan whispers to Jenn, "but all I can see is Xanaducks."

Jenn stares for a moment. "Now that's all I can see."

"Welcome to Speed Dating at Xanadu," says Raymond, lifting his arms in a praise gesture.

"Xanaducks," whispers Jenn.

Ryan laughs. Her playfulness is encouraging. As she sat on the bed earlier and cycled her way out of reality, he thought the meltdown might mean the end of their trip. Maybe not the end of being there, but the end of their enjoyment of it. Creeping at the edges, though, is the truth of what waits for them at home. The reality. A reality that now doesn't include the twelve hundred dollars or so they'd been expecting from unemployment. Twelve hundred or so for the last two months. Twelve hundred or so this month.

He shakes his head to clear his mind a bit. Narrowing his focus like the beam of a flashlight, Ryan turns his attention back to Raymond Horne, who is explaining the complicated geometry of how Speed Dating will work. Raymond seems more wiped out than would be expected on day two. His voice is hoarse, and he has the pallor of a man nursing a hangover. His verve is gone.

*Must've had a lot of sex last night,* thinks Ryan. Why else would you become a host of something like this, if not to have a lot of sex? He wonders how a person manages to build an empire upon getting laid.

"Everybody here will get to meet everybody else," their host assures the masses. "*If* you all promise me you'll be good campers and slide on down when I blow the whistle." He holds up a shining silver whistle. He waits. Waits. "How about a 'we will' from you lot."

Ryan joins the chorus affirming that they will be good campers.

"Last rule," Raymond says. "Do not discuss the following." He holds up a finger for each of his points. "One, where you are from beyond a simple statement of fact. Two, how or when you arrived at this resort. Three, when you are leaving this resort." He leans forward and puts his hand beside his mouth, as though offering a private aside to his audience. "Unless you are leaving immediately after Speed Dating, it's far less relevant than you may think. And four, God help me, what you had for breakfast. I shouldn't have to say all of this. But we human animals are often woefully unprepared for quick conversations, so rarely do they hold much meaning. To help you along, as you only have two minutes, I recommend the Mildest and Wildest game."

Raymond may have seemed a touch diminished when he began to speak, but he has revved himself up now to evangelistic fervor. His pause seems only to whet the audience's appetite to hear more.

"What's that?" calls someone in the crowd.

"I'll tell you," says Raymond with a grin. "You should lead by telling the folks you're paired with, or foursomed with, rather—"

One of the triad members points out "Or fivesomed."

"True, you'll all be fivesomed at least once," agrees Raymond. "And threesomed, if Mia decides to play..." he extends his hand toward a seat near the riser, where a woman in a tie-dyed floral dress sits, tablet in her lap.

She looks up. "No, Raymond, I'm planning to observe."

"As Sigourney Weaver in *Gorillas in the Mist*."

"Let's hope it doesn't come to that," says the woman, turning back to her screen.

"That's Mia Benjamin!" says Jenn, with some enthusiasm.

"Should I know who that is?" asks Ryan.

"Where was I?" asks Raymond.

"She's the blogger I was telling you—"

"Mildest and Wildest," cries the audience.

"Yes! So, you should lead with two things – and I encourage you to start thinking of your answers now, as they'll generate much discussion, and two minutes is an unbearably brief time. Think about yourselves, leaving this resort in a week—"

Groans come from the audience.

"I know, I know, but picture it. You've passed through those horrible sliding glass doors, you're waiting for your shuttle to the airport. But you have smiles on your faces. You're thinking back fondly. What is the mildest thing that could've happened to you this week that would bring those smiles, and similarly, what's the wildest?"

He grins at them. "For example, my mildest would be to find a connection with a sexy woman or couple and just hold space with them. Exist in their sexiness." Raymond pauses. "Too woo-woo?" He laughs. "Never underestimate the sensuality of holding space! But let's see, my wildest would be to find two women in need of discipline, suspend them from the struts on one of the beach or hot tub beds, and thoroughly flog and fuck them."

That seems to satisfy the audience, and they reward Raymond Horne with a roar of approval. Ryan nearly feels whiplash from the sheer breadth of space between their host's mildest and wildest preferences. He looks to Jenn for support and finds her grinning widely.

"You have yours, I guess," he says.

She nods. Her grin subsides. "You're not stressing about this, are you?"

He shrugs. She knows.

"From our conversation last night, I think you might have a wildest."

This is true. He nods. "But what does that actually encompass?"

"That's up to you. What're you looking for?" She presses herself against him. "What turns you on?"

He looks around the room, at the variety of women around him. Age, body type, height, ethnicity. Features ping his radar, attracting him. The hair of this woman, that one's glasses, the tits on her, and the ass on her!

The men, though... "Men just all sort of blend together, into...man."

Jenn laughs, then covers her mouth.

Ryan looks away, feeling the heat of embarrassment.

His wife grabs his shoulders. "Oh, no! Hon! I'm not laughing at you!"

He looks back at her.

"I promise." She leans in close and looks out at the crowd with him. "What piques your interest? With the guys?"

Ryan feels at a loss. He looks at the men in the room, trying to see them the way he looks at the women. With many of the women in this room, almost most, he wagers, he can identify at least one thing about them that he finds attractive. "It's different for the men."

"What makes it different?"

He makes a subtle gesture at a couple near them. The woman, in a wheelchair, has rich black curly hair. Her red and black polka-dot dress shows off exceptional curves, leaning into her clear pinup style with a bow. Standing next to her is a very handsome white-haired man, dressed in linens as bright as his hair, looking every bit like he stepped off some yachting magazine cover.

"Those two," he says.

"Yeah, I noticed them last night at dinner, they're *sexy*."

He looks at her and nods slowly. "Yes. Objectively I can see he's very attractive, handsome, well-built, etcetera."

"Well-built?" She elbows him.

"But when I look at her, well, I mean, it's different. A whole different reaction."

"The boobs, right?" asks Jenn.

He rolls his eyes. He can't deny that the ample cleavage on display initially called his attention. "Well, yes, but...I mean. Her style. Look how pretty—" He scowls and stammers.

Jenn nods. "Look, hon, I get it."

"Yeah," says Ryan.

"No, I really do! I didn't quite know how to look at women. Didn't really know what I found attractive. Or when I did know that I found someone attractive it made me feel guilty but also..." She smiles. "Tingly."

"I don't get that from men."

"You know that you don't have to explore this." She smiles. "I promise no one will make you. And no matter how hot I might find the idea, I will not be disappointed if you don't."

He closes his eyes for a moment, thinking back to his mildest twinges of interest. From feeling an urge to masturbate with a friend back in junior high, to the discovery of the lurid adventures that could be had in online chat rooms in high school. Everything came with shame. Not on the surface, and not because he felt he'd done anything to truly be ashamed of... But down deep, down below, it was there. The incidental contact he's had thus far hardly could be counted as exploration. As he and Jenn had gotten closer to Paige and Bruce, things had become more flexible and fluid. He's had Bruce's penis in his hand once or twice, but always to guide an insertion elsewhere. Those moments, though. There were blips.

"Maybe I just want to play with a cock," Ryan says, and instantly feels a pall of shame settle down over him.

This time Jenn manages to stifle her laugh.

"I'm going to need you to put your game face on here," he says, taking a deep breath.

"I'm sorry, I know. Honey. If you want to play with a cock, you should play with a cock." She appears thoughtful for a moment. "What about with Bruce and—"

Ryan shakes his head. This is a no-go, him and Bruce. The quick little thoughts have suggested this possibility to him, as well, more than once. But always the concern. "What if something happened? Or I really didn't enjoy myself, and it ruined something between the four of us?"

This gives Jenn pause. After a while, she nods. "Okay, I get that."

"I think the best first exploration would be with someone new." He says this aloud, but to himself.

"Well," she says and sweeps her hand at the masses in the room. "Let's see what we can find for you in a 'new.'"

# 18

## CRISTA

W hat are they doing here?

So many people. So much pressure.

And how much can you truly find out about someone in two minutes, even with this absurd mildest and wildest ice breaker? Crista racks her brain and cannot come up with anything.

Not. A. Thing.

She looks to Allie, seated in a chair she lifted down from the stacks to the side, watching Raymond Horne detail the mechanics of this speed dating frenzy. *It'll be a frenzy, alright,* thinks Crista. She absently crosses her arms over her breasts, wishing that she hadn't gone along with Allie's suggestion that topless was just the right way to meet and greet their fellow travelers. She steps back, next to Allie's chair, as Raymond passes out...something, she can't quite see what...to the other couples in the room. Are they all contestants? Is this a game?

"*Mi amor?*"

She looks down at her wife, who is smiling up at her, dark eyes shining.

"This may be too much for me," says Crista, speaking quickly, and at a higher register than she'd like.

"Then we'll go." Allie stands and offers Crista her hand.

Crista stares at it. This is the moment, isn't it? The moment to choose how they meet many of these people, how they first appear to them. The moment to see them. To be seen. "No," she says, quietly. "We should stay."

Allie's arms slide around her. This is safety. A snippet of an old song plays in her mind, something about "my lover's arms around me." Or was it "surround me?" The safety of this lover's embrace has allowed her so much.

When Crista decided to leave journalism behind, Allie supported her choice. When she came out to her family, Allie sat on the couch beside her, holding her hand. When she wrote her op-eds on marriage equality, helping fight that fight just a few years ago, Allie read every word, unafraid to offer honest criticism. Maybe that's what she needs now?

"I need you to tell me I'm being silly," says Crista.

"I don't think you are, *mi amor*, but tell me more about what you need."

Crista nods, cracks open the can, and lets her insides spill out into her lover's, her wife's, ear. "I'm not as pretty as you I'm not as smart as you I'm not as sexy as you I mean look at your boobs you were born to be topless where I look like a gawky teenaged boy and what was I thinking with this haircut and what am I going to say to these people and who wants to talk about children's books in a sexy environment no one wants to hear that I write the *Kolcarrot Rabbit Mysteries* no one needs that to take away from their fun and if I tell them anything else all they'll want to talk about is the war or terrorism or Gaza and I don't want to talk about fucking Gaza or fucking Iran because that's also not fucking sexy like me and they won't want to play with us anyway because we offer nothing for the men who can't understand that we just don't want..." She is distracted by a kiss on her neck, first just below her ear, then a nibble on the back in that oh-so-right spot.

Crista shivers.

Allie's lips brush her ear. "Your feelings are all valid, though I think you're projecting."

Crista nods. She knows.

"As I said, if you want to leave, we leave. We can go grab some food at the lunch buffet. We can see what the hot tub looks like in the bright light of day. We can go to the bedroom and munch on each other."

"I think we should stay," says Crista, entirely unsure of herself. She may not quite believe it, but some portion of herself that she used to trust and call "journalistic instinct" suggests that this is the best use of their time.

"Sorry to interrupt, ladies," says Raymond Horne, holding out a condom in a shiny purple foil packet.

"Thank you," says Allie.

Crista just nods.

"Look, *mi amor*, we're sixty-nine!"

She laughs. The condom packet on one side has a sticker with the number sixty-nine, on the other, the logo for this trip. The one that also adorns the shirt Raymond is wearing. Xanadu X. Try as she might, Crista finds it incredibly difficult to separate that name from the hours she spent watching Olivia Newton-John on VHS in her parents' basement. She reminds herself that she can still do the dance.

The realization hits, though, pulling her out of the fog of memory. "If we're sixty-nine that means there's way more than fifty couples here." A fresh batch of nerves crawls up inside her.

"Alright campers!" Raymond climbs back atop the stage. "I need numbers one through thirty-six to step against the wall and thirty-seven through seventy-two to— Man, seventy-two." He laughs and shakes his head. "Cluster in here in the center, please. Time is of the essence."

"We're doing this, yes?" asks Allie.

Crista looks from her wife to the glass door separating them from the freedom outside, to these couples trying to quickly align themselves based on numbers. The Clash rings in her head. She opts for double trouble and nods. "Stay." She grabs Allie's hand, and they move to the center of the room.

Raymond organizes his two groups into concentric circles, outside and inside rings. They'll have two minutes and then rotate to the next. After everybody in the outer ring has met everybody in the inner, the circles will split and form two separate scale models of the first rings. "Then, everybody meets everybody," says Raymond, raising his arms toward the lofty ceiling of La Fiesta. "Are you ready?"

"Here we go," says Allie, as she pulls Crista into their spot, in front of a couple they have not met.

Raymond's whistle blows, and Crista takes a deep breath. Out of the corner of her eye, she sees him press the button on a stopwatch. Her wife is already introducing herself to the young couple before them.

"Beth."

"Andy."

Crista looks around, feeling the room spin. She closes her eyes. The sound becomes muffled. She feels Allie's hand on her arm and knows that her wife is speaking for her. Not apologizing, no, because there's nothing to apologize for, but introducing her, and detailing their version of swinging. She catches glimpses of words from the muffle. "—with the wife—" "—happy for the husband to participate with his—" "—just not into—" "—understand that may not work for every—"

She rouses herself back to the world, to look at Beth and Andy. She's surprised to find that they aren't as young as she'd initially thought, likely older than she and Allie. They're one of the brave couples who have decided to do this thing naked. Beth is nondescript, with smallish breasts and a gentle curve of belly. Her mound is bare. Her blonde hair is tied in a ponytail, her face devoid of makeup.

Andy is lanky with a chest mostly free of hair. Below he's bushy, the curls almost hiding the flaccid penis that seems to Crista to have nearly turned itself inside out. You'd have to be quite confident to walk around like that, wouldn't you? And hell, all she's doing is standing here topless. Very unlikely anyone would notice the nipple that inverts itself whenever it pleases. She nods and smiles at the couple when they address her, though sound still hasn't come back.

Bits of what Beth is saying reach her. She catches the words "soft swap" and tries to rouse herself to the world, the conversation. To reassociate. Soft swap has been good for them because many soft swap couples prioritize what they often irritatingly call the "girl-on-girl action," and there's no penetration outside the relationship. They've had far less trouble with men in soft swap relationships. No last-minute demands. No "accidental" attempts at insertion.

"Mildest and wildest," says Andy. "We really have no idea."

"But we're excited to be here!" Beth says in such a chipper tone Crista can't help but smile. She's reminded of one of her mother's friends who used to sell Tupperware, back before those home businesses became all about makeup, health shakes, and mediocre vibrators.

"I'm not sure at all about mildest and wildest either," confesses Crista. The couple leans in at Crista's first words to the conclave. She's momentarily self-conscious but continues. "Being naked outside yesterday was pretty wild for me."

"Oh, I know!" Beth's eyes are wide, her nod nearly spastic. "We decided to come naked today because, well, it's hard to worry that people will judge you when you take your clothes off if they meet you with your clothes off."

Crista blinks. She's been so caught up, so worried about being judged by others for her body, for the contrast between herself and her gorgeous wife, for their unique brand of swinging... To hear someone else express similar concerns, particularly since Allie seems to share none of them, fills her up.

"Can I hug you?" she asks.

Beth laughs. "Never been asked about a hug. Yes!"

They hug, and Crista makes a point to fully experience it. The scent of this woman includes sunscreen of course, but also something citrusy. The feel of her warm body, their breasts touching, allow both to take a deep breath and connect their sigh. She feels Allie's hand run along her back. *Okay,* thinks Crista, *this is nice, I could do—*

A whistle shrieks silencing the room, with a laugh blooming from the silence. "Okay, campers, let's do like Alice and *Move down move down move down!*"

The machinery of these two circles has not yet been well established, and the inner circle flexes with people unclear of the direction they should go.

"To the right to the right to the right to the right!" shouts Raymond through laughter. "That's my fault!"

The inner circle lurches to the right, and the game begins again.

As every successive couple passes through, Crista finds her mind drifting into her old habit of cataloging crowds, observing them, to write about them. (*The Erotic Vacations of Swingers?*) The age range of the group is vast, as is relationship style and body type. She recognizes that obnoxious young podcaster couple in their mid-twenties ("Have you seen the film *Koyaanisqatsi?*"). A few older couples, who've clearly been coming here for ages ("Of course, then it was called Aphrodite's Atoll, and really leaned into the kitschy atomic age design." "Which was already two decades out of fashion..."). The hot pinup girl in the wheelchair. Then there's the triad, whose relationship structure intrigues Crista, even if their lack of a woman who's into women makes them an unlikely fit for play time. While Crista finds it difficult not to compare herself directly, she's pleased that she feels at least somewhere in the median attractiveness level. The variety of reasons for being here also impress her. For every couple here for the first time or brand new to the exploration, there are veterans of this lifestyle, this resort.

Amongst the vast gulf of differences, though, Crista sees the patterns emerging. Many of them grew up religious, marginalized, she hesitates to use the word oppressed, even in her own mind, but somehow...held back. There are quite a few divorcees in the group, people who tried monogamy and found themselves cheating, people who were cheated on, those who tried to walk the path that had been expected of them and in the end simply could not.

As the central circle breaks out into its separate smaller circles, Crista is acutely aware that she hasn't said much. "Oh, God, has everybody thought me rude?"

Allie laughs. "I don't think anyone thought you rude. Quiet, but that's alright. We've had an even influx of quiet on the other side of the circle as well."

"Yeah," Crista says, "most couples have the talker and the quiet one."

"The mouth and the heart," Allie whispers into her ear with a snicker.

Crista laughs to herself.

"Have you seen anyone you like?"

"I—" Crista begins, but is unable to finish. She's been observing and collating data but somehow missed that detail. "I think objectivity has robbed me of the attraction goal."

"Well, don't worry," assures Allie, "I've earmarked a few in my head."

"Oh, good."

"Oh, shit," Allie's smile calcifies into something harder, and Crista looks where she's looking.

Oh, shit, indeed.

"Hello again, sexy ladies," says Will, taking Allie's hand. He kisses it.

Though he addresses them both, Will doesn't show any attention toward Crista.

"I'm Madison!" exclaims last night's schoolgirl next to him. "I've heard about you two."

Crista looks her up and down. She's wearing a bikini in that shade of blue they used to call electric. Her smile and eyes seem to take up all the real estate on her face, and her light brown hair is streaked with blonde. Her face is so earnest, enthusiastic, Crista finds it hard to do much other than return her smile.

"How did you two meet?" Crista asks. Will still doesn't look at her.

"Will came into my Starbucks every day and ordered the exact same thing."

Will nods, his whitened teeth gleaming.

"Venti double shot," says Madison. "Every morning."

"She's on my way to the dealership," adds Will.

"And then two weeks ago, he comes in, and he looks so sad," Madison says, her eyebrows drooping like a cartoon character's.

Crista feels an absurd need to comfort Madison, as she's clearly been more affected by whatever had happened than the grinning ghoul next to her.

"My wife was fucking her boss."

"Were you two in an open—"

He cuts Crista off with a glance, finally, in her direction. His eyes are bright but icy. "No," he says, flat.

"And instead of coming in once a day that week, he came in twice a day. Then he took me out for drinks and asked me to come here! Free! Can you believe it?"

"I can," says Allie.

The whistle blows. "Move down move down move down!"

"Can I tell you something?" Madison takes Crista's hand.

Crista leans in, wanting to pull this girl along with them down the line.

"We need to go," says Will, again kissing Allie's hand before she can slide it away from that smarmy grin.

"I think you two are *so* sexy," she says, in a way that makes Crista worry that this girl might use up all the O's in Mexico. "And if you wanted to do something this week. I'm sorta new at the whole girl-girl thing, but—"

"These girls don't play with men," says Will, latching his arm around Madison and tugging her away. "Time to move down."

Madison looks over her shoulder at Crista as they move to the next slot down the line. The look on her face suggests that even right next to them, the gulf is terribly vast.

"Well, hello," comes a familiar and sexy voice.

Crista turns back and finds herself in front of Jenn, the younger woman from last night. She accepts the hug readily.

"That was a lot of information, wasn't it?" she asks her wife, after Speed Dating has ended, walking down the beach in the direction of the bar.

Allie nods. "Three hours of meeting people is exhausting. But, important question, are you glad we did it?"

Crista shrugs, thinking about the couples she saw, seventy-one of them, if that count was correct. So many blurred together. Some, like Beth, like Jenn... Some stood out a bit.

"What would you like to do now?"

Crista isn't sure. "Beach maybe? Get some sun? Or the pool. We haven't done that yet."

"You know what else we haven't done yet?" Allie slides her hand down beneath Crista's sarong.

"No, honey, not now."

Her hand slides back out, and she nods.

They walk hand in hand up the beach, not looking at anything in particular. Not looking at each other.

# 19

# BRUCE

And after such a pleasant afternoon, it all went to shit because of Emily.

*No, that's not it,* Bruce reminds himself. Emily didn't make him sit on the bed with his phone. Emily didn't force him to answer. All Emily did was text. All Emily did was call. Should she have done either? No, this was true. But he never should've removed the phone from the safe. Not after last night at dinner. Not with Paige feeling so overwhelmed, so stressed. The least he could have done here was be sympathetic to her feelings.

"She asks so little of me," he tells the quiet dark beach. The waves lap. The resort behind him is hopping, setting up for tonight's theme, something about millionaires and mansions, trying not to infringe on any Playboy copyrights.

Bruce stands on the beach, wearing his sport coat and slacks, ready for dinner. So why isn't he there? Why isn't he at Rakuen with his wife, with that gorgeous couple? The last words Paige said to him ring in his ears "I don't like this." Firm, pained.

She asked him with her eyes to put the phone away, back in the safe. To not answer at all, because this phone call was a gross violation of their embargo. Of course, the embargo had already been broken with texts. He had allowed that. Flagrantly ignored the statute.

Instead of following his wife to dinner, he is standing on the beach. His cell phone is back in the room safe, where he should've left it in the first place. When he ended his call with Emily, he had maybe a quarter battery left. He has no intention of charging it tonight. "Maybe it'll just die in there," he tells the water. "Then we'll be done with this."

*Will* they be done with this, though? Even if the phone does die, and there's no more communication with Emily this week, what will happen when they get home? Will she be done with him? Will he be done with her? He'd held Emily at arm's length when she'd come back into Paige's life last year. He hadn't felt it his place to be involved. Uninterested in meddling, and hoping that maybe, somehow, things could get back to how they were once. Way back. Before she married. When they could've been whole.

Jennifer complicated things. The newness and deepness of the relationship she shared with Paige. Emily being Emily complicated things more. When she vanished from Paige's life again, his text to her had been short and to the point. **You can't do that to her again.** After a moment, he'd added: **I won't let you.**

Overprotective, very *mannish*, sure. He'd received a single word response: **Sorry.** No explanation beyond that. Just sorry. With a period. Typical Emily.

On the beach, he chides himself again. Is that fair? To classify Emily's behavior as typical her? Is he once again passing the buck down the line?

"I fucked up," he tells the surf.

His voice echoes back to him, and a passerby asks, "What?"

Bruce waves the question away and waits until the passerby is halfway to the next resort before continuing to criticize his handling of the situation. He did indeed fuck up, both in general and specifically tonight. He glances at his watch. Paige left the room over a half hour ago. She'll be in the middle of dinner right now, with the incredibly sexy Alexis and... He pauses, about to chide himself again when he pulls out the name, "Malcolm. His name is Malcolm. Fuck," he says to himself and turns from the surf toward the night-lit buildings of Aphrodite's.

He avoids revelers on the paths, easy to do, since their suite and the restaurants occupy the southern portion of the resort. He'd have to go north to get to the party, and Bruce Shepard is not really feeling the party right now.

Standing before the glass door of Rakuen, the red neon chopsticks color his blue shirt purple. Inside is a long thin center table, backed by a fish tank. Along either side are tables for two, with a Hibachi grill near the tank at the back. Bruce doesn't need to go inside to see the grill seats are occupied. A flame erupts from the Hibachi in front of Paige, who sits between Malcolm and Alexis. Malcolm serves Paige salmon. She smiles and kisses him. Alexis's hand slides beneath the fabric at the back of Paige's dress.

Bruce puts his hand on the brass door handle but doesn't pull. He decides to let them be.

*So, what's to be done now?*

As he feels too late for the party in Rakuen, and doesn't have much interest in either mansions or millionaires, Bruce returns to their suite. He tosses his blazer on the bed, throws off his shoes, and opens the mini-fridge in the tall cabinet near the TV. Dos Equis, Coke, Diet Coke, Sprite, and water. Out of the corner of his eye, he sees the tan rectangle of the safe. The red blinking display informs him that it's currently locked.

*It should stay that way,* he tells himself.

He closes the fridge and sits on the bed. Room service is only a phone call away. Drinks. Food. Often the same food being served in the restaurants. Eduardo, their personal butler, would bring him a smorgasbord. He could revel in the perks that come with Aphrodite Platinum Membership.

"That make you feel good about yourself?" he asks with a snort. "Aphrodite Platinum?"

He shakes his head. Butler service in their glorified time-share is something he doesn't deserve now. Another glance over at the safe. Still locked. He nods. Time to get the fuck out of the room. Go somewhere where the safe and his phone aren't.

The festivities grow louder as Bruce walks. He skirts along the outside edge of the courtyard, avoiding the throngs of women dressed in stockings and bunny ears, and men wearing suits or silk robes. He is not in the mood for such orchestrated fun. Not just now. He follows the path that winds behind the stage all the way to the other side of the courtyard bar. With most of the guests standing and sitting on the side of the bar facing the stage, this side is sparse enough to sit, to think. He orders a *cerveza*.

"Bruce!"

He turns to see Raymond Horne at the end of the bar, in the seat furthest away from the throng of people. Bruce waves.

"Join me?" Raymond asks, gesturing to the empty stool on his left, then to the one on his right. He shrugs.

*Why not?* Bruce thinks. Is his plan to just sit and wallow? What good would that do? Why not spend time catching up with an old friend?

"Absolutely," says Bruce.

They met Raymond before Xanadu, back when he was taste-testing the resort for a weekend at *In the Lifestyle*'s annual takeover. Bruce saw in the man a blind and hungry ambition to do something good, to make people happier, and took a natural shine to him immediately.

"How goes it, my friend? I was hoping I'd run into you."

"Oh," begins Bruce, elongating the word until he figures out what to say next. Should he just say, 'Good?' That'd be the easiest, wouldn't it? To play it off and drink in silence. Then wander back to the room. To the safe.

Miguel sets a Dos Equis in front of Bruce.

"Not so good, Raymond," he says instead. The safe fades from his mind. "I fucked up."

Raymond nods and clinks his beer against Bruce's. "Me too, man," he says. "Me too."

"I heard that Colleen..." Bruce isn't sure how to put it, so he lets the name hang.

"Left? Yeah." Raymond shoves his beer around the glass bar top, trailing the condensation ring behind it.

The men sit in silence.

"You don't have to talk if you don't want to," says Bruce after a while. "But if you need to..."

"How'd you fuck up?" Raymond asks.

Bruce looks at him.

"You don't have to talk if you don't want to," says Raymond, a weary smile appearing on his face. "But if you need to..."

"There's a girl. A woman. Back home. We had a relationship with her a while. She left, then came back, then left again. Really hurt Paige last time." Bruce frowns. "She's been texting. She called tonight."

"You didn't answer, did you?"

Bruce doesn't reply.

"Shit."

"Shit," Bruce agrees. "I just want to help her, you know? She's going through a divorce right now. Or will be." He's not sure. *That right there ought to be a wake-up call, no?*

"You have a savior complex."

Bruce looks up at him.

"I mean, I get it, 'cuz I'm a savior." Raymond pours the rest of the Dos Equis down his throat and pokes two fingers at Miguel.

"I don't think of myself as a savior," Bruce says.

"Oh, no," smiles Raymond, "you misunderstand. Having a savior complex isn't about actually saving anyone."

Bruce nods slowly.

"It's about the need to save. The actual person being saved is often incidental." He hands a fresh beer to Bruce, who looks at it, then takes it, finishing his own.

"She meant a lot at one point."

Raymond nods.

"What happened with Colleen?"

"Like that, is it?" asks Raymond.

"It is."

"Well, Colleen thinks I'm broken," Raymond tells him, taking a long swig. "And she's right, I am broken."

"I feel a little fractured, myself," admits Bruce.

"She left to shove me toward fixing myself."

"And how will you do that?"

Raymond shakes his head. "It's sorta like monogamy, isn't it? Routine. Complacency. Stasis. When not presented with a need to change, we usually don't." He looks at his beer, as though waiting for something, some insight. "Like, monogamous people often stay together because it's just what they do, and they can't see life outside it. They can't figure out how to *not* do it. Then they wake up at eighty-five realizing they've missed out on life." He wipes his mouth. "And I'm not knocking monogamy there, of course."

"Of course," says Bruce, knowing the party line. "Monogamy is absolutely fine if that's what you want."

"Absolutely," says Raymond.

"Are you missing out on life?" asks Bruce.

Raymond shrugs. "Have you ever heard of anhedonia?"

Bruce shakes his head.

"You hear it in there? The root? Hedon. Like hedonism?"

Raymond grins, but there's no mirth in it. "Anhedonia is a form of depression where you're unable to feel joy, to feel pleasure. Most often you lose enthusiasm and feeling for things you once enjoyed. Colleen thinks that yours truly, the king of the swingers' ball, the libertine, the debaucherous leader of Xanadu, *Bacchus Humanus*, the grand high poobah, head counselor of the Xanadu Home for Wayward Hedonists, suffers from anhedonia."

Bruce gives his friend a once-over. He's still wearing the T-shirt and khaki shorts from much earlier today. That means he hasn't been to dinner, since all three restaurants have a long pants policy. "And what do you think?" he asks.

"Bruce," says Raymond, "I think she's right. Though I'll never ask anyone to pity me my scores of sexual encounters."

"I don't pity you."

"Good," says Raymond and he guzzles the last of his Dos Equis. He stumbles to his feet. "Now, can I give you some advice?" he asks, slurring a little.

"Please," allows Bruce.

"Keep your fucking phone in the fucking safe. And go and apologize to your wife." Raymond steps closer to him, and now he can smell the evening's worth of beer. "And this woman, the one who called..."

"Emily," says Bruce, not liking the taste of her name.

"Emily," repeats Raymond. "You can't save her. And even if you could, she's not worth your marriage." He takes a step away, a longer one than anticipated, staggers and swerves, grabbing for one of the log columns along the bar.

"Can I help you some—"

"Don't be a fucking savior, Bruce. Just be yourself."

"Well," says Bruce, "me, myself, would help you to a chair, or your room."

"I intend to sit on the beach and watch for meteors. Leonids are this week, you know."

Bruce nods. "Tribune says they're supposed to be good viewing this year."

"The moon will have nearly waned completely," says Raymond.

"Watch out for crocodiles," Bruce tells him.

"You too."

Bruce doesn't help him to the beach, but does follow at a distance. Once he's sure Raymond is safely seated in one of the lounge chairs near the beach beds, he wanders back, making sure to let the security guard know that the host of this trip is alone on the beach.

He wanders aimlessly between the buildings, where the evening's festivities have graduated to disco and hot tub. He reaches their building and pauses, looking through the gauzy sheer curtains into the room beneath theirs. On the bed in that room is his wife, receiving and giving at once, the center of a threesome.

He hears the rising calls of her orgasm.

He hopes she'll forgive him his foolishness.

He climbs the stairs to their suite and opens the safe.

# 20

# RYAN

Ryan's wife looks exceptional tonight, and he hopes she knows it. Whether or not she would acknowledge her objective hotness, Jenn can't be missed in a feather-light cotton dress clinging to her lithe body. Unlike those obviously aware, strutting as if all eyes should be on them, Jenn still looks from side to side, as though questioning why everybody in La Grande Fête is looking at her as they sit for dinner.

A woman walks past their table, six feet tall, with breasts that exceed her impressive stature. Jenn's eyes rise to look at her. Ryan sees her internalize something. Some remnant of inferiority, that emotion Jenn spins most often?

"Hon," he says.

She looks back up at him.

"You look gorgeous."

He sees it blossom across her face. First, her eyes light and she smiles just a little, but she is a woman transformed. She tucks the hot pink lock behind her ear.

Swinging lit a fuse within her, but Ryan can still see the shy girl from before. He sees it in every glance. When she turns inward to process something. When she looks down. She's not so very far removed from where she was in the before times, before the lifestyle, before they held hands and plunged into the deep end. He still sees the little nuances that resemble Jennifer Lambert, even the distant vibrations of Jennifer Straub.

"The change has been dramatic," he told Bruce sometime last September. Their difficult period had come and gone by then, and this thing called swinging had begun to feel truly right.

"You never know what comes out of the paradigm shift. You remember what that is, right?"

"Complete change in the way of thinking," said Ryan, smiling at his friend's ability to be utterly pretentious without knowing it. "Heliocentric versus geocentric, etcetera." He spun his hand, saying, "Continue."

"Well, look at you," smiled Bruce. "Anyway, that shift tends to send its tendrils down deep inside." He pokes his fingers at his diaphragm. "When we look deep down there, we see who we truly are. Sometimes it's not who we thought. Sometimes it's much more."

Jennifer transforming into Jenn had been merely a way to put a name to the phenomenon. She developed some of Paige's mannerisms and ways of speaking, became far more outspoken and self-advocating.

Soon they will be entering their fifteenth year together. Not all those years have been good, of course. The two of them spent a whole lot of years cruising at fine, and a few at mediocre. The paradigm shift had been their decision to move from monogamy to non-monogamy, and the echoes of that shift carried right into the present day. The only bad stretch was that time after he threw her dress and his keys at her, dragging her out of that big swinger house party. He'd been drunk, but that was no excuse. He'd been jealous and angry. And stupid. Looking at her now, he marvels to think that had nearly cost him everything. That had nearly cost him her. The woman sitting across from him in La Grande Fête, holding his hand, still smiling at his compliment.

"You're not looking too bad yourself," she tells him. "Oh, and I wanted to tell you..." She leans forward across the table. "You up there, with Lydia, I was impressed."

*Oh, stop*, reaches his lips, but he doesn't say it.

At hot-tub-happy-hour, he was distracted by a woman with tattoos covering much of her body. The distraction was so great that he came to a full stop, clogging the small Gulf Stream of people moving from one end of the bean-shaped hot tub to the bar and back. Behind him, a man with four tumblers of something neon blue grumbled and griped.

Ryan stood, his two espresso martinis hoisted in the air over the heads of those submerged in the hot tub, and watched for a moment. The woman leaned against the side of the tub, the water just below two large and buoyant breasts with prominent brown nipples. She wore Ray Bans Wayfarers with purple frames atop her head, holding an expanse of unkempt wavy brown hair out of her face. Listening to her orations from lower in the water, their faces at breast level, were that Will guy, the one with the young woman with him, and two other men he didn't know.

He didn't know what the tattooed woman was talking about, just that he wanted to listen.

When he finally reached Jenn with her martini, she grinned at him.

"What?" he asked.

"I saw that," she said and gestured toward the tattooed woman, who seemed to have finished her oration and was sitting on the edge of the hot tub against a glass rail that overlooked the ocean. Ryan could see two large tattoos, one on each of her thighs, but still couldn't quite resolve what either of them were.

*Maybe I need glasses,* he thought fleetingly.

He also saw a large bush of curly black hair between her legs and felt his flaccid cock twitch.

"Do you want to go talk to her?"

He looked from his wife to the tattooed woman. He wanted to talk to her, but mostly, he thought, he wanted to listen. He nodded. The woman with the tattoos looked down at her legs in the water, kicking them back and forth. Her disciples had wandered off; Will found the bar, but the other two were nowhere to be seen.

"Why don't you?"

Why doesn't he? "Maybe you could—"

"I'm not going to pick her up for you," Jenn said with a soft laugh. "I mean if you *really* want me to, I will go talk to her on your behalf, but—"

"No, you're right," he said, "I can't keep hurling you at people I'm interested in."

She nodded. "You can do it! You're looking good! You're obviously intrigued."

Intrigued, yes. Looking good? Ryan gave himself a once over. He'd lost the excess weight he'd put on last year during the most stressful portions of their exploration. Maybe fifteen pounds more, on top of that. He'd never be mistaken for someone who worked out, and his pale skin had already begun to lobster on his arms and shoulders. He flicked his gaze back to the woman with the tattoos still staring at her toes. At her creamy white skin beneath those tattoos. What was the worst that could happen here? Will might come back. She might be uninterested. But Ryan found the momentary vision of her knocking him down and stepping on his balls under the water highly unlikely.

"She can't say yes to any naughty thing you wanna do unless you actually ask her to do it, you know," Jenn whispered in his ear as she wrapped her arms around him from behind.

"That's very true."

"Go on. Say, 'hey.'"

Hey.

His first, very mild, "Hey," went unnoticed by the tattooed woman. The clearing of his throat also didn't rouse her attention from her feet in the water. "I'm Ryan," he said, sticking his hand out, directly into her line of sight.

She looked up at him and squinted, the evening's sun setting over the Mexican countryside blocked only by the sheer curtains of the beds behind him. She dropped her Ray Bans down over her eyes, unleashing her hair to poke out in several directions at once, captured by the rooftop breezes blowing across the hot tub.

"Hi there, Ryan," she said. "I'm Lydia." She grabbed his hand and gave it a good firm shake.

"I was very intrigued by—"

"The tattoos?" she asked, with enough edge for Ryan to infer how often men have lead by asking her about her tattoos.

"Well, yeah," he said. "But you just looked so engaged when you were talking." He looked down at his espresso martini, feeling that he'd pursued the wrong tactic. "Looked like you had something to say, is all."

"I've been known to say things," Lydia said, hopping from the ledge into the water and putting her hands on her hips. "How about you?"

"Nonsense often streams from my mouth."

"Nothing wrong with a little nonsense now and then."

"Relished by the wisest men," said Ryan, almost on instinct. He chuckled.

Lydia's smile grew, and she nodded. "Very nice."

"I wasn't sure about coming over here, didn't want to interrupt—"

"Interrupt nothing. They listened, so I talked. Though at least two of them would've listened to anything I had to say from their tit-level vantage point." She flicked her thumb, nail covered in chipped midnight blue polish, in the direction of Will at the bar. "That one was only listening at all 'cuz I told him I didn't want to hear his opinion on the subject. Also, I think 'listening' is generous, he was more waiting to talk."

"What was the subject?"

"Rape culture."

Ryan blinked. "Intense."

"It is," she agreed.

"And what was his opinion?"

"Regressive misogynistic foolishness."

Ryan nodded and smiled at her. She smiled and nodded back.

"Was that all you wanted to say?" she asked, cocking her head to the side.

Even behind the tinted lenses of the Ray Bans, he could see her squinting. He felt the tug to just agree, thank her for her time, and return to Jenn. This had never been his strong suit. But the part of him that was intrigued by her tattoos and her gesticulations and her pubic hair, that part rooted him in place.

"You intrigue me," he said to the water.

"Do I?"

He nodded. *Spit it out, asshole!*

"I'd like to talk to you, and hear what you have to say."

She nodded slowly.

"And I think you'd be fun to make out with."

Her nodding intensified.

"And maybe do other—"

"You should kiss me," she said, pressing herself against him. As her arms encircled his neck, he felt warm hot tub water drip down his back.

The stud in her tongue slid along his. She tasted fruity and tropical. *Much better than I do,* he thought. *Espresso martini flavored.*

When they broke apart, he smiled at her.

"How was that?" she asked.

"Excellent," he said.

"Good, I thought so too."

Will returned with two transparent plastic cups, each containing only about an inch of light liquid. "Tequila!" he said, in what Ryan supposed was intended to be a Frito Bandito-style Mexican accent.

"No thanks," said Lydia, without turning away from Ryan.

"What's up?" asked Will.

Ryan sized Will up. "Lydia and I are talking." He paused. "And after making out with her, I intend to invite her over there." He pointed past Will, to the beds with their billowing curtains.

"Just for the record," said Lydia, "she would accept that invitation, were it offered."

"So why the hell was I off waiting for the good tequila all this time?" Will asked, his eyes narrowing.

"I don't know." Lydia shrugged and took Ryan's hand. "I didn't ask for tequila."

As he and Lydia walked toward the hot tub's ladder, Ryan looked to Jenn for approval, for confirmation. Sitting between Bruce and Paige, with both arms on the outside rim of the tub, she beamed at him. With a tilt of his head, he asked her if this was okay. She nodded and smiled even wider, then blew him a kiss.

On a bed, they kissed. Lydia's tongue moved with passion, and he felt her hand grab at the short hair on the nape of his neck. His hands went from her hair to her neck, to her arm. Finally, his right hand found her breast. Her deep breath through her nose answered his worry about whether she liked it.

Then she pulled back and looked at him, a frown appearing. "Look, buckaroo, I was supposed to meet my husband downstairs about—" She leaned back to look at the clock, "Fifteen minutes ago for our dinner reservations. And this," she pointed down at his hand on her nipple, "will lead to something if I don't go now."

"Oh," said Ryan, unable to hide the disappointment in his voice. "It will?"

"It will." She put her hand on his face. "I want to make that explicit, so you don't wonder once I've gotten up. I think you're cute, and I loved the way you got all shy when you came up to me, and I enjoyed kissing you. I never make promises about sexual stuff, so I'm not going to tell you that I'll fuck you in the future, but I'll say, without question, I want to continue this at a future time." She looked away, then back. "Like tomorrow?"

He nodded and gave himself a moment to sweep his eyes over her tattooed front, immediately spying the *Ghostbusters* logo on her right shoulder, a pinup girl drawing, the Cheshire Cat below her left breast. Much more he couldn't readily identify.

"Does that work for you?"

He looked into her eyes as she returned the Ray Bans to the top of her head. They were the palest shade of green he'd ever seen.

He nodded. "That works for me."

"Maybe we can get Ted and your lady in the mix too. But if that doesn't work, that's okay. We play mostly separately anyway." She smiled. "But he's awesome, so maybe."

He felt guilty asking. "One kiss for the road?"

She crawled across the bed to him, sliding her legs onto his lap. He felt himself stiffen as she grabbed his face in both her hands and gave him a soulful kiss. When they broke apart, she fixed her eyes on his. "To be continued," she said, then bit her lower lip with an, "Unf."

"To be continued," he agreed.

"I don't know that I did much of anything," Ryan says at dinner, wondering if he deserves his wife's accolade.

"You approached," Jenn retorts, "and you asked."

"I did that."

"And that's excellent, hon." She leans across the table to kiss him, the scoop neck of her dress exposing everything beneath, including exceptionally perky nipples. His wife clearly enjoys his adventuring.

Ryan smiles, enjoying her enjoyment.

# 21

# JENN

"**D**o you have any concerns about ditching condoms?" Jenn asks her husband after considering the question herself for quite a while.

Ryan, who'd been savoring a mouthful of his lobster ravioli, swallows quickly and coughs.

"Sorry," Jenn says, "out of left field, I know."

He gulps down some Riesling and nods, his face flushed and eyes wide. "For us," he asks, "or..."

"For us." She grins.

He chases his Riesling with water.

"I'm not asking if you have philosophical concerns," she reinforces. She should've prefaced all of this. Maybe waited until he finished chewing. She folds her hands on the table in front of her and lays out her reasoning. "I've got the Mirena now, and that's pretty much foolproof. And we're both STD free. Is it just inertia at this point?"

Her husband takes that in. The flush has receded from his face. He doesn't appear antsy or anxious. This is good. "I can't think of any argument for keeping condoms that doesn't sound dramatically paranoid," he says after a good long think. "Even more paranoid than usual for me."

She smiles and leans forward, about to suggest that after they finish their lobster ravioli, which is just as good tonight as it had been last night, and after they finish their creme brulee of course, they find one of the chairs around the pool and get closer in a way they haven't before.

"Hello, awesome people," says Kendra de Martolos, arriving with inconvenient timing.

Jenn pauses longer than intended, an image of herself and Ryan fucking on the chairs near the pool, the flickering light from under the water illuminating them, still in her head.

Kendra's eyes widen. "I do hope I didn't just interrupt something serious."

"Oh," says Ryan.

Jenn smiles and shakes her head. "No, no."

Kendra smiles. Her shiny satin dress, vivid maroon, is cut down to her navel, and her ample cleavage seems to defy gravity, two cantaloupes suspended on nothing, pressing against each other in the slit. All at once, Jenn wants to motorboat, to press her face between those glorious breasts and just feel every bit of their weight and softness as she rubs from side to side. The thought makes her a touch self-conscious.

Kendra, who considers herself mostly straight and very rarely finds the desire to play with women, had established a buddy relationship with Jenn. The two of them go to movies, occasionally dancing. Not the way she dances with Paige, though. Then there's the way they left things. The way Kendra and Ryan left things. With Kendra's husband Vince so often out of town, Ryan had gone on several dates with Kendra before getting frustrated by their soft swap status.

While Jenn and Ryan had thrown themselves right into the deep end, full swap, really-for-real penetrative sex with people other than their partners, Vince and Kendra practiced a specifically lighter style since they'd started. For them, swinging usually involved petting, oral sex with others, then coming back to each other for the deeper things.

"Sometimes it feels like high school," he confided to Jenn, one night after a date as the two of them lay in bed, looking at the ceiling where once there'd been a crack.

She nodded.

"I'm not sure if I want to keep doing this."

"Look," said Jenn, "I like Kendra, I do." She waited for him to indicate that he believed her. A nod. A smile. After a moment, he gave it. "But if she's not what you need, she's not what you need."

Ryan frowned. "They're fun, right?"

Jenn attempted to be magnanimous. "Sure."

Ryan met her eyes, his look begging for truth. Begging for her to not fuck around.

"Okay, look," she took a deep breath. "I enjoy hanging out with Kendra. But her lack of interest in me makes our relationship very different than yours."

"I know."

"And I enjoy our dates with the two of them, too. Vince treats me well. "But with him so busy, and with my relationship with her so platonic..."

Her husband nodded again. "Is it okay to not be satisfied?" Ryan asked, his tone meek.

She put her hand on his face, turning him to meet her eyes. "It's okay for you to recognize that this relationship isn't fulfilling your needs. It is *not* okay for you to continue doing something that doesn't fulfill your needs. Especially if you're leading her to believe it does."

He said nothing.

"What was our mantra? No longer content, something something." She couldn't quite remember the mantra their old couple's therapist Dr. Petrillo had given them, back when things were bad, when they'd found themselves passing through day after day like zombies.

"No longer content to just live." Ryan looked back at her. "But this is different, isn't it?"

"Is it?"

"She's not my partner."

"No," said Jenn. "So why would you be content to 'just live' with her?"

"I don't want to hurt her feelings."

Jenn nodded. "The longer you wait, the harder it'll be."

Hurt feelings and awkwardness came when Ryan told Kendra that he wasn't getting what he needed from their arrangement. If the hurt feelings hung around, the de Martoloses certainly weren't showing it here at Aphrodite's, though Jenn still finds herself on edge around them.

"Can we join you?" Kendra asks.

"Please," Jenn says, hoping her grin looks genuine.

Mateo, their waiter, appears almost immediately, with two menus for the new couple. He's trailed by another waiter and waitress who set silverware and glasses. "*Bienvenido,*" Mateo says and takes their drink orders, disappearing quickly back into the darkness of La Grande Fête.

"So," says Kendra, not rushing to follow the beginning with a middle.

"Kendra and I were talking," says Vince. He also seems hesitant. "And, we thought that this place might be a good place to… Dear?"

She takes the ball. "To take the next step."

"The next swinging step."

They appear to be waiting, though Jenn isn't sure what for. Are they looking for encouragement? Permission? "We also think this is an excellent place to take next steps," she puts her hand on Ryan's, recalling the brief condom-free discussion they'd begun.

"Well, that's great! Because we're ready for full swap," Vince spits out.

"And we want you two to be it," follows Kendra.

"Hey," says Ryan in such a boisterous tone that Jenn is suddenly certain he'll follow up with *mazel tov*. He doesn't, instead just repeating, "Hey."

"That's exciting!" says Jenn, feeling tension in her chest.

"I mean," says Kendra, "no pressure." She sits back in her chair. "Sorry."

"No, no," says Ryan.

"Just surprised," says Jenn.

"Let's just say this," Kendra offers, "if the opportunity presents itself, and all four of us are on board, it's a thing that's on the table."

Jenn is amused when Ryan does say, "*Mazel tov,*" while raising his glass. She shoots him a look and a wink that says, *I know you so damned well, Lambert.*

All four toast, to new explorations, to exciting advances in their sex and swinging lives, and to the rest of the week at this place.

She drinks deeply of her wine, an Amarone.

"It's from Valpolicella, just north of Verona, actually," Bruce told her of Amarone, way back at the beginning, the night they met.

"Fair Verona, where we lay our scene," she replied, well past tipsy.

She blushes now at the memory.

She's happy to be among friends – even with the bit of awkward, she genuinely likes Vince and Kendra – but itches to discover more *new*. She wonders what Lydia is up to after dinner, and how hard it would be to wind Ryan up and point him in her direction. That'd be something to watch, if not participate in. One mustn't make assumptions about someone's sexuality, lest one be quite disappointed.

She sips her wine again, thinking that *L'chaim* would've been a better touch of Hebrew. She gives herself a private toast, *L'chaim, to life!* To a life less monogamous. To a life unburdened by regressive spoils. To a life in paradise, even if briefly.

To a life unafraid.

Unafraid.

Jenn hopes so.

22

---

## PAIGE

*That was a foursome, wasn't it?* Paige asks herself in the afterglow of her wild time with Malcolm and Alexis. She doesn't think the couple that so generously overlooked her missing husband at dinner and beyond noticed the replacement fourth, the additional woman there, but she'd been in the mix just the same.

Emily.

Not the entire time, thankfully. Not after Paige's first major orgasm. For a while after that, Emily vanished, snuffed out like a candle. Gone. The oral sex train was just the first course, too. Though in between drifting thoughts of Emily, Paige returned to her husband again and again. He should be here with her, with them. He should be here in her mind instead of Emily. Here in this room instead of in their suite on his phone, Emily's gateway into this resort. Into their lives. Again. Once upon a time, it'd been easier to ignore such things, such people. When you left your house, you left the telephone, too.

*Way to sound your age,* says her snarky inner voice, the one that always reminds her that next year will mean fifty, whether she still runs a company or not. The snarky voice sounds a lot like her mother.

During dinner with Alexis and Malcolm, she looked over her shoulder, toward the glass door at the other end of the restaurant, so many times. That wistful longing that at some point

Bruce would stroll in and do that thing where he unbuttons his blazer with one hand, even though he'd just buttoned it moments before, because one should make an entrance. He'd apologize profusely for being late and toss off one of those meaningless excuses that make eyes glaze over and the listener understand that the reason isn't important.

"The important thing is that you're here," they'd say.

And Bruce would throw his blazer over the back of his chair and take the empty fourth seat on the end in front of the Hibachi. He'd find the fried rice they'd ordered him, and the glass of pinot noir.

But he never did come to dinner, did he?

"We've had an incredible time," said Malcolm after dessert was finished. "We're not sure what your plans are now, or your situation."

Paige wasn't sure she could detail what her situation was at the moment. Her husband refusing to ignore their ex, the ex who'd escalated from texting to calling, despite being asked to do neither by both of them. And this was enough to miss dinner with two very sexy people? To miss—

"I have no plans," said Paige, making her decision quickly. "Have any to offer?"

If this was to be her last time at this fabulous resort, unlikely but possible, then she would experience all it had to offer. This would be her week to live deep and deliberately. Once, probably as recently as last year, it had seemed as though this lifestyle, this place, their lives, would never cease to produce dividends. How frighteningly naive they'd been. What devastation a few bad months could wreak.

But that wouldn't be her, not this week. Bruce could do as he pleased. Let him spend his week here talking to that woman at home, that woman who'd stay and say the right things, and cuddle up, and be there, just as long as it took to get what she needed and then, *poof!* Gone like a magic trick, leaving behind only a lingering implication that they were both so very slutty.

Or at least Paige was.

"We have some champagne back in our room," offered Malcolm. He slid his arm around her waist. Alexis mirrored the movement on her other side. "And I would very much like to taste you."

*Unf*, thought Paige, letting her eyelids flutter. Having the two of them to herself, indulging in some selfishness for a change. Just the thought made her tingle. Maybe not *just* the thought. Certainly, having them on either side of her, in the warmth of the late evening, their hot breath on her ears and neck. Their kisses. Their... Was that a nibble from Alexis?

She felt her own warmth, wetness, the slow drip down her left thigh.

"I'm a yes for that," she told them. "Let's make haste before the party starts right here."

They made haste, and combined and recombined in various delicious configurations. Alexis's orgasms took their time and seemed to expand inward instead of out. Malcolm refused to allow anyone near his impressively large penis until both women assured him they'd been thoroughly satisfied.

Then, together, they devoured him.

Throughout it all, though, Emily had

(slut)

made her presence known, as though she'd knocked down a wall, set up a tent, and demanded squatter's rights in Paige's brain.

And for Bruce, she just wished that he'd been there.

Returning to the evening now, with the cool breeze coming off the ocean, Paige sees that the lights are off in their suite, directly above Malcolm and Alexis's. She takes off her heels and steps down to the beach.

She knows she ought not stay down here long – evening is the domain of sand fleas and chiggers and mosquitoes, and if you believe the signs, crocodiles. The allure of the beach offers her no other choice, though. The possibility of seeing fellow travelers defiling the beds, the soft sand beneath her feet, the sound of the waves lapping lazily.

The fingernail moon hangs just moments above the horizon, reflecting a winding trail of white on the water. Below it, she sees the hulking phantom shadow of a cruise ship, three lines of dim light defining decks.

As she nears the center of the resort, where the empty bar bisects a row of beach beds, she hears the quiet music of the evening. The steady *umph-umph* has given over to something vaguely tropical and inoffensive, always played just low enough to be indistinct, unidentifiable, forgettable. A mild soundtrack for the last drinks and BLTs.

Lying on one of the lounge chairs, which in the evening are usually drawn up near the rails, Paige sees a mass that resolves itself as she nears. "Good evening, Raymond."

He's still wearing the T-shirt and shorts from earlier in the day. Paige feels a swell of motherly concern, hoping he's put on bug spray. But he is her peer and has been here nearly as many times as she has. He either knows better...or he doesn't.

"Hello, Paige," says Raymond. He turns his head to look at her and gives her a weary smile. "You look stunning this evening."

"Oh," says Paige, "piffle."

"I'm meteor watching," says Raymond.

Paige looks up at the sky. On the darkened beach, still several miles from Cancún proper, the field of stars is vast and the vague painterly smudge of the Milky Way ekes out visibility. She takes it in, noticing constellations that she remembers from way back in her high school's astronomy club.

Look! The Pleiades! Look! Orion.

"Seeing many?" asks Paige.

"A handful," he says. "Sometimes the vastness of the sky here can be overwhelming, like I might fall into it. Sometimes it makes me feel hopeful."

Paige doesn't know what to say to that. "Have you seen Bruce around?" she asks instead.

"Saw him at the courtyard bar about..." he trails off and sticks his thumb out toward the moon. "About one thumb ago."

She smiles in the dark and considers pulling a chair next to their host, sharing his troubles, sharing hers, here with the Milky Way to bear witness.

Maybe another night.

Instead she thanks him and moves down the path between buildings, listening to the late night snackers and drinkers communing around the courtyard bar. This is where she finds Bruce, his blazer thrown over the back of the empty chair next to him. Phone in hand, he types with his thumb.

But, of course, that chair isn't empty at all. Emily is there. Non-corporeal, but there. Maybe she won't leave this time.

Would that be better? At all?

Raymond's meteor watching suddenly seems a better bet. She could just leave, too, because if he's been talking to Emily, or texting with her all this time, then surely, it's deeper than simply,

"Can you help me fix this problem." She's gone around the bend toward, "I need you," and, "I want you," and probably a photo of that shaved—

Bruce's eyes meet hers, and now she can't just slouch back off to the beach, not without him following. The pristine quiet and calm would be torn, because oh, would there be a confrontation. His face falls as she feels hers tighten.

He holds up his phone, facing her. She can't quite see the screen, but sees immediately that the telltale green and blue text bubbles are absent. As she walks closer, it resolves itself into a Sudoku puzzle.

"How has your evening been?" he asks as she steps up near him. He gestures to the chair holding his blazer. "I've been saving it for you."

She looks at the chair, unfolds and refolds her arms, doesn't sit. "Your phone is—"

"Out of the safe," he says. "I know." He points the phone back toward her. "But look at the battery life." His battery indicator has gone red, and the little percentage number reads seven. "I'm going to kill it, and then it will join your dead phone in the safe. Two little corpses of our life beyond this resort."

She still doesn't sit.

"I apologize," he says, "profusely. For all of it. For dinner, yesterday. For missing dinner, today. For missing what looked like an incredible experience with Alexis and Malcolm."

"It was," she says, terse, "pretty spectacular, actually." She looks down at the dying phone. "She's very flexible."

"Will you please sit?" he asks.

Paige looks at the cluster of couples at the opposite end of the bar, including their friends, their lovelies, the Lamberts. Jenn gives her a small wave.

"Listen," says Paige, unwilling to sit just yet. She waits a long time before continuing. During the silence Bruce remains, hands folded, ignoring every *bloop!* of his phone as the battery grows weaker. "I will not tell you not to talk to her."

"I don't want to talk to her."

"Stop."

"Okay."

"I will not tell you not to, because you are a grown-assed-man and can make your own decisions." Paige fixes her eyes on his and waits. She's not entirely sure what she's waiting for, but finds the moment ripe for a dramatic pause.

He nods. "I don't want—"

"Want it, or not," Paige says, "she has a hold on you. I know that hold, I've felt that hold." She takes his hand on the bar. "I don't blame you."

"She does have a hold," he admits.

"That said, I need to excise her from *my* trip." Her words come fast, and she doesn't look up from the bar as she says them. "From here on out, my rules of engagement – and this isn't for engaging with her, but is for engaging with me – are as follows: I don't want to hear her name, what she's doing, how her divorce is going, how it's not, what she needs, or that she's sorry for what she's done or is doing to me, to us, or anything."

"Okay."

"This is what I need to be able to enjoy this trip. Which could be our last. It's essential." She waits a moment, then raps her knuckles on the glass bar top. "She already had an uninvited position at that threesome back there. Made it a foursome without consent from our lovely friends." Paige laughs wanly. "Guess she took your spot."

Bruce returns a similarly weak laugh.

Now she looks him in the eye and tries not to let her voice betray her. "I can't have her in my life. Not after the last time. The way she— It was once too many, once too far." She looks back at the bar. "If you can agree to that, I think we can call this a blip and move down to the other end of the bar for pizza and BLTs."

Bruce looks away, sitting thoughtfully for a while. She's always appreciated that he doesn't hide his need to think, to process. She appreciates now that it is happening. They've always understood each other's need for autonomy, and have tried very hard not to make what other swinging couples term their *rules,* what some more advanced or long-term swingers downgrade to *boundaries.* As a couple, they state their needs, and do their best to understand, validate, and follow.

"I won't speak to her again this week," he says. He taps his phone. "When this phone dies, she'll have no way to reach us."

Paige hears what he's actually saying. *I'll want to talk to her, I'll want to fix things for her, but I'm cuffing myself to the radiator.*

"And you understand my needs?" she asks. If Bruce tumbles

from the wagon – she hopes he won't, of course, but can understand why he might – she needs assurance he'll abide by her request.

"I do. I won't mention her again."

Paige decides to leave it there and concedes to sit.

"I love you," he says, but it sounds more like a question to her.

"I love you, too," she replies, then puts on a smile and shows it to her friends across the bar, who've been joined by Crista and Alejandra. "She's not allowed to ruin our evening. And I have a powerful craving for bacon, lettuce, and tomato."

He nods. "I'm sure that can be arranged."

# 23

# ALEJANDRA

"No, honey, not now."

The words spoken hours ago by her wife still reverberate in Alejandra's head. She shouldn't be surprised and isn't sure why she is. It's not the first time she's heard those words, just the first time on this trip.

"Are we the cliché, *mi amor*?" she asks her martini, giving it a quick stir with the middle finger of her left hand. She lifts that finger to her mouth and sucks off the gin. Across the bar, she catches Paige's eye.

Paige winks. Alejandra returns it, though the flirt has gone out of her, here at the courtyard bar at nearly three in the morning with a dirty martini and a pepperoni pizza, sharing the bar with the final crowd before the early crowd. They're the overnighters now, aren't they? A quartet of raccoons skirts the trees around the bar, desperate to approach, but hesitant.

Alejandra recognizes perhaps half of the people at the bar, from direct contact (some more direct than others), from up to three minutes of conversation at speed dating. Several martinis deep, Crista mingles with fellow overnighters. Next to Paige is Manic Panic, er, Jenn. Alejandra'd spent a copious amount of time making out with the young woman, but it still gives her a kick to call her by the rebellious nickname. Jenn's husband gobbles pizza next to her.

Crista pops between Jenn and Paige, also flanked by her own

husband, the incredibly giving man whose name she cannot quite remember. *Starts with a B,* Alejandra thinks, as her wife nuzzles to the left, nuzzles to the right. Alejandra cocks an eyebrow. *Paige and Bruce, yes, that's it.* They've just moved to that side of the bar, after what looked like a rather intense conversation on the other end. Alejandra noticed him sitting alone earlier, and had wondered rather moonily when he might be joined by his sexy wife. And then, behold, she appeared.

Madison, the unicorn, is being doted upon by that couple with the podcast Alejandra can't stand. As a lesbian scraping her way through the world of bi and hetero swingers, there's really nothing she's found more annoying than the distinctly hetero-normative and bi-appropriating musings of cis couples like that one. *But I wouldn't know anything about that,* Alejandra sneers and sips her martini.

She wonders how long it'd take for her wife to say, "No, honey, not now," to these new friends. To Paige, Strawberry-Blonde herself. To Manic Panic.

Alejandra raises her eyebrow as Crista runs her fingers along the unicorn's shoulders.

*You* really *need to start using people's names here,* she tells herself. *This isn't a convention, after all – you might want to fuck some of these people. Though,* she reasons, *it wouldn't be so out of the norm to fuck one of those people...* That was how she'd met her wife, after all. Convention, journalism award banquet, it's all the same, and sometimes kissing the right asses leads to...kissing other parts.

Madison looks up at Alejandra's wife lovingly.

Two weeks before the trip, Crista said it, "No, honey, not now," as Alejandra began to kiss her at the mirror before bed. Crista left the bathroom just after, but the words lingered, stuck. They always seemed to be delivered with that cadence and tone. Always the same. As it was in the beginning, so it is now and ever shall be.

Alejandra went to the door of their bedroom and found her wife already under the covers, her tablet casting dim light onto her face.

*Do you want to start this?* she asked herself. She wasn't sure, but the pressure had been mounting for weeks. With the trip coming up, things needed to be said. Essential.

"Do you think you'll ever want to fuck me again?"

The tablet fell from Crista's hands. "What?" she asked, alarm in her voice.

"'No, honey, not now,'" Alejandra repeated back, an almost perfect mimicry. Ought to be, she'd heard it enough.

"I'm tired," Crista said.

"Me too."

"I don't think I need to be pressured..."

Alejandra sat on the side of the bed and put her hand on her wife's knee through the layers of duvet and sheets. Whenever possible, de-escalate. "I'm not pressuring you. I'm sorry if my phrasing was intense just then."

"S'okay," said Crista, quiet.

Alejandra chose her words carefully. "We have a lot of fun with other people."

"We do."

"And that's great."

Crista waited.

"But I'd also like to spend more time playing with my wife."

Her wife looked at her lap where the tablet had fallen and said nothing for a while.

Alejandra wasn't interested in letting this conversation be the kind where she said everything and Crista listened, so she waited as well. *I'll wait all night.*

When Crista did speak, it was almost inaudible. "I'm sorry I'm not all over you all the time."

"Oh, *mi amor*, you don't have to be 'all over me all the time.' It just would be nice to have you touch me and look at me the way you did Alyssa last weekend."

Crista nodded, still looking down.

"When we swing together, and we fuck sexy bitches—"

Her wife blurted a laugh.

Alejandra smiled and continued. "When we come together during orgy time, it's amazing."

Another nod.

"I'd just like to have some of our amazing time not be entirely wrapped up in others," Alejandra said slowly. "Sometimes one on one."

Crista looked up. Her face showed fear; Alejandra had seen it before.

"I'm not going anywhere," Alejandra told her. "Our dynamic

is our dynamic, and it doesn't change how much I love you. I want you. More Crista. I'm addicted."

Now here they are in paradise, on a trip that would, of course, include plenty of sex with other people if they got their way, but is also supposed to offer time for them to be together. Just as two. Just themselves. To hear those words here knocked her back. And then to watch her wife flirt... Alejandra turns to her fellow night owls, distracting herself in fantasy. A black couple appears next to Paige and Bruce, giving hugs and kisses before they vanish back into the night. She takes a good long look at that amazingly tall woman walking away. *Hate to see you go,* she thinks. *Maybe Paige could introduce us.*

Paige catches her looking and smiles. Alejandra wonders if she could book some private time with Strawberry-Blonde. This time maybe Alejandra could wear the harness. She imagines herself showing up at Paige's door with her bag slung over her shoulder, unrolling the options like an old-fashioned knife roll so Paige could select the dick she'd wear.

*Choose and perish,* she thinks and snickers. She returns Paige's smile. The connection with Paige floods relief into her with surprising force. Relief? Relief about what? That she is not, in fact, sitting alone at one end of the bar while her wife, the introvert, the quiet one, the shy one, the... She realizes the word and immediately rejects it. There's no way, even in silence, even to herself, no way at all she'll refer to her wife, the love of her life, her everything for six years now, as *plain*. Alejandra gulps down the last of her martini. It's true, though, isn't it? She takes a deep breath. Crista *is* the plain one and Alejandra is the glamorous one. They both know it. Everybody can see it. There's nothing wrong with admitting to one's self the real facts about one's relationship. Every pairing has certain dynamics, and the fundamental truth is that Crista's role is the shy, plain woman who doesn't want sex very often.

A flush crawls up Alejandra's face, as though those on the other side of the bar might see inside her, hear the things she's thinking. She turns, again catching Paige's eye. The woman gestures with her head, asking silently for Alejandra to come over. She wants to be with them, with this group. Crista is already making out with Manic— Jenn.

She remembers sitting on the white pressed sheet in Crista's hotel room the night they met, when she'd received that award.

She can't remember what it was called, but it looked like a hideous acrylic flame, sitting on the desk in the corner. The physical award might not have been impressive, but the history of the woman was. The journeys, the courage. Where she'd been, and where she was going.

When Crista came to her, after a post-sex shower, Alejandra dove in immediately. Fingers and tongue. They devoured each other. Over and over. And again, the next week. Over the interim years, the change had been so gradual. Has the novelty worn off? Steadily ramping up the excitement, first with BDSM, then with swinging. Is swinging now too boring to save them from the dreaded and horribly cliché inevitability of Lesbian Bed Death?

The pizza scorches her mouth, but something about its greasiness soothes her. This is exactly what she needs right now, this late at night, this early in the morning. She'll eat a slice and then go to bed. Let Crista stay up and flitter like a fairy to her heart's content. On her way to bed, she'll step up next to Paige and whisper in her ear. Whisper that she'd love to fuck her tomorrow. Whisper it with the hunger and ferocity found at the very beginning of a relationship, whatever the type. When everything is still new and fascinating, and you're still finding out, "Oh, you like *that?* Interesting."

There'll always be love between her and her wife. That wondrous companionship she'd never felt before. Support, and understanding, and all those other platitudes that Alejandra is too weary to continue plucking this evening.

The quartet of raccoons waiting for crusts get fearlessly closer. Their little hands grasping at the air, as though they're imagining holding a slice. "Here you go." Alejandra tosses them her crust. The foursome pounce and fight over the sliver of pizza. "Can't we all get along, trash pandas?" Alejandra asks them, then stands, kisses her wife on the cheek, and whispers good night to her.

She'll tell Paige her desires tomorrow. Not sure she could conjure much ferocity at the moment.

No, honey, not now.

# PART IV

*Monday*

# 24

# JENN

The bedside clock reads 6:47, earlier to rise than the day previous. Jenn longs to return to the comfy dream that featured Crista, Paige, and Rachel Maddow, that cute lesbian newswoman. There was something at the end, though, Jenn can't quite remember, but she thinks it may have been Grace from HR coming to interrupt the Sapphic pleasures of her lady orgy.

Jenn looks at Ryan, sleeping on his back with his mouth yawning open. She notices the bulge and peeks. Ryan's cock is rigid, like it is most mornings, lying against his stomach. She could just take it in her mouth, or, hell, climb on, fuck away the jittery, anxious feeling. But has it even been an hour since they returned to the room? Let him sleep, since he can. Grace likely won't wander into *his* dreams to fire him.

She stands on shaky legs and satisfies other biological needs. She can smell in her urine the many espresso martinis she consumed last night, this morning, a few hours ago. She sways after wiping herself and clutches the edge of the sink. She could shower here, but thinks it might be more pleasant at the edge of the beach. The budding morning sun rays edge along the floor.

Yes, a shower in the sun would do nicely.

Jenn slips the coil of stretchy plastic attached to her key over her wrist, grabs a floppy hat and her sunglasses, and relishes the moment she realizes that she needs nothing else. Maybe her tablet? Sunscreen.

*Okay, a few other things*, she concedes and scoops up the beach bag with the trip logo silk-screened onto it. *With your $4,000 donation, you'll also receive this Xanaducks tote bag, isn't it just the living end? Where else can you find quality orgies like— I may still be drunk.*

Bag, keys, check. She throws a glance over her shoulder at her husband's morning wood. She'd left it uncovered. He could get cold. She rushes back, throws the sheet over him, and drops a kiss on his cheek. Bag, keys, kiss, check.

*I'm outtie.*

The sun welcomes her. Not completely up yet, but really, neither is she. In a moment, she's on the beach, looking at the ball of fire at the horizon.

"Good morning," she says, squinting at it. "Another day in paradise." She assures herself that regardless of an unsettling dream, this *will* be another crazy day in paradise. Today is the foam party. She's never been to a foam party. Surely that will violate some morality clause somewhere, won't it? When the foam gets thick, how can there not be shenanigans?

Shenanigans sound great.

Swinging has not always been a constant source of joy for Jenn and Ryan, of course. There was Beck, the gonorrhea scare, some mediocre encounters with mediocre people.

But Bruce and Paige.

Paige.

Jenn sighs, putting her feet in the water. Her body soaks in the rising sun, skin prickling as it heats.

Paige has been like nothing else, no one else.

"Hey," Jennifer Lambert said, sometime late last year, as they lay in bed next to each other.

Paige turned toward her, the rainbow silicone dong in its leather harness bumping against Jennifer's leg. "If we do it again I think you'll need to wear the cock. My thighs are burning!"

Jennifer laughed. "Totally," she said. "But that's not why I heyed."

Paige's arctic blue eyes fixed on hers, and they shared a long quiet moment. Jennifer wondered if what she was going to say needed to be said after all. Didn't Paige know it? But no, Jennifer recognized the value in vocalizing things and said, "I love you."

She didn't look at Paige as she said it, finding herself instead fixating on a hazy patch in her bedroom ceiling, where once there'd been a crack until Ryan and Bruce had fixed it.

She'd only said, "I love you," to one person before, romantic love anyway, and that person was her husband. To say it to a woman, to this woman, she felt the waves of so many different emotions. The lingering shame that still cropped up at unexpected times and places, the one that whispered the word *lesbian* the way she'd heard her aunt whisper it when she was little. The fear, mild though it was, that their love wasn't acceptable.

They'd said it before, so many times, but they'd substituted the word "heart" for "love" in the beginning.

"I less than three you," Jennifer had said once, immediately caught between exultation and annoyance at how twee it was.

Paige had stared at her, thinking it out with a smile on her face. After a moment, the smile had broadened. "I less than three you, too."

Then "less than three," the simple emoji in their text conversations, had replaced the word "heart." So, of course this, "love," wasn't out of left field, was it? When you're saying, "I love you" consistently already, just as **I <3 you** or "I heart you."

But after she said it for real, the time waiting for response felt like eons. Paige reached up and put her hand on the side of Jennifer's face, the side facing away, and pulled Jennifer toward her. They shared the same pillow, nose to nose, eyes to eyes. Paige's had tears in them.

"I've wanted to hear that," said Paige. "I wanted you to feel okay saying it."

"I do," said Jennifer.

"I love you, too, Jennifer."

Paige's thighs found strength for another round, this one slow and deliberate, with unwavering eye contact. And when they came, they showered each other with love.

Something is going on with her girlfriend, here in paradise. She's seen little glitches, little hesitancies. Jenn is uncertain what it might be, but knows that when Paige is ready, she'll tell her. If Paige needs her, she'll ask. After all, sometimes people need to process on their own before they can bring their concerns, their issues, to those they love. Paige knows something is going on with Jenn as well. And can assume what it is. They'll talk, at some point, when there's time alone.

"I should ask for that," Jenn says to herself as she walks the beach, "should ask for that time." Time with Bruce and Ryan involved is wonderful, but would never match the time alone, just the two of them. With the woman she loves.

"One should always ask for what one wants."

She jumps, startled. *Who said that?* For one wild moment, she's sure it's the resort itself talking to her. Her logical side doesn't bother to point out the absurdity, instead asks *Why would Aphrodite's have a male voice?*

Now she sees him, covered in two white beach towels, a distressing number of red mosquito bites on his face. Their host, their Bacchus, Raymond Horne, lies in a chair in front of a bed near the center beach bar. She realizes it, but asks anyway, "Did you sleep out here?"

He staggers to a sitting position, squinting at her. "I did indeed. This was not part of my plan." He presses the ball of his palm to his right temple. With his other hand, he points at her. "Jennifer Lambert."

"Jenn," she corrects. "Yes."

"You're up early." He swings his finger around to the sun. "It's ball-of-fire in the morning."

She smiles. His mosquito bites aren't as bad as she initially thought. Several on his cheeks, a couple on his forehead. "I have After Bite," she tells him, looking into her tote bag and finding the itch relief pen at the bottom. She holds it out to him. "You can borrow it."

He smiles and takes it from her, still squinting. She watches as he presses the tip to each of his bites, wincing as he winces, feeling the paradoxically exquisite sting. She absently wonders if she has any bites of her own she could apply it to, then laughs at herself, *weirdo*.

"Do you need anything?" she asks. "Anything else?"

He shakes his head at her. "Tell me you're having an enjoyable time?"

"I am."

"Room okay?"

"It is."

"Is there anything I can do to help make your trip better?"

*Kill the HR manager at my old job?* "Point me in a direction," she says to him. She's not sure why she said it, or why she's being obtuse, but there it is.

He squints at her, and in that look, she knows that he understands that this isn't about being pointed in the direction of breakfast (which should open soon), or where to sign up for snorkeling. "Where do you want to go?" he asks her with gravitas.

She thinks a long time, feels her voice catch as she tells him, "I don't know."

"Well," he tells her, warmth in his voice; none of the pretension and theatricality she's seen in him so far. "That's something we can certainly work on. Figure out."

"I'd like that." Jenn returns her gaze to the sun, sloughing off its fire on the horizon.

## 25

---

## RAYMOND

Raymond Horne's face itches. He scratches it absently, admiring the ass on Jenn as she strolls down the beach, and feels a stirring beneath his shorts.

*At least I didn't sleep naked,* he thinks with a surge of relief.

Thankfully, Jenn Lambert has left the bite stuff behind, so he can apply it as needed. The welt right on his temple not only itches but throbs, and it's hard to medicate without ammonia dripping near his eye.

He should *not* have slept on the beach last night. This is not a lesson he feels he needed to learn, either, but something he should've known in the first place. This isn't exactly his first rodeo. The sting of the After Bite hastens the throbbing in his head. Too much to drink, too little sleep, poor sleeping conditions. That about cover it? He nods to himself.

Something should be done here. Thankfully, nothing that his campers will notice if he doesn't do today. Today is the foam party, and the resort puts that on themselves. His presence is not even remotely required. Maybe he'll pop by and make an appearance, but until tomorrow's big playroom orgy, there are no Xanadu exclusive events on the schedule. Perhaps he should hose himself down.

*Maybe I should go back to sleep,* he thinks, noting the time at just 7:20. People do rise this early on a Xanadu trip – something he's never quite understood – but not many. Most are folks who have a morning exercise routine to stick to. Others are people who can't make the shift from their regular workday schedule. Then there are the time shifters, their friends from Europe and Australia, who are always having a devil of a time just trying to regulate, only to find themselves, just as they're getting the hang of the place, passing back through those sliding glass doors (the sign next to them, placed by Raymond, "Did you remember to dress?") on the way out.

He throws off the towel covering his legs and inspects them for bumps, thankful to find only a few. He applies After Bite to them, wincing at the sting.

"You need to make a cross."

Raymond squints at the silhouette in the sun. The white hair on her head blazes, back-lit with orange flame. He smiles. "Good morning, Debra."

"Good morning, Raymond." She doesn't move from her spot between him and the sun. He can feel her eyes on him without seeing them. "Rough night." It's a statement, not a question. "You make a cross, with your thumbnail," she says and waits.

Raymond still doesn't know what she's talking about, and she walks over to the bed. She points at the bite on his leg, then, with a flourish, pokes her thumbnail into it.

"Yow!" he says with a wince.

"Oh, don't be a baby."

He sees the divot left by her thumbnail for a moment before she turns her thumb and presses a second divot over the first, making a small plus sign.

"Now it won't itch so much."

He claps his hand to the freshly crossed mosquito bite and rubs it, a scowl on his face, feeling foolish. He supposes it's alright to feel like a child when the woman scolding him is twenty-six years his senior.

"Need me to do the rest of them?" she asks, a sadistic smile on her thin lips. He notes that she has put on lipstick to come down to the beach.

"No," says Raymond, pulling his legs up, "no, I'll get them."

"Suit yourself," she says. "I've come down for some pre-breakfast sun." She points a rolled up white towel at the beach chair next to him. "Mind if I join you?"

"Not at all," Raymond says with a smile.

"Good," she replies. "Didn't want to shuffle all the way down to the chairs in front of our bed."

"Oh? Where are you?"

She stops unrolling her towel and points vaguely up the beach toward the start of the beds. "Second row down there."

"You got a back row? Want me to get you moved?"

"Back row's good for canoodling," she says, without irony in her voice, a sly smile on her face.

Debra and her husband James showed up randomly on the second Xanadu trip. When he asked them how they heard about him, she shook her head. "We haven't the foggiest idea who you are. We called our travel agent and said we want to go to one of those naked resorts," she told him. "And not the namby-pamby nudist ones. A real sex resort!"

"Our agent referred us to someone else," James added, "and here we are."

Debra pulls off her crimson wrap, revealing the slight frame beneath. Seventy-seven years have been kind to this woman. Her small breasts have sagged only a little, and the pouch of belly is barely there. She's made a point of spending an hour in the gym on every day he's seen her at the resort, and he assumes that this year will be no different. Her husband, James, doesn't join her in the gym, and his body shows its age more. Despite being almost ten years her junior, he is always mistaken for the older one. The shiny bald head rimmed by white hair might be part of that.

Raymond has always admired the Koonzes. Their willingness to explore and jump in, their complete lack of societal shame about their bodies. He notes, with a smile, that Debra has trimmed her white curly pubic hair into a small heart.

"You keep staring at my pussy, I'm gonna make you eat it," says Debra, following his gaze with a cackle as she lies next to him.

He laughs too.

"You're sadder this trip," she tells him. "I don't like it."

"I don't like it either, Debra."

"I heard Colleen left. You've got that woman who lost her kids here instead."

"Well," he says, wondering how on earth Debra, a woman who, as far as he knows, still doesn't have an email address, could possibly know about Mia's custody battle after being outed publicly. "That's sort of—"

"You don't need to explain."

He nods. But he wants to explain. He wants to tell her that Colleen cried when she left. When she told him he needed to get back to who he was before, when he was good. When he was happy, productive, positive, and a real leader.

He asked, "Who was I?"

Colleen folded her arms.

He knew the look she gave him, the cocked jaw and smirk. It was her calling-Raymond-on-his-bullshit look. Her I-don't-have-time-for-this look. All the while, the tears glistened in her eyes and on her cheeks.

"You're just going to leave, after all this," he said, sounding accusatory because he felt accusatory. He knew at that moment if he could just find the right button and push it, close the right circuit, she'd stay. She'd stay because she couldn't bear to leave. That's what her tears were telling him. "What kind of an example is that to set?"

She laughed without humor, slid her fingers up into her blonde hair, and for a moment he thought she might yank out handfuls. She closed her eyes and breathed. In through the nose, out through the mouth. Repeat.

"I thought we said we could work through anything, and now you're leaving." The failure button. Your failure, Colleen.

"Yes, I am, Raymond," she told him and got close. "I'm leaving because you stopped being fun."

"Fun?" he asked and dug in. "I'm sorry, I didn't realize we were children on a playground." There it was. The right button.

Wrong result, though. Colleen left without another word, and Raymond put his hand through the glass coffee table.

In the tropical sun, he can see the faint pink lines of the scars on his hand, though the deeper pink-red bumps of the mosquito bites hide them nicely. "I don't want you to think less of Colleen or anything," he says to Debra.

"I won't," she retorts. "I always liked her better'n you anyway."

He turns to her, sees one side of her crimson mouth turned up.

"People leave, Raymond. For the wrong reasons, or for the right. Which was this?"

"I think she left for the right reasons."

"Think she'll come back?"

"Not until I'm better."

"And can you get better?"

Raymond thinks about it a long time. As he thinks, he feels her hand on his arm. A comforting squeeze. He looks back toward her, and the smirk is gone. Her hazel eyes see right into him, and he feels as though he might weep. "I don't know."

She squeezes his arm again and gives him a quick nod. "*I* think you can," she tells him.

They sit in silence, looking out at the water.

"My ex-husband left," she tells him after a while, "back in ninety-six." She nods again, as if in assurance that this is the real truth. "Said I was frigid. Ran off with a secretary. Least it wasn't *his* secretary, though I couldn't tell you why that's better. I hated him for a while, you know?"

Raymond nods.

"You know how you hate the people who point out the things you don't want to believe about yourself?"

Raymond knows. Stasis. He says so.

"Good thing, though. If he hadn't, I wouldn't have needed to get a job, wouldn't have waited on that darling man back in our room, wouldn't have screwed him in the hotel across the street from the restaurant."

Raymond snorts a laugh. "Well—" he begins, but she cuts him off.

"Even with him, though. Got frigid after a decade."

"Frigid isn't exactly a term people like to—"

"Oh, knock it off, Raymond. So polite. James and I also had sexual difficulties. That make you feel better?"

"The term? Yes," he says, "the difficulties, no."

"You know what it was?"

"I have an idea that I do."

"So smart." The smirk has returned.

"You both wanted to have sex with other people," says Raymond. That old chestnut. That classic. The one people don't talk about.

"Bingo." For a moment, he thinks there are tears in her eyes, too. She looks away, puts her hand back on his arm and squeezes. "Trip saved us. This place."

Raymond thinks about that.

"Saved us from just repeating the cycle again." She nods. "If we hadn't come here, we wouldn't have known where else to look."

They gaze out at the horizon a while longer. He reaches over and takes her hand.

She squeezes it. "I'm old enough to be your grandmother," she says, "but I'd jump you just the same."

"I'd say mother is more likely," he tells her. "Is that an invitation?"

"I think you've got stuff," she says, poking a finger to his forehead, "and maybe we can't trust your decision-making at the moment."

"I do have stuff." Without question.

"When you work that stuff out, maybe next trip, the one after, I'll be here."

He smiles at that. "Yeah?"

"I'll always be here," she tells him.

They share a comfortable silence, hand in hand, as the sun rises.

# 26

# PAIGE

From an elevated vantage point lounging on her beach bed, Paige watches Jenn stroll through the surf. Her girlfriend glistens in the morning heat, moving in and out of the water on the shore, apparently unaware of being watched.

*How could she not know?* Paige wonders. *How could she not at least assume?* That woman is gorgeous. She'd said so the day they met. The moment they met, in fact.

"I'm Paige, and she is gorgeous!" she said, after Ryan introduced them in the foyer of Barbara Watkins's house, though she immediately regretted not saying it directly to Jennifer. Perhaps it was best she didn't, though, as the poor girl was so flustered by the comment she could barely speak. Effusive compliments toward sexy people could be risky, after all, and she and Bruce were supposed to be on their best behavior that night.

Vanilla is as vanilla does.

They couldn't help it, though, she and her lovely husband.

Apparently, swinger is as swinger does. You never can tell in the wild, either. What people are into. *Who* people are into. It's why she and Bruce so rarely put out feelers in the "real world." But there was something about the Lamberts, Jennifer and Ryan. Their sweet awkwardness. Their innocence, though Paige was loath to call it that. It wasn't about corruption, but potential.

From the moment they met, Paige saw a spark in Jennifer Lambert. The awkward stammer when Paige winked at her. The attempt to cover it up while extolling how great Paige looked while discussing gym memberships. But one mustn't assume other things either, Paige reminded herself. Even if she was interested in non-monogamy, like really for real interested, she might not be interested in women.

First, Paige knew, you had to gauge receptiveness to flirting. And you could always find people receptive to flirting who are very interested in cheating on their partners, so you had to look for that bit of nervousness with the flirting. The sense that even while here with you, they're still somewhere mentally with their partner. Jennifer returned Paige's flirting, though Paige didn't think the young woman even knew she was doing it. But there was the odd little ping of not only interest in other people, but also interest in Paige. Something about how utterly flustered she got, over and over. How she'd hold eye contact, then look away.

There was something there. A potential swinger in the wild.

Paige wonders if she'd been that for Emily, herself? Emily in her triad relationship? Emily who didn't know that Bruce and Paige were swingers, even if the newborn had taken swinging off their plate for a while. Babies will take a lot of the exploration out of you.

Emily held her breath and put herself out there, taking all the risks at once. The non-monogamy risk, the asking for what you want risk, the bisexual risk.

"I have a new assistant," she told Bruce in bed the week after she hired Emily, all raven hair and peasant blouses and long billowy skirts.

"Oh?" he asked.

"She's something!" Paige said, with a dramatic flourish that would've made her high school drama teacher cringe.

Bruce laughed. "Now, what does that mean?"

Paige didn't know, and she told him that. She'd felt a draw the moment Emily Laurel walked through her door. Her black hair hung down to the small of her back. The thin cotton of her blouse did little to hide her large breasts. Paige needed to turn away more than once, to be the disinterested boss.

"It means that I have a crush on a girl."

He nodded.

"Girls in general or just this girl?"

Paige didn't know. She'd only occasionally wondered, only occasionally felt the tingle.

"This girl for sure," she said. "But I'm her boss!"

"That is a wrinkle," Bruce agreed. "Though you're also everybody else's boss."

"Isn't that *extra* bad?"

Bruce pursed his lips and nodded. "Probably."

Paige watched from afar. She watched up close. She got little inklings from Emily. Moments where they'd touch. Not anything unprofessional, but little electric fingertip touches. It only grew more complicated when Emily became their nanny.

She moved into their lives, spent long hours at their house, even the occasional overnight. Then one night she dumped it all on the table. "I don't know what it would mean, but I want to have a relationship with you both," she told them in their kitchen. "Like, more than friends."

Paige didn't know how to respond, how to say that she'd been wanting that too, for months. She marveled at Emily's bravery. To say it with all the blind risks, not knowing their sexuality or their proclivities. Just getting a sense. Instinct.

Maybe that's what it was with the Lamberts as well. Seeing them. Their wide eyes, their nervous awkwardness. Maybe Paige just knew. Which was why she sent Jennifer off with Bruce to find wine. He'd be able to figure her out. To see how deep the possibility ran. Her feeling about them could have just been neurons misfiring, after all. She could have misjudged. She'd done it before.

On the beach, a stiff breeze catches Jenn Lambert's hat. She bends to snatch it back up, then chases it down the beach.

Paige can't help but smile at the view. That apple-shaped ass, flush of pink between her legs. Oh, there's the tingle. She could invite Jenn over. Could do so many things on the nearly empty beach while much of the resort still sleeps. She doesn't, though.

"They shouldn't feel beholden to us," she told Bruce when the Lamberts announced via email that they'd decided to come along on the November Mexican adventure. "Like, they can play with us if they want to, but they also can do that at home."

"Spread their wings and fly? Always a delicate balance," agreed Bruce. "Though I don't think Jenn could ever have her fill of you."

"Stop," Paige giggled, climbing atop him.

Paige flattens out on the bed. If Jenn sees her here, she'll feel compelled to come over. She'll do it regardless of whether she wants or needs a few solitary moments. When there are people we know, people we care about, we go to them. So she'll leave Jenn be, let her have her time of contemplation on the beach. That's why Paige is here too, after all. Her morning on the beach while Bruce sleeps.

Both of their phones are dead, face-down in the room safe, with the stacks of two dollar bills for tipping and their passports. Emily's umbilical into their trip has been severed. She exists here only in their minds and memories now. How much damage can she really do from there?

As Jenn passes, Paige feels a wash of regret. The rest is right too, isn't it? Even if we need solitary moments, if someone we love, or who loves us, is hurting, aren't we obligated to go to them? Someone she loves is walking across the beach. Someone she less than threes.

Does she still love Emily? After all of it? It's surprisingly difficult to answer, even though she thinks she ought to be able to do so. Especially after the dinner that hadn't happened last year.

She sat, alone, at the Horn Lodge. Emily of old never would have been interested in that place, but this new version of her was different. Wilder. Emily Fitzgibbons ate steak medium rare, and ate pussy in bar restroom stalls.

Paige picked her phone up off the fresh linen tablecloth. 7:23.

"Still good?" asked the server, his dark eyebrows cocked in different directions. The expression on his face didn't feel remotely subtle. It asked her, without saying a word, when she was going to give up the charade, admit her date wasn't going to show and leave, or admit her date wasn't going to show and order. Either way, the single glass of pinot noir she'd been nursing wouldn't make up for holding a table this long.

Defiantly, Paige put her fingers on the rim of her glass and said, "I'm good." The server held her look for a moment before disappearing back into the darkness of the restaurant.

She looked at her phone again. Only two minutes had passed, but that made an hour since she arrived at the Horn Lodge, fifty-five minutes since her date was supposed to begin. "It's not happening," she whispered to herself, tossing the phone down.

She'd tried to remain objective at Bruce's request, to take things slow. Hadn't even made a big deal out of it. Because why make a big deal, if it was just going to end the way it always ended. Suddenly, randomly. That was how Emily rolled, after all.

But somehow, after their three dates in one week, despite Bruce's warnings and requests, Paige had fallen right back down. Right down deep.

When Emily Fitzgibbons had shown up at the Lamplighter that first night, after the, **i'm in town. drink?** text, Paige had lost her ability to be prudent, to be guarded. Emily's raven hair was short, curling around her freckled face. She still wore very little makeup, just hints. Nobody's lips were naturally quite that color. Forty had looked good on her.

That night at the Lamplighter, Paige had forgotten all the bad and seen the administrative assistant who'd added nannying to her résumé when Paige went back to the office, who'd added lover, partner, third to her emotional résumé shortly after that. The middle was blank; only the beginning, the good parts, shone hard and bright. Paige had felt all the love rush back. The hope they could be that again. The promise of maybe.

*How would it work with Jenn?* Paige had asked herself before falling, but she'd fallen even knowing that she didn't have a clue.

Emily had bought the first drink, then the second, then shots. And then they were digging into each other in the second stall on the end. Remembering each other's bodies, inside and out. Emily had changed, to be sure; Paige had, too. But they still fit together. *She even tastes the same,* Paige had thought, licking her fingers.

At the Horn Lodge days later, there was none of that reverie as the time crossed 7:40. Emily was not coming. That was evident.

Paige tossed back the last of her wine. She threw two twenties on the table, not interested in seeing the smug satisfaction on that server's face. He had been right, of course. So had Bruce.

Emily did that. Emily ghosted. Some people would invent excuses, make it clear that they'd at least thought about the person they stood up, let down; Emily would just say sorry and hope it'd suffice.

*I shouldn't be surprised*, thought Paige.

"Bear with me," she said as she leaned against her SUV in the parking lot, "I am much forgetful." The line came from something by Shakespeare, but she couldn't remember what. Jenn would know. Her Jenn.

When the **sorry :(** did come later that evening, Paige didn't know how to respond to it.

**Where were you?** she asked, after staring at her phone for a while.

The ellipses indicating Emily's typing lasted quite a long time, then vanished, then appeared again. They stayed that way until morning. Ellipses with no resolution.

An email from Emily's husband came the next day. **Emily has come back home. She doesn't need you or your husband filling her head with ideas of where she'd be better off. I don't know who you think you are, but fucking a man's wife in the bathroom at a restaurant is really fucking shitty. Leave her alone.**

Paige was aghast, and didn't respond to Mike Fitzgibbons. Instead, she sent, **are u ok?** to Emily.

**i am okay.**

**Do you need anything?**

The fucking ellipses appeared again and remained for nearly an hour.

**i can't be what you want me to be**

Paige rubbed her temple, where a headache had sprung that she hoped wouldn't climb into migraine. **I just want you to be you.**

**I'm home. I want to be here. i want to make my marriage work.** Then, after another twenty minutes of ellipses, **ur a bad influence. i'm not a slut anymore.**

At seeing that text, Bruce raged, stammering, around the living room. She showed him the email after and he became even more furious.

Then Paige shared with that beautiful woman down the beach with the pink in her hair.

"You're not a bad influence," said Jenn, "and she's a fucking adult."

Paige nodded.

Jenn's ire rose. "No, really, she's a grown-assed-woman who made choices and then excused her rudeness by blaming you." She scowled. "And implying that you're a slut? Fuck her!"

*Fuck her*, thinks Paige on the beach. She climbs off the beach bed to head to the bar, to have Celia whip up a bloody Mary to help shore up her defenses. Brace for impact.

Or maybe, hopefully, just enjoy the day.

# 27

# BRUCE

"Good afternoon, angel," says Bruce, when Paige joins him at the swim-up bar in the pool.

"I did not intend to sleep so long," she tells him with a yawn.

"Was it good sleep?"

She shrugs.

He supposes that's good enough on the first day without Emily. "Behold," he tells her. "It will soon be *La Fiesta de la Espuma* time." He points at the giant machine on the far end of the pool, surrounded by both Aphrodite's staff and two gentlemen wearing red shirts with *Fiesta de la Espuma* emblazoned on them in yellow.

"So it seems," says Paige.

"Hungry?" he asks.

She shrugs again.

He nods to himself. His wife may be sitting next to him, nude save for rainbow bikini bottoms, but her mind is elsewhere.

"Are you still upset with me?" he asks after a long silence.

She turns, surprise on her face. "No, I'm..."

He waits.

"She's inside me too, you know."

"I know."

"Did you know Raymond slept on the beach all night?"

Bruce laughs. "That I did not know."

"Welts," she says, gesturing, "all over his face."

"Poor guy."

"Poor guy, indeed. We're starting over, today?" he asks, an intentional hesitance in his voice.

She looks at him with worry and exhaustion, the stress of the outside world that has tagged along on this trip. Her eyes are bright, though. "I want to go hunting. I crave an afternoon tryst."

He smiles. "That's my girl."

"Have you seen anyone who might meet our occasionally less than vigorous screening process?"

He laughs. "I think our process is thorough, if flexible."

"Oh, it is," she says, face severe. "But let's be honest. Sometimes a tight little ass and just the right pouty expression makes us both weak in the knees."

"You speak rightly," he laughs. "If we're exploring bad decisions, there's that one right there."

She looks, but doesn't seem to see who he's implying.

He throws his head a touch forward and to the right, in the direction of the deck chairs. "Two o'clock," he tells her.

Now she sees.

Bruce focuses his eyes just to the right of the man in his midforties, and his twenty-something...what was she anyway? Date? Traveling companion?

"Oh, yes, Mr. Shepard, I think anything connected to *him* would be a spectacularly bad choice."

"I feel sorry for her," Bruce says.

"Don't feel too sorry," Paige retorts. "She got a trip to Mexico. And I have a feeling she's better at fending off his advances then he expected."

Almost as if on cue, Madison swats at Will's hand, crawling like a spider heading up her thigh toward her bikini bottoms. She doesn't so much as glance at him, keeping the vast lenses of her sunglasses trained on the sky. Will, on his side, penis only half erect and losing its turgidness, purses his lips, then flips to his back.

"Someone isn't getting what he'd hoped out of the bargain," Paige says.

A series of bangs draw Bruce's attention back to the far end of the pool, where a slow dribble of foam drips like pre-cum from the foam machine's spout. The tallest man in red whacks the machine with a hammer a couple more times. He steps over, picks up an extension cord and shakes it, then drops it back to the deck.

"There are a surprising number of extension cords poolside," says Paige.

"A little threat of death reminds us we're alive."

She laughs, gazing again at the bad idea. "He is a fine specimen of manhood, if you only look at his body and face, and ignore his personality."

"He shaves his chest," Bruce says. "There was stubble at the bar last night."

"Just because chest hair looks good on you, doesn't mean every man should have it."

"I'm just saying— Thank you, by the way. You're not in the habit of looking beyond severe character flaws. Doesn't even have that big a dick."

"Are we threatened?" asks Paige, her smile sly.

"Not at all."

"But we're comparing dick sizes here. Not *that* big, meaning it is big, because it was worth mentioning the size."

"Forget I said anything," says Bruce.

"How can I forget?"

Bruce attempts to change the subject. "What could she be, after all, a couple years older than Adam? Twenty-two? Twenty-three?"

"Are you getting old, darling?"

He fixes his eyes on his wife. The poking, the niggling comments. She might say she's fine. She might believe she's fine. Most likely, she's just made the decision to be fine, reality be damned. He learned long ago not to question it. *Take yes for an answer, Brucie*, he thinks. Take "I'm fine," for an answer.

After several false starts, a fan whirs and the red machine blurps to life. The trickle becomes a flood and is met with a rousing cheer from those on the deck and in the deep end of the pool.

"Here comes the foam," says Bruce.

"Lookie, the triad," Paige tips her drink toward them. Rory, Terrence, and Marley, each with a towel around their neck, circle a pair of beach chairs, exploring their trio of tote bags.

"The three of them look like they could be the cover of

*Polyamory Magazine,* published somewhere in the Pacific Northwest," he says.

"Probably Portland. I'll bet they're from Portland."

Every time Bruce has seen the triad, they've been in the hot tub. Now he gets to see them in full, their toned bodies. Terrence wears swim trunks, but they hang low enough to showcase what Paige calls the "crotch lines."

"Like they point to your junk," she'd said once.

"Junk?" he'd asked.

She'd stuck out her tongue.

"I wouldn't mind getting to know that one," says Paige, pointing with her drink again subtly and flicking her head to the left.

"The naked one?" asks Bruce.

She nods.

"Well," he says, looking at the naked one, Rory, with abs and an almost distressingly long hanging penis. "I'm sorry to tell you that the naked one, Rory, is also the gay one."

"But he's so pretty," says Paige, mock sobbing. She bangs on the bar top for emphasis.

"*Señorita?*" asks Javier, folding his hands on the bar.

"Oh," she laughs, "no, I was just—" She stops herself, then points to the drink of the day, blended in three parts with layers of red, white, and blue. "I want this."

"*Sí,* yes, okay," Javier replies and goes to work with the blender.

"Pretty, indeed," Bruce agrees with a wink. "Marley?"

"She's pretty, too," says Paige, with the air of someone who doesn't want to move on.

Marley is quite lovely, her hair buzzed short on each side of her head, the top, blonde, hanging down. A broad smile, with lips that appear naturally pink. Breasts, large handfuls, atop a toned abdomen. Between her legs, blonde hair and prominent lips with a shiny hoop piercing. Pretty, indeed.

"I wonder how they play," Bruce says.

"It's their first time here, right?"

"I think so. With so few bi men around, must be difficult for—"

"So few *out* bi men," Paige corrects.

Bruce agrees. His own bi leanings have ebbed and flowed over the years. Never something he's sought out, more of an in-the-moment thing. He knows that seeing him with another man turns Paige on. It turns him on too, as a matter of fact. Just not a priority. Not something he fantasizes about.

"That was a poke at you. Eff. Wyy. Eye." She pokes him. "Both verbally and physically." She takes a long, loud slurp of her drink and winks at him.

"I'm aware," he says. "Heard it and felt it. Would you like more time with them?" he asks, nodding toward the lunch tables where Malcolm and Alexis dine with Debra and James.

"So you can have a go?" she asks.

"Your playfulness is barbed," he says, his smile fixed.

Paige takes a moment to consider. "I'm sorry."

"Not necessary," he says.

"I didn't realize I was doing it," she says. "Yes, I would like another round with Malcolm and Alexis. And I told them you weren't feeling well, so I'm sure they'd be open to bringing you into the fold."

"Thank you," he says. He takes her hand on top of the bar. His wife, his love, his angel. "Thank you," he repeats, lifting her hand to his lips.

"You know," she says, "I wouldn't have any problem with you going off and finding some shenanigans of your own to get into. Between Crista and Alejandra, and last night, there hasn't been a lot for you to do yet this week."

"I was thrilled to watch," Bruce says. "And last night—"

"No, I know, and last night. And I know you enjoy watching, but you can't tell me you wouldn't have rather climbed inside that ball of women."

Bruce smiles. "We could always chat with those two," he says.

Paige turns to see Ryan and Jenn ambling up to the pool. Ryan makes a wide berth around the red foam machine and its extension cords. They mill about a while before finding a single empty deck chair.

"I don't want to pressure them," Paige says, with a nod for emphasis.

"I don't think they feel pressured," says Bruce, "but alright."

She turns her full body toward him and puts her hands on his thighs. One of her hands is cold from her drink, and his cock springs to half-mast. "Are you doing okay?" she asks, a serious-ness in her voice that surprises him.

"I," he says and stops. Her concern is genuine. With Paige,

verbal traps are incredibly rare. This has to be about him leaving Emily in the safe, at home, disconnected. After her firmness about not wanting Emily to be part of this trip, he's unsure how to proceed.

"I know it's hard," says Paige. "She's difficult to..." she trails off and looks out at the growing mass of foam and bodies on the other side of the pool. "She's difficult to forget. Difficult to let go." She doesn't look back.

Bruce nods, slowly. "I'm okay," he says after a while.

Paige grins again, her seriousness gone. She hops off the stone stool into the water and knocks back her drink. "I've been summoned," she says and kisses him with icy, syrupy-sweet lips.

Jenn stands at the edge of the foam, grinning, bouncing, her small breasts moving only slightly, but ever so pleasantly. She waves at him. He waves back.

"You mind?" his wife asks.

"Have fun," says Bruce.

"Join us if you'd like," she says.

"Nah," he replies. "She wants you. And I think that's perfect."

Paige grasps hands with Jenn and the two women disappear into the billowy white.

# 28

# RYAN

J enn is welcome to plunge herself into the mess of bubbles steadily filling the pool. Ryan has no interest. Instead, he lays on the deck chair, feeling himself sizzle. He glances down his body and the belly he's worked all year to jettison. The last six months have been good for his diet and exercise, and the belly is little more than a slight paunch now. More than he'd like, sure, and he wouldn't be winning any "best abs" awards, but that doesn't seem like the kind of thing Aphrodite's guests focus on.

"Never forget the best reason to lose weight," said Bruce over a whiskey.

"What's that?" he asked.

"Makes your dick bigger."

Ryan cocked an eyebrow. "I'm not sure that's true," he said, hesitant about correcting the man he knew was usually right.

"Well," Bruce shook his head, "it doesn't make your dick *actually* bigger. That's foolishness. What it does do, though, is remove a lot of the latent fat around the area, allowing the portion of your dick hidden below that fat to introduce itself to the world."

Ryan laughed.

"Some say it's about a quarter inch for every ten pounds."

He did some quick math then, with the forty pounds he wanted to lose before November. Jeez. Ryan had never worried all that much about the size of his penis. He'd recognized early on that the monstrous sideshow cocks in porn were certainly not the median line, and he knew from reading that he fell almost two inches over the national average.

The prospect of an additional inch, though...

"Well, then," said Ryan, holding up his glass, "here's to a bigger dick!"

Bruce's laugh echoed around the Shepards' living room, and he clinked his glass to Ryan's.

The weight loss hadn't been as easy as Ryan had hoped, but he'd managed to drop thirty-four pounds in the ensuing months. Looking down now, with his flaccid penis just below the belly paunch, he can be satisfied with it all.

*Never had any complaints, either,* Ryan reminds himself. About the weight or the cock size. He feels a sudden rush of something unfamiliar, a feeling he realizes must be confidence. He looks at the mountain of foam, and the confidence leaves him. How enclosed things must be in there, under that foam. Weighty, like it's smothering you. How could you breathe? How could you get anything but soap bubbles in your mouth and eyes?

He draws in a deep breath and lets it out slowly, looking away from the foam monster that has consumed half of the pool. At the swim-up bar he sees Bruce, who smiles and tips a glass at him. Ryan nods back. He could go over there, hang out with Bruce, his friend. But retreating to the safety of friends, wouldn't that be a waste of that weird confidence spike he just felt? It rode on the back of the fact that he talked to a woman last night without prompting, without being thrust into it. He spoke with a woman last night, without needing to lead with, "Have you met my sexy wife, Jenn?"

Lydia. He's kept an eye out for her all morning and through lunch, seeing her once off in the distance, bent over to pick up drinks off a table in the courtyard. She disappeared down a trail between the trees and buildings shortly after. He wonders if he'll be able to find her.

This morning he had no intention of going to the foam party, and he certainly isn't interested now in going in. But when he found Jenn on their newly assigned beach bed (way down at the end, close to the boat rental shop) she made the salient point: "C'mon, it's the only event this afternoon. If Lydia's an event person, she'll be there. If she's not, you can wander around the resort to see if she's elsewhere."

*Not here*, he thinks, *but somewhere on this resort is a woman who seems really into me.*

He stares at the machine as it belches foam into the pool. The machine's handlers keep adjusting dials and looking from the foam, to the machine, to the foam, to the machine in such a manic fashion, Ryan thinks they're just trying to appear helpful to the Aphrodite's staff members who are looking from them, to the machine, to the foam, them, machine, foam.

"I'll do a lap," he says to no one in particular, reminding himself that both Jenn and Paige are in that foam. He thinks he saw Kendra disappear into it as well. Plenty of people who are into him. He nods at his own logic and lays out his towel on the deck chair in a way that clearly says this chair is taken. He gives Bruce a quick salute and strolls off.

The pool is flanked by the three restaurants and the lunch grill and buffet. Beyond the pool, there is the sand, the beach, the ocean. He passes between the two buildings that house the biggest suites on the resort, even larger than Bruce and Paige's. He wonders who can afford them and is disappointed when he can't see through the sheer curtains to peer inside. Beyond are bungalow style buildings, rattan and grass roofs hanging low enough to brush against his head, even near the middle of the walkway.

Guests in various stages of undress are everywhere today. Some are clearly heading toward the foam party, carrying goggles and even a respirator, others are heading away. A couple makes quiet love bent over the railing of a balcony as he passes. He marvels that the resort can feel so big and yet so small, at once. People everywhere and nowhere. Almost every group has people he's met in it. Sometimes the rest seem to fade to scenery.

As if to confirm his thought, he sees the podcasters coming down the path, Kitten's flaming red hair pulled up into two tiny pigtails at the back of her head. He feels himself stiffening as he looks at her body, those breasts, the curves.

"Watch it, man," says Strom, "you'll put someone's eyes out with that thing." He points at Ryan's penis. Ryan looks down in time to see it shrivel in embarrassment.

"They'd have to be on their knees already, Eric," says Kitten, giving Ryan a wave and a wink.

With that, his cock is back in the game, and as he walks, he's acutely aware of it, bouncing with each step, slapping against his thighs. He emerges from the path to the largest of the resort buildings, two floors of rooms and a seemingly endless stairway up to the hot tub. Then onto the courtyard, with beds, bar, lobby, and shop. He waves to the older couple sitting nude at the courtyard bar and hopes he'll feel as comfortable with himself when he reaches their age.

Back onto the path, he winds between buildings housing smaller rooms like their own. He finds surprisingly few people on this path, and those he sees, he doesn't know.

Then he's traversed the resort and turns right down the final path that drops him at the very northern edge of Aphrodite's stretch of beach. There's a sign in front of him: **Warning: Clothing Optional Beach Ahead**. Below it, in smaller lettering is ***Advertencia: Playa Nudista Adelante***. Ryan is amused by a little clip-art-style graphic of a child reacting with horror to the sight of a man's bare ass.

He heads down to the waterline and turns south. Out in the water, he sees two separate clusters of people and one couple off to the side, apparently fucking, based on their movements. Someone in the second group waves to him, but he can't quite tell who it is. He waves back.

Ryan stops at the beach bar, where Celia hands him a rum punch before he can ask, the same drink he's ordered every time he's come to this bar. "That's some excellent service," he tells her.

"I saw you come down the beach," she tells him with a smile.

"*Muchas gracias*," he says and makes a mental note to bring her a big tip later.

"*De nada*," she replies.

Ahead is a catamaran. Two-thirds of the triad (Marley, the woman, and he thinks the guy is Terrence) are working to put up the sail with an Aphrodite's staff member in a white polo with the swoopy logo on the breast.

Ryan sits on the beach bed that they've claimed as their own. Marco told them when he showed them to it that they might not be able to keep it for the rest of the week, but to try early *mañana*. For now, though, he sits at the edge, dangling his feet, and sipping his rum punch. A complete lap and no Lydia. He sighs. Oh, well, maybe she'll be in the hot tub later.

"Mind if I sit and wait here?"

He looks up and sees the remaining third of the triad. "Not at all."

The man puts his bag down in the sand, throws a towel on the edge of the bed, and parks his naked ass. Ryan reflexively glances down and notices that the man's penis, while flaccid, is almost as long as his when hard. He cautions himself not to extrapolate, remembering the aptly named Mr. Johnson from freshman year health class telling the boys (while the girls were off watching the "other film") that size when soft and size when hard were very different things.

"Rory," says the man, holding his hand out to Ryan. The twinkle in his eye suggests he is aware of Ryan's gaze.

"Ryan."

"I've seen you and your partner around," Rory says. "You're cute together."

Ryan smiles. "Thanks."

"Swingers?" he asks.

Ryan nods.

"Not a lot of friendly room in the swing community for..."

"For?" asks Ryan.

"Bi guys." Rory looks away, grabbing a royal blue swimsuit that looks as tight as Ryan's boxer-briefs. Without turning back, he adds, "As a gay man, there's not a lot for me in that community."

Ryan nods.

"Some straight men bristle at anything but full on hetero men in the lifestyle. They don't like the idea that they might get treated the way they treat women," he says. "Maybe they'll get pressured into something they don't want to do. The way they pressure—" He fixes Ryan with a long gaze. His eyes are hazel, his cheeks meticulously manicured to look unkempt, his smile warm but distant.

Ryan doesn't know what to say.

"Sorry, a pet peeve of mine. A place like this, mostly full of swingers, lots of bi women and hetero men." Rory pulls on his swimsuit and adjusts himself once inside it.

*Like he's smuggling a python*, thinks Ryan.

"And I can't help but think of how nice it'd be if someone who was interested said as much, rather than be afraid of the stigma of being a 'bi guy.'"

"I didn't even realize there was a stigma." Ryan contemplates this information.

"Don't you think it's odd that in a community where at least eighty percent of the women identify as bisexual, there are so few men who identify as the same?"

"I," Ryan begins, then admits, "never thought about it."

Rory nods and stands. "We rarely think about things that don't affect us directly. Call it straight privilege."

Has he just avoided thinking about this? Has he been oblivious? Ryan doesn't know.

"Oh, hey," says Rory, "seriously, wasn't trying to throw guilt at you or anything. Sometimes I'm a pretentious ass. Just want to put out there that if someone is interested in me, I hope they'd tell me."

Trying not to get conversational whiplash, Ryan considers. This man is quite conventionally attractive, isn't he? Without question. Ryan has seen the looks Rory gets from women as he passes, often followed by the disappointed whisper, "He's the gay one." Why would Rory be telling him all of this, unless... *This is one of those moments,* thinks Ryan, *one of those opportunities to try things, to say yes to things.*

"Listen, we're heading—"

"Yeah," says Ryan.

Rory waits.

"I'm curious."

Rory waits.

"I've never been with a guy, and I'm curious," Ryan admits, then draws a long slow breath.

"Hard to say some things sometimes," says Rory. "Didn't realize you were that new. Thought you were just closeted bi." He grins, and Ryan feels self-conscious. "No, no!" he says. "Jesus, I'm a tool. Listen, it's awesome that you want to explore."

"But," says Ryan, waiting to hear what the "but" will be.

"But nothing, it's awesome," Rory tells him, running his fingertips down Ryan's bicep in the gentlest of strokes. "And I dig it," he adds. "Well, okay, yes, I guess there is a 'but.'" He flicks his finger toward the catamaran, now with its sail fully raised.

Marley sits on the side of the vessel, arms folded, watching Rory and Ryan.

"But!" he says, laughing, "Another but. But we're here 'til

Saturday, and if you're interested, for real, we should do something about that curiosity."

Ryan nods and smiles, sure that if he opens his mouth, it'll be all stammers and platitudes and reasons to not try something. Rory sits next to him and leans in, putting a hand on Ryan's thigh. Ryan's cock twitches.

"Well, look at that," says Rory. "Can I give you a kiss?"

He thinks of the moment Jennifer first kissed Paige back at the Horn Lodge nearly two years ago. "That was the moment. The change began there," she confided later. The change that led to swinging, to dating, to eventually this entirely new persona, Jenn. "One of these days, Ryan, you have to give yourself over to new things," she told him, days before this trip, as he lamented living in fear. "Saying yes quells the fear!"

"Yes," says Ryan.

Rory's lips press against his. The kiss is chaste, and Ryan takes in the uniqueness. He feels the bristles of Rory's beard. Tastes cinnamon mouthwash. Smells mingled cologne and sunscreen. Rory's tongue slides between his lips, but only for a moment.

"Woo!" hoots a female voice, probably Marley, behind them.

"You know we've only got this boat for two hours, right?" calls Terrence.

Rory pulls apart from Ryan but stays near him. "Thanks for the kiss," he says. "They're fuckers. To be continued?"

Still afraid he might chicken out should he be allowed to speak, Ryan just nods.

Rory returns it and runs over to the catamaran. "Seriously, fuck you both. Cock blockers."

Ryan watches them disembark and sits in silence for a while. *That was something,* he thinks. Something new, something different. Not life changing, but he's not sure what life changing would feel like. All he has to go on are Jenn's assurances that she knew everything was different from the moment she stepped out of her hetero shell.

"Everything doesn't feel different," he tells himself. "But everything doesn't need to change for something to be a valuable experience." He hops down into the sand, leaving his tumbler behind.

Another sensation washes over him, pride. Sure, he hadn't initiated the conversation or put things out there. He hadn't even asked. It had all been handed to him. But he'd done the most important part of the exploration. He'd said yes.

With a new rush of confidence, Ryan walks up the two steps to the pool deck, avoids the troublesome extension cords, steps beside the thunderous red machine, and drops into the pool. When he breaks the water again, he holds his breath and steps beneath the cascade of foam.

Time to try new things.

# 29

# CRISTA

"Please don't walk away from me."

Crista stops with her hand on the door handle, the door ajar in front of her. She's ready to quit this room and burst forth naked into the sunlight. It's far too gloomy in here. She turns back toward her wife. Her gorgeous wife.

She doesn't blame Allie for her frustrations, but Crista has lived with her uneven sexual desires for a long time, has been embarrassed by them, has apologized for them, has fought to keep them from consuming her and from destroying relationships. As tempting as it would be to blame her high school boyfriend, and his notions of "what's mine," she can't.

"I'm sorry my sex drive doesn't work like yours," says Crista with a sigh, not letting go of the handle, and not closing the door.

"That's not," Allie begins, but stops and looks away, "that's not what I'm saying. You don't need to apologize for that."

"Clearly you need me to apologize for something." Crista loosens her grip on the handle and stands opposite her wife, sitting on the end of the bed.

"No, I just." Again, a dead stop.

"You knew this about me when we started dating," says Crista. She lets go and walks forward, stopping mid-way between the bed and the door, closing behind her. She folds her arms across her breasts. "My drive is different."

"You seem to be doing just fine out there." Allie gestures toward the door.

Crista squeezes her lips together and narrows her eyes. Is Allie jealous? That seems such an odd prospect, almost impossible. For Alejandra Vargas to be jealous of Crista Norris. For that to be jealous of this. She begins to ask the question, getting as far as, "Are you," before recognizing what a triggering word *jealousy* can be for both of them. The big J came up a lot, early on in their lives together. Crista jealous of Alejandra's accolades and adoration, both professionally and personally, the constant turning of heads as she'd walk by. Allie had it all, especially once Crista left journalism for the far quieter, less prestigious world of children's books.

"There's a lot of," she begins, trying to find a word other than "energy" that doesn't sound foolish in her mouth, but can't, "energy here."

"There is," agrees Allie. "I wish you'd turn some of it toward me."

*But I can fuck you at home.* Crista doesn't say the words because they feel selfish. More triggering than the J word. They also feel true, though, don't they? When you only have so much sexual enthusiasm day-to-day, when you have a diminished sex drive like she does, wouldn't you want to spend it on people you don't live with, see at home? *I'd never go see a movie on vacation either,* she thinks, cementing the idea, her rightness. How to say it without saying it? How to explain—

"I wanted this to be for us." Allie looks down at her lap and momentarily becomes very interested in her right thumbnail.

Crista feels the knot in her stomach. Here she is, actively hurting her partner, her lover, her wife. Actively hurting her by... *By just being me? By needing my needs and wanting my wants?* This might be a time to be silent. To just be. She sits on the bed next to Allie and takes her hand. They sit in silence awhile.

"Do you still want me?" asks Allie, breaking the silence.

"Yes," says Crista.

"As much as the rest?"

"Yes. You're different than them, and they're different than you."

"Different."

"You're my partner, you're my wife," she says.

"That doesn't make me feel you want me more."

"Let's not fall into the hetero stereotypes for a moment," says Crista, more tension in her voice than she'd intended. "We believe that no one person can fulfill each other's needs, yes?"

"Yes."

"And that there are all different levels of excitement and attraction?"

"Yes."

"And that me wanting to fuck someone else doesn't equate to me not wanting to fuck you."

"Yes, fine," says Allie, exasperation showing, "the starvation economy bullshit."

Crista waits.

"Just because I believe all that doesn't for a moment mean I don't want my wife to want to fuck me." Allie looks away. Quieter, she says, "To tell me she wants to fuck me."

"I don't—" Crista stops when she hears her voice echoing back from the ceiling. She takes a long breath. "I want to fuck you."

"Then how about you say yes occasionally?"

*Shit.* "I do," says Crista, deflated.

"Why haven't we had sex yet on this trip?"

"But we have!" she protests.

"Just us," says Allie. "Doesn't count if there are other people."

"How can you say that doesn't count?"

"Okay, yes, it's sex, it counts. But it's not *us*."

Seizing on a potential solution, or at least an end to the current tension, Crista offers, "Do you want to have—"

"No," says Allie. "Right now, I really don't."

Again, the silence consumes them; hands clasped, lips pressed together.

"When you say no to me, then I see you flirting and kissing and—"

"When you asked me yesterday, I was overwhelmed and fried from meeting so many—"

"You could've suggested it later," says Allie, "once you'd gotten over that. When you were dancing around the bar."

"Why didn't you say something?" asks Crista, surprised.

"I'm saying something now." Allie takes a deep breath and puts her hand on Crista's thigh. She doesn't look up from it. "Look, I know you feel self-conscious and unattractive, and that makes you less likely to ask for sex."

"And—" begins Crista, but Allie's quick squeeze of her thigh stops her.

"And I know that your sex drive is responsive and situational."

"Yes," Crista says, very quiet.

"But when you tell me, 'No, not now,' again and again and then go after all the other women, the ones who look different from me—"

"I'm not—"

"Stop!" says Allie. Her voice also echoes.

Crista stops.

"I need you to show me you're attracted to me. And at bare minimum, I need you to occasionally say yes when I ask, if you're never going to do the asking."

Crista nods.

"I won't be this cliché. This walking example of lesbian-bed-death paired with the couple that only fucks when they swing." Allie stands. "So right now, I'm going to leave. I'm going to go to the foam party, and I know you don't want to be there, and that's fine." She leans down and kisses Crista, who sits in silence, unsure what she could possibly say to make this better.

When Allie's hand touches the door, though, Crista sees it spiraling out of control, sees down the timeline leading to another future where another relationship reaches another end, not because of lack of desire, but because of—

"Wait!" says Crista.

Allie stops but doesn't turn back toward her.

"What if I came with?"

"You don't want to go to the foam party," says Allie, still facing the closed door, hand grasping the latch.

"But what if I did?"

"If you ignored the germs and claustrophobia and came anyway?"

Crista pushes away the feelings those words bring up, the feelings that caused her to say them to Allie hours before this conversation, this argument, this standoff. "Yeah," she says with a weak laugh.

"Well," says Allie, finally looking back, "that would be nice if you did."

Seeing the opportunity to smooth things over, Crista grabs her tote and key and steps up beside Allie. "Let's go."

"You don't have to go in if you don't want to," Allie tells her as they step out the door.

"I know."

They walk the path through the less affluent subdivision of buildings, past the courtyard and lobby, past that silly sculpture that Crista can admit is beginning to grow on her, past couple after couple, to the pool, where the foam party is already in full swing.

Crista stares at the sheer volume of foam sitting atop the pool like the world's largest whipped cream-topped drink. She sees chemicals and potential pink-eye and most of all that crushing feeling when you're surrounded and can't breathe.

Her wife's arms slide around her shoulders, and she can feel Allie's now bare breasts against her back, hot breath in her ear. "I know it's hard, feeling that things are expected of you."

Crista reaches up and holds Allie's arms against her chest.

"I don't want anything from you that you don't want to give freely and without guilt."

"I do want you," says Crista.

"I know. And saying that occasionally works almost as well as doing anything."

"I'll try."

"Thank you." Allie kisses Crista's ear and then whispers the most fabulous thing: "I swear you don't have to go near that foam for me to be happy. Just coming here with me is enough."

Crista smiles and doesn't join Allie in the foam.

# 30

# JENN

And just like that, in a sea of white foam, her body pressed against her girlfriend's, Jenn is content. With Paige in her arms, against her lips, their breasts together, holding each other, the stressors drift out of her mind. The unemployment, the lack of direction, the things weighing so heavily on her that she barely had two hours of sleep last night – in a moment, all lost. Lost in those arctic blue eyes.

"You're just grinning at me," says Paige.

"Sorry," says Jenn. She looks away, a quick glance into the abyss.

"Sorry?" Paige laughs. "Oh, my dear."

Paige holds Jenn's face in both her hands, turning it back to her, then places a kiss on her lips.

Jenn's grin returns. "You have a super power," she says.

"Oh really?"

"You can kiss away fears, stress, panic."

Paige laughs. "Would that I could."

"Like that first time you kissed me, actually kissed me. When I was spiraling, you caught me." That kiss, at The Horn Lodge, when the idea of swinging had overwhelmed her, when it all seemed too big and too real and too impossible and too scary, Paige's lips drew her back. Back to the date, back to the world, back to herself. Paige's kiss made it all okay.

Here in the foam, hands and lips and bodies pressed together, her kisses had the same effect.

"It's like you take the stress from me," Jenn says. "You take it and hold it."

"And synthesize it down to squirtable fluid," Paige says with a very serious expression.

Jenn blurts a laugh.

With the same serious look, Paige puts the back of her hand next to her mouth and whispers theatrically, "There seems to be a lot of alcohol in the drink of the day."

"I'm just trying to say thank you."

"Anytime, hon."

Muffled words, a female voice, travel through the foam to them. "Because I don't want you to, okay!" They sound as though they are nearby, but acoustics in the foam are distorted.

"Ooh, drama!" Paige says with a giggle. She pushes her ear into the foam, ostensibly to hear better, and puts her finger to her lips. "Shhh!"

"You're shushing me?" asks Jenn. "You're the one talking."

"Look!" comes a male voice, "You're not being very fair."

"Fair?" the first speaker replies. "I'm sorry, I didn't think there were strings attached."

"C'mon, a guy brings you to Mexico for free and you—"

"Seriously?"

Jenn mouths, *Madison*.

Paige mouths back, *I think so*.

"Did you expect me to be your fucking concubine here? Take care of your needs?"

Paige's theatrical whisper again, "I don't think she's using that word correctly."

Jenn shushes her.

"Alright, alright," Paige says, putting her finger in front of her lips and shushing herself.

"You could show some appreciation."

"Fuck this!" Madison emerges from the foam wall in a burst of bubbles, bumping into Paige. Her hair is dark from the water and plastered down against her face. Her makeup has run. She looks between them and apologizes.

"No need," says Paige.

"Fucking guys, right?"

"Madison!"

Paige and Jenn close the gap between them, putting their backs to the spot where Madison just emerged from the foam. They link their arms and brace for the impact, which comes directly. Will appears out of the foam, his erect cock grazing Jenn's hip.

"Watch where you poke that thing!" Jenn says.

"Whoa," says Will, putting his hands up.

"Are you rubbing your cock against my girlfriend?" Paige demands.

"What? No, I—"

"It was like getting speared," says Jenn.

"That was an acci—" He sees Madison, arms folded across her breasts, and holds his hand out toward her, between Jenn and Paige. "Madison, let's go talk."

"No, I'm fine."

He lets his hand hang there and frowns. Paige and Jenn slide closer together, forcing him to withdraw his arm. "Are you two making a fucking wall?"

"We're just enjoying the foam party," says Paige. "Aren't we, Jenn?"

"We absolutely are," agrees Jenn. "When we're not getting poked by pricks."

Will's frown expands as he narrows his eyes. "Okay," he says. "Excuse me. But you know that was not intentional."

Jenn shrugs.

"I'd really like to talk to my date," he tells them.

"I'm not interested in that," says Madison.

"Well, I feel that it's important, as the person staying in my room, that—"

"Madison, you're welcome to stay in my room," says Paige.

Jenn laughs, but is surprised by the tiny prick of jealousy she feels.

"Hey, wait," says Will.

"Not now, Will. You can go back into the foam, and we'll talk later." Madison stares at him, tightening her arms over her breasts. Jenn thinks they look like they're about to emerge screaming over the top of her forearms.

"And see who else you can poke with your cock," says Paige to Jenn, late, as though she's on a tape delay, then snorts with laughter.

Will holds Madison's stare for a moment, then flicks grumpy

glances at both Paige and Jenn. "Fuck it, fine." He spins, Jenn sliding away from his cock as he turns, and flails back into the foam. Then it's just the three of them again.

"Jesus," says Madison to herself. When she looks up and sees them looking at her, she stammers and defends. "He's usually nicer."

"Well, that's good," says Paige, her tone indicating she doesn't believe it at all.

"You know you don't owe him anything," Jenn says. "For bringing you here, I mean."

Madison's hazel eyes are wide. "Oh, of course I know that! I told him that when he asked me. Said 'I'm not going to fuck you just because you bring me to Mexico, you know.' Said it way too loud at Starbucks. Courtney heard me and everything. She's the other barista. There was a to-do. I might fuck him," she says, "but not because he brought me here." Her lips purse and she clenches her hands into fists, putting her arms down to her sides. "But I'm sorry if I don't want chlorine and bubbles inside my pussy right now!" she shouts into the white.

"What?" asks a voice beyond the foam.

"I don't want that either," agrees another, "and I'm not sorry." Muffled laughter.

Madison takes a deep breath and nods. "I'm getting another drink."

"The drink of the day is especially potent," suggests Paige, with a few too many esses in "especially."

"I'll take that recommendation." Bouncy youthfulness returns to Madison and she bounds forward, leaves a quick kiss on each of their lips, then disappears into the foam.

"Did he actually poke you with his cock?" asks Paige.

"Yeah," says Jenn, "but I don't believe it was on purpose."

"Still, he's a skeezeball," says Paige.

Jenn agrees.

"I feel like you were saying important stuff, before we were so rudely interrupted." Paige's grin returns.

She had been, hadn't she? Jenn nods. "When I'm with you, I feel safe," she says.

Paige's grin falters, her eyes widen.

Jenn's intent hadn't been to be so earnest, not during the foam party, not to drunk Paige, and not after coming between Will and Madison. That safety is why their time apart early on –

after Jenn crossed lines of jealousy and foolishness, when she and Ryan were still green and new, when they hadn't figured themselves out yet – had hurt so much. Paige, from the beginning, had created safe space for Jenn. Here in the foam at Aphrodite's Resort and Spa, fifteen hundred miles from her former job, from the people who had judged her, kicked her to the curb, and then denied her unemployment, Paige's touch was soothing.

"I love you," says Paige. "Always and forever."

"I love you, too," says Jenn, conjuring the moment they confirmed their relationship, put a name to it.

"So, we see each other multiple times per week," said Jennifer over ice cream, sometime in mid-September of last year, about two months after the dark time.

"We do," agreed Paige, catching Jennifer's eye before sliding her tongue around her scoop of Moose Tracks as seductively as it was possible to lick ice cream.

"Without the men," added Jennifer.

"Yes, it's nice to get out without them, isn't it?"

"It is," she agreed. To ask this meant putting herself out there, big time. They were swingers, right? Swingers get together as friends and fuck, they don't... They don't... "Are we dating?" She blurted out.

Paige stopped, tongue pressed against her cone. If she was surprised by the question, she didn't show it beyond that moment of pause. She finished her lick and then focused those steely eyes on Jennifer. "I think so," she said.

"Oh."

Paige laughed. "Oh? Not the answer you were looking for?"

"It is, actually," said Jennifer, processing her surprise. "Just didn't expect it to be so easy."

"I'm easy, baby," said Paige with a laugh.

Jennifer's face must have shown her introspection as she considered the next part, the next important question. Paige nodded and put on a serious face. "As you said, we go on dates multiple times a week sans boys. We often have sex. We get all smoochy, even sometimes in public if we get carried away. So, hence, I'd say, ergo and such, we're dating."

"Does that mean you're my girlfriend?" asked Jennifer.

"Do you want that?" asked Paige.

Jennifer flushed. "More than anything."

Paige smiled. "I'd love to be your girlfriend."

Under the foam, a year and change later, Paige asks, "What're you thinking?"

"About my girlfriend," says Jenn.

"Shucks," says Paige.

"And the stuff I'd like to do to her."

A sly smile spreads across Paige's lips. "And what stuff might that be?"

"I want to eat you up."

"Ooh," says Paige.

Jenn takes her hand and together they emerge from the foam, finding themselves only a few feet from the bar. Paige blows a kiss to Bruce, who's talking with a woman they met at speed dating. Her name eludes Jenn.

"Where do you want me?" asks Paige.

Without a word, Jenn leads her to their empty deck chair. *Ryan must have found Lydia,* she thinks with a smile, feeling a gleeful relief at the thought. He seems to finally be pushing himself out of his shell, exploring new things, asking for what he wants. This trip is good for him.

Paige lies down, and Jenn climbs on top, kissing her, beginning with her lips and cheeks, down to her neck with gentle nibbles. She focuses on each nipple for a moment but doesn't linger. She traces her tongue down, around Paige's navel, to the patch of red. She pauses, nuzzling with her nose, feeling the curly wetness, smelling the unmistakable scent of this woman she loves. She doesn't hesitate long, though, and her tongue slides along Paige's lips, slips under the hood and feels her clit becoming erect. There are fingers in Jenn's hair, nails dragging over her scalp. This pushes Jenn past the point of teasing, and she slides her tongue in deep, past the slight taste of chlorine from the pool, to the place where she can drink deep of her lover. She tastes Paige entirely, sliding her tongue along the inner walls, feeling every fold, every fabulous turn of the lip, exploring it all. A swell of fluid slides across Jenn's face, flooding the towel below them both. It drips down her chin and chest, warm, smooth. Paige turns the orgasm inward, as she sometimes does. Jenn sees her eyes pressed shut, feels the last few bucks of her hips, finishing her orgasm against Jenn's face.

When Paige's eyes open again, Jenn is right there. They kiss, deep and soulful. Jenn rests her head against her girlfriend's chest, listening to her heart, to her breathing. Across the pool, she sees Ryan returning. He walks up to the machine spraying foam into the pool, stands there a moment, then drops into the water.

*Well, look at that,* she thinks, then feels she should join him. Reward the exploration, reinforce the value. Maybe...do the thing.

"Can I..." Paige begins as her breathing slows.

"Yes, but later," says Jenn. "Is that okay?"

"For you to eat me out and take a rain-check on reciprocation?"

"Yeah," says Jenn, trying to hide the worry from her face.

"My darling girl," says Paige, "you worry too much."

She kisses Paige again. "Thank you," she says.

"Quit thanking me for letting you do that! Seriously!" Paige laughs, and Jenn does too.

"I'm going to go fuck my husband without a condom."

Paige's eyebrows go up. "Oh, really?"

"Yeah," says Jenn. "It's time."

# 31

# ALEJANDRA

lejandra watches but doesn't participate as the glow party begins. She sits alone at the back side of the courtyard bar, sipping her third drink of the evening and admonishing herself for feeling lonely. "After all," she points out, "there are people everywhere."

In a flipped nighttime version of the foam party, the courtyard has been transformed. The evening lights have been extinguished, and three large light-posts, topped with black light fixtures, send an ethereal purple glow over the crowd. The people have come prepared, too, with headbands, bikinis, clothes of white and yellow and blue.

Luis the manager, who'd been there to welcome them at check-in, stands on the other side of the glass doors. His arms are folded, and he wears a polite smile on his face as he watches the rave-like revelry from the safety and air conditioning of the lobby.

In front of the doors stand entertainment staff members. They're obvious, Alejandra notices, because of how beautiful and fit they are, not to mention the white polos they wear instead of the button-down uniform shirts of the rest of the staff. To the right of the doors, *Señor Entretenimiento* has a chiseled jaw and an expert fade haircut leading to just the right amount of artificial bed-head up top. His polo is tight enough to contour to his abs, and his shorts leave little question about what he packs below.

*Señorita Entretenimiento*'s polo is also too small. *I can see your under-wire*, thinks Alejandra. She's wearing khaki shorts that barely reach the bottoms of her ass cheeks. For a long moment, Alejandra loses herself in the jiggle as *Señor y Señorita Entretenimiento* distribute glow sticks, glow necklaces, glow bracelets. Then she turns her attention back to the crowd, trying to pick out people she knows, though the dim lights and strangely purple smiles make the game difficult. She wishes Crista were here, so people wouldn't think there is something wrong, that she's sitting alone. On reflection, that doesn't strike her as a good reason for her wife to be with her.

"But you don't mind if I go out," she asked Crista as they walked back from dinner.

"No," said Crista, "of course, please."

"Because I'm tired, but—"

Crista waved a hand at her. "Seriously, hon, I'm good. Just exhausted. Today took a lot out of me."

Alejandra found it difficult to not hear the comment as accusatory. That their conversation (it hadn't been an argument) ruined Crista's day. It had been draining for Alejandra too, of course, but a second wind brought her back down to the courtyard bar. She wanted to see what a Glow Party looked like and found it to be nearly exactly what she'd expected: a rave, put on by people who'd never been to a rave.

She smiles, catching Miguel's eye. "*Agua, por favor.*"

"*Sí, Señorita* Alejandra." Miguel produces two tumblers of ice water for her.

"*Gracias.*"

When both tumblers of *agua* have vanished, Alejandra stands. She looks down at the sheath maxi dress she wears, a chocolate brown scoop neck with spaghetti straps. Beneath it, nothing, of course, and she laments the sag in her cleavage from lack of wire support. She grabs both sides of the dress at her waist and tugs downward. The line of cleavage elongates pleasingly as the spaghetti straps stretch. "There," she says to herself. She gives Miguel a wave and taps the three dollars she's left on the bar top.

"*¡Muchas gracias, Señorita Alejandra!*"

"*¡De nada!*" she tells him and looks around the courtyard. *This is foolish*, she thinks. Maybe, but she could use a bit of foolish at the moment. What better place to seek validation than among the swingers. Especially when the only validation she is after just now would be to kiss a few women. The courtyard is her playground, to say nothing of the disco or playroom upstairs. Though the playroom might be pushing things too far.

"I want you to have fun," said Crista in their room, as she grabbed her tablet off the side table and climbed into their queen-sized bed.

Alejandra frowned at her wife, wondering if this would be one of those times where Crista told her to have fun but didn't really want that, or if she genuinely was being given permission to go out and find someone to play with. "You're not going to be upset—"

"I'm not going to be upset..."

They looked at each other.

"But kiss me before you go."

Alejandra walked to the bed, bent down, and kissed her wife three times. First light and quick, then deep and long, and then a final light kiss. She stood again.

"Have fun," Crista said.

"You too," said Alejandra.

"I think it'd be most amusing to write part of the next *Kolcarrot Rabbit Mystery* here." Her wife smiled at her from the bed.

Alejandra laughed. "The swingers were always bad guys on *CSI* and *Law & Order*."

Crista nodded without laughing, then drifted back to her tablet. Alejandra longed for one last moment of eye contact before slipping out of the room.

She sees Jenn dancing with her husband in the courtyard, wearing a white T-shirt tied below her breasts, emphasizing them beyond their modest size and showcasing her flat and oh-so-white tummy.

"I need to stop and tell you that you look very sexy," says Alejandra.

Jenn stops dancing and turns to Alejandra, eyebrows sloping outward, the look of someone who has no idea how to respond. Ryan, dancing a very white boy dance behind her, grins.

"People clearly don't tell you that often enough."

"I," she begins, "I mean," then stops.

"Can I kiss you?"

Jenn nods, eyes still very wide. Alejandra leans in and presses her lips against Jenn's. Before long, Jenn's hands slide up to Alejandra's neck and into her hair. She catches one finger beneath the knot of curls pinned up on the back of Alejandra's head. "Sorry," she whispers directly to Alejandra's lips.

Alejandra responds by slipping her tongue into Jenn's mouth. They linger together for a while, Alejandra sliding her hand under the taught T-shirt, running her fingers up and down Jenn's spine. The woman shivers at the sensation. When they separate, Jenn's eyes don't seem to focus.

"Thank you," says Alejandra.

"Thank you," repeats Jenn in nearly identical inflection.

"*Very* sexy," says Alejandra again, then slides away. A glance over her shoulder as she nears the lobby reveals a wide grin on the young woman's face as she returns to her goofy dancer husband. Alejandra likes those two, and thinks they'd be a good couple to play with again this week. He hadn't seemed to have any issues with the whole nature of their arrangement. He'd hung back and watched, sure, but he'd had that look on his face she always loved seeing.

Awe.

"Now," she tells herself as the song changes to Usher, "the next one shouldn't be someone I've played with."

Out of the corner of her eye, Alejandra notices a man lingering. Watching. Ever since she turned thirteen, people have told her that she's attractive. Back then, she was a tall, thin, eighth grader in Arizona with voluminous breasts crammed under too-small uniforms. Many of those expounding her beauty had been her own age, boys from the high school. Even then, Alejandra knew the compliments grew progressively creepier as those dispensing them got further from her in age. The creepiest were her teachers, men who'd say, "Looking good," and wink.

The man whose gaze follows her from the bar reminds her of those men, his shiny navy blue shirt and black slacks making him nearly vanish into the black-lit dark. She wonders where Madison is, as *that* could be a kiss to remember, and keeps her distance from Will. Men like him were almost non-entities to her, though. She wasn't interested. Didn't know much about what she was interested in, back then, though. It hadn't helped that her rapid development caused anger and jealousy in so many of her friends. And there was the chronic back pain that still plagues her.

But there'd also been Maria, who'd tried to hide her gaze

while everybody else openly stared and judged. Maria, who'd barely budded. Maria, with her glasses. Maria, Alejandra's first burning, confusing love. They shared their first kiss behind a row of lockers in the swimming pool locker room. It was awkward and impulsive, and rather foolish in retrospect, and of course they were seen. Seen and judged. Judged and reported. Reported and admonished. Admonished and punished. Punished and banned. Being told they couldn't talk to each other just inflamed their primal pubescent urges, as confusing as they were. Gay was a concept she'd just barely confronted. Lesbian sounded even more foreign.

She'd known that she felt nothing looking at the boys, no speck of interest in them, with their weak dirty-lip excuses for mustaches, always grabbing at the crotches of their jeans as they dealt with their own early developments. When her friends whispered curiosities about what the boys might have between their legs and told campfire stories about something called jizz, all she could hope was that she'd never have to touch one of their things, let alone allow it between her legs. While many of her friends lost their virginity at fourteen, fifteen, and sixteen – many willingly, some not – to sweaty and desperate boys, she managed to avoid the whole ordeal.

Now, looking at the sea of bodies around her on this resort, she regards the hanging phalli the same way she regards any other part of a man. She can appreciate the aesthetic appeal, especially when they've shaved it bare, but is detached from the appreciation, the way one appreciates a fine statue of the human form. She wouldn't wank off the statue of David either.

Crista wasn't much help in unraveling this thread, having lived for many years as a "straight girl" in Kentucky. Her sexual experiences were vast and varied before she announced her bisexuality to family and friends. She hadn't really gone all-in on a relationship until she'd met Alejandra at a certain awards ceremony, and hadn't even intended that to be more than a one-night-stand. It's a mild ego boost, having been awesome enough to convert a one-night-stand into a relationship, then into a full-fledged "gay marriage" when it became the law of the land two years ago. Hell, their wedding invitations had even said, "Come watch us get gay married!" The invitations had the intended effect of keeping away those who'd judge. Including Isabel Vargas, her mother, who'd banished Maria

Castillo, and who, to date, has never visited Alejandra and her wife.

*The first time the three of us are in a single room, it'll likely be the parlor of a funeral home*, thinks Alejandra. *And you'll be in the box, Mamá*. She scowls and leans against the sliding glass door. That fourth drink may have been a mistake, as it seems to have led her down this dark alley. She shakes it off, swings by the bar for another *agua* from Miguel, and surveys the crowd dancing in the courtyard. She finds Will almost immediately, still pretending not to watch her, hiding his mouth behind a short glass of whiskey.

As she moves between couples and triads and foursomes, she sees someone she's met, but cannot remember a name. The woman sits alone on one of the hanging beds, crossing and uncrossing her ankles in the highest heels Alejandra has seen all week. She wears bikini bottoms that glow brilliant yellow in the black-light. The hair on one side of her head is cropped close enough that a drill Sergeant would approve, but the other side is straight and long. In the purple-tinged light, her lips are black, her face pale. There are flowers painted up her modest belly to her nipples, two large sunflowers, petals stretching to cover the entire pendulous bosoms.

"I love the body painting," says Alejandra, standing and leaning against one of the four posts holding the bed aloft.

"Thank you," the woman says and smiles a purple-toothed smile up at Alejandra. "I like your dress."

"We met at the..." Alejandra says, trailing off in that way that always feels so manipulative to her but never fails to produce the desired results.

"On the shuttle," she says with a nod. "I don't know if we shared names. Katrina."

Alejandra shakes the hand that Katrina extends. "Alejandra."

"You're the—" Katrina cuts herself off and looks away.

"We're the lesbians," Alejandra finishes. "You needn't be embarrassed. Helps to advertise what we want and don't, I think. Let the legends of Aphrodite's Lesbians proceed us."

Katrina laughs a nervous laugh.

"Can I sit?" asks Alejandra.

"Please," Katrina says, rubbing her hand over a spot on the sheet.

Before she sits, Alejandra glances over the full expanse of

purple, realizing she's looking for visible splotches. Too much time reporting on crime scenes, maybe? She's impressed by the Aphrodite's laundry. "Must use a lot of bleach here," she murmurs as she sits.

"What?"

"Nothing worth repeating," says Alejandra. "I saw you across the courtyard and thought you looked like you might enjoy a kiss."

Katrina grins bashfully. "Yeah? Maybe."

"Maybe."

"I'm waiting for my husband," she begins, then stops.

"I won't take up too much of your time."

"Oh, no," says Katrina with the face of someone who's not sure why she said the preceding sentence. "I just meant," she stops again. "I don't know. Yes, yes, I'd like to kiss you."

Alejandra does, and it's entirely different from her kisses with Jenn. Katrina uses her tongue infrequently and nibbles lightly on Alejandra's lips. Unique, different. *Not totally my thing.* "Thank you," says Alejandra when they separate.

"No, I," returns Katrina, appearing to look for something more substantial, then smiling quietly. She nods.

"Maybe I'll see you tomorrow," says Alejandra. She might, of course, but the nibbling method didn't match her, and she's unlikely to seek out a second kiss. She's known women who bite because they think it's what their partners want or like, and those can be molded with instruction and suggestion. But in Alejandra's experience, the ones who include nibbles in their kisses by default will leave bite marks and blood when the next level kicks in.

"I hope so," says Katrina, who leans forward and plants an impulsive kiss on the corner of Alejandra's lips.

Alejandra smiles, wondering if she's misjudged the woman, but stands when Katrina's husband returns, in dark slacks and a bowling shirt, apparently uninterested in the glow party.

"Hi again," he says.

She gives him a smile and a wave and slips between two clusters of bodies working to take the glow party up to a glow orgy.

"I've got something for you," says a man behind her.

She spins, ready to address the voice assuming she needs what he's got. "Listen, Will," she says with bite, but stops at seeing Raymond Horne, a small confused smile on his face, holding up a headband with two glowing loops in the shape of Minnie Mouse ears, with an outlined bow between them.

"Hi there," he says.

"Hi, Raymond." She looks down at the headband. "Do you really think that's me?"

He shrugs and absently scratches at a welt on his cheek.

"Jesus, what happened to you?"

"Let's just say, don't forget your bug spray," says Raymond.

"Oh, I don't."

He sniffs the air. "I smell Skin-So-Soft," he says.

Alejandra laughs despite herself at the man who has just smelled her and identified her specific brand of bug spray. "Yes, smells better than the ones with DEET."

"Jesus," he says to himself. "Remember how a minute ago I pulled a Hannibal Lecter on you by smelling you?"

"Indeed," she responds.

"Can we pretend I didn't?"

"Of course," she says.

"Is Will bothering you?" he asks, glancing behind her.

She's certain if she follows Raymond's glance, she will see Will, sipping his whiskey to prove just how nonchalant he's being. Certainly not following her around the courtyard tonight. "I'm not sure he's bothering. Irritating. Following."

"I've had a couple similarly vague almost-complaints," Raymond tells her. "You'll let me know?"

"I will," says Alejandra.

Raymond stares absently at the mouse-eared headband. She takes it from him and puts it on her head. "Thank you so much for the ears, Raymond."

"We aim to please," he tells her.

She sees his distraction. It must be hard to run something like this, to monitor and help. She touches his arm. "Hey, Raymond?"

"Yeah?" He brings his attention back to her, but she can see he's still only half there.

"You're doing an excellent job," she tells him and gives his arm a quick squeeze.

He looks down at her hand, and then into her eyes. Now he's there with her, and she's not sure if he's going to cry or embrace her. "Can I give you a hug?" he asks.

She nods and opens her arms to him. He's warm and smells

nice, refreshingly free of cologne. She smiles, recognizing a touch of ammonia. Poor guy with his bug bites. "You're a good hugger," she says.

"Hosting cuddle parties'll do that," he says. "You'll tell me if Will crosses a line? Not because I don't think you can take care of it yourself, but because I—"

"Of course," she tells him.

She leaves Raymond as he's pulled into a cluster of dancing women. His moves are more refined than Ryan's, than most of the white boys she's watched dance, and it makes her smile.

She ends her night back at the courtyard bar, after the black lights have gone off and most of the guests have disappeared up to the disco or hot tub. She sips a Coke, enjoying the real sugar of Mexican Coca-Cola. A few couples have approached as she's sat here, mostly feeling out her willingness to be their unicorn for the evening. She told two of the couples that she'd be interested some other time; with another, she's certain the man didn't understand when she told him that she simply doesn't play with men. Regardless of interest, though, she's begged off on all offers, taking the currency of appreciation and letting it nourish her.

"Um, hey." Madison steps up to the bar and folds her hands on it. She stands close to Alejandra, close enough that their shoulders touch.

"Hello, Madison," says Alejandra.

"So, I," Madison begins, looking intently at her fingers.

"Yes?" Alejandra asks.

"I'm headed to bed," she says, without looking back at Alejandra.

"It's late," Alejandra says, noticing the clock has carried them over into Tuesday. But is 1:00 AM actually late here in this dark paradise, where dozens of people still dance their sweaty dances at the disco and fuck their sweaty beautiful fucks in the playroom next door?

"Nah," says Madison, as though she can read Alejandra's thoughts. "Not late, just tired. Too much dancing."

Alejandra can see a sheen of sweat on Madison, who has ditched all but her bikini bottoms and spike heels. "You don't take off the bottoms?"

Madison looks down, then back at Alejandra. "I'm a little shy," she confides.

Alejandra nods.

"Are you asking me to take off my bottoms?" the girl asks, suddenly quite interested in her hands again.

Alejandra grins. "I'm not asking," she says. "Though I'm sure I'd enjoy seeing you fully naked."

"I'll show you mine if you show me yours," says Madison, a wild grin appearing on her face out of nowhere. She pinches her thumb and forefinger on the green tie at her left hip.

"Alright," says Alejandra, standing. She reaches down and grabs two handfuls of the brown sheath, pulling it up over her head, and in a flash, stands naked.

A whistle of appreciation from men across the bar. "Nice!"

Alejandra takes it and puts it in her confidence vault. She cocks her head at Madison. "Your turn."

Madison nods and pulls the tie. The bow vanishes, and the bottoms fall.

There's a discordant moment, where Alejandra's thoughts about what Madison might look like fully nude don't match up with the reality. She'd expected college girl pussy: bare, tiny lipped, a closed clamshell. Madison's trimmed dark landing strip points down to a brilliant pink *labia minora* dangling from between two very pale *majora*.

"I hate how it hangs," she tells Alejandra, scratching absently at her thigh. "Guys don't like it."

"Whoever told you 'guys don't like that' meant *they* don't like it," says Alejandra, leaning closer to Madison. "And one must never forget how stupid guys can be."

The girl laughs and presses her thighs one over the other, as though trying to hide.

"I didn't mean to make you uncomfortable, asking you to take them off."

"Oh, no, you didn't," assures Madison. "Some of the rest have." She moves her hands to cover up.

Alejandra leans in and whispers. "Why don't you put them back on."

Madison does.

"Thank you for sharing," Alejandra says.

"I want to kiss you," says Madison, after re-tying her bottoms. "Would you be into that?"

"I would indeed," says Alejandra, taking Madison's chin in her hand and kissing her softly. Their lips part, but their tongues don't join. It is a kiss full of potential. It is a kiss of comfort.

Madison thanks her, then laughs and rolls her eyes at herself.

"Get some sleep, beautiful girl," says Alejandra.

She nods, plants another kiss on Alejandra's cheek, and disappears into the night. Alejandra catches a glimpse of Will, who meets her eye with a frown on his face, then looks away. He follows Madison into the dark.

Alejandra takes a deep breath through her nose, slowly letting it past her lips, then smiles to herself. *Successful experiment.*

When Gabriella asks her if she'd like a pizza, she finds that she would.

# 32

# RYAN

The hot tub is nearly empty when the rain begins to fall. At first, it's only small droplets, making Ryan wonder if it's just splashes up from the hot tub. As the rain gets heavier, and a crack of thunder rings out, the people occupying the beds opposite the hot tub scatter, call their play on account of rain, and walk in various stages of dress downstairs. Two couples and a single male scoot over to a small seating area next to the hot tub bar, shielded from rain by the grass roof. One couple dashes to hop into the hot tub. They stay down at the opposite end of the bean, what people this week have dubbed the "cold end." It is by no means cold down there, but definitely the furthest one can get from the main heating jets.

Ryan and Jenn remain at the opposite end next to the bar. His arms extend along the outside edge of the tub, rum punch in one hand, getting steadily watered down by droplets of rain. Jenn leans in, tucked into the crook of his arm, with her head tilted back, eyes closed. Rain rolls down her smiling face.

"Clearly the rain doesn't bother you," he says.

"Not at all," she tells him. "I used to love going out in the summer rain when I was little. Always comforted me."

Ryan closes his own eyes and leans his head back, though the pelting of raindrops on his face doesn't strike him as comforting. Maybe it's just the thing. The thing on his mind.

"I think we ought to talk about Vince and Kendra," Ryan says.

"I don't know how I feel about their," Jenn searches for the word, "plans?"

"The full swap," says Ryan

Earlier this evening, as Ryan waited on the balcony for Jenn to finish her makeup before dinner, he noticed Vince walking below and waved.

Vince returned the wave and asked what the Lamberts would be doing tomorrow.

"Not sure," said Ryan, feeling unexpected reluctance. "Going to the orgy?" The orgy was scheduled for the middle of the week, threatening to take over both the disco and the adjacent play-room. Ryan still hadn't been up to either room, having found plenty to enjoy just in the courtyard, the beach beds, the hot tub.

"We're not sure," said Vince. "We'd *really* like to play with you both, though."

"We should hang out," offered Ryan, feeling the reluctance deepen. "No expectations." He said it, the progressive swinging mantra, the encouragement to simply be, to experience, to not need or demand or expect. Ever since that party where he felt left out, and the subsequent fallout, he'd tried to make "no expectations" his creed.

When Vince and Kendra had booked their trip to Aphrodite's, he'd still been dating Kendra on a relatively regular basis. After Ryan and Kendra stopped dating, the frequency of interaction had lessened. They hadn't seen the de Martoloses in almost two months before this trip.

"An awful lot of presumption, too," says Jenn.

"For them to show up after two months and announce that they want to full swap," says Ryan.

"I feel like a dick," says Jenn, her eyes still closed, the droplets of water appearing more frequently on her face. He waits. After a while, she opens her eyes and stares into the sky. "It's pretty impressive that they trust us so much that they want us to be their first full swap."

Ryan agrees.

"But at the same time, it's a lot of pressure. They just decided this is how it's gonna be, didn't even ask us if we'd be interested. Told us. And I kinda don't want to do that."

Ryan thinks about this a while. "They're sweet, genuine people."

"They are."

"And we've had fun with them in the past."

"We have."

"But," he says.

"But," she agrees. She looks up at him, one eye closed in the rain, and asks, "So we're not doing that full swap?"

He takes a deep breath. "I don't want to."

She nods again. "We should tell them that."

"Yeah," he says. He kisses her, deep and long.

The clouds burst, and the downpour becomes torrential. Squeals and shouts from the others in the hot tub, rushing under the rattan roof to gather their things, then for reasons Ryan cannot begin to understand, back out into the rain to brave the stairs, which are slippery even under normal circumstances.

Gathering the tumblers around the edge of the tub into a stack, Andres leans over to them from behind the bar. "*¡Relámpago!*" he tells them, then rushes down the stairs himself.

Ryan and Jenn look into the dark night sky.

"Should we go downstairs?" he asks.

"I can barely handle those stairs when I'm not also dealing with a hurricane."

Ryan agrees. They emerge from the hot tub, from hot water to tepid rain cascading down upon them. The wind blows it up from the sides, and at once Ryan feels as though he's wandered into one of those storm-at-sea movies, where men who look like the Gorton's fisherman in large yellow rain slickers and hats battle the elements. He has no such slicker, and their robes are in a cubby with their towels, under the bar roof. Standing in the rain, wetter than when he was in the hot tub, he grabs Jenn's arm as she moves past him.

She stops and turns back to him. "What?"

He cocks his head toward the beds, mattresses stripped of their sheets, probably by poor Andres before he quit this roof, shining their vinyl, water-proofed shine.

She laughs. "Really?"

"Not like we need to go get a condom or anything," he tells her with a grin.

She returns the smile, grabs his cock, and leads him to the bed. She flops backward onto it, sending up a splash.

"Reminds me of a slip and slide," he tells her.

"Shut up and fuck me," she tells him.

She winces as he slides inside her.

"Are you okay?"

"Yeah, it's fine. Gentle, though. Between the pool sex and the hot tub and no lube...just be gentle."

He agrees, and they move together. Her hips, his. He grabs at her back and her ass, and she slides across the vinyl mattress. The movement is slow, and he can feel her warming up to him, her juices begin to flow, making inside nearly as wet as out. He slides her up and down the slick mattress, doing less and less thrusting and more and more sliding. Their tempo and pace pick up, and now the water is coming from below as well as from above, as they splash their bodies over the drenched bed.

"Ryan," she says, "fuck!"

"Yeah," he agrees, never quite knowing what to say on such occasions, but, "yeah," usually does nicely.

"Harder," she says, impatient, "c'mon."

"You told me gentle!" he says.

"I reserve the right to change my mind and I'm telling you harder now!" She grips his arms, and in addition to the sliding, begins to thrust upward. Her thighs slam into his. He feels their pubic bones bumping together. She throws her head back. A mouthful of water sends her coughing, and he stops. "Don't, (cough!) don't you stop!" She reaches around, grabs a handful of his ass, and does the thrusting for him. He picks up her rhythm. The sliding, the thrusting, the pounding, all beneath the curtains of rain. When she comes, her whole body is clenched, her teeth bared, eyes squeezed shut. He pulls back and out, the action taking him over the edge as he spasms and sends one, two, and a thin third shot out over her belly, bush, and thigh. It's washed away almost as quickly as it arrives. Jenn's orgasm intensifies, the cork out of the bottle, and he feels his lap and knees flooded with warm liquid, contrasting dramatically with the now-chilly rain. He kneels before her through her spasms, one hand on the back of her neck, one on the small of her back. Slowly she loosens her grip on his arm and ass, and her eyes open. She looks deep into him, and she's laughing now. Laughing and coughing and coming, as a second, third, fourth wave hit her. New warmth runs down the vinyl mattress over his legs and onto the concrete deck below.

The rain has mostly subsided by the time they return to the hot tub, drips and drops in cool counterpoint to the warm waters of the tub.

"I wonder if this'll hold me," Ryan says, pulling himself up onto the granite bar top.

"Had three girls on it earlier for body shots," she reminds him.

"True."

He swings his legs around over the bar and drops down to the rubber mat below. He throws a towel over his shoulder, folds his hands on the bar, and asks his wife, "What'll it be?"

She giggles. "Surprise me."

He nods, and, with the limited supplies remaining after Andres's hasty exit, whips up two pineapple-upside-down-cake martinis. "It's not cake vodka," he tells her, regretfully. "Vanilla will have to do."

"We'll survive somehow."

They clink their plastic tumblers together and drink. Vanilla does nicely. Ryan catches a glimpse of the clock on the wall. "Jesus, it's nearly four."

Jenn laughs. "What day?" she asks.

He has to think about it for a moment. "It's Tuesday, now, darling."

"Tuesday," she repeats, disbelief in her voice.

"Already Tuesday, or?" he asks.

"*Only* Tuesday," she says.

"Happy Tuesday." He offers his tumbler for a plastic clack.

"Happy Tuesday," she replies, kissing him, then tapping her tumbler against his.

As they finish their martinis, the rain slows to a trickle. They towel off, throw their oversized robes on, then head to the court-yard bar to close down the pizza oven with the other stragglers. Already it feels like habit, routine, but a glorious routine.

Home indeed.

# PART V

*Tuesday*

# 33

# CRISTA

The dim light of morning has just begun to crawl across the floor of the suite when Crista sits up in the middle of the king-sized bed. She's naked under the sheet between the sleeping couple, both facing the outside of the bed. The man's hair is dark and salty, the woman's is nearly white blonde in an elaborate, now messy, up-do.

*That'll hurt when you take it down,* thinks Crista, a distraction from the fact that she has absolutely no idea who these two people are, a distraction from the old familiar burn down below, inside. She lowers the sheet and examines her vulva, the vivid pink shade of "freshly fucked." A headache blasts from behind her right ear to above her left eye, and she presses her hand against her forehead, closing her eyes. It doesn't go away, but does mellow. She slides down the valley between the couple, to the cold tile floor, staggering as she steps down from the bed riser. The room is still dim, but she can make out a coffee table, a sectional couch, clothes in a few piles on the floor. She sees a dress she's reasonably sure is hers and picks it up. *Yes!* This floral pattern, the giant hibiscus. She remembers pulling this from her closet, hours ago.

In her room the night before, after finishing the roughest outline of a new mystery for Kolcarrot to solve – this one centered on Mayor Badgerton's rutabaga patch – she flipped over to the internet and browsed aimlessly. When a sidebar ad promised topless photos of a celebrity she vaguely knew, she felt the tingle. She wouldn't click there, because there lay spyware and pop-ups, but she could look at her porn feeds. She clicked her daily photos folder, and let it feed and nourish her hunger. Animated GIFs presenting gloriously sexy moments in time. She liked these so much more than straight-up porn, especially since most porn featuring women was produced specifically for a male gaze. She sometimes found some tingles at Crash Pad, or Girls Out West, though. Those women looked real. Looked like her.

Her hand found its way to her vulva, and she inhaled deeply as her middle finger slid between her lips. She swiped the index finger of her other hand up the tablet screen before her, catching both animated and still images. Here, a young tattooed woman with blue hair slid a black gloved hand out of a bigger woman's pussy; her vulva quivered at the vacancy. Crista's own moistened. She stayed there for a while, swiping and fingering, swiping and rubbing, a continuous feed of captured sexual moments marching past her. Some good, some bad, all feeding the need that had risen to the surface of its own accord. It struck her that she could go outside and find her wife, who'd happily service that need. Perhaps with the help of others.

"And it's all available just outside your door!" she said to herself, affecting an old-timey travelogue announcer's voice.

She paused, middle and pointer finger on either side of her clit, which seemed to have doubled in size since she'd begun. *Get up. Get up and go out. Get up and start your vacation.*

In the closet, she grabbed the first dress she saw, light blue, covered with huge magenta and white hibiscus flowers. She pulled it over her head and went to the drawer for panties, stared at her simple options, and shrugged. "What fun is that?" After all, the rarest of flowers, her sexual appetite, had just bloomed independently, triggered by random happenstance, and she felt the hunger she so rarely felt. Her sex drive, which she'd learned was considered "responsive" from a helpful book called *Come as You Are*, frequently eluded her. She'd never really know when the desire, the urge, the hunger, would show up.

Masturbation was often a means to an end, something she did when bored, when procrastinating (procrasturbating) between writing and drawing the Kolcarrot books, something that always felt exceptionally exhilarating and naughty. Usually, when presented with the opportunity to have sex, she threw herself in and enjoyed it thoroughly. The higher intensity the opportunity, the more likely she'd go with it, and the more likely she'd ask for it herself. It's why swinging worked so well for them.

But, did it?

She shook her head, ignored the question, slipping her hand through the scrunchy ring of her key and stepping into the humid evening in search of misadventure.

In the room of the unknown couple the morning light grows stronger, but only barely. Or maybe Crista's just getting used to the dim. She sees the yellow rubber coil attached to her key and exhales relief. Behind her, the man takes a deep breath and smacks his lips, then rolls over to face the center of the bed. She holds her breath as she watches him run his hands over the place she has vacated.

*Don't wake up, don't wake up,* she wills him. He doesn't.

She can see his face now, covered by a short salt-and-pepper beard, more salt than his hair. A name swims to the front of her mind, projected out of focus on a white screen. She squints, and her eyes burn from sleeping in her contacts. She closes them for a moment and focuses on the name.

"Sergey," she says. She has no idea how loudly she has spoken, but loud enough to echo. Neither party in the bed wakes. "Sergey and Polina." She examines the compounded name in her mind and agrees it's correct. They'd met for the three minutes of speed dating, then not seen each other again until last night on the beach.

The scent of pot was unmistakable, and Crista wondered why the silhouettes on the beach with the glowing red cherry hovering between them were so unconcerned about the roving security guard. She'd wanted to bring her own, had gotten pretty good at traveling while carrying, back when she still traveled for work. Some of the worst edges of the world could be blunted with pot. Maybe she should find Allie, and they could both join this group smoking up.

Maybe they'd sell her some.

"Evening, party people," she said as she approached. The silhouettes resolved to three distinct shapes. She smiled, recognizing that one of them was their fearless leader, Raymond Horne.

"Good evening, Crista," he said. "Have you met my friends Sergey and Polina?"

"Briefly," she replied and waved.

"We are celebrating," said Sergey, his voice doubling down on his heritage.

"We have sold our house," Polina agreed, grinning. She took a long, slow drag on a device the size of a thick credit card.

"You're not worried about—"

"I gave Alberto fifty bucks," said Raymond. "He's more concerned about miscellaneous people getting into the resort than patrons smoking up on the beach."

"Especially with feefty dough-lars in his hand!" Sergey said, accent thick, laughing.

Crista smiled.

"Join us," said Polina, offering Crista the vaporizer.

She looked at the trio, all smiling and happy, and thought how nice it'd be to get outside herself for a while. Maybe when she got back to the room, her new Kolcarrot mystery wouldn't involve the murder of the badger mayor's aardvark aide. Though she wondered if anyone would be interested in her crime scene sketch, which strongly implied the murder weapon had been an unusually large zucchini.

She took the vaporizer, pressed the button on top, and inhaled. *Oh, yes, hello my friend.*

In the room, her eyes adjust to see the top of the coffee table, covered in revelations and answers to unasked questions. A headache snakes across her brain like lightning and lingers with thunder. On the table are two empty bottles of vodka, the vaporizer, pills of various sizes and colors, and what looks like the end of a line of coke.

Crista brings her hand up and pinches her nostrils together, then takes a long deep breath through her nose. "Don't think I did that," she whispers to herself, barely audible. The chanting, "Shots," echoing in her ears indicates she likely enjoyed plenty of the vodka. Her headache agrees.

A female moan draws her attention back to the bed, where Sergey seems to be sleep-fucking his wife in the spooning position.

*I have to get out of here,* she thinks, feeling that burn again between her legs, the one that only comes from sex without lube. Endless drunken sex. Stoned sex. The kind where she's too far gone to read the signals, and so dehydrated that her body shuts off the waterworks. Since she'd read the tea leaves of her own life and slid down the Kinsey scale all the way to six – "Exclusively Homosexual" – only once has she done the drunken-sex-with-a-man thing. Her therapist cautioned her not to read into it too much, and reiterated that it did not mean that she was actually bisexual. "Our drunk selves want what we want in the moment; often it's meaningless. Pure Id." As she heads for the door, she wonders what drunk and stoned Crista had wanted last night.

Something rubbery on the floor trips her, and she almost face-plants on the cold tile, catching herself on the cabinet that houses the safe, refrigerator, and television. She crouches to get a better look and sees a long red dildo still attached to a harness. She lifts it by the harness and brings it closer to her face, inhaling deeply. The scent on it, barely there now, is definitely hers. She feels tension she hadn't realized she was holding leave her body.

She remembers the moment Polina pulled off her dress to reveal a boyish frame, milky pale, with pink nipples atop cupcake breasts. Her ribcage beneath could be seen in relief, her stomach concave, her pubis prominent with a smudge of light yellow hair. She stood, wearing only a cockeyed grin on her face, her soft blonde hair shooting out from the up-do at the back of her head. Her husband on the couch behind her, leaning forward to the coffee table and making a long *sniiif!* From behind her back, Polina produced a massive red dong.

Crista thought that dildo could split her right in half. But at that moment, sitting on the tile riser that surrounded the bed, she wanted it inside her. Wanted this woman to strap it on and fuck her. She reached down and spread her lips for Polina.

"Yom!" said Polina with a grin. "Give me the straps," she told her husband without looking at him, just snapping her fingers in his direction.

Sergey pinched and rubbed at his nose, then stood and staggered toward the closet. He lumbered forward, headlong, and Crista laughed at the erection curving out and downward. She'd always found real penises to be rather amusing. But she wondered how it'd feel in her hands. Was the skin baby soft? She knew better than to ask, though; he'd never understand that her interest was in the aesthetic only, that the thought of putting him in inside made her tummy rumble in the not-so-good way. That big scary red thing, on the other hand...

When Sergey returned, he held a nest of black leather straps and buckles in his hands. He spent a few minutes trying to untangle the mess before Polina snatched it from him.

"Get her shots," said Polina.

Crista laughed. "Oh no." She had no idea how many she'd already had, but knew it was more than three in quick succession. The dryness of her lower lips made her momentarily consider getting a bottle of water from the fridge.

"Shots, shots, shots, shots, shots!" said Sergey, dancing away from his wife, scooping up three shot glasses from the TV stand, and plucking the vodka bottle off the table.

When Crista looked back, the proud red cock protruded from Polina's pubic bone, surrounded by radiating leather straps. She walked seductively toward Crista, throwing her small hips back and forth as she did so. "You want me to fock you," she said, more than asked.

Crista did want that, and said as much, though not with words.

Slipping out of the door, Crista squints in the harsh morning light. She finds herself on the opposite side of the resort, near the pool. The sun is half of a white circle, obscured almost entirely by hazy morning clouds over the ocean. She's up before the music, but the tropical birds are chattering in the trees. She sees two staff members in button downs and reddens. This is the walk of shame now, isn't it? A walk of shame where she'd been out all night after telling her wife she'd be right in the room. Where she couldn't be one hundred percent certain that she hadn't had a real penis inside her, along with that fake red cock. She doesn't think so, is very close to certain, but the reel missing from the middle of last night's film is the part after Polina climbed atop her and slid that red cock deep inside, the exquisite pain turning to orgasmic pleasure, but never disappearing entirely. Even now the pain lingers. The shame crawling in her stomach, and in her burning vulva, and in her dry throat, all lead her home, to the second-floor balcony, to their room, where she slides in her key and turns the handle. Where Allie waits for her.

Crista's shame turns to tears as she slides down the inside of the door, onto the cold tile floor of their room. The tears stream down her face, and Allie, sitting in bed, wide awake, eyes red, doesn't rise to comfort her.

# 34

# JENN

"Can we make calls to other rooms?" Jenn asks Ryan, who is lying on his side in their bed, facing away from her. "I want to call Bruce and Paige."

He grunts noncommittally and waves his hand as though trying to wave her back to sleep. It's early, true, but not terribly early. Not as early as yesterday. Jenn has never slept well outside her own bed. Even in friendly confines, she finds it difficult to relax the way she can in their bedroom, in their bed, on their mattress. For half of the night she spent at Paige's house while Bruce was out of town, she stared, wide awake, at the light fixtures on the ceiling and the shadows they cast. Having barely slept, she rose before Paige, covering by going out for bagels.

"Do you think I can call them?" she asks.

This time Ryan doesn't offer a grunt.

Last night she slept well, unlike the nights previous, unlike other times in unfamiliar places. Short sleep, still, as they were out so very late, but happy sleep, without worry. She knows that the stress of the job, her reality, will return soon, but for now, she really feels she can enjoy paradise, for at least a few days. What she wants today, more than anything, is the safety and comfort the Shepards provide. "With Vince and Kendra at dinner, and then Crista and Alejandra...after...we haven't had any time, just us and them."

Ryan clears his throat.

She looks at the back of his head. "Is that an answer?"

"What time is it?"

"Eight-forty."

His grunt suggests that this is the end of his contributions at this time.

She considers reaching around and grabbing him, but thinks better of it. The last time she tried surprise morning sex, she startled him out of sleep so deep he literally shouted, "no!" to his unknown attacker. He spent the better part of the next half hour explaining that she hadn't done anything wrong and that he hadn't thought she was attacking. Besides, if she coaxes him awake with a hand job, she'll want to climb aboard when he rolls over, and just now her vagina isn't feeling very welcoming. She looks across the room at the bottle of silicone lube she used in the pool yesterday, but hadn't had with at the hot tub during the storm last night.

*Helps to take the lube out with us,* she thinks. She looks at the phone, next to the clock, next to her charging cell phone on the bedside table. She could call them from her phone, but she remembers Paige saying something about the fiery pink death of her battery, whatever that means. *Means they probably shut off their phones.*

The Shepards' room number is 1111. She could just dial it and see what happens. Or she could call the front desk, tell them to connect her. Would they do that, this early? Would they judge her? Tell her to get off her ass and walk over there? Surely not, but something about them *knowing* she was interested in fucking the Shepards made her uncomfortable. Though how they'd know it was anything other than a social call is beyond her. And is play-time anything other than a social call, anyway? Angry vagina and all, playtime for the four of them sounds divine to Jenn. The experience has grown rather rare as of late. The last time she remembers all four of them, Ryan and herself and Paige and Bruce, together in the same bed for playtime, well, must have been two months ago now. Two-and-a-half? It hasn't been for lack of desire, rather lack of time. As Paige's work stresses grew, she spent more nights and weekends at the office. After Jenn lost her job, Ryan picked up extra work to push back the eventuality she doesn't want to think about, when the buffer in their emergency fund runs out. All this business has resulted in more twosomes and threesomes lately than foursomes.

She pines in the direction of the phone. Bruce and Paige probably aren't even in their suite by now, she realizes. They've been up early in paradise to greet the day.

"Like me," she says and snorts. Greeting the day in a panic yesterday, after just over an hour of a fitful nightmare filled sleep, and today just under five hours of erotic-dream-filled get-the-juices-flowing sleep. Maybe tonight, and into tomorrow, she could hit six. She wouldn't mind more dreams of Paige and Bruce. Especially dreams like the one that had Bruce sliding into Ryan. Those dreams would be just fine indeed.

Ryan's insistence that Bruce shouldn't be the one he experiments with is valid, of course. But, if he likes his exploration elsewhere, it could open a whole new avenue for their foursomes. She feels a tingle at the thought. Even if Ryan and Bruce never play the same way she and Paige do, she can still run that specific fantasy over and over in her mind. Just think of the masturbation to be had.

Her husband stirs, and for a moment she's certain he can feel her projecting her fantasies onto him. While his head does follow his body to point in her direction, he coughs once and smacks his lips, remaining asleep.

Greeting the day, for the Shepards, typically means the gym, then the beach. She doubts they've had breakfast yet, probably just fruit smoothies. Maybe she can waylay them, and they can all have breakfast together.

She slides from the bed, grabs her phone and the red coil attached to her key (Ryan's is purple), plants her sun-hat on her head, and grabs the door handle. *Sunscreen!* She nods to herself, scoops up her tote bag, and steps out into the day.

The morning is hazy but bright. No lingering after-thought of the storm from last night. The beach is beginning to crowd. The clothed tourists always walk right along the waterline. She grins at the uncomfortable looks on their faces and wonders why they hadn't stopped at the sign.

She skirts close to the line of beds when she sees the one next to the bar, the one she found poor Raymond in front of yesterday, is today occupied by Mia Benjamin. Jenn knows her from her blog, *A Kind of Beautiful Agony* which she stumbled upon while searching for more information on what specifically triggered squirting orgasms after Paige told her it was a mystery to her. Mia had done as extensive research as was possible through surveys with no funding. Her research, though, had been cut short earlier this year, when her ex-husband sued for custody of their son, citing her blog, and the fact that she had very explicitly included herself as one of her research subjects, as creating an unfit environment for children. He won, and Mia Benjamin, now sans a blog, has been embroiled in an appeals battle ever since.

Jenn brings up her hand in a tentative wave that Mia doesn't appear to see. After a moment, the blogger does look up from behind her sunglasses and smiles. She returns the wave. They stare at each other. Jenn feels her cheeks reddening. This isn't just anyone, this is Mia Benjamin. She may not be Time Magazine famous, but people sure know her online! And besides, Jenn knows more about this woman's pussy and masturbation habits than she knows about anyone's! Including Paige!

Mia beckons, and Jenn slides her feet as she walks over.

"Hi," says Mia.

"I read your blog, before—" Jenn wills herself not to be stupid. "I found it because of squirting. I'm a squirter." She feels herself nodding too much. "It's terrible about your ex-husband. What an asshole." *Dial it back, Jenn.* "I mean, anyway, hi."

Mia laughs and repeats, "Hi."

"I know how it feels." Jenn grimaces. How on earth does she know how it feels? How *what* feels, in fact? You don't tell a mother whose child has been taken away that you know how— "What I mean is..." *Yes,* she thinks, *what the fuck do you mean, Jennifer?* "I lost my job," tumbles out.

"I'm sorry to hear that," says Mia. She puts down her pen.

Jenn only just realizes she had been writing. "Sorry."

"Sorry for what?" asks Mia.

"For interrupting you," says Jenn.

"Nonsense. Why did you get fired? I assume you want to tell me, or you wouldn't have brought it up."

It's true, she does want to tell Mia. Mia who writes about the beautiful agony, who helps people with their lives, with their sex. "Morality clause," says Jenn.

"Ah," nods Mia, "the dreaded morality clause."

"Do you ever help people figure out what's next?"

Mia tilts her head to the right and waits.

"Like, what to do?"

"Like a life coach?" Mia asks. "Because I *do* do that."

"Is it expensive?" asks Jenn, feeling a knot grow.

Mia smiles at her. "Tell you what, why don't we sit down and chat, and then you can decide if you think I'd be helpful, and then we can figure out what that would cost."

The worry still lingers, but Jenn nods. "But not now," she says. "You're working."

"Indeed," says Mia. "If you want to do it here, though – *here* being Aphrodite's, I mean – we can."

Jenn nods. "Yeah," she says. "That'd be really great."

"Excellent."

"I'll leave you be," says Jenn, recalling the original reason for her excursion. She squints at the bed down at the other end of the beach, revealing possibly up to two Shepards.

She thanks Mia and heads that way, waving to several couples in beds. Some she knows, like Nancy, the beautiful pinup sitting on a bed, her wheelchair beneath, and Madison (thankfully, Will is nowhere in sight), some she spent a forgettable three minutes with and cannot remember details, many she doesn't know at all. She realizes that even the largest events here wouldn't be able to accommodate all one-hundred-and-eleven couples.

"Eleventy-one couples would be far too many," she says with a snort, then covers her nose and reminds herself that the beds are much too far away for anyone to have heard.

"Well, look, my darling, Neptune has answered our call and sent us a goddess," says Paige when Jenn strolls up.

Bruce, lying on his back, side-eyes Paige. "Not sure that's Neptune's forte, angel."

"Well, I thank whichever god brought you to us," says Paige. "Good morning, beautiful."

Jenn wishes them both a good morning, first with words, then with kisses. "Have you had breakfast yet?"

They shake their heads.

"Want to have breakfast with Ryan and me? I mean, not now, 'cuz he's still sleeping, but when he gets up."

"Sounds great," says Bruce. "We can eat on the patio around eleven. Do the brunch thing."

"Awesome," says Jenn.

Paige reaches out and grabs her hand. "We're okay," she says.

Jenn squints, uncertain. "Sure?"

"I mean, we don't want you to feel obligated," says Paige.

"Wait," says Jenn, still not quite understanding, "what're you talking about?"

"You know, it's your first time here."

"Yeah."

"I'm sure you want to be out meeting other people, having meals with—"

"Oh!" It becomes clear in a rush, why the Shepards have seemed to be staying on the perimeter. Not quite avoiding her and Ryan, but certainly less *around* than she expected on a resort this size. Even a resort that can house one-hundred-and-eleven.

"'Cuz you can fuck us at home," says Paige.

"I mean," begins Jenn, marveling at the idea that Paige is trying not to pressure them, "I appreciate it, that you're thinking of us."

Paige laughs. "You're being diplomatic."

"But, seriously!" exclaims Jenn. She hurls herself onto the bed between them. "Let me be clear," she says, "Ryan and I would very much like some quality time for the four of us today." She waits a moment, and then self-consciously adds, "If you'd be into that."

"After all this time," asks Bruce, "do you really think we wouldn't be?"

Jenn smirks and cocks her head to the side. "After all this time, do you really think *we* wouldn't be?"

"Fair," says Paige.

"I less-than-three you both," says Jenn.

# 35

## PAIGE

The scream causes everyone at the table to turn toward the waterline. Paige stands, feeling the pumping adrenaline, those years as a lifeguard at Birchwood Pool flooding back. She sees the pixie with red hair pulling a man up onto the sand. "The podcasters," she tells the rest of the table.

A party captain in a white polo rushes to the couple on the beach.

"Fuh-fucking jellyfish!" screams the man on his back in the sand.

"Strom," says Paige. *Good,* she thinks. Jellyfish stings, while painful, aren't dangerous, and that guy is kind of obnoxious.

"I got stung by a jellyfish our, what was it, angel? Second year here?" Bruce doesn't look up from the plate he's turned back to.

Paige nods absently, continuing to watch. A small crowd has gathered around the podcasters. The man in the polo rushes back behind the grill, into the resort's backstage area.

"Oh, good," she says, seeing Will jogging across the sand in his best Hasselhoff impression. Twenty yards from the small cluster, he yanks down on the waistband of his board shorts. In a fluid motion that Paige begrudgingly finds impressive, he leaps from the shorts as they slide down his legs.

"Hurts, though?" asks Ryan.

"Oh my God!" screams Strom in the sand.

Bruce nods. "Hurts like fuck. They keep a whole jellyfish kit on hand to treat it. Ammonia. Something to dull the pain. It's nothing compared to their strep throat kit, though." He laughs. "That even includes—"

Will wraps his hand around his bouncing flaccid penis as he makes it to the group. "Let me through!" he shouts, with the practiced confidence of someone used to getting what he wants.

"Oh, no," Paige says and laughs despite herself. Her companions stand to watch.

"Is he...?"

The small cluster of people part for the man aiming his penis in their direction.

"Wait, no!" screams Strom.

"*¡Señor!*" yells the staff member in the polo shirt, already jogging back, a cleaning caddy with a big bottle of ammonia in his hand.

Jenn claps her hands to her mouth.

From their vantage point, just yards away at the edge of the lunch grill patio, they watch it happen in slow motion. Urine spills forth from Will, first wildly because he is still running. The droplets glint in the sunlight, and the cluster of people around the podcasters spread *way* out.

"He's getting something!" screams Strom, raising his hands to his face, another scream of pain combined with one of horror.

The impressive fountain arcing from Will causes much of the patio to go silent.

"Jesus," shouts Kitten, shoving herself back from her boyfriend, naked and in pain on the sand.

The stream hits Strom squarely in the chest, splashing everywhere. He shields his face and yells, "It's my leg, you fuckhead!"

"You know, urine is not actually all that helpful against jellyfish stings," Bruce says. Everyone continues to stare, mesmerized.

Paige nods. "Ammonia concentration is too low."

Will has finally come to a halt, and he redirects his cock downward to Strom's legs. The stream holds for what seems like an eternity.

"You pissed in my mouth!" yells Strom, hacking and coughing in the face of this unsolicited golden shower.

"*¡No, señor!*" The staff member puts his hand on Will's chest and shows him the kit.

"I've got this," says Will.

"No, asshole, let him do it!" yells Strom. "Fuck, fuck it hurts." He takes a deep breath and unleashes his fury at Will. "You're not helping!"

Will's pee finally ebbs until it is just dribbles in the sand. The crowd has grown, but keeps their distance. Those at the epicenter stare at each other. "I just..." says Will, looking between Strom, Kitten, the party captain with the jellyfish sting kit, Strom, Kitten, Strom's face, Strom's leg.

He slinks away.

The party captain kneels beside Strom, taking a towel from his shoulder to dry off the urine. The crowd begins to disperse as excitement subsides, and Paige sits back down at their lunch table. "Well," she says to Bruce and the Lamberts, "where were we?"

"Dessert," says Ryan. "Then sex, I think."

Paige agrees, and dessert is ordered.

Later in their suite, she unbuttons Ryan's shirt and slides it off his shoulders. She alternates kissing and nibbling, beginning at his neck before moving to his shoulder, down his bicep, and back up, catching the scent of him as she passes from his armpit to his chest. She takes his nipple into her mouth and feels his cock grow hard against her knee. She makes a mental note of this additional information and moves along to his other nipple.

On the other side of the bed, she sees Jenn lying face down as Bruce rubs coconut oil into his amazing hands. He starts in small circles on her shoulders and back, spiraling out.

Paige is pulled back to Ryan when his hand slides up the nape of her neck into her hair. She feels the firm tug as his hand makes purchase. She leans her head back and exhales warm breath over his left nipple. She looks up at him, he looks down at her.

"What would you like?" he asks her, putting his hand on her cheek.

She nuzzles against the hand for a moment and tells him, "I want you inside me." She encircles his growing erection with her hand, noting the softness of the skin on his shaft, the dramatic texture and color shift at the coronal ridge. She presses against his urethra with her thumb, and he shivers.

"That sounds great," he says.

Without looking, Paige reaches into the pile of condoms haphazardly strewn across the step that surrounds the king-sized bed. She tears open the package with her mouth, holding eye contact with him, this lovely boy who'd once been so scared of her. That wasn't fair, though. He'd been afraid of life, and that night in the laundry room at Barbara Watkins's Christmas party, Paige Shepard had represented a life he wasn't living.

She pops the condom between her lips and teeth with a wink and drops her head down. She pinches the tip with her tongue and slides it onto his cock, feeling him moving deeper and deeper into her mouth. A little further and a quick gag produces the very best saliva. When she removes her mouth, he's dripping and clad in what she's amused to note is an opaque black condom.

"Huh," says Ryan.

"You like?" she asks.

"What you did? Yes," he tells her, eyes focused on his erection. He bounces it twice for good measure. "It looks like a dildo."

"It does." She laughs. "A big black dildo." On his face, she sees that the word big has had its intended effect, so she leans back and spreads her legs in his direction. "Come get me."

As Ryan kneels between her legs, Paige turns to look at Jenn. Bruce has moved down to massage the small of her back and her ass, and she glistens from the coconut oil. Paige leans over and plants a kiss on Jenn's ass cheek. A giggle from her girlfriend lets her know the gesture was appreciated.

She hears a squirt of lube, then feels Ryan's cock pressing against her. He rubs his head over her clit, sending tingles up and down her spine. She turns her head back to meet the intensity of his gaze. He slides the full length of his cock up and down. Her lips spread as he slides, and she feels the first wave beginning to draw up within her. Without a word, he repositions himself. Her lips part and she takes him effortlessly. She feels him moving within her as he leans over her to kiss between her breasts. She grabs the back of his head and pulls him to her nipples, which he greedily sucks.

She nibbles her lip as a wave of pleasure shudders through her, then grips him on the inside.

"Whoa," he says, his eyes wide.

She grins up at him and nods.

His thrusting slows, and she feels every bit of him slide through her internal grip. She releases the hold and her breath.

"That's new," he says.

"Something I've been working on," she says, grabbing him again.

"I'm not. Going to last. Long," he pants. "If you. Keep doing. That."

She shakes her head at him. "Come whenever you feel it, love." She squeezes as hard as she can and feels the orgasm pulse down the length of his shaft, exploding into the condom. She wraps her arms around him as he collapses atop her, his chest heaving.

She whispers in his ear, "Thank you, baby."

"Thank. You." Haltingly, he moves back to his kneeling position and reaches down to pull himself out. "I think you're trying to keep the condom," he whispers to her.

"Oh," laughs Paige. She lets go, feeling the condom pop out of her, and the release sends a profoundly unique and pleasurable shudder throughout her body.

Ryan slides to her right, drops the condom in the trash, and lies on his side next to her. Paige puts her hands on her stomach to feel the pulsing spasms. "Well," she says, "that was something."

Ryan concurs, still wide-eyed.

She kisses him, then turns opposite to look down Jenn's body, toward her head. Bruce is kneeling on either side of her thighs, inside her, as he continues massaging her back. Her moans of pleasure alternate two distinctively different pitches. Listening to her is lovely.

Paige kisses the instep of her foot as she comes.

# 36

# RAYMOND

Raymond Horne lies on his back atop a round ten-foot-diameter cushioned bench in the center of the Aphrodite's Resort and Spa playroom. With his left hand, he strokes the long shaft of a man named Vince whom he just met this morning. His right hand is outstretched, fingers inside a tall, slender woman named Alexis. He's talked to her and her husband once or twice, but never extensively. Squatting above his face is the female portion of the triad, Marley. Her pierced labia rubs against his nose through a sheet of plastic wrap, there for "safer sex." He's only sucked it into his mouth twice and is making a conscious effort to breathe through his nose and keep the queening going. Down his body, a wonderfully curvy woman named Nancy is riding his cock, bouncing her ass in his direction as she rides. Thankfully she is doing all the work, since his thoughts are elsewhere.

He's nearly immune to the experience, could disassociate entirely should he choose – leave his body and observe, or more likely go elsewhere, go home, go to that spot of sun in the bedroom where he lay with his partner not so very long ago. His partner, his friend and lover. When he still had those things. Not so very long ago.

His prostate tingles, experiencing a flesh and blood cock for the first time in ages after a parade of dildos. Mädchen's cock is thin and long, ideal for anal stimulation, and the woman it's attached to is fantastic. He hadn't known she was trans until she asked to fuck him.

"I don't always stay fully rigid, but I'm cycling my T-blocker this week, and I've taken one of those friendly blue guys," she told him. "You game?"

"I'm game," he said.

As enthusiastic as his consent had been, as involved and invested as he had been when this conglomeration of sexy descended upon him, he finds himself unable to remain in the moment. It could be the many banana daiquiris he's had since lunch. It could be the pot, provided by Sergey and Polina, that he smoked. But Raymond knows the truth: He's a pathetic man, because only a pathetic man would spend his time at the center of an orgy feeling sorry for himself. Sorry because nothing can be good since Colleen left.

*Jesus*, he thinks, *I don't fucking deserve these amazing sexy people.* He contemplates tapping out, but Vince has begun to fuck his hand, Marley rides harder, periodically cutting off air to his nose in that oh-so-wonderfully dominant way, he's found Alexis's G-spot, and it's growing ever more engorged, Nancy may be coming now, and Mädchen continues to prod his prostate. *Boom boom boom!* The shakes! Oh, those prostate shakes. Deserving or not, he's in far too deep to pull the ripcord and bail. Not now. Not yet.

When Mia offered to oversee the orgy, that would've been the time to change things.

"No," he said instead, insistent. "I need to do it."

"If you're only doing it because you think you need to, then you definitely shouldn't."

He narrowed his eyes at her psychobabble.

She grinned and shrugged. "I'm giving you an out."

He considered Mia's offer for a while, even going as far as seeking her out on their beach bed. That would've been the way to handle this, right? Accept her help, and take some down time to figure things out, at least a little. At least before his hands were full of genitals and there was a cock in his ass. Before someone sat on his face, on his cock. That would've been the time, then. Instead, upon seeing her expectant face, he just told her he had this and gave her a wink. *He had this*, planning to wander into the orgy Rodney Dangerfield-style. "Hey everybody, we're all gonna get laid!" Journey blasting from the speakers.

"Your brio doesn't play with me," she told him and returned to her tablet.

"You think it's a bad idea?"

"I'm not the boss of you, Raymond."

"But..." he said, deflating. After staring down the beach, squinting in the sunlight for what seemed like an hour, she lowered the tablet and turned her large sunglasses in his direction.

"Is there more?" she asked. "Are you waiting for my approval?"

Was that it? "No," he said.

"If you want my opinion as a friend, I think you've got things to let go of. Big ones. If you want my opinion as an educator, you may not be well equipped right now to lead the bacchanal you want to provide for these people. If you want my opinion as a guest of this trip, people seem to be doing alright finding their sexy all by themselves."

He opened his mouth to respond, but she continued.

"And if you want my opinion as an outsider who hears things, you're different, discordant. They don't know exactly why, may not even feel it consciously, but subconsciously, people know something's up, something's wrong. It's not just those two podcasters talking about it."

Raymond grumbled. Those two podcasters had released another episode this morning, complaining about the organization of the foam party, wrongfully placing the blame at his feet, when that was one of the events he hadn't planned this week, and again lamenting "the fall of the once-great Raymond Horne." But, if it wasn't just those two podcasters, "Who else?"

"You're focusing on the wrong thing," she told him. "Doesn't matter. When people are talking, it's usually because there's something worth saying."

He scowled. "I have an orgy to throw."

"Godspeed."

On the round bench in the playroom atop the building, Mädchen's nails dig into his ass cheeks. She expels three explosive breaths as she comes.

He hears Nancy's partner say, "That was incredible to watch," and a few people nearby agree.

There's some shuffling movement on the bench. Marley slows her grind to a halt. Mädchen pulls back and reveals a vacancy within him. He feels hot breath near his ear, a pant in her voice, "Thank you for that, you sexy man. I've been fantasizing about it ever since I saw your ass on Saturday."

He tries to thank her, but it comes out garbled, most of the sound disappearing into the plastic-wrapped vulva above his mouth. To better facilitate, Marley rises off him about an inch. "Thank you," he tells Mädchen.

"I'll leave you all be, my husband craves... mmm...something."

*Another satisfied patron of Xanadu,* he thinks. His laugh is stifled by Marley's vulva. His prostate pulses with orgasm, the tell-tale shakes, but overall rather muted. He's confident that, had he not popped his own little blue pill earlier, Nancy wouldn't have anything to be riding. Thankfully, his hands are not dependent on his ability to focus.

Would these beautiful sexy people feel bad if they knew he was just barely here? His physical form, sure – that's what they're all using and enjoying – but emotionally checked out. *Video 29: Conscious engagement.* That's the one that talks about doing things because you want them, being present. That's the one he can almost hear playing in his head. The one he should heed. Whether they can tell or not doesn't matter, does it? It's still unfair.

*How?* he argues with himself. Mädchen got what she wanted. Vince is about to get what he wants, if the erratic nature of his thrusting is anything to go by. Marley hasn't come yet, but her grinding ebbs and flows, and at the very least she's getting to top.

"I'm a Domme," she told him, "and I want to queen you. I like to be able to control the breathing of powerful men."

He nodded.

"I'm not particularly sexually attracted to you," she told him, in such a refreshingly matter-of-fact fashion that he smiled. "Don't usually get a smile saying things like that."

He shrugged.

"I'm very direct."

"I'm a fan of radical honesty," he confessed.

"Well, try this on. I want to lie you on your back, and I'll squat over your face. I'm not going to squat all the way down because you're going to lift your face to me. You'll lift your head and lick my pussy for as long as I'd like. And if I tell you to, you'll hold your face there until you can't breathe."

Raymond thought this sounded like a fine idea.

"Gyuhh!" shouts Vince as a shot of fluid hits Raymond's arm and chest.

"Oh, yeah," says Nancy, and the vigor with which she rides intensifies.

He feels a hand dig into his hair and yank. "You're not going to come, do you understand."

He leans his head back, to give himself a moment, and agrees. "Of course not, Mistress."

She doesn't know that he'll be unlikely to come whether she allows it or not, and he hopes she doesn't decide to bestow the ability on him at the end of this encounter. He won't. Hasn't all week. Hasn't all month, in fact. Just one more thing he can't quite figure out how to do anymore.

Nancy slows to a stop, exulting, "Fantastic," before accepting her husband's offer of help off. Raymond's cock flops from the warmth of her body into the chill of the room. A moment later, he feels a warm mouth surround his cock and assumes it's still her.

He hears the voice of Alexis's husband, low and sensual. "I'd love to bring you over here for a spell, my darling."

"Oh, yes," comes the reply, and his hand feels chilly all at once, exposed to the air, soaking. A mouth slides along each finger. "To be continued," she says, a question mark implied.

He changes his two-finger salute to a thumbs-up.

A painful groove has been worn on his lower lip by Marley's twin labia piercings. That's alright, though, it's good to feel that, to feel the submissiveness, to not be in charge. He's aware at some point that his cock is no longer being sucked, and he assumes that the reason is that it has gone flaccid. He knows from experience that, firm understanding of penises or not, it still feels sorta shitty when one goes soft on you.

Marley lifts herself off, and he sees her standing above him on the bench through hazy plastic wrap smeared with fluids. She reaches down and plucks the barrier off his face. "You did good," she tells him without real praise in her voice. "You can do that again before the end of the trip."

He nods and thanks his Mistress.

Marley steps over his head and with a thump leaves the bench.

The sounds of pleasure come from everywhere. If he took a moment to allow all this to wash over him, to appreciate not only what has just happened, but that he's conjured this tribute to Bacchus out of nothing, then maybe he'd be able to take some stock, see some value. After all, Xanadu might not be firing on all cylinders, but it's bringing people together. Maybe he'd be able to convince himself that he is alright. He's a lesser human without Colleen in his life, but she hasn't always been with him, and he'd done okay, once upon a time.

One thing Raymond knows with absolute certainty is that he feels nothing as he lies here. He's gone from the center of a sixsome to the wet aftermath so quickly. Perhaps the anhedonia diagnosis, despite not having come from someone qualified to diagnose such things, should be considered. Maybe the asshole judging other people's qualifications to make diagnoses should take a hard look at himself, acknowledge his deep depression, and understand how he works within those parameters.

Maybe Xanadu Ten should be the last one.

*If someone said this to you, how would you advise them?* he asks himself. When things are darkest, he's always recognized that he is the absolute worst at doing what he ought to.

"I'd say," he whispers, "I'd say don't make any major life decisions while in the valley of depression."

No one hears his voice amid the cacophony of sexual exuberance around him.

Raymond Horne lies on his back atop a round ten-foot-diameter cushioned bench in the center of the Aphrodite's Resort and Spa playroom.

He is alone.

# 37

# RYAN

Observing from the side of the orgy, Ryan wonders if he has a place within. He sits with a rum punch in his hand, his second since the bacchanal began, finally feeling that slightly sloshy feeling. He hasn't been up to the play-room before on this trip, and he's not sure why. Whenever he's passed below the red-curtained windows atop the lobby, he's gotten the strangest "keep out" vibe, that it wasn't for him, he wasn't invited. But now here he sits, in his shiny crimson boxer briefs that are his wife's favorite. He feels oddly exposed, para-doxical after being nude in the sun. He is, however, rather fond of the pronounced bulge in the front. Now, if only someone else would notice and become rather fond of it.

When they arrived at the top of the stairs and stepped under the curtains into this den of iniquity, this room of hedonism, he immediately scanned the sea of bodies looking for Lydia. He saw all of them and none of them, saw them enough to see what they all lacked. There were tattoos here and there, swallows diving, roses on lower backs, tribal swoops on arms. Nothing as elabo-rate as the artistry that covers Lydia in almost haphazard fashion.

He stayed on the outskirts as Jenn moved magnetically toward the sea of people, already pulling her dress over her head with her free left hand. The dress slid down her right arm and stopped where their hands met, holding. Here, his wife could be in her element, could forget about her troubles amid the distraction of hedonism. That would have been unfathomable only two years ago, but here, now, it makes a kind of obvious sense. His wife, after all, had taken to openness like a fish to water, or rather like a woman who realizes in all sorts of surprising flashbacks at the end of the film that she'd been a fish all along. Or something like that.

She turned back toward him, still holding his hand. Their arms were outstretched to the limit. She cocked her head at him, eyes wide, then grinned. The "is everything okay?" grin. The "can I play?" grin. And of course, he wanted her to go and frolic and find playtime. If he would take a deep breath and follow her into the writhing collection of bodies positioned every which way on the furniture, on cushions, over to the side in a sex swing, he'd find fun too, wouldn't he? The two of them hunted well together, after all.

As their swinging lifestyle had evolved beyond couples dating, they'd explored the many different varieties: playing together at parties, playing separately, dating separately, going on the kind of dates that Paige and Bruce had taken them on, once upon a time, the "we're into you, are you into us?" dates, the "want to come back to our place and get into some trouble?" dates. Time didn't allow them to date together as often as they would have liked. But when does time ever truly allow for anyone's desires in full? Instead it keeps us humble, parceling out moments, making them precious.

If he would go into the flesh with her, they'd find the fun, either with others or just the two of them. Some of their best sex, some of Ryan's favorite, has come after he's seen the full extent of her exhibitionism. When she notices a glance, or people just watching, and her little orgasmic calls become bellows, her gentle glides become bigger, and when she lets go, and the waves break, she never holds back. Not in a crowd. Like a show with that comedian that smashes watermelons, hope you brought your ponchos, 'cuz the first few rows *will* get wet.

He could tell that exhibitionism was what she was after tonight, as she waggled her eyebrows at him, flung her head off to the side to ask, "Comin'?" Subtle she was not, and he loved her for that. "Or are you looking for Lydia?" she asked, her pink tongue appearing briefly, gently mocking, between her teeth. "Lydia, the taaatoooed lady!"

Ryan hushed her and pulled her close. No one had heard, and Lydia was nowhere in sight. His heart pounded all the same.

Jenn wrapped her arms around him. "You're wearing too many clothes," she said.

"Am I?" he asked.

She nodded and unbuttoned his shirt, sliding it off his shoulders.

"Better?"

"Almost," she said, unzipping his fly and unbuckling his belt. His pants dropped, and she claimed them as well, flinging his clothing over her naked shoulder.

Then he stood in just his underwear. "You look good," she said, elongating the O's.

He smiled back. "Thank you."

"Do you want me to stay with you?"

He shook his head.

"Want me to rustle up some hotties?"

He smiled and kissed her. "Go have fun."

She held both his hands in hers as she moved away from him, not breaking eye contact, not breaking touch until she'd be unable to move further away. She threw him a wink, then turned toward the party and lifted her arms as though this was her church. He imagined an orgasmic hallelujah spilling from her.

He doesn't regret sending her off, sitting on the margins. After all, is he truly alone when surrounded by friends? Or those who could become friends?

Ryan watches the centerpiece of the orgy, a cluster of five people all engaging with one. He thinks the man on the bottom is Raymond, but he can only really guess at that based on the pale blond hair beneath Marley's distracting rear end, sliding back and forth over his face. He's happy that Vince is engaging, though finds it curious that a man he's been told is quite hetero is getting a hand job from the prone party host. Seems less-than-hetero? He feels a flash of discomfort at the thought. The judgment comes so easily, doesn't it? He should work on that, especially since he wants to explore without judgment. Why should he be anything but thrilled by the fact that both Vince and Kendra are occupied here? Kendra's with a muscular man on a red cushioned bench off to the side. Her attention elsewhere is reassuring, it means that he won't be corralled by her and asked to do the thing, to make the swap. The anxiety accompanying that thought suggests that he needs to reconcile himself to the fact that is becoming more and more apparent, that his and Jenn's sexual relationship with the de Martoloses has run its course. Nobody's fault, after all. Just one of those things.

He sees Jenn sipping a drink and flirting with a short woman with bouncy black curls. He smiles, recognizing the way his wife moves her head and body when trying to attract. The way she flirts. The subtle head tilt to show she's truly listening, that little crease between her eyebrows. Her hair is almost too short for her to twirl around her finger now. Almost.

He strolls through the playroom, surveying the writhing bodies like Caligula. Momentarily he stops, fascinated by a tableau: Terrence sitting on a cushion, Rory in his lap, sliding up and down as Terrence runs his hands around his lover's chest. Rory slides his flaccid penis in and out of his right hand as he moves rhythmically, the motion almost mesmerizing. Ryan hasn't seen much sex between men, and only porn, never in person. Rory opens his eyes as he rides, meeting Ryan's. They hold his for a moment, and Rory grins and winks, tilting his head in a way that could be interpreted as inviting Ryan over. He might just be adjusting, though. If he wanted to invite Ryan over, he'd probably use a finger, or hell, his voice. Ryan's heart thumps, and he decides that the lack of explicit request means it wasn't Rory's intention to include him in his time with his boyfriend. And even if it had been his intention, Ryan isn't sure how he feels about that. Not yet, anyway. That will take more time, more contemplation, a mostly sober head.

He sees Raymond, alone now on the round cushioned bench, the last of his playmates having wandered elsewhere. Raymond's face drifts, beginning contented and satisfied, then losing the gleam, the sparkle leaving his eyes, the smile leaving his lips.

Ryan sees emptiness flood in.

He wonders if he should say something. Go to him and put his hands on his shoulders, tell him things are okay. No, that would be an assumption, an invasion. They don't know each other, after all, not more than a little. Would he appreciate, "Are you okay?" Not everybody would.

"Hey there," says Lydia, sliding up beside Ryan.

He looks at her for the first time since their kiss two days ago. The one person, besides his wife, he's wanted to see most.

The person to whom he finds his thoughts drifting. "Hey," he says.

"Any interest in going somewhere quieter? Orgy isn't my scene."

"Oh? You came up here—"

"Looking for you," she says.

It's the thing he wanted her to say, his hoped-for reason. He feels the flush of vacation crush, the momentary thrill and excitement of a headlong dive into a relationship destined to evaporate once the confines of the trip have been quit. But that's a future concern.

"Let me tell Jenn," he says, "my wife."

"Please do," she replies.

As he walks toward Jenn and the bouncy haired woman, he notices that Raymond has left the center stage and breathes a sigh of relief for the man who looked so sorrowful.

# 38

# BRUCE

"Comin' up to the orgy?"

Bruce looks up from his crossword puzzle.

Debra leans against the courtyard bar, nude except for her sun-hat. She brings her drink to her lips, pink and orange with a small green umbrella stuck on the side. She flicks her eyes toward the umbrella. "Oh, I bring them from home. I enjoy their festivity. Want one?"

"Not sure it'd go with my coffee," says Bruce.

"It's at least Irish, I hope."

Bruce holds his thumb and forefinger up to indicate a smidge.

"Good."

He puts down his pen and smiles at Debra, giving her body the imperceptible glance he's worked years to perfect. He hopes he looks as good as her when he reaches her age. Hopes he'll still be coming to places like this. He wonders if he ought to tell her that; would she appreciate it? "I'm taking an afternoon break," he says instead. "Pacing myself."

"That's a good idea. Orgy started a while ago, anyway."

"You heading up?" he asks.

"Might peak in, but nobody wants the old farts at the orgy."

Bruce opens his mouth to disagree.

"'You're not old,'" she says for him, deepening her voice to an approximation of his tenor.

He smiles. "I was going to say..."

"You were going to say that's not true," she says and sits on the stool next to him.

"Right," he says.

"It's exaggerated, what I said. But you know as well as I do that this lifestyle gets younger every year, and those on the one end aren't so keen on playing with those on the other."

He blinks at her. There's a rumbling inside him. Gruff and blustery denial. He is, after all, only forty-eight.

"Now, now," she tells him, putting her hand on his, "I wasn't lumping you in with the seniors."

Still surprised by the amount of concern he'd felt, he again opens his mouth and says nothing.

"We've had some wonderful experiences in this place. A couple this week, in fact," she tells him. "But I've got eyes, I can see. I don't let it bother me, either. I get fucked plenty, both by James and by other suitors." She leans closer to him. "Even a couple ladies."

He takes her hand and kisses it. "You have a zest," he tells her, then wonders if that too is offensive, if it implies that he's surprised by it because of her age.

"Well, thank you, Magnum." Debra winks at him and stands again. "Bet you're wondering, now, 'Is she calling me 'Magnum' because of the PI or because of my dick.'"

He laughs.

"Maybe a little of both, though I haven't spent enough time with the latter to judge adequately." She toasts him with her drink.

He smiles at her, contemplating whether she is indeed hitting on him, or if this is just her playful style. And if she is hitting on him, what is his interest? He's uncertain. The Koonzes have been the "elder statesmen" of their trip for the last several years. It's an unfair place to slot them, though.

"*Señor* Bruce," calls Luis as he emerges from between the sliding glass doors, holding his dark hand up in a wave.

"*Hola,* Luis," says Bruce

"You have an emergency call," says Luis, "I tried your room, but no answer."

"Oh my," says Debra.

"Fuck," says Bruce, jumping to his feet. He turns to Debra. "The boys. My kids."

"Go, go!" She shakes her head and waves her hand. "I hope everything's alright!"

"Yes," he says to Luis. This is why he always keeps his phone on. The resort number, the "vanilla" number that rang the ambiguous "Aquamarine Travel Group and Spa," that was for absolute emergencies, but his phone, that would have been the boys' first call. He runs things through in his head. It's Tuesday, so Hunter would probably just be getting home from school. Adam would also be finishing his classes on Loyola campus. School or not, emergencies happen. He rushes to the sliding glass doors and stops when the air conditioning hits him.

"Can I..." He gestures toward his naked body. The lobby is one of the few places on the resort where nudity is not allowed.

Luis looks down at him, then over his shoulder into the lobby where Marisol and another staff member sit at the desk, then shrugs. "Is okay, emergency."

The repetition of "emergency" crawls right up on top of him. Could've been a car accident on Hunter's way home from school. Or maybe Adam didn't get back to Loyola after all. Bruce tries to remember if his son's first classes of the week are on Monday or Tuesday. He thinks Tuesday, because Adam had been so proud of his ability to condense his college schedule into just a few days.

This isn't helping. Bruce takes a deep breath as he walks past the two couches which usually contain sad folks who've already checked out, waiting for their shuttles to arrive. Marisol looks up with concern as he follows Luis into the business center. She's worried too. It'd have to be bad, if Luis had shared it with the rest of the staff.

Luis lifts the receiver and passes it to Bruce in what seems like slow motion.

He takes a deep breath. Luis gives him a nod. Paige should be here too, if it's an emergency, she should be here, in case it's bad. "Did you go to look for—"

"*Señora* Shepard, *sí*."

"Thank you, Luis."

"*De nada*," says Luis, leaving him alone in a small nook with one computer and one printer, aspirationally called the Business Center.

Bruce looks at the blinking light over the number two. *Dos,* he thinks. He presses it. "What's wrong?" he asks, knowing that he should be Dad with a capital D here, the strong dad, calm and collected, because whoever is calling with an emergency, they'll be the panicked one.

Crying.

He takes another long, slow breath. "What can I do?"

"He kicked me out."

Bruce momentarily tries to connect the dots. To figure out whether his younger son has kicked the older out, but that didn't make any—

Emily.

The situation snaps into focus quickly, his stomach lurching along with it. A wave of relief that his children aren't the ones having an emergency, followed by a wave of anger that Emily has again violated the promise.

The third wave of emotion hits him hardest, as the sound of her crying pulls him all the way back, years back. Over a decade. Christ. They sat on opposite sides in the den. Bruce in the armchair, Paige in the love seat, a box of tissues by her side, nose red, eyes wet, glimmering in the firelight. He regretted starting the fire. It felt so inappropriate. Emily sat in the center of their couch, barely taking up an entire cushion, looking so tiny and alone. Her raven hair hung in a pair of pigtail braids down her back. She looked between him and Paige, crying.

"This is really hard," she said, making it about herself.

Bruce scowled at her.

"I don't think either of you appreciates—"

"How can you—?" Paige had begun but cut herself off, folding her arms, looking away.

Emily waited for her to say more, then turned to him.

"Let's not pretend that your engagement to—" Bruce paused, feeling his voice getting rougher. *Be the bigger man here, Brucie. Be the grown-up.* "To a man you just met. Let's not pretend—" He stopped. "Forget it."

"Forget what?" Emily asked, fear in her eyes. "Look, we can still spend time to—"

"I don't want *just* friendship." Paige's words were no more than a whisper, but they carried a whip crack. Both Bruce and Emily waited.

"I wish you were happy for me."

"I wish you didn't play the 'suddenly, monogamy' card and let us find out about your engagement from your sister," Paige snapped back.

Emily looked down.

"Let's," begins Bruce, to the Emily on the phone, over ten years removed from Emily on the couch, "let's start with telling me if you are physically in pain. Have you hurt yourself?"

"No." The voice is a ghostly whisper between sobs.

"So, this is not an actual emergency."

"I don't have anywhere to go! He shut off the accounts. Put fraud alerts on the credit cards."

Bruce frowns. "Well, he can't just do that," he tells her. "Not if they're joint accounts." He puts his hand against the wall, on a flier full of numbers for local shuttle and taxi companies. He presses his forehead against it too, dropping the phone to his side.

He hears the sniffle, the cough, the sob, "Bruce?" quietly from the receiver. He should tell her that he's sorry he can't help her. He doesn't need to be sorry, true, but it's the courteous thing to say, the right thing to do. Be sorry, be sympathetic, get off the phone and get out of here before Paige— Before Paige what? Gets here? Bruce looks around the small room furtively, as though his wife might pop up from anywhere, give him her disappointed look, and ask, "You want to help her, don't you?"

Does he? Yes, but *why* does he want to help her?

"Bruce!" the small voice on the phone demands.

"Did you call your bank?"

"Yes, he told them I was behaving erratically and he would send over a note from my doctor."

Bruce squinted. "I assume there is no doc—"

"Of course not!" she screams into the phone.

"Emily," says Bruce, affecting his most calming voice, "I need you to recognize that the person who called the resort I'm staying at in Mexico and said it was an emergency, when it is not, *may* be behaving erratically and there may be doctor willing to say so."

She says nothing for a while, then, begrudgingly, "Okay."

"Go stay at a hotel and resolve this in the morning," he tells her.

"I don't have money! Do *you* carry cash?"

"I do."

"Well, most people don't these days."

He concedes that silently to himself. Her husband can't lock her out of their accounts for long, but he can do it for long enough to be difficult. Especially if he's reported their credit cards missing or stolen. Even if she has the right to use them, she could still be shit out of luck. He sighs, knowing where this is heading, trying to steer around it. "Do you have any friends you can—"

"No, Bruce, I don't have any friends here." Her voice seems pointed and hurt at once, and shoves him back down the timeline into the kitchen of their first house.

"I don't make friends quickly," said Emily, holding Paige's hand. "I only ever have two or three in my life. But you two walked right into that spot. You became what I needed. And I didn't even know I needed it."

"Bruce?" she asks, and he's back in the Business Center.

He signs, resigning himself to the inevitable. "Do you have a pen?"

"Yeah."

He gives her his Visa card number, expiration, and confirmation code. "Book on your phone, and put my name on the room, too."

"Thank you! I don't know what I'd do without—"

"Yeah, Emily," he says, "yeah." He hangs up the phone and rubs the spot between his eyes that has begun throbbing. He takes a minute. Emily wouldn't con them, would she? Of course not. She's many things, but inconsiderate is probably the worst of them. He wonders if it'd be best to not mention this, not right now, not in Mexico. To let things lie. Maybe Paige doesn't need—

"What was Emily's emergency?" asks Paige from behind him. "And why did you give her our credit card?"

Bruce opens his mouth and finds that there is nothing to say.

"*Señorita,*" says Celia, rousing Paige on the beach bed from a dream that vanishes quickly. "There's emergency phone call!"

Adam. Hunter. Something. She leaps from the bed. *Focus, Paige.* Emergencies need focus. "Where?"

"Lobby," says Celia. "Hope everything's okay!"

Paige rushes, to the steps, to the path, to the courtyard, to the lobby, trying not to run scenarios in her mind. An emergency could be anything. And maybe the Aphrodite's staff is exaggerating. They might treat every call to the vanilla line this way.

Luis is solemn in the lobby and points her toward a door off to the side. She rushes through, just in time to find Bruce, naked, reciting their Visa card number into the phone. Maybe a car broke down, maybe a wallet was stolen. She catches her breath in the doorway, waiting for him to finish.

"Book on your phone, and put my name on the room, too." A pause, then, "Yeah, Emily, yeah."

Paige feels the floor drop. She sways in the doorway.

Emily.

Bruce hangs up the phone and stands there, head downcast, fingers touching the receiver.

She wants to rage at him. To yell. To get on that phone and *69 and ask Emily who the hell she thinks she is. To demand that she stop trying oh-so-very-hard to ruin this trip. Emily and Bruce, the both of them. In conjunction. In cahoots. She takes a deep breath instead. "What was Emily's emergency?" The levelness of her voice surprises her. Tense, sure, but level. Reasonable. "And why did you give her our credit card?"

Bruce doesn't respond, doesn't even turn to look at her. He just stands with his fingers on the phone, looking down.

She waits.

Waits.

Then leaves.

Paige feels his fingers whisper past her arm as she strides across the courtyard toward the beach. She pulls away and ups her speed.

"Paige," he says.

She doesn't turn to look at him. "I am not going to discuss this with you here." She pauses a moment, then resumes her walk. Between two buildings, down onto the beach next to the bar. She walks past Celia's pleasant, "*Hola*," probably intended for some miscellaneous guest who hadn't just come from an emergency call in the lobby. Who didn't just have an invasion from Emily. To Paige, Celia asks, "*¿Señorita, cómo estás?*"

Paige flashes the briefest of smiles and says, "*Así, así*," without breaking her stride.

She hears Celia say, "*Hola, Señor Bruce.*"

She storms past bed after bed, relatively empty just then. *Well, they're all at the orgy,* she thinks. *The orgy we could be at, with our friends. Fucking. If you'd just let cunting Emily Laurel go!* Her heart races. A furious glance over her shoulder reveals that Bruce has dropped back about twenty feet behind her. He keeps pace but gives her the gap. She reaches their building and stomps up the stairs to the second-floor entryway, slaps her card into the lock and throws the door open. She steps onto the cold tile floor. The door bangs into the wall then closes on its own. She stands in the dark air-conditioned silence and breaths. In, out. In, out. *What are we really mad about, here?* she asks herself, knowing she has just moments to figure it out. In moments, he'll open the door, and they'll have to talk about it all. In moments, she'll have to decide whether she is mad at Emily or him. "Both," she says to the empty room. She walks over to the bed, sits on the corner facing away from the door, and waits.

The lock beeps, then Bruce stands in the open doorway. He remains there motionless for what feels like hours, saying nothing. When he finally closes the door, he walks across the room. She feels the bed move as he sits on the opposite side. In the silence, they don't look at each other. Paige sees from a glance that he's looking down at his lap, the way he does when he's ashamed. How long will the silence continue? She doesn't know, but she'll be damned if she's going to break it. The air conditioner seems as loud as a jet engine.

"I'm sorry," says Bruce, and the engine evaporates.

She takes a deep breath and decides to wait, instead of playing along and asking what he is sorry for.

"I shouldn't have..."

Still, she waits, but he does too, and he's silent for longer than she can bear. "You shouldn't have," she agrees, she keeps her voice level, her cadence measured. If she doesn't, she knows, this will all spiral out of control very quickly. "She shouldn't have. I shouldn't have."

"I don't know why," he offers.

"Yes, you do," she returns.

"I don't think she can take care of herself."

Paige stares at the back of his head, boring holes with her eyes. "Why are you responsible for taking care of her, Bruce? Why are *we?*"

Maybe he senses that she's looking at him, because he looks up from his lap, but still won't turn to look at her. Maybe he feels ashamed. *He should,* she thinks. "Let me just recap here," she tells him, "I told Emily, after she vanished on me last year, after she called me a fucking slut, that I needed her out of my life for good. At your suggestion, may I remind you. So, she comes back and, knowing she would find a closed door over here, reaches out to you."

He turns to her with a surprising emotion on his face. At first, she can't read it, expecting the usual gamut of sad and regretful. But it's anger. "Not being able to reach out to you isn't why she reached out to me." His voice rises. "I'm not fucking plan B, Paige. I'm not her consolation prize."

"We were *always* her consolation prize!"

He opens his mouth to retort, but she doesn't let him.

"She didn't get what she needed from her two boyfriends

back at the beginning, and here was this on-their-way-to-successful couple, so why not try that out for a couple years. A couple years of promises. A couple years of assurances. A couple years where we were all she needed, all she ever wanted!"

"Paige."

She ignores him. "And then the moment she's presented with Mike, with the *normal* life he represents, it's monogamy now, just 'cuz, and 'hope you didn't take me too seriously when I said I'd be here forever, because I'm gonna take this train.'" Paige stands and walks around the bed to stand in front of him. "Oh, but, of course 'I'll still always love you,' sure, 'that hasn't changed!' And then, again, when things aren't working out in monogamyville, she walks right back over to us, and I fucking *fall for it!*" Paige feels the tears coming but doesn't want to let them fall. Why can't she be angry, but not hurt, not in pain, not full of the same regretful *bullshit*—

"She—"

Paige shows him her palm and he stops talking. "But, of course, when the E-train is leaving the station, guess who doesn't get invited to come. Me. You. Us. Plan B doesn't matter. Plan B *never* mattered enough."

He stares, waiting. He rubs his hand down his face, pausing a long while over his mouth, letting her continue.

"Now you're plan B, Bruce. You're it. And she's ruining your vacation. And she's ruining my vacation. And she's doing the same old Emily shit. Calamity after calamity, with only one constant. One single unifying factor between all the bullshit she's ever come to us for help with."

He nods. "Her."

"Emily can't be fixed. But she can break us." She folds her arms across her breasts, suddenly feeling exposed, topless from the beach, sarong around her waist.

"I know how you feel about her," he begins, "and—"

"Do you?"

He holds her eyes. "Yes. You love her. Despite all of the shit."

Paige tries, desperately to hold the tears back.

"And so do I. I think we always will."

She shakes her head.

"This, specifically, was a problem that maybe I could help with. She got kicked—"

"You think this is about whatever you did for her back there? On the phone? With the credit card?"

"Isn't it?"

"Are you fucking *high?*"

He scowls.

"You told me, when you were furious last year. You told me she'd never change! And now she's got you. Christ, she wasn't *that* good a fuck, was she?"

"Petty doesn't look good on you, Paige."

She knows that he's right, but fuck him for saying so.

"She is scared and alone right now." His voice is clipped, angry.

"I'm scared," she yells. "Me, Bruce. Your wife. The one who didn't fucking vanish on you. Her marriage is ending? Her random        knew-him-for-ten-minutes-before-I-married-him husband turned out to be an asshole? I'm so sorry she realized she's not the center of the fucking universe for a change."

"I can't fix what you're scared about," he says, the admission deflating him.

"How about you pretend like you want to try!"

"I do want to! It kills me, Paige, that I'm failing you. That I can't take care of you. That I can't make it better for you. I feel like such a failure. The orchestra is worthless."

"It's not," she says, losing most of her bravado.

"I can't fix it for you, Paige. And that hurts so much." He falls back to the bed, but looks up at her with darkness in his eyes. "So, when I see something I can fix, maybe even for a night? It's nice to feel useful. It's nice to feel like I *can* help."

She opens her mouth and lets it hang. "It's not my job to make you feel useful. And I'm sorry that my problems, which I thought were *our* problems, are so—" The rest of the sentence vanishes as she stares at her husband of twenty-five years. Twenty-five tomorrow, in fact. Lying on his back on their bed, angry at her for having problems he can't fix? She smiles so hard her teeth hurt. "You know what? Do what you want. Spend the rest of this fucking trip on the phone with poor little Emily. I can't stop you. You're a grown-assed-man after all. I plan to squeeze every last drop from this place, in case this is the last fucking week we ever get here."

She steps outside and slams the door so hard that something

clatters and falls. She takes a moment. A moment to take all the pain created by Bruce, by Emily, take it, acknowledge it, let it fill her for a moment, then put it aside. She visualizes setting it on the ledge of their balcony, overlooking the ocean, then shoving it right the fuck off to splatter on the concrete patio below.

"You should know," says Lydia, her hand against his chest as they sit on the bed. Her green eyes are wide, like they may take over her face. Her sheer white billowy dress barely hides the dark shadows of her tattoos, can't come close to hiding her erect nipples. "I don't really have penetrative sex often. PIV, I mean. Penis in vagina. Not even with my husband."

Ryan nods.

"I just want to be upfront about that, because it often will cause gentlemen callers to either go along assuming that they'll be the aberration and I'll go for it, or to decide that I might not be worth their time, when there are so many other sexy ladies around who'll have no problem taking them in, as it were, when the time is right." She blinks at him.

He's unsure if he should respond yet, or if she's going to continue. He wonders if his silence will be construed as sliding into one or the other of those categories. Instead, he looks at her, open, waiting, still clad only his red boxer briefs.

When he checked in with Jenn in the playroom, she was hanging in the sex swing, head back, with the curly haired woman's face between her legs. He kissed her upside-down face. "Do you mind if I go with Lydia?" he asked. "I don't know where."

She returned an enthusiastic nod.

As Lydia walked him across the courtyard toward her room, he admired the silhouette of her nude body under the dress. She held his hand and threw looks over her shoulder, a contented smile on her face. She led without talking, and he followed without questioning.

On the bed in Lydia's room, she moves her hand from his chest to his arm. "I hope you stay, though. Because there are oodles of things that we can do."

"I am," he says. "I will."

"Good," she replies.

"You really don't have penetrative sex often?" he asks, not sure if he's looking for clarification or deeper layers.

"I don't. Internal scarring." She tilts her head and narrows her eyes the slightest bit, as though sizing up his reaction. "It's from quite a while ago. But makes insertion painful."

Ryan contemplates this. The chalkboard of his mind holds many small crude sketches of himself and Lydia in various positions, mostly involving penetration. There's a moment of forlorn acceptance, the slightest bit of disappointment. He sees her eyebrows go up, expectant. "It's fine with me," he says.

"Good," she says.

They sit in silence. Ryan looks around Lydia's room, the mirror image of his and Jenn's. Bed in the center on a small stage, columns at the front two corners. A small bench seat with drawers, a small table, mirrors along one wall. He looks at himself in the mirror, at her. Bruce, he knows, would offer her a massage, or put his hand on her thigh. He wouldn't be sitting, waiting for someone to speak. "I, uh," is the best he can manage.

Lydia smirks.

"How long have, uh, you and," he pauses. Panic washes over him as he realizes that he cannot remember her husband's name. Something with a T. Or R? Is it Robert? That's got both.

Her smirk grows, and she lets him panic a moment more before saying, "Ted."

"Ted! Yes!" He pokes his finger at the ceiling, then dials back the enthusiasm he's shown for her husband's name. *Way to emphasize that you forgot, doof.* "How long have you two been swinging?"

"We don't swing," she tells him and waits.

"You...what?"

"We're not swingers."

He frowns and squints.

"I enjoy watching you parse."

Ryan snorts a laugh and smiles. "Well, I'm glad you're enjoying yourself."

"We're poly, Ryan. Ted and I. Polyamorous? We have loving relationships with—"

"Yes," he tells her, "I'm aware of poly."

"Good." She slides her hand down his arm to his hand, enmeshing her fingers in his. "Now before you get all parse-y and concerned I brought you here to indoctrinate you into a relationship..."

Ryan chides himself for the internal monologue suggesting exactly that.

"We also have casual sex."

"Like swingers," says Ryan.

She laughs. "Yes, of course, because swingers have cornered the market on casual sex. We're chimeras. Half swinger, half poly, all sensual."

All sensual is right! Even standing in the hot tub looking bored by three suitors, she had a sensuality about her that he couldn't describe, hadn't even been able to even give name to. Sitting here with him, holding his hand, she embodies that sensuality. The peasant dress hangs about her curves in the stark white light of the room. He can see her tattoos beneath, the curves of her breasts, the hard brown nipples, the black patch of hair, her legs tucked beneath her on the bed.

Maybe sensing his focus, she reaches up to the white linen tie holding the dress over her breasts. As she pulls, the bow vanishes and the dress slides off her shoulders and down to her waist. The hand hovers there, running one of those deep blue nails up and down her sternum gently. He returns his eyes to her face, and she waggles her eyebrows at him.

"I'd say you like what you see, but I don't generally play with that kind of hubris."

"I do," he tells her.

"To get stuff out of the way, I last tested in October and don't have HIV, HPV, HSV one or two, syphilis, gonorrhea, or anything in the Hepatitis family. I play as though everybody has one of those things, though. Not saying you do, but it won't change my play style." She points to the end table showcasing a roll of plastic wrap, a box of nitrile gloves, and an assortment of condoms. Also, seemingly out of place on the safer sex table, a paddle. "Gloves, barriers, etcetera. I assume you're good with that?"

He nods.

"Excellent. So, in addition to the aforementioned disinclination toward PIV, it is also unlikely I will come during our time together today. And that, my handsome man, has nothing to do with you and everything to do with my at times uncooperative body. If we somehow manage it, I will treat you with a praise dance and sing 'Rah-rah-foo-ferah.'"

He laughs.

"But, as it is a rarity, it is not my end goal, and therefore I tend to focus in the moment. I'm a top, if you play those games. But I'm not a serious top, so I don't call myself a capital D Domme. Really, I'm just someone who likes to tell people what to do, how to do it, and sometimes hit them if they're," she drops her voice and says with a deep British accent that calls to mind Tim Curry, "naughty. Now," she says and twirls her hand in his direction. "How about you?"

He blinks and takes a deep breath. "Okay. I've gone over these things with other playmates before, but never so extensively. Or quickly. Or...matter-of-factly."

"I believe in efficient and effective communication."

"Indeed," says Ryan. "Well, I get cold sores, but haven't had one in a few years. I, uh, am fluid bonded with my wife. We always use condoms with other people. I've...used a dental dam once." He pauses and stares at her, looking for validation, maybe an okay.

She smiles and nods. Encouraging.

"It doesn't bother me to use stuff."

"Good."

"I...haven't ever done the whole dom/sub thing."

"Interest?"

Is he interested? Suddenly, he's worried. Suddenly there are too many and too few options at once. What does one do if they don't eventually have sex? How do they know when they're done?

"You okay?"

He nods. "What, uh, what do you want to do?"

She stands and drops her dress to the floor, then steps out of it. He smells soap and a touch of salt from the ocean on her nude body. The combination is stirring. She steps closer and he puts his hand on her thigh over one of the larger tattoos, a small hill with a round door, and ornate text below. **In a hole in the ground there lived a hobbit.** He slides his hand over her soft skin, around to her back, where he cups her ass and pulls her closer. His face and her bush meet, and he runs his nose through the thicket of hair, then up to her belly button, which he kisses. He looks up at her as she looks down at him, her breasts hanging between them. He moves up and suckles. When he stops, their eyes connect.

"Would you like me to tell you what to do?" she asks with an inquisitive look.

The idea has such merit. If she tells him what to do, he won't have to ask or make moves. If she tells him, he won't even have to worry about it. He nods.

"Gonna need verbal confirmation here, Ryan."

"Yes," he tells her.

"And when I tell you what to do, will you thank me?"

He smiles. "Yes." A thought occurs to him. "Should I call you Mistress?"

She smiles. "Oh, gender norms. Just go ahead and call me Master."

"Yes, Master," he says, trying it on. He likes the way it feels.

"Is anything off limits?"

"I don't know." He thinks about it. "No, not with your caveats and safety methods."

"Well then, I think you're going to be my toy. You know. Here for my amusement?" She tousles his hair and bends down, bringing her lips right next to his. He tries to close the gap between them, but she pulls back. "Ah, no. My amusement, toy."

Suddenly, he's unsure.

She must hear it in his breathing. She takes his face between her hands and lines up their noses. Her eyes have flecks of brown in the pale green. "Hey," she says. "I won't push you deep. I won't hurt you." She laughs. "Unless you let me. The submissive is always really in charge, okay?"

He nods, his breathing returning to normal. She gives him a kiss, first light, then another harder, then another deeper. When she pulls away, she looks at him with concern, asking again with her eyes.

He nods again and smiles. "Just new."

"This is why we play, yes? To discover the new."

"Yes."

"Time-in?"

He laughs, then fixes his eyes on hers. An intense look, a serious look. "Yes, Master."

The concern leaves her face, voracious hunger arrives. She moves her hand from the side of his face to the back of his neck. This time when she kisses him, she slides her tongue almost impossibly deep into his mouth. She reaches down with her other hand, tucks her long cold fingers beneath the waistband of his shorts, and wraps them around his very hard cock.

He gasps into her mouth, and she nibbles on his lower lip.

She pulls back, abruptly, and points at the bed. "All fours," she tells him. "Lose those."

He drops his underwear to the white tile floor and climbs onto the bed.

"I'm going to blindfold you," she says, a proclamation, not a question. Then, with her back turned, searching through a suit-case on the side bench, she adds, "Of course, if a toy didn't want that, that toy could always speak up and say so." She appears to find what she wants in the case, but doesn't turn back.

Ryan says nothing. A toy *does* want that.

She returns with a long black scarf, sheer, but when doubled and trebled and wrapped around his face not once but twice, the world goes dark. For a moment he worries, for a moment the anxiety is very present. But she presses her lips against his ear in a kiss. "You don't have to do anything, you know. Nothing is expected of you. You're just my toy, and I'm going to play. If you're hard, you're hard. If you come, you come. If you decide, as toys sometimes do, that the time has come to put away childish things, then we do that. You don't have to say anything unless it's no."

Again, a toy says nothing.

Her hand grips his cock between his legs, pulling it back toward her. He feels chilly lube dribble up and down his shaft, then she's stroking. He's never felt this before, at this angle. There's pain, but only a touch, not enough that he'd stop her because it's also...so...

"Wow," he says.

She says nothing, just continues exploring his body, sliding her hands around him, squeezing, tugging, evaluating, kissing. She nuzzles against the hair in his armpits. She runs her teeth over his shoulders. She slides her nails down his back and across his ass cheeks. She spreads them and he draws a slow breath, unsure what she might do. He hears a quiet rip and feels something light, almost weightless, pressed between his cheeks. Then the warmth of her tongue, running in circles, as she returns her hand to his cock. She strokes faster and faster, tonguing him through the plastic wrap. The sensation makes him shudder.

"I'm, uh," he says, trying to warn her.

She understands it, her grip on his cock tightens, and when he comes he feels a fullness. "Just needed to get something under you," she whispers and relaxes her grip. Now he shoots, then again, again, again.

The bright white of the room is almost blinding for a moment as she unwraps him. He blinks up at her, standing above him.

"I'm going to need you to eat my pussy," she tells him, then emphasizes, "It's so great to have a toy that'll do that for me."

"Yes, Master," he says as she climbs onto the bed next to him. She spreads her legs, her pussy glistens beneath a thin sheet of transparent plastic wrap. With a smile, she tells him to get to work.

He kisses her in her doorway when they part for the night.

"Did you have fun?"

He nods with enthusiasm.

"Something new?"

"Yeah, that was..." he can't find the words.

"Any interest in," she looks down, "I dunno, doing some more stuff before the end of this sojourn?"

"Yeah," he says, confused by her downward glance. "Were you embarrassed to ask me that?" he asks before he realizes the question might be rude.

"Hey!" She pokes him in the chest. "Can't be confident all the time."

"I guess that's true." He takes her face between his hands and looks deep into her eyes. "Yes, I'd love to play with you again. Do the toy thing again."

"Other things might be fun."

"I'm game."

"Good," she says, tipping her face up to kiss him again. "Goodnight, Ryan."

"Goodnight, Lydia."

One last kiss and she closes the door.

Ryan wanders off to the courtyard bar, to have a drink and recall what he can. Then maybe he and Jenn can hit the hot tub.

"Good day?" asks Jenn.

"Great day," says Ryan.

They clack their tumblers together.

The rooftop hot tub is far busier than it had been last night, and Ryan and Jenn sit on the stone stools below the waterline at the bar. Jenn glances at the clock on the wall. It's just past 10:00 in the evening. There is a scattering of couples and singles at either end of the hot tub bean, and three of the beds on the opposite side of the platform are occupied. When they first arrived up here to talk through their experiences, the day people were still out and about, having late dinners, dancing post-orgy at the disco. Now, the crowds have begun to arrive, and people watching can begin. To the left end of the bean, three men have climbed up on the ledge, and two women make their way up and down the row. Suck and move, suck and move. She giggle-snorts.

"You're getting a little loopy," says Ryan with a smile.

She looks down at her tumbler, now only a third full of the drink of the day: orange and grapefruit and pineapple with rum. She holds up her fingers to indicate how much of the glass is empty, then shows them to Ryan. "I only had that much."

He laughs. "Julio has kept you flush with refills."

She stares at the glass, swaying a little. She slaps her hand down on the marble bar to steady herself.

"Whoa," he says, reaching out for her.

"How many have I had?"

Ryan glances up and to the right, counting. "Three."

"Three?"

"And that one," he says, pointing to her tumbler.

"Three and two-thirds."

"Yes.

"Oh, my." She stares at the tumbler, tasting the rum on her tongue, then finishes the last of it. "I may need a spacer."

"Excellent idea," says Ryan. "*Agua, por favor.*"

She grins at her husband, who smiles warmly back.

"You're very content, aren't you?" he asks.

She nods and sips her spacer. "I feel good about so many things right now."

"Would you like to share?"

Her grin widens. As it happens, she would very much like to share. "I love knowing that you had so much fun. Like, you picked up a girl and went off without an assist."

"You encouraged."

"Yeah, but you did it. You asked. You got." She sighs. "The feels are strong. The compersion."

"Are we drunk enough to be making up words?" he asks with a laugh.

She narrows her eyes at him. "You know that one."

"I don't," he says.

"Paige told me, and I told you."

He smiles and shakes his head.

She frowns, certain she has shared the word.

"You could tell me about it now, though," he offers.

"It's kinda like the opposite of jealousy."

"Opposite of jealousy."

"You know, an overwhelmingly positive sense of joy and thrill, knowing your partner had fun."

"You feel that?"

"I do."

"Me too." He leans forward and kisses her sweetly, running his fingers through her hair, giving the pink lock a tiny tug before tucking it behind her ear.

"And I love knowing that there's a unique new dynamic we can maybe play with in the future."

"Oh yeah?"

"Wanna be my toy sometime?"

"I do," he says.

"That, and Zoë, I'm losing track of time and space." She laughs. "Letting go and letting flow in front of so many appreciative people." She knows her sigh is theatrically dramatic but doesn't care. The warmth of the day has overwhelmed any inhibitions. "And, of course, the awesomeness with the Shepards earlier."

"Oh yeah," he agrees.

"Our financial life may be in shambles," she says, her laugh a bit wild as she raises the brand-new tumbler Julio has deposited next to her, full of that glorious orange and pink concoction, "but somewhere along the line, we got rather decent at this stuff."

He follows her glass with his, tracing its path, before he's able to clack his against hers.

"It's still Tuesday, right?" she asks, leaning forward.

"For about ninety more minutes, yeah."

"Do we have to go home?"

"Well, not until Saturday. Three full days still."

She feels her breath catch in her throat. "Doesn't feel like long enough," she tells him, wiping at her eyes.

"Oh, hon, I know," he says. "What would you like to do? How shall we grab hold of this late hour?"

"We should find cool, sexy people to make out with."

He nods and smiles. "Sounds great."

The night is interrupted by the sound of someone pretending to be a trumpet, then a voice, "Presenting Queen Nancy!"

Jenn stands to look, swaying a bit, but steadies herself on the bar. She sees the face of Nancy, the beautiful pinup, appear above the rails of the staircase, far higher than expected. Her grinning face rises and rises until turning the corner for the last bit of stairs. Then, Jenn can see the full breadth of the spectacle. Four men, including Nancy's husband, surround her wheelchair, each having hoisted it to waist level. Nancy covers her mouth as she giggles. The men stop at the top of the stairs, and slowly lower Nancy, in her chair, to the ground. She kisses each one of them in thanks, then wheels herself up to the dry side of the bar.

"Like an Egyptian queen," says Ryan.

Jenn nods, still awed by the spectacle. "I'd make out with her," she says.

Ryan laughs. "I think she has several suitors at the moment."

Indeed, the men who carried her up to the rooftop in her wheelchair now surround her at the bar, doting on her, swooning over her, offering kisses.

"So it would seem."

"How about them?" He points toward a couple on the far end of the hot tub, near the ladder.

Jenn follows his finger to a couple they met briefly at the welcome party. Abigail, she thinks, and his name starts with a C. Abigail leans back against the side of the tub confidently, her breasts poking above the surface like two pale mountains. Her long dark hair is plastered to her shoulders and arms. Jenn can picture moving in front of her, bending down, and the first kiss, the gentle, tentative one, before you know how the other person likes it, before you really...

She shakes her head and smiles. "Got in deep for a second there," she tells him. "I like her." Abigail and Chris, that's it! And the couple next to them is Brooke and Josh, she thinks, but they met so many people at speed dating, and she did her best to keep up. "Though I believe that they're occupied."

Ryan agrees. "What with the flirting? Yes."

Brooke's face is freckled with a dusting of cinnamon, a high ponytail of brown hair trending toward red. Jenn finds her beautiful, in that no-makeup effortless "I just got out of bed" way that she at once loathes and loves.

"I want to kiss her too, actually," says Jenn, pointing discreetly.

"How about the guys?"

"Hmm?"

Ryan laughs. "You like the girls."

"I do," says Jenn, turning to face him, a warm smile on her face. He has a smirk on his, and she's unsure why. "What?"

"Top five sexiest people in the hot tub."

"My top five?"

"Yes."

She's still uncertain, but she nods. She'll play along. She pokes a finger into his right nipple and grins. "Number one."

"Pssht," he says, expelling air. "Okay, let's say five sexiest people you don't live with. Deal?"

"That's fair," she grins again. Fun game. She does a quick scan of the hot tub, now host to about twenty couples and a scattering of singles. Nothing compared to peak hours, when it feels like the whole resort might be there, but bustling nonetheless.

"Have you gotten a good look?" he asks.

"You have to play too," she tells him.

"Of course," he says.

"Okay, one: Brooke."

"Which one is Brooke?"

She shushes him loudly, drawing more attention than Ryan's stage whisper. "Reddish brown hair and freckles."

"She's your favorite?"

"Oh, I was making five the best. Building, you know?"

"Fair enough. Number two?"

She looks around, making a point to see if she can discern the people on the deck beds or deck chairs. She can't and Ryan did say *in* the hot tub. She covers her hand and discretely points down to the opposite end of the bar. "The one that looks like Veronica over there."

He gives the woman a quick glance and turns back, grinning. "I met her and her husband Steve yesterday. Her name actually is Veronica."

"You're fucking with me," Jenn says, dropping her jaw. "I read the Betty and Veronica Digest books all the time in junior high!"

"Yeah?"

"I was totally on team Veronica."

Her husband smiles. "I was a Betty fan, myself."

She pokes him again. "You just like big tits and blonde hair."

"Stop poking me," he says, swatting at her hand. "And so do you! So that's two."

"Can't believe her name is Veronica. I should go talk to her. Even back then I wanted to make out with Veronica."

"You should, but first you need to give me the top three sexiest people in the hot tub that you're not currently sharing a bed with." Ryan looks around, pausing a few times. Jenn thinks he may be sussing out her type.

She takes a deep breath. He thinks he knows her so well. Okay, let's look for someone he won't expect. Finding the sexy. A woman across the tub, rather boyish in face and body, a shock of magenta hair slicked back in the center of her otherwise close-cropped head. She's seen the woman once or twice throughout the week and always been very intrigued. A small gold hoop arcs around her right nostril. "Her," says Jenn, holding up three fingers. "Number three!"

"Hmm," says Ryan, making the sound go up at the end like a question.

"Hmm," repeats Jenn, with the same inflection.

"Wouldn't have called her as your taste."

"She's intriguing," insists Jenn, hearing in her own voice a touch of belligerence. She picks a second tumbler of *agua fria* up off the bar, and nods to Julio, who grins at her then moves to take another order.

"I also find her intriguing."

"Okay, then."

"Seriously," says Ryan, putting his hand on her shoulder. "I wasn't calling your taste into question."

"Okay, then," she repeats and begins to scan for the top two. "Do they all have to be in the hot tub?"

"No, my love," he laughs, "they don't."

"'Cuz I really think Paige is my number five." She frowns and looks down.

"There's nothing wrong with that, hon."

"I feel like I cheated!" She's conflicted by the choice, but it isn't really a choice at all, is it? "But Paige is sexy, the very definition for me! Her confidence, her poise, her control. The way she flirts, the way she kisses. The way she," she drops her voice, almost coughing on the words, as she realizes how loud she's talking, "licks me. She's so...pretty, and sexy, and I love her."

Ryan nods, lips pursed, eyebrows sloping out. "I know, my love, I know. You didn't cheat."

"Oh! Nancy!" Jenn exclaims.

"Queen Nancy indeed," agrees Ryan, giving Nancy a saucy look across the bar.

She runs through the list in her head and scans around the hot tub. "That's my five."

"Okay," Ryan says. "Brooke, Veronica, the woman with the magenta mohawk is named Sonja, by the way..."

"Sonja," repeats Jenn, wondering what it'd be like to run her hands over the sides of her head.

"Then Nancy, and Paige."

Jenn runs through the names in her head, repeating Sonja to herself a few times. Veronica would be easy to remember. "I wonder if we could find a Betty here at the resort. That'd be quite the," she pauses and sways, grabbing for the bar, "sandwich. Jesus this drink climbed on top of me."

"Okay," says Ryan. "What do all the people on that list have in common."

Jenn glances from one to another, conjuring a phantom of Paige in the tub with them. All are pretty, all are sexy, but the five of them have few shared characteristics. Facial structure, beauty, body type, breast size. Almost all different. "Is your point that I don't have a type?"

"No," he tells her. "That's not quite my point. They're all women, my love."

Jenn blinks at him. "Yes," she agrees, "they are, but—" Then it hits her, what he's saying. That she looks around this hot tub and sees men and women, sure, but the ones she *really* sees are the women. "What, uh," she asks, a waver in her voice, "what does that mean?"

Perhaps sensing that she's becoming unmoored, he takes her hand. "I wouldn't worry about it. I just think it's interesting, don't you?"

"I still find you attractive," she insists. "You are very sexy!" She leans forward and kisses him.

"Jenn," he says, taking both her hands. "I know in the past I've been a little...nervous...occasionally. And maybe read too much into things. But I know that you think I'm sexy. Thank you, of course, for reinforcing it. But it doesn't worry me that you find women sexier—"

"Is that it?" she asks quickly. Is it that she truly finds women sexier?

"I think you might—"

"When I masturbate, I fantasize about women," she says, not to him, or to anyone really, just saying it to hear it, to put it into the world. "When I watch porn, I look at the..." The thought hits her, and she asks the question before processing it. "What if I'm gay?"

"Okay," says Ryan, affecting his calmest and most comforting voice. "Maybe I shouldn't have mentioned this after four of those." He points to her drink. "And!" he exclaims, "I forgot about the espresso martini I got you downstairs."

"But—"

"I don't think you're gay."

She shakes her head.

"I think you just might be," he looks up at the night sky, apparently searching for the right thing to say, "*more bi* doesn't make sense. Not *on* the fence, but just...on the other side of the fence you thought you were on."

She runs through scenarios in her head, of the times she's been engaged with the men around her in the lifestyle. At the beginning the scales had tipped in the hetero direction. Since, there have been far more frequent times where she's beelined for the women with the men as an afterthought. "Is that okay?" she asks, a slight pleading note in her voice.

"It's wonderful, my dear. It's you."

She smiles at him, knowing her smile is weak and unconvincing. She wishes Paige were here, she'd know what to say, how to understand all this.

"Truly," he tells her, his voice calm and reassuring. "Just let it be a new thing to see. No decisions need to be made, no new ID cards or registration changes at the post office. Just...a touch different than expected."

"Different can be good," she tells him, hearing herself trying to be convincing.

"Different *can* be good," he repeats and kisses her. "Would you like to go to a bed and have sex with me?"

She very much would. She says so, and they do.

# 42

## ALEJANDRA

Alejandra stands on the balcony entryway to their room, leaning on the high plaster rail and smoking a cigarillo she's bummed from one of the staff members. She would've preferred a cigarette, but it was all Reynaldo had, and beggars looking for a fix can't be choosers.

"Quite a day," she says to the dark, exhaling a long plume of gray smoke. It dances in the hanging grass of the roof before drifting skyward.

Their room is billed as a "garden view," and she sees the garden below her, between the two buildings. Small budding palm trees and other tropical plants, vivid pinks, oranges, and greens, fill the patch of greenery. One building over would've raised their rate significantly for an "ocean view." But she can see the ocean. Sure, from here it's a small square of blackness off to the left. She can only see it by stretching up and out, leaning over the edge, farther than she ought to.

Alejandra thinks it's Wednesday, now, but she's not certain. She's been on the balcony for quite a while, more than an hour, maybe two. They're into the back half now. The trip is waning, and she wonders if their marriage, their relationship, is also waning. This balcony and the last beach bed on the end have been her only two destinations all day, and Alejandra thinks she ought to go get some of the late-night pizza. Her stomach lurches. It's the first insistent hunger she's felt today, and it's a bit of a relief to feel something new. She's so drained by the survival question.

Does everybody get tired of sex eventually? Or just of sex with her?

She knows, without question, that she could go up to the hot tub right now and pick up any number of different women. Despite her reluctance in general to do such things, and some nagging Catholic guilt about having pride in her appearance, there isn't really a question.

Before Crista, Miranda also went cold, but that'd been in the days of monogamy, when cold meant no sex and hiding masturbation from each other.

Going to the hot tub, going for sex, though, that'd mark an end for her. It'd be revenge. For last night, for this morning. A point of no return, where she's checked out, closed up shop on the relationship. Wouldn't be the first time for that either, would it?

*We may be close to that point, but I'm not jumping off it,* she thinks.

Her wife's arguments and defenses were nothing new. Alejandra was exhausted before this morning's fight, er, conversation, even got going.

"I'm so sorry. I didn't intend to do that, I promise," said Crista, in the doorway, fingers hooked into her shoes.

"What was your intent?" Alejandra aimed for calm but instead found clipped. Clipped was okay. Terse, also fine. Deserved, surely. An understandable tone to use for addressing the wife who didn't bother to come home at all.

"I don't know."

"When I woke up, and you weren't here, I was about to call the front desk and report you missing. Lucky you came back. Could've been a manhunt. So, what was it? Who was it, to keep you out?"

"Polina," she said, refusing to make eye contact, "and Sergey, the Eastern Euro—"

"I've met them. Did you fuck them?"

Her wife stammered. "I fucked her. I don't, I mean I don't think—"

Alejandra sprang from the bed, jaw so tense she could hear the throb of blood rushing in her ears. She shoved past her wife through the open door and slammed it behind her. The morning sunlight was diffuse and vague, still not having crested the building between them and the ocean. She grabbed hold of the rail with both hands and breathed deeply. A glance down revealed her nudity, surprising her. She'd been so focused on the rest. So angry. Angry at her wife, who'd fucked— well Polina wasn't the problem, was she? Circumstances were the problem. And if she'd fucked...him. That man. Of course, *he* wasn't the problem either. "No," said Alejandra. "The fucking situation is the fucking problem."

She banged on the door to be let back in.

Crista opened it, standing off to the side to allow Alejandra the widest possible berth.

She sat on the edge of the bed, a frown on her face. She took a long deep breath. She didn't look at Crista, standing in the corner near the door, and when she spoke, her voice was calm. "I think I need to make a few things clear here. I am not upset about you fucking Polina. I'm not more than reasonably upset that you fucked Sergey. I—"

"I don't think I did!"

Alejandra sat in silence, and Crista followed suit. "I am *concerned* that you aren't sure if you had sex with a man last night." The silence loomed. "But that is also not why I am upset."

"You're upset that I had sex with other people and not you," said Crista. "Or one other person."

Alejandra felt the weight of it. This woman she loved so very much. This woman she loved kissing and touching and caressing and fucking. This woman. "I'm sad," she said. "I'm sad that I wanted you to come out with me last night and you didn't. But then you went out on your own and did stuff. And we could've done it together." She laughed humorlessly. "Polina's got that Nordic Ice Queen look going. It's very sexy."

"Yes, it is." Crista's voice held hope.

Alejandra looked up at her wife, into her terrified eyes. "If I only get to fuck you when other people are around, then you need to bring me with you when you fuck those other people. Or you at least need to tell me why you don't want me there. I think you owe me that."

Crista's face fell. "It's not that I don't want you there."

"Then what is it? Why is it? You say you have a responsive sex drive, then—"

"Why do you put it like that?" Crista asked with an edge. "That I *say* I have one. Why don't you say, 'You have a responsive sex drive'? Because I do. That's what I have. That's how I'm built."

The semantic argument was exhausting, but Alejandra just breathed for a moment. "Fine. You have a responsive sex drive. I recognize that that means other people have to jump start you. And once upon a time I could, but maybe I got boring—"

"You didn't get boring."

"Well then, something. And now you need others. And I want to be clear, I like fucking others. It revs me up, too. But I don't need it. Not all the time."

Crista moved closer and closer, finally pointing to the bed next to Alejandra. "Can I sit here?"

Alejandra nodded, and Crista sat.

"I'm sorry."

"It's not the first time. Or the second."

"I know, I'm sorry."

"This seems to be us," she said.

"It does," Crista agreed.

"And at some point, we're going to have to decide if that's what we want."

"Wait," said Crista.

"I'm not sure it's what I want, anymore."

"Hold on," said Crista.

Alejandra stood. "I need to think."

Crista tried to stop her from going. They should keep talking, they needed to keep talking. Her words blurred into a soup of pleading and empty assurances. Alejandra held up her hands and went.

She sat on their beach bed and thought, she lay on their beach bed and thought, she slept on their beach bed, succumbing to stress and exhaustion. When she returned in the evening, the windows were dark. She walked inside and found Crista sitting on the step that surrounded their bed, lights off.

"You came back," said Crista.

"I needed to think," said Alejandra.

Crista nodded and wiped her face with both hands, sniffling.

She'd been crying, and Alejandra's instinct was to rush to her, hold her hand, comfort her. Not now, though.

"I need you to hear me," said Alejandra.

Crista stared at her, eyes wide.

"I am not okay with a sexless marriage between the two of us."

"Okay," says Crista.

"I don't know if you've just stopped being attracted to me, or—"

"No, that's not—"

"Then what?"

Crista sat in thoughtful silence. "I'm like a boulder, at the top of a very shallow slope."

Hands on her hips, Alejandra narrowed her eyes skeptically.

"It takes a lot of pushing to get me rolling, and even once I do I only move slowly."

"Like getting blackout drunk and fucking a woman and maybe fucking her husband."

Crista stopped.

"I don't think I should have to always shove you. I don't think that should be my job."

"It's not your—"

"It feels like my job."

"I still find you attractive," Crista whispered.

"I know."

"I'm just fucked up."

Alejandra ignored the blatantly manipulative "feel sorry for me" phrasing.

"All the shit growing up, and—"

"I know," said Alejandra again, with a frown. She agreed, some of the stuff from Crista's past was absolutely appalling and could rightly put someone off sex. But that wasn't quite what was happening here. Alejandra wasn't sure exactly what was happening, but asexuality wasn't the cornerstone. "What I need," she said, "is for you to initiate when you want to have sex with me. Something you say you want."

"I do."

"And failing that, I need you to say yes when I ask you, because you say you want that, too."

"I do," she said, quieter.

"And failing that, I need you not to say you're uninterested in sex and then go out and fuck other people."

This time Crista said nothing.

"If you're just not interested in having sex with me some night, you're going to say that." Alejandra stopped short, then looked away. "Or you're going to find another wife."

Crista flinched, then nodded solemnly.

Alejandra sat down on the step next to her. They sat in silence for quite a while.

"What do you want to do?" asked Crista in a whisper.

"I don't know," said Alejandra.

"Will you hold me?" asked Crista.

Alejandra nodded, and the two moved to the bed, arms around each other. After a while, the bodily warmth and darkening room lulled them both to sleep.

When she awoke after ten, Alejandra slipped out of the room to the balcony, where she looked at the night, thinking nothing. The nothing feels comforting.

"Hey," says a voice, a pale figure climbing the stairs. Her strawberry-blonde hair catches the light from above their neighbors' door.

"Hello, Paige," says Alejandra with a tired wave.

"You don't appear to be having fun."

Alejandra sees that Paige's eyes are red, and there's no warm smile on her face. "You don't either."

"I'm not," says Paige, without hesitance. "Sometimes things are just shit."

Alejandra nods. "Were you looking for me?"

Paige points to the door in front of her, next to Alejandra's. "Jenn." Their lights are dark.

"Ah," says Alejandra. "Didn't realize we were neighbors."

"She's not here," says Paige, "and honestly, even if she was, I don't know what I'd say to her." She stares at the door, her face growing sadder, before finally choking out a single sob then flipping back to anger. "My fucking marriage."

Alejandra laughs mirthlessly. "Mine too, want to talk about it?"

"No," says Paige.

"I think mine is in a shaky stasis right now, and going back in there again won't make it better." She flicks her thumb toward their door.

"I'm done with fighting for the night."

"Me, too. Want to get a pizza and eat it on the beach?"

Paige looks back up at her as though it's the best idea anyone's ever had. "Yes," she says. "Yes, I want to do that."

"Let's do," says Alejandra. She follows Paige down the stairs.

# PART VI

*Wednesday*

# 43

# PAIGE

"I thought he knew better, that's all. Kinda disappointed he doesn't. More than *kinda*, actually. Really disappointed. I know that's not fair. He shouldn't be held to a higher standard than I am. He shouldn't have to be that guy. We're supposed to both be that, for each other. Bruce is my hero. Truly. He's the gentlest and most giving man I've ever met. Former cheerleader here, too, so I've met more than my fair share of shit heads. The way he acts with our sons, as though every interaction is molding them, shaping them to be better men. Better than manly or masculine. Better than the idea of 'man.' Better." Paige looks out over the twin bows of the catamaran, off to where the turquoise water breaks to white. She feels the droplets of ocean spray on her face and body, smelling, tasting the salt in the air. She realizes that her monologue has lasted since they left the shore, when she'd waved goodbye to Jenn on the beach and wiped away tears. "I've been talking too much," she says, turning to her boating companions. Hector, slender and dark from decades in the sun, sits at the back near the mast, squinting into the horizon. Closer to her, much closer, sits a beautiful Hispanic news anchor named Alejandra wearing Gucci sunglasses, lenses shimmering rainbows, and nothing else. Thankfully asking nicely and throwing him several bills, made Hector decide that life vests weren't necessary and Alejandra's beautiful body didn't need to be hidden. Paige barely tries to hide her leer behind her own sunglasses.

"Not too much," says Alejandra. "I'm thankful I haven't had to talk, honestly."

"You don't have to," Paige tells her, wondering what it'd be like to bite the point where her neck meets her shoulder.

This morning Alejandra knocked on the door of their suite and woke Paige. Bruce, who was sleeping on the sectional sofa, didn't stir. He'd always been the heavier sleeper.

"I've chartered the catamaran for the morning and afternoon. I don't know if my marriage could survive eight hours at sea without any escape except into the deep blue." Alejandra scratched her wrist and looked away. "Wanna come?"

Paige did, but first called the front desk and asked them to prepare a cooler with cheese and sausages and fruit for them. "What's the use in paying for foolish extravagance if we're not going to use it, right?"

Alejandra agreed.

It had been difficult, on the beach, when she saw Jenn, lovely Jenn, walking toward them, white hat on her head, tote over her shoulder. If the catamaran hadn't already been drifting several yards from shore, Paige would've beckoned her on. Asked her to join. Had to explain. Instead, she blew her a kiss and waved as they moved toward open water. Jenn stood and watched for a while, a perplexed, somewhat hurt look on her face.

"Jenn thinks so highly of us," Paige says to Alejandra, "to tell her would be like admitting to a parent that you're a fuck-up, you know."

"Second generation Catholic Mexican immigrant," Alejandra says, "who had to tell *mamá y papá* that I'm a lesbian in high school after they repeatedly insisted I go to prom with Elias Rosales, terribly confused about why I wouldn't take them up on their offer of a later curfew and a rented limo. Did not tell them I would have used both the curfew and the limo to see how many fingers I could fit inside my girlfriend, Reena. Poor Elias."

"Not only a girl, but I'm guessing not Hispanic?"

"Jewish."

"You win."

Alejandra laughs, and Paige wishes she could see her eyes beneath those sunglasses. The laugh sounds pained.

*Mine probably does as well,* thinks Paige.

"I was just throwing in my 'admitting stuff to parents' tale of woe," says Alejandra, "not invalidating the pain of telling a loved one you're not perfect."

"I think I disappointed her, though," Paige says. "By hardly talking to her yesterday and leaving out from under her today."

"You don't owe her—" Alejandra stops mid-stream. "Never mind. I'm projecting."

"You're right," says Paige, "I don't owe her an explanation, but I want to give her one."

"She'll be there when you return."

"She will."

An hour into their excursion, and several mini bottles of mediocre pinot grigio from her Xanadu tote bag down, Paige feels herself scowling as the face of the intrusion swims up in her mind. Emily. Emily, so beautiful, so sexy. So naughty. *Fuck.* "I get it," she says, suddenly enough that Alejandra jumps. "The draw for him with Emily I understand. It's intense and internal."

"Firsts can do that to us," agrees Alejandra. "She was your first..." She leaves the sentence open.

"She was the first for so many things. The first woman I genuinely connected with. The first person we shared our life with. Like full-on poly shared."

"Poly frightens me," says Alejandra after a while.

"Do you think Crista would meet someone else? That's always the big fear."

"No, I think I would." Alejandra looks away, toward the horizon, where a cruise ship looms like a mountain come unmoored.

Paige nods and grabs a handful of grapes. She lies on her back on the taut fabric platform suspended between the two pontoons, looking up at the vivid blue sky, broken by only the smallest puffs of clouds. She wants to tell Jenn all of it, about Emily and Bruce. The emergency call. How it makes her feel. Because they talk about things. Because they love each other. Shutting her out feels terrible, for both of them. But Jenn thinks she and Bruce know how to do all of the things, navigate all the bumps. And doesn't it entail getting deeper into last year, too? Talking more extensively about Emily's trip back through the picture. How she'd been helpless with lust for this woman from her past. Dipping her fingers back in to get a taste of the old times, despite her better judgment.

(slut)

She can admit wrongness, foolishness, embarrassment to Jenn. But what had that been last year? Pure stupid lust. Would Jenn understand? Would she understand being led to believe everything was hunky-fucking-dory yesterday? When the four of them... She wonders what Bruce will do with his day. How much of it will be spent on the phone with Emily, working out her issues, dealing with the shit that seems to always follow her? All while Paige is managing the collapse of her family's company. Not her fault, probably, but on her watch. Feeling the loss of her husband's focus, out here, in one of the few places she feels honestly herself, is too much. Things are supposed to be frivolous and fun out here. At Aphrodite's. In paradise. This is where they go to get away. Every single vacation since their first visit here, aside from their yearly family trip, had brought them back to Aphrodite's. To this bit of ocean, this stretch of beach, this bastion of excess and hedonism. Where they can unwind the way their parents might have in the Summer of Love. Or had hers been too busy producing her?

Bruce was the first child in his family, so his parents could well have spent their time indulging in the peace, love, and free sex of the sixties. Before their politics shifted and they grew old and conservative. A common occurrence. But not for Paige. Not with fifty looming next year. Not with the very real possibility that their trips to this paradise will become far less frequent.

"I was thinking about a gang bang," she says later, turning toward the beautiful woman sunning next to her.

"There are only two of us," Alejandra replies, squinting over the top of her sunglasses at Paige.

"I want to take all this resort can give me."

Alejandra laughs, loudly. "Will I have to take a number?" she asks.

"Do you think I could make that happen?"

"Paige," says Alejandra, in a tone of voice that suggests she can't believe she must say this, "you ask for a gang bang back on shore, and you'll have a line across the resort."

Paige smiles, picturing herself on one of the beds in the courtyard, pillow under her ass, legs spread and held by patient men and women waiting for their turns. The sea of hard cocks and brilliantly colored dildos all ready to plunge into one of her hungry orifices, the line of cocks-in-waiting stretching between the buildings all the way down to the beach. How lovely that would be.

(slut)

She shoves the voice way-way down. Emily will not ruin this trip for her. Not any longer. She's not invited.

"I'm serious," says Paige to the smirk on Alejandra's face.

"So am I. I want a low number. Before the frenzy."

Paige rolls to her side and kisses Alejandra's cheek. "You lovely woman, you can have number one."

"Now, that's an excellent offer," Alejandra replies and rolls toward Paige.

Paige runs her fingernail from Alejandra's neck, along her clavicle, around her left nipple and down to her tight belly. She holds it, just above the line of her waist. Above the trimmed hairs, above the brown lips of her vulva, smooth and inviting. Paige holds her position and stares at Alejandra, stares into her sunglasses, past the rainbow alien shimmer of the lenses.

"Are you waiting for an invitation?" asks Alejandra, after an almost interminable amount of time.

Paige nods, feeling relief that this thing she wants is alright, a surprising feeling just now, out here. Emily's voice remains silenced, held back and pushed down as Paige focuses on the sexy woman in front of her.

"I'm a fuck yes, Paige," says Alejandra.

That's all she needs to hear.

# 44

# JENN

As the catamaran launches from the beach, Jenn has no doubt that's Paige sitting with her feet dangling over the side. Her hair is fiery, back-lit by the rising morning sun, and the sarong around her waist is the one that Jenn gave her a month before the trip. Blue with black flowers. Jenn has its match. An extra-long squint and stare confirms that the woman on the other side of the catamaran, wearing no clothing at all, is Alejandra, wife of the woman who fisted her, one of the participants in their amazing all-woman orgy. A smile drifts across Jenn's lips as she nears the launch point. She waves at Paige, who notices and waves back, but the boat is on the move, and five feet of water becomes ten, fifteen. Jenn stops walking, nearly at the waterline, no longer any point in going further. She waves again. Paige waves back. After another dozen feet or so Paige turns away, and the moment opens a floodgate inside Jenn, filling her with sadness, loss, regret, swarming together in combinations she doesn't quite understand but readily recognizes as jealousy.

Why should Alejandra be out there with Paige, instead of her? The question consumes her for a while. She's still considering it at breakfast. In front of a plate of waffles and bacon, Jenn looks out at the ocean and can no longer see the catamaran. She tries to make sense of this emotion. In the time they've been together, been girlfriends, so much has happened and changed, but once Paige opened up, Jenn has never felt separated, at arm's length. Paige has always been there to help guide her. Her name alteration had even been Paige's idea.

"You're not that girl anymore, that's why it's strange for you," she told Jennifer as they finished their steaks at The Horn Lodge.

"Can people actually change so fundamentally?" Jennifer asked.

"I think they can. I believe you did."

"I guess I keep waiting for the pendulum to swing back. Like I went from almost-virgin to—"

Paige snorted in her wine and covered her face with the back of her hand. "Sorry."

"What?" asked Jennifer, feeling worry creep in. "Are you laughing at me?"

"No, darling!" Paige reached across the table and took her hand. Only for a brief time now had they been girlfriends, and it still felt odd to apply the term. Odd and lovely. Lovely and tingly. "I just find it rather incongruous that the woman I had my hand inside last night was something she terms 'almost virgin' when we met."

Jennifer grinned at the memory of Paige, flanked and assisted by Ryan with lube and Bruce with water, sliding her hand all the way in, past the last knuckle, then flexing her fingers. The sensation had been unlike any she'd ever felt, fullness, a blast to the G-spot. Exceptional.

"Well, that's my point, isn't it," said Jennifer when she regained focus on the world in front of her. "That I did nothing, and—"

"God said 'let there be swing?'" Paige giggled.

"*Someone* said 'let there be Paige.'"

"D'aww."

"And now everything is different. Can I be so different, while still on the outside appearing the same? I'm still Jennifer the shy quiet sister, cousin, daughter, friend."

Paige looked at her for a long while. "Do you want to tell them?"

"Tell them?" asked Jennifer. "Oh, about— No! No, I don't need to be out like that. I mean, they don't really need to know, right?"

"Not unless you want to bring me home for Christmas."

"I'd like to unwrap you for Christmas," said Jennifer.

"You can unwrap me early!" Paige giggled. She took a long sip of her pinot noir and folded her hands under her nose, vivid blue eyes full of love. "You should do something simple, symbolic. Change something external about yourself to reflect the new person you are internally."

That night Jennifer became Jenn, and understood her transformation a bit more. Family asked questions, but she avoided, and when pushed she could shrug and say, "Just felt like a change..." Being Jenn felt more accurate. When she cut her hair after the Westin's Appearance Policy no longer held any hold on her, she saw the face of Jenn in the mirror. The truth. The transition complete.

Paige should be here with her now, for breakfast, to talk about this thing Ryan had said last night, about the liking girls more than boys. Because it's new, and it's big, and it's scary, and she needs her girlfriend. Instead, Paige is out on a catamaran with Alejandra. *Which is fine*, she reminds herself. She just misses Paige. Just needs her. Paige would even be the one to talk to about these feelings of abandonment, this compersion imbalance. She was so happy about Ryan finding joy and passion with Lydia, so why this growing pit in her stomach over Paige being on a boat with another woman? She scowls at the phrase. *With another woman* sounds like a line from a teaser for a late-night Cinemax infidelity drama. Of course, the person with the other woman would probably be Antonio Sabato, Jr.

"Morning sads?"

Jenn looks up into a smiling freckled face that spent a significant amount of time between her legs yesterday. Zoë's curly hair is pulled into an explosive ponytail on the back of her head. She wears a light green sundress and holds her breakfast.

"Hi," says Jenn. After a moment of smiling at each other, Jenn notices the three empty seats at her table. "Would you like to join me?"

"I'd love to," says Zoë, sitting next to Jenn.

"Your breakfast puts mine to shame," says Jenn, eyeing her dining companion's egg white omelet flanked by cubes of cantaloupe and watermelon.

"Shush. I ate a stack of bacon Monday so big I could still taste it yesterday."

Jenn laughs, the admission giving her an odd sense of relief and permission.

"You didn't answer," says Zoë.

"Answer?"

"You seemed sad when I walked up." She shakes her head. "Never mind. It's none of my business."

"Oh," says Jenn, not certain how much she wants to share with this woman she barely knows, despite having rather intimate knowledge of her vulva. The paradox momentarily distracts Jenn. "Just some jealous feels. Missing someone."

"The jealous feels are very real."

Jenn watches her eat for a moment, remembering the end of their encounter yesterday. Jenn thanked Zoë for her skillful tongue, and Zoë expressed hope that they could have more time together, in some vague and unspecific future.

"Yes," Jenn told her, "there'll be more time."

Today Jenn doubts her answer. "I hope you didn't feel blown off yesterday."

"Blown off?"

"The way I left, after you..."

"Oh! No, no, absolutely not."

"I didn't know if you wanted me to— Right then. Or a strap-on or something."

"Honestly," says Zoë, "my flower is enjoying a nice break."

"Your flower?" Jenn laughs, then covers her mouth. "Sorry, didn't mean—"

"Oh, whatever," she says and waves it off. "It's a silly name. My older sister always called hers that."

"Flower," repeats Jenn.

"Kohl was very enthusiastic the first few nights, both in the pool and the hot tub."

"Aha!" says Jenn, familiar with that rawness.

"Yes," Zoë says, "and when he's drinking, he takes so much longer and forgets lube."

"So it's just all thrusting," comes a voice from behind Jenn. Zoë and Jenn look at each other.

"I'm not eavesdropping," the woman says, "you two are loud, and these tables are too close together."

Jenn turns in her seat and the white-haired woman behind her, sitting alone, grins. Jenn looks back at Zoë and shrugs. "There's room at our table if you'd like to join us."

The woman nods and moves opposite Jenn with her plate of jellied toast. "Debra," she says.

Zoë smiles. "We met at the—"

"Oh yes, speed dating. I apologize, I'm not nearly as good with names as I used to be."

Zoë and Jenn introduce themselves as Debra resumes spreading jelly on her second piece of toast.

"It gets worse as they get older." She leans in and drops her voice. "Gets worse as we get older too. The waterworks get less efficient. We dry up, and they take forever." Debra looks them up and down and shakes her head. "But you've both got a long way before that. You especially, sweetie," she tells Jenn.

"How do you deal with it?" asks Zoë.

"I ride less pole."

The women laugh.

"You know how sometimes lube feels like a luxury right now?" Debra asks.

Jenn nods.

"I think I'm past that stage," says Zoë.

"Well, lube is a fundamental human right and should be applied by the bucketful. Stupid TSA laws or I'd have it in every bag." She lowers her voice again. "Did you know they have lube now with marijuana in it?"

Zoë nods. "Some was going around between the ladies at work."

"Must be a progressive place," says Jenn.

"Oh, it's government, but a building full of scientists is a building full of tryers."

"A government building full of scientists," Debra says, leading toward a question she doesn't ask.

"I try not to talk too much about it. I work for NASA."

Jenn stares at Zoë, the woman who ate her out so magnificently. "NASA! Are you a rocket scientist or something?"

"Aerospace engineer," says Zoë, looking down at her plate.

"Aerospace en— That's a fucking rocket scientist."

"Okay," says Zoë.

"Well," laughs Debra, "here I thought I was bringing the knowledge of age to the table. Didn't know I had to compete with a— A what?"

"Aerospace—"

"Aerospace engineer! Lordy."

Zoë takes a drink and nods, a pained smile on her face. "This is why I don't tell people. Can we go back to talking about pussies, please?"

Debra dabs crumbs off her plate with her last morsel of toast. "Well, that lube with canna...something."

"Cannabidiol," says Zoë.

"Yes, that. It helps. Get some."

"Doesn't really make you high, though," Zoë tells Jenn.

"Does if you use it in your butt!" The old woman winks. "Otherwise take breaks, and don't fuck in the water so much."

"Yes," says Zoë, pointing to Debra. "That. So much that. Hence my flower's hiatus."

Jenn nods.

"That doesn't mean I'd be opposed to reciprocation," says Zoë with a grin.

Jenn smiles back.

"Also," says Debra after a moment of silence, "if you look for the men with smaller dicks. You can fuck more of them."

The women laugh.

"The science on that is sound, I think," says Zoë.

Jenn sees Ryan waving and pointing toward the buffet, but she catches him first with a hug and a kiss.

"You look like you're having an enjoyable morning," he says.

She shrugs.

"Ladies table," he says.

"They're fun." She sighs. "But Paige is on a boat trip with Alejandra."

He nods.

"And I'm feeling complicated things."

"Do you want to talk about them?"

She shakes her head. "No, just wanted you to know about them."

"Okay." He kisses her. "You'll let me know if you need me to beat somebody up."

"Always. Do you want to join us?"

"I'm thinking breakfast on the beach bed, actually."

Jenn smiles. Her husband. Doing things on his own. Unpushed, unburdened. "That sounds nice. You enjoy that."

"Let's have dinner together tonight," he says.

"It's a date."

# 45

# BRUCE

Bruce Shepard has never trusted people who claim their relationships are problem-free, thinking them either bald-faced liars or desperate to cover up their insecurities about very real problems. He has never claimed this about his relationship with Paige as it never has been. Still, those in their orbit, their friends and family, their playmates, often insist otherwise.

*Isn't it harder to deal with problems when people think you're perfect?* He knocks back the shot of tequila and taps the bar next to it. Javier pours another. He lifts the shot to his lips and turns toward the pool before downing it. *Let's stop there, Brucie.* He rolls the pale brown remnants around in the bottom of the shot glass and nods. Great idea. He leans back against the bar and slides his feet through the water around him. "Twenty-five years," he says, in awe of the time. But he and Paige are still children, aren't they? They still go out to play all the time, after all. He can see the years between, all the time. He can see his sons going from diapers to driving permits, and now his youngest is finalizing his college plans. *Jesus. Hunter, going to college now.* He doesn't rail against the march of time. He basks instead in memories of their twenty-five years of marriage, plus a handful of years before that. They were whole, a team, partners, everything, he and Paige. Their problems still seem so insignificant when cast in relief against that timeline. A quarter century.

His own parents barely made it to fifteen, and the family collapsed so spectacularly that he didn't see his siblings after going away to college, not for a while. Paige's parents went strong until her father died at seventy-one. Just over half a century. Now the widow Norton, the matriarch, holds court over the clan of children and grandchildren, and soon a great-grandchild.

Twenty-five years is no accident, nothing to scoff at. It certainly owes an enormous debt to their open marriage.

"Join you?" asks Raymond.

Bruce nods to him, and their host plops his bare behind on the submerged stool next to him.

Raymond asks Javier for a melon ball. "Everything okay?" he asks Bruce. "Heard there was an emergency call last night."

Bruce shrugs and shakes his head. "Today is Paige and my twenty-fifth wedding anniversary."

"Cheers! But that doesn't sound like an emergency."

"Well, as you can see, today I'm sitting alone, present company excluded, while she's off on a boat with someone else because I—"

"You didn't keep your phone in the safe, did you?" Raymond tips his melon ball at Bruce and gives him a look; not accusatory, just knowing. He looks away, at a game of chicken going on at the other end of the pool. When he turns back, his face is grave. "Look, man, I just lost a vital relationship. And who knows how many others along the way."

"I know."

"Last thing I want to see is something external wrecking things for you. Internal conflict, sure, that's an excellent reason to separate, try time apart. Some relationships run their course too, and the participants spend the first half on their way in and the second half on their way out. That's not you."

Bruce shakes his head in agreement.

"Can I join you two?"

He looks up at Ryan and nods wearily. The Lamberts have become their closest friends, but even so, it's hard to let them in all the way. They see so much of the good, but the bad is hidden away, behind the curtains of Oz.

"So," says Ryan dramatically, "why don't you tell me what's going on. You two have been avoiding us since yesterday."

"No," says Bruce. "No, I promise we haven't."

"Then what is it? Seriously. Why did Paige go off on a boat with Alejandra and ditch Jenn on the shore?"

*Crap,* thinks Bruce. That one is hard to dance around. He'd known Paige left early, of course, but not that Jenn had been there to see.

"It's my fault," says Bruce. "I upset Paige. A lot. And she's taking some time away from me."

"On your anniversary."

Bruce nods.

"What'd you do?" demands Ryan, who then seems self-conscious about his tone. His face mellows. "I mean, if you want to talk about it."

Raymond watches the exchange.

"Emily, our ex..."

"From way back?"

Bruce nods.

"She's going through a divorce, she's been texting and call-ing." He looks at Raymond. "Emergency call last night was from her."

Raymond blinks in a way that shows he'd expected the answer.

"She called here?" Ryan's eyes are wide, as though he can't fathom it.

"She got kicked out by her soon-to-be ex-husband. I gave her my credit card number for a hotel."

"Sounds like a savior thing to do," offers Raymond, turning away to sip his melon ball.

"Thank you, Raymond," says Bruce. "I'm aware that I fucked up."

"That sounds like a helpful thing, though," says Ryan.

"Would be, if this wasn't Emily's same old shit and Paige hadn't explicitly asked me not to talk to her this week."

"And her making an emergency call to the resort probably didn't help," says Raymond.

"Oh," says Ryan.

"Unfortunately, now, I get to spend the day of my anniversary in time-out. Thinking about what I've done."

"Can you fix it?" asks Ryan.

Bruce shrugs. "It's done, it's a thing. The fix is about not making it worse. Don't apologize, just don't do it again, right?"

"Should probably stop trying to save Emily," says Raymond.

"You should probably stop moping about Colleen," says Bruce.

Raymond nods. "Touché."

"You two are a fun pair," says Ryan. He looks between the two of them and frowns, folding his arms across his chest. "Look where you are. There are naked women trying to push each other into the water. Everywhere, naked people. Sexy naked people. Smart, geeky, fun naked people! But if you want to boil it down to objectification, we can do that, too! Like bush? There it is. Like bare, we've got that too. Big boobs, small boobs, perfect handfuls. Glasses. Blonde, brunette, redhead. I mean, look at that redhead!"

Bruce follows Ryan's finger to the other end of the bar where the petite redhead who Bruce met as both Lena and Kitten lies on her back on the granite bar top. Javier runs a line of chocolate syrup from her sternum, a figure eight around each nipple, down to her vulva. Then he pours a brown drink out of his cocktail shaker into her belly button. Three women descend on her, licking, sucking, drinking.

"All I'm saying is, there are worse places in the world to be a fuck up," Ryan continues, not taking his eyes off Kitten's giggling face. She looks up and makes eye contact with the three men.

"Ah, to be a young swinger again," says Raymond, and he toasts Ryan with the remains of his melon ball. "I used to be fun, a long time ago..."

"Oh, stop feeling sorry for yourselves," says Ryan. "As a subscriber to the grand tradition of feeling sorry for myself, I get it. I also know that there's little less attractive than people feeling sorry for themselves. Which makes me think you both ought to knock it the fuck off."

Bruce stares at Ryan, finding it hard to believe this is the same man he counseled about jealousy in his living room. The one he talked through various meltdowns. "You know, there's a nice way to say all that," he says, unable to bring himself to acknowledge Ryan's rightness.

"Fine, here: It'll probably be okay. You and Paige have twenty-five years of inertia if nothing else, and I think you've got a lot of 'else' on top of that. You, Raymond, I don't really know other than your videos...but what would *you* say if someone was moping about whatever the way you are."

Bruce can't help but offer, "His ex."

Raymond sips his drink.

"Some of us can't afford frequent trips here. Especially if Jenn can't get a job quickly. But we're trying to leave that at home and wring out every bit of awesome this place has to offer. It might help, if you tried to do the same."

"It might at that," says Bruce.

"But," adds Ryan, toasting toward the men with his own tumbler, "twenty-five years is a very long time, excellent, and should be commended."

Bruce returns the toast, scrambled flashes of the twenty-five years in his head. Paige in white, red roses in her hands, walking down the aisle of her parent's church. They'd believed *something* then, though it hadn't been capital G God. But they'd known the value of keeping one's family happy with little discomfort. Is that it? The secret? A little personal discomfort is sometimes all it takes to keep family, friends, partners happy. The look on Paige's face the first time she watched someone go down on him. Her expression the perfect mixture of awe and wonder and lust. Hunger. Hunger to share. Their first threesome. Picking up a unicorn in the wild.

Emily, of course. She was more than a playmate – she was a fixture for a while. She became a part of the family. She woke up with them in the morning after fucking them silly the night before. So unique to their habits, unique to the swing. Plucking a relationship from nowhere.

The years after her departure had been hard, with a few ill-advised attempts at replacement, to fill the hole she'd left. No one fit, but really no one could fit. When you have a spot to fill, you're defining boundaries instead of building a relationship. And wasn't it about pushing boundaries? Escaping boxes? Expanding, growing?

Jennifer, now Jenn, came the closest to filling that hole for Paige, after they stopped looking. Then Emily leaped back in, as though she knew they were finally getting over her, and wreaked devastation.

"How does she keep grabbing hold of me?" asks Bruce to the two men sitting with him.

"Sometimes we hold on to people because they remind us of a better time," Raymond suggests. "Emily was a tremendous part of your life. But she's not that anymore. She's divorcing, which is hard. She's needy, which is hard. But even if she walked back in, right now, today, and everything was fine with Paige and you, and all bad feelings were wiped away, these things usually don't fit back together." He frowns and looks away from them. "Sometimes things just were, and they can't be again."

"Do you guys wanna help clean me off?" calls Kitten from the bar. Her torso and mouth are smeared with chocolate.

"No thanks," says Raymond. He taps his chest, adding, "Anhedonia." She frowns and blinks back at him as he gives her a big photo-worthy grin.

"What's anhedonia?"

"Sorry, my dear," he says. "I have things to set up!"

Bruce also shakes his head, still considering Raymond's suggestion.

Ryan looks from one man to the other.

"Just because *we're* moping doesn't mean *you* should turn down an invitation like that," says Bruce.

"Watch out, though – they broadcast everything on their show," adds Raymond, putting his index finger to the side of his nose.

Ryan nods. He fixes his eyes on Bruce and puts his hand on his shoulder. "It's going to be okay," he tells Bruce. At this moment, Bruce kind of believes it.

Ryan heads down the bar to lick chocolate off a petite podcaster.

# 46

# CRISTA

With Allie by her side, wandering through Aphrodite's – hanging out, just being – still caused intense anxiety for Crista. What did the people around her think of her? What did they want from her? Now, without Allie, she finds herself in a constant game of avoidance. At the bar, in the courtyard, at lunch, it seems that everyone, even people uninterested in play, make small talk at any opportunity. It's all a distraction, though, from thinking about yesterday. The damage is significant, maybe greater than she can patch. She lies on their beach bed after lunch, her tablet in front of her face but turned off, just a buffer discouraging the banality of talk without purpose.

*Who'd want to talk to someone with that attitude, anyway?* she asks herself.

Occasionally she glances over the top of the tablet, out at the vast plane of blue in front of her, interrupted by naked people nearby, snorkel boats out at the break, a line of sails just in front of the horizon, the hulking cruise ships at the edge of the world. She imagines she can see the Aphrodite's logo on one of the sails but knows that's folly from this distance. Allie is out there, though, on a catamaran that launched from this beach, right over there. Crista wonders if she's out there by herself, or if she's invited others to her boating party. Others who might match her energy and enthusiasm. Others who might have a handle on their fucking libido. Others who know what they're doing, who know themselves, who don't fade into the background at the slightest opportunity and hide from the wonders on display.

Her wife has never quite understood Crista's introversion, the way quiet contemplation often does more for her problem-solving than discussion. It's probably for the best that Allie has taken the boat trip without her. Gives them both some space and distance.

She feels exposed here on the beach. Do the people strolling in the water, the ones at the bar down the way, know? Know how she fucked up. Will they whisper, and point, and talk about how the lesbians' relationship blew up yesterday and now the hot one is off on a boat trip without the other one?

The hot one and the other one. The hot one and the plain one. No one has said it. The phrase exists entirely within her head. But Allie is tall and gorgeous. The flowing hair, the mesmerizing eyes. "Cleavage for days," Crista whispers to herself and laughs. And here, on this resort, without clothes getting in the way, it's easy to see that forty-two years have been incredibly kind to Alejandra Vargas.

And in this corner? Plain Crista Norris. Slender to the point of skinny, breasts that barely fill an A cup, a dusting of freckles, dull eyes and duller hair. Exactly the kind of person who fades into the background. The introvert's super power. She has spent a lifetime using plain to her advantage. In high school and college, people underestimated her and thus were always more impressed by her work than they might have been otherwise. As a reporter in the field, she blended. When people talked to her, they felt comfortable. No one is truly candid with someone significantly hotter than themselves.

Crista sees Beth walking down the beach, as naked as the last time she saw her, and the woman seems to have found more sun since speed dating. Her shoulders and the tops of her breasts are the shade of pink that means a painful morning shower. Her ponytail is pushed through the back of a black Xanadu cap. Beth may be hiding her eyes behind sunglasses, but Crista knows when she's being observed. Beth hesitates once, twice. Briefly stops and looks out at the water.

Crista smiles. She's seen this behavior before, from people who have stories to tell that scare them, things they're not sure they should say to her. Beth has something to say that she's uncertain about, and Crista would be lying if she tried to convince herself she isn't interested in what that might be. Instead of waiting, Crista lowers her tablet and looks directly at Beth, who is all *um*s and stops, standing between the bed and the horizon. Talk that's anything but small. An actual distraction, perhaps, to take Crista away from her thoughts.

"You look like you want to ask me something. If the question is where Alejandra is, I, unfortunately—"

"No, I was looking for you, specifically."

Crista blinks at her. "What can I do for you?"

"I know that sometimes lesbians don't like to play with women who've never been with other women before."

"It's more that they don't like to *date* women who've never been with other women before, because they're more likely to just be exploring and go back to the default."

"Default," Beth says, flatly, though Crista hears the noninflected question mark.

"Default is usually hetero. If there's a gray area, anyway. People drift toward the norm, not the fringe." Crista gives her a lopsided smile, hoping she hasn't just ruined this conversation by ignoring the obvious reason Beth has come wandering.

Crista has done some wandering and drifting herself, too, hasn't she? Before Allie, there'd been women, sure, but not girlfriends. Lovers, not relationships. They'd often been accompanied by men who would push to be included. The hetero dream, the FFM threesome. Punctuated by double blowjobs and men unable to fuck both thanks to lack of orgasm control.

"Would you like to. Come back to my room?" asks Beth, stilted. "Or we could get a drink first."

Crista smiles at Beth, though it is a façade at first. How nice it feels to be asked, not as a couple, but her, specifically. Beth had sought *her* out, not The Lesbians, not Allie, but her. How nice it'd be to check out of her brain for a while. Disappearing into a dark, chilly air-conditioned room sounds like an excellent alternative to the afternoon heat, quickly approaching the nineties. A creeping question, though: is she deserving of the reprieve? That responsive sex drive kicks into gear. Could she both get laid and hide at once? How appealing. "Why don't we grab drinks and go to your room."

Beth nods enthusiastically, relief crossing her face. She stands taller. As they wait for Celia to produce a rum punch for Crista and a Hurricane Aphrodite for Beth, they go over the necessary precautionary measures and testing. Beth and her husband have had little experience sexually beyond each other, and both were tested the week before the trip.

*They don't even get cold sores!* marvels Crista.

"And we brought a roll of saran wrap, 'cuz we heard on *Swingerqatsi* that it's good for oral sex with women."

"It is indeed," says Crista with a slight laugh.

Beth's room is chilly and dark, and Crista stands in the darkness for a moment as her host scrambles to figure out why the light doesn't turn on when she flips the switch. She snaps another one in the corner, and the white room glows brightly.

"Would, um," Beth looks away again, "would you mind if my husband watches?"

Crista shakes her head. At this point, she's been watched by countless husbands and boyfriends, as she and Allie treat their partners to orgasms in ways they've often never heard of. "Fine with me. Just so—" she stops, realizing she's about to slam down their lesbian swinger caveat. *He's not touching me.* It's strange, without Allie here, to say that, to be firm. Instead, Crista asks "But it's just you and I, right?"

"Oh, yeah," Beth says. "He loves to watch me, and he'd love to watch us together."

Crista nods.

Beth goes to the door and waves Andy in. He's long and lanky, a sheepish smile on his face. He gestures silently to the couch and looks at them. Beth gives him an emphatic nod, and he sits. His dick juts from a patch of light brown hair between his legs, quite a bit larger than at speed dating, though she imagines that's to be expected. They are rather unpredictable, if she remembers correctly. And this one seems to only be about half way there.

The women begin kissing, heavy, intense. Crista wonders if Beth is trying to kiss like a man. As they sit on the edge of the bed, their hands explore a little, Beth cupping one of Crista's breasts, then the other, then back to the first. *Second verse, same as the first.* Crista thinks about how rarely she's the one leading the exploration. It's Allie, always Allie, full of "Okay, now let's..." and "I have an idea."

Channeling her wife, she takes Beth's hand and slides it between her legs. Beth cups her vulva and pubic mound, but remains motionless. They stop kissing, and Crista looks into her eyes, green, nervous. "It's okay."

"It's okay," repeats Beth, seeming entirely unconvinced.

"Treat mine the way you like yours to be treated." The words appear without forethought, and Crista hears them echo back to her, sounding like her college roommate, who said those words initially, who told her that it was a bad idea before sticking her tongue down Crista's throat, then taught her how to play with a pussy that didn't belong to her. It had indeed been a bad idea, and a cold war followed after a couple months. The back half of freshman year had been quite difficult. The orgasms, as she explored others, reminded her why it had been worth it.

Here and now, Beth slides two fingers inside her, making Crista wonder when she'd managed to get lube. She gasps as her G-spot begins to awaken, feeling the early tingles. She should tell Beth, though, so there won't be hard feelings.

"I probably won't come from that," she says.

"Do you want me to stop?"

"No," says Crista, "please continue, just don't expect..."

"I don't expect anything at all," says Beth.

Crista lets go of a knot inside that she hadn't noticed before. How nice it is to find someone without expectations. After a while, they progress to oral, Beth insisting that she's more comfortable on the bottom. They pull off two sheets of plastic wrap, and Crista rubs lube all around Beth's bare vulva and surrounding area. "To help stick the wrap to you," she says and Beth nods, wide-eyed.

When she climbs on top of Beth, she realizes that the couple inches of height difference positions her vulva perfectly in front of Beth's face, rather than atop. "You double tap me, if you can't breathe or need anything," says Crista, then double taps Beth's left butt cheek.

Beth taps an affirmative and then slowly slides her tongue along Crista's vulva through the saran wrap. Crista shudders. She pulls the wrap tight against Beth's pussy and licks and sucks. Very shortly Beth begins to buck her hips and moan against Crista's pussy. Crista wraps her arms around the woman's thighs, taking it as a personal challenge to continue.

After the bucking ceases, Crista looks up. Andy, still across the room on the couch, wears a grin that seems to consume the entire bottom half of his face. He strokes his dick briskly, tugging it downward, toward the floor.

Crista watches, then whispers. "Do you think he'd want to fuck you with me here?"

A garbled but incredibly enthusiastic, "Yes!" drifts back up to her.

To be a part of this couple's big moment, to let them reconnect in the middle, that gives Crista a thrill. She might have royally fucked her own relationship over in the last few days, but today she could be here for this, and isn't that something? "Would you like to fuck her?" Crista asks Andy.

A vigorous nod, then he bolts to a standing position, hand still gripping his dick, and moves to the edge of the bed.

Crista peels back the plastic wrap from Beth's vulva, keeping the top portion in place so she can continue. His dick seems huge, and she wonders if it's truly as big as it appears to her, or if she just hasn't been this close to a dick in a while. Beth's licking intensity halts as Andy slides into her. Once he reaches near full insertion, she begins to lick again.

Andy looks down and whispers to Crista, "Can I put my hand on your arm? I don't know if I'm supposed to touch you or not."

"You can touch me," says Crista, "just not—" She stops, unsure what she was going to say. Beth's intensity is just right, the clit focus even better. "This is you and your wife, not you and us."

"Got it," says Andy, and with his hand gently and barely on Crista's shoulder, he begins to fuck his wife.

Crista watches the act, marveling at the close-up, that she gets to witness this incredibly personal thing from this vantage point, merely an inch away. She runs her tongue in circles around Beth's clit, feeling the bucking ebb and flow, watching Andy's long penis disappear and reappear again and again. Mesmerizing. So close she could lick it if she wanted to. But she doesn't want to, of course. Right? Crista lifts her head up, pulling back.

"Everything okay?" asks Andy quietly.

"Yep," says Crista. She rolls off Beth to the other side of the bed. Beth turns to look at her, eyes going from wide and concerned to closed and orgasmic and back.

"Are you—"

"I'm good," says Crista. "I'd like to just watch you two, if that's okay. My body is..."

They both nod, and after another moment of looking at Crista, they turn their focus toward each other.

She watches them fuck. Watches Beth come twice more while rubbing her fingers around and over her clit. Crista notices the dimples in Andy's skinny butt as he gasps through his own orgasm. Beginning inside, then pulling out to shoot his cum onto her belly.

Crista can smell the salty, sweaty scent from across the bed.

"Thank you," says Beth, after several heaving breaths.

"Yeah, that was probably the sexiest thing I've gotten to do since we started," says Andy.

"My pleasure, you sexy people," Crista tells them. As she leaves their room later, she begins to wonder exactly what her pleasure is.

## 47

# RYAN

"She likes it when you stick your tongue in her ass," says the whisper.

Ryan freezes, his tongue in a puddle of espresso martini in the navel of a petite redhead, unsure how to respond to this information. He's not about to stick his tongue into the ass of a woman he hasn't said more than a handful of words to, and certainly not at the recommendation of the man grinning at him as he turns from Kitten. Strom waggles his eyebrows Groucho style.

Javier says, "Neeeples!" and squeezes two dark chocolate syrup rings around Kitten's very hard nipples.

Kitten calls, "Woo!" and turns her head toward Ryan. "Help a gal out?" she asks him with a smile.

He returns the smile, and lightly licks his lips. He would indeed like to help a gal out.

"Lick it all," says Strom, dropping his voice back into a skeezy whisper.

"Dude!" says Ryan.

Kitten's lips drop in a pout.

"What?" Strom asks him.

"You're being very pushy!"

"Don't you want to lick her nipples?"

"I—"

"I'm just asking."

"I think I'll let someone else have a turn," says Ryan. Before he leaves the bar, he bends down to Kitten and says, "Thank you for the invitation."

"You're invited for more," Kitten tells him. "A kiss before you go?"

Ryan kisses her, tasting the chocolate on his lips, the mango drink on hers. Then he makes his way deeper into the pool, where he sees his wife talking to a couple. She laughs broadly, throwing her head back. On the prowl. He approaches slowly. He can't clearly see the woman; she is eclipsed by the man, leaving only two small nipples to indicate her presence beyond him. Jenn touches the man's arm. He clearly lifts weights. His chest is bare and shows off lines of definition. His jaw is solid, with a few day's growth of salty beard. His dark hair hangs to his shoulders.

Ryan pauses, wondering why he's so focused on this man. He asks himself the important question: Is this man attractive? He stares. *Or am I just trying to find him attractive?* He supposes that trying to force attraction might be a bit foolish, but how bad could it be? Bottom line, though, this man, while attractive, isn't necessarily attractive to him.

The one that is attractive to him, or at least intriguing, in that subtle rumble sort of way, is Rory of the triad. As if on cue, Rory and Terrence sit down on the edge of the pool. "Well, that's just obnoxious timing, isn't it?" says Ryan under his breath.

He looks back at his wife and the couple. The man is laughing, and finally moves back slightly. Ryan sees the woman next to him, recognizing her magenta mohawk and nose ring immediately. He wouldn't have paired Sonja with this man, though. "Huh," he says out loud. He thinks Sonja told him her husband's name during their short hot tub conversation, but he cannot remember it.

He looks back over to the side of the pool where Rory and Terrence sit. Terrence runs his fingers up and down Rory's leg as they talk. They point at various people in the pool. Ryan notices that both of their cocks are poking straight out from their laps. He could walk over there, right now. Walk over and say something. Suggest that his ambiguous, "to be continued," with Rory the other day could be continued now. Or, if not now, soon. They're there on their own, after all. No one talking them up.

Ryan moves toward them. He hears Jenn's laugh and pauses, looking back. His wife wears an enormous smile on her face and is failing miserably to cover it with her hand. *So demure*, he thinks. Sonja whispers into Jenn's ear, and she laughs again. Ryan smiles wide himself, lost in the one on Jenn's face. She holds eye contact with the man, and Sonja's arm is around her waist, chin on her shoulder.

Turning back toward the pair of men on the edge of the pool, he catches Rory looking at him. Rory winks in his direction, and something in the pit of Ryan's stomach rumbles so suddenly that he wonders if it's the fabled Montezuma's Revenge. He tries to remember if he accidentally drank any of the tap water. Maybe brushing his teeth. The heat in his cheeks indicates something else, though. He waves offhandedly back at Rory and heads again toward his wife.

What the hell was that? Whatever it was, it still holds space in his stomach and chest, a tightness he can't fully identify but doesn't like. *Maybe I'm not quite ready for that,* he thinks. Ready or not, though, he ought to try to control his facial expressions around people who've shown interest. He nods and turns back toward Rory with a grin. Rory nods back. Ryan points discretely toward Jenn. Rory nods again, then holds up his empty wrist and points at it. *I know!* mouths Ryan.

Turning back toward Jenn and the couple lessens the pressure. At the very least, he hopes he hasn't given Rory the impression that their interaction terrifies him. *This'll be another hold my breath and jump thing, won't it?* Ryan asks himself, knowing the answer. It's so new, so different. Perhaps even more different than watching Jennifer suck Bruce's cock for the first time.

"You look deep in thought," says Kendra, running her finger along his arm.

He turns to look at her. Her smile is genuine but barely hides her worry. Her blonde hair has gone dark from the water, plastered to the sides of her face and neck. Her pendulous breasts are buoyant in the pool, and he feels a tug of interest. "Yeah," he says, not holding her look, glancing toward Jenn and the couple.

"Tell me about it," says Kendra, mirroring another conversation between the two of them, another time he looked deep in thought. He came over for their every-other-Tuesday date and sat on the couch without saying anything. She asked him to tell her about it. At first, he didn't. With enough prodding,

Kendra using some of her therapist phrases to draw him out, he spilled.

"I don't think this is working for me anymore."

She flashed between the professional and the personal. Both coexisting on her face, then neither. Then she haltingly asked him, "Tell me more about that."

In a fit of stops and starts, he told her what was on his mind. "It always just feels so...unfinished."

"Unfinished," she said, "because we don't do penetration."

He felt heat in his cheeks but nodded anyway. It *was* how he felt, after all.

"And you want to stop?" The irritation in her voice was loud and clear despite her apparent desire to hide it.

He didn't really want to stop, he wanted to advance, wanted them to move beyond soft swap to full. Mostly he just wondered what it'd be like to fuck Kendra. Lay her down, spread her legs and feel her fully. He knew it was selfish and petty. He didn't want to say that, and, attempting to avoid the pressure of "next level" talk, he let out the petty instead. "And the drive over here is..."

"Is what?"

Ryan frowned. He should stop there. Should absolutely *not* say the rest of that sentence. But he did, regretting it as he went. "So long." Her face changed, surprise in her eyes. That phrase, so innocuous, changed things. They stopped dating.

"I feel like I should try something new, but it's scary," he tells her, months removed now, in the pool.

She nods. "I feel the same," she says and smiles. She mouths *full swap*.

*Oh, yeah, right!* The conversation they haven't had. Might need to have it sooner than later, if he doesn't handle this—

"What do you want to try?"

He's not certain he wants to tell her, or anyone, really. It's a massive thing, a scary thing. He waffles. "Oh, a few different things. Some BDSM, some other stuff."

"What's holding you back?"

"You know me," he says.

"I do," she agrees, letting her hand drop beneath the surface of the water and brush against his cock.

"Have you found some fun here?" he asks, pulling himself back a touch, not enough to be noticeable, he hopes.

"Oh, yeah," she says, "but we're still waiting for the main event."

"Main—"

She mouths *full swap* again, and Ryan wonders why she won't say it aloud, here of all places. In a pool at a resort full of swingers. She'd had no problem interrupting their dinner with it the other night!

"Yeah, right," he says and desperately looks toward Jenn. She's in the middle of a deep kiss with Sonja, whose husband stands behind her, kissing the buzzed portion of her head. He wants to be over there, to be a part of that. Or over with Rory. Hell, anywhere else, just to not have to say, "I don't know if we really are on board with that."

Kendra's smile vanishes. "I thought that's what you wanted."

"What?"

"I thought that's why you stopped dating me!"

Ryan glances around to see if others have heard, are looking. "That's not—"

"Too far to go to not get to fuck me, I think it was." She folds her arms and cocks her head.

"Look," he says, then can't figure out how to follow that.

"Look," she repeats, mimicking his tone perfectly. "I'm waiting. Tell me more about that." The phrase sounds exceptionally pointed here.

He should tell her more about that, shouldn't he? Ryan feels the dam crumble then break. "Look, you can't just decide that you're going to go full swap with us!" He's sure he's speaking louder than he ought to.

She frowns.

"I mean, you have to see the pressure that puts on us. Here, on our vacation, surrounded by people. You've decided for us! Decided something's going to happen without asking first. Tell me you see that's unfair!"

"I see how you might feel that way," she allows, begrudgingly.

He hears a sigh escape his lips. "It's not that we don't wa—"

"No, it's fine, Ryan." She holds her hand up.

"I'm just trying to be hon—"

"Honest, yes," she says. She looks down and away for a moment, then back up at him. Her smile doesn't appear genuine. "Thank you for your honesty."

He opens his mouth to reply, but she's already turned and is making her way back toward the bar. Vince, sitting near Bruce and Raymond, gives her a smile that gradually fades.

"Well, shit," says Ryan quietly. He glances to where Rory and Terrence were sitting, but the men are gone. When he looks back toward his wife, she waves him over. He takes a deep breath, puts on a smile, and drifts in her direction.

# 48

# ALEJANDRA

"I have to ask," says Paige to Alejandra. "What is a 'gold star lesbian?'"

Alejandra looks up. From this vantage point, her companion is all pale skin and breasts. She lifts her head off Paige's torso and moves to a sitting position. "A gold star lesbian," says Alejandra, pausing a moment.

"Yes, it's something I've heard you say," says Paige.

"It's a lesbian who has never been with a man."

"Aha. No experimentation, no early straight phases."

"Exactly."

Paige nods. "Huh." She stares at her for a moment, looks out at the ocean and shrugs.

"What?" laughs Alejandra.

"So, you've never had any interest in men?"

"Academically?"

"Physically."

"No."

"No?"

"No." Alejandra, feeling a little self-conscious, looks at Hector, the only representation of manhood in sight, with his thin mustache and dark skin. His muscles strain against his white polo. "Nothing."

He notices her looking and nods, flicking his first two fingers off his forehead in a quick salute. She smiles back at him. "I see it, aesthetically," Alejandra admits, "but no. Men are rough and smell funny, all sharp angles. And I don't have to explain my sexuality!"

"No, you don't," says Paige, smiling wide. "Not in the least. I was just curious."

The smile cools Alejandra's defenses. She breathes for a moment.

"Touchy subject?" asks Paige.

"In this lifestyle, people are always trying to convince me that if I were truly open, I'd be able to play with a dick and not mind."

"Not mind."

"Yeah! I want to ask them if they think so little of themselves that they want to do something with someone who just 'doesn't mind' it."

Paige shrugs. "I think it's rather easy to find people who don't practice mindful swinging. I've seen plenty over the years."

*Mindful swinging.* Alejandra chews on the phrase for a moment.

"I won't fuck anyone if it's not a full-throated joyful 'fuck yeah,' you know?" Paige sighs. "Not worth my time. I'm going to be fifty next year."

"No, you're not," Alejandra says. There's no way the woman in front of her is that old. Not. A. Chance.

"Oh stop," Paige says, poking Alejandra's side.

"You don't—"

"Let's not play those games out here on the ocean. I think we're both clearly attracted to each other, and I imagine that neither of us particularly likes compliments..." Paige pulls down her sunglasses to reveal sea foam blue eyes.

"True."

"So, let's not do it. Let's accept the mutual attraction and not feel the need to dress it up and take it for fancy dinner to impress it."

Alejandra laughs. "Fair enough. Though I'm shocked to hear you're fifty. And I would say so even if I weren't trying to get... well, not *into your panties*, because you're not wearing any."

"I'm not."

"Me neither. I'll also just say that I have not once, in my entire life, thought that I'd like to take one of those dicks and put them inside me. Not in my mouth, my vagina, or my ass. Not once." She realizes the caveat. "I mean, specifically, the ones attached to men. If a woman is wearing a glittery blue or purple dong, I'm quite a fan of putting those inside me."

"Shame we didn't bring one," says Paige.

"Who says we didn't?" asks Alejandra, reaching over to her tote bag. She lifts the flap slightly, giving Paige the briefest glimpse of a purple dong and leather harness inside.

"Seems you had something planned for today. Besides licking each other while Hector watches."

Hector glances at them. "*¿Sí? ¿Necesita algo?*"

"We're good, Hector. *Estamos muy contentas.*" Alejandra smiles at him, and he smiles back.

"Okee dokee," he says and gives them a thumbs up.

"How much of that do you think he sees out here?"

"Last year we caught Celia, from the beach bar, on her way out of the resort for the night and asked her to get a drink. Off resort, of course," says Paige. "She told us stories about people trying to get her to have sex with them, of people flagrantly disregarding the rules. People fucking on the lobby bar. Anal sex on the beach. I mean, Alejandra, tell me, who the hell has anal sex on the beach?"

"A genuinely exfoliating experience."

Paige laughs and lays back, resting her head on one of the life jackets they'd bribed Hector not to require them to use. He'd been insistent that they bring them, of course. "I can't imagine eschewing dick forever."

"Good thing no one's asking you to," says Alejandra.

"True!" Paige says. "That said, I definitely skew more toward woman. Wasn't always that way, but opening up helped adjust my focus."

"Seems to be a common theme."

"Monogamy doesn't usually allow for experimentation with sexuality."

"It doesn't."

"The strongest relationships I've had since we opened up have been with women."

"See," says Alejandra, "women are awesome!" Her grin hardens a bit as she remembers why she's out here with Paige and not her wife.

A sly smile crosses Paige's face. "But the best I've ever been fucked was by a man."

"Bruce?"

"Nathan Fullerton," Paige says, her expression turning wistful, eyebrows up, the fingers of her left hand tracing circles around her nipples.

"I thought the unspoken lifestyle rule is that the best sex is always with your partner."

"Let me be very clear, Bruce is a fantastic lover. He's stunning with his tongue, and with his hands, and he knows exactly what to do with his cock."

Alejandra stares at her, smiling. It's refreshing to hear such honesty. In the clubs she and Crista have been to, and with the couples they've been out with, she's always found it hard to open up, really connect with anyone on a level beyond sex. People are liable to say anything they think you want to hear if it means they might get to fuck you. And, she reluctantly admits, Paige's enthusiasm for the male member certainly does make it sound good. But gold star is gold star, and after being phallus-free for over fifteen thousand days, it seems like it'd be such a cop out to touch one now. Besides, she doesn't really *want* to. Interesting, maybe; enticing, no. Not something she much wants to consider longer. "Was it just that once? Your shining time?"

"We've played a few times, but very rarely. He and his wife are incredibly busy. He's bi, though, and Bruce is sorta...situationally bi."

"I've met women like that. We tend to avoid them."

"Ah, yes, but when you're a rare bi man, situational bi is like a bounty bestowed upon the right connections. Haven't seen them since early last year. Had some fun at a party." She smiles again, a wistful hand tugging at her fiery bush.

"How about the best experience with a woman?"

"That's tougher," says Paige. "Some of my best experiences were the firsts with..." She waves her hand dismissively.

"Emily."

"Yeah. A lot of emotion caught up with that."

"Sorry," says Alejandra, regretting having brought it up.

"Nah," says Paige. She expels a long sigh. "Emily was, to speak in clichés, a firecracker. She's the one I'd get carried away with in a bar. One time she ate me out under the table at a TGI Fridays. I came just as our waitress asked if there was anything else she could do for me." Paige's focus drifts again, out over the water. "I'm very lucky right now. Bruce, when he's not an idiot, is a wonderfully considerate partner. And Jenn. It's like she spends our entire time together, both sexual and romantic, trying to impress me."

"I noticed that about her," says Alejandra, thinking about that play time on night one. When things had still been good. Before the crash.

"I tell her it's not necessary, that she can just do what she likes, but still she tries to outdo herself." Paige wipes at her eyes beneath her sunglasses. "I should've asked her to come with us. I just needed... It wasn't my place to invite, and I needed some time without anyone I'm in a relationship with..."

Alejandra reaches out and puts her hand near Paige's, close enough to bump fingers. Close enough for an invitation. Paige takes it, grasping her hand.

Looking out on the ocean, Alejandra remembers how Crista had yearned to impress her, early on, trying new things every time they were together, working her ass off to get Alejandra to come.

"I haven't been doing this as long," Crista said. "I need to catch up." Then, smiling, she dove back into Alejandra's pussy, licking and sucking with wild abandon.

That night, their first night, Alejandra came more than she ever had with another woman. She didn't count her solo time with the magic wand because, well, no one was that good. But the enthusiasm of this young woman, this award-winning journalist with her ugly-as-sin acrylic flame sitting on the hotel room desk, using her fingers and tongue and face, was stunning. By the end of that evening, Alejandra was already beginning to fall in love, despite all her internal caution alarms blaring.

"Would you like to go on a date?" Crista asked as they dressed the following morning. "Not for another two weeks, 'cuz I'm going to the Vatican."

"To atone?" laughed Alejandra.

"I don't much do atonement, but I'd happily flick my bean while thinking of you."

"In the Vatican? How wonderfully wicked."

"You didn't answer my question," Crista said, eyes full of caution as she pulled a shirt over her head.

"I would love to go on a date with you when you return from the Vatican." Alejandra reached out and caught the bottom hem of Crista's shirt, lifting it to reveal a curly brown patch. She looked in Crista's eyes, then back to her vulva. "When do you have to leave?"

Crista threw a nervous glance at the bedside alarm clock. "I need to be in the lobby in seventeen minutes."

"Then sit on my face."

The happenstance of it all. Alejandra almost hadn't attended the banquet, had only done so on a whim, and for the food, and so she could get a little more info from a journalist friend of hers about a potential opening at CNN. And then there she was in a suite the morning after, Crista's vulva blooming like a flower above her face, already bright red from all the attention. A bead of nectar stretched from one lip to the other, and suddenly there was nothing Alejandra wanted more in the world than to drink deep. The taste was heavenly.

Dressing fourteen minutes later, Crista hastily threw out her caveats. "You should know I've not really...dated women."

"That's okay, I imagine you're busy."

"I am tremendously busy. But that's not what I mean. I haven't dated women because," she frowned, "because I haven't met many women. To date."

"That's okay," said Alejandra.

"Look," said Crista, scrunching her face, "I've dated both, and the women have been less frequent. But I'm looking for women right now."

"Okay," said Alejandra, squinting, a warning bell sounding. *Bi girl.* The kind that'll love you and leave you as soon as a husband in the suburbs presents himself. But it wasn't as though she'd had a whole lot of reliable lesbian women to date lately, was it?

"Is that okay?" asked Crista.

Alejandra agreed it was okay, and they were out of the door.

She sighs, loudly enough to rouse Paige from her perch on the side of the boat.

"Heavy thoughts for you too, eh?" asks Paige.

She nods. "Was hoping the boat would clear my head." She looks down. "But having you here has been..."

"I get it," says Paige.

They smile at each other, mutually agreeing to keep avoiding the sources of those heavy thoughts for a little longer. Paige glances at the tote bag mischievously and raises an eyebrow. Alejandra raises one back at her.

"The question is," asks Paige, "who gets to wear the cock?"

"Dealer's choice," says Alejandra, hoping Paige will want to wear it. Hoping she can lay back and feel. Hoping Paige will hold down her wrists, bite her neck, and *fuck* her. She watches, rapt, as Paige pulls the leather straps up her legs, carefully tightens them, then kneels in front of her with eight inches of purple dong jutting from her leather covered pubis.

Alejandra spreads her legs and takes every inch.

To the hilt.

# 49

# JENN

"Okay," says Brooke, "no one can sit next to their partner." She is unrelentingly perky, with dark reddish-brown hair. Jenn has a vague sense that she's lusted in the woman's direction, possibly in the hot tub, but she doesn't remember having interacted with her before this. Brooke's hands are up, fingers spread wide, as she tries to hold the attention of the four couples, all milling in a crowded open area next to the large round table in the back of La Grande Fête.

Jenn feels Ryan squeeze her hand.

They could still bail, couldn't they? Bail and find comfort with people they know. But who? Paige is God knows where. Bruce seems glued to a seat at the pool's bar. Vince and Kendra? She doesn't want to open that door. Jenn sighs.

"Preferably sit next to someone you don't already know," Brooke continues. "It just works better that way. Though I know with a group this size that's more difficult, I think each couple here only has a single connection to the whole."

*We don't get to sit together or with Kyler and Sonja?* thinks Jenn. She knows it's an attempt to force the mixer, getting people outside their comfort zones, but would it be so terrible if they just sat next to Kyler and Sonja, with their perfect hair? Would it? Jenn looks at their new friends, who'd invited them to dinner, then at the rest of her potential dinner companions, Brooke and her husband, and a dark-haired uncomfortable-looking couple.

The decision is made for her as the couples begin to slide in around the table. Jenn and Ryan are the last two to sit, only air between them thanks to the gap in the round bench surrounding the table. Ryan sits next to Brooke, who is talking about how many times she and her husband have been to the resort. Jenn's neighbor is the man of the dark haired, nervous people. She plasters a smile on her face. This will be fine. She looks at Ryan, finding a similarly forced and nervous smile on his as well.

"This is one of our traditions," says Brooke. "We invite and ask others to invite, so it spreads out like a whip. I'd love it if we all could say our names, our relationships, our Aphrodite's status, and one interesting thing about ourselves."

Jenn takes a deep breath, thinking she'll likely either be first or last. *First or last, Jenn? Well, first means people might have forgotten you by the end, but last has to live up to all the other—*

"Jenn," she says, making the decision subconsciously. "Husband is Ryan." She points at him. "By Aphrodite's status, you mean—"

"How often you've been here," says Brooke.

"This is our first time," says Jenn.

The man next to her leans over, she can smell his aftershave. It's musky, but not overbearing. "Ours too," he confesses.

"We're swingers, but do some poly too. Interesting thing..." Her mind goes blank. She scans the table top, seeing the butter and salt and pepper, water glasses and wine glasses. The light twinkles in what might be crystal, but is probably just glass. The white of the table linens seems so bright. What's interesting about her? That she's a squirter? Half the women here are squirters. That she's bi? Jeez Louise, you couldn't be less interesting than that. That she— *Fuck*. "I was fired after a unicorn we fucked sent a picture of her and I to my HR department. Morality clause." She puts on a tight-lipped smile, then slowly takes a sip of her water while her dining companions react with a mixture of platitudes and shock. She feels so exposed now that they know. She crosses her arms over her scoop neck, hiding her cleavage because she *can* hide that. *Can't hide from the truth about work, though. Not when we're the ones talking about it, can we?* She feels Ryan's foot find hers under the table and breathes out slowly. She flicks her eyes toward him and winks. *Everything's fine.* He smiles back. She turns her attention to the man next to her, with close-cropped salt and pepper hair just beginning to recede. It looks good on him, and his round face is warm.

"David," he says. He gestures toward the dark-haired woman across the table. "My wife, Mona. Been married since 1990, swinging since," he pauses and locks narrowed eyes with Mona, "February?"

She nods.

"First time here. Haven't played yet."

"With other people," amends Mona.

"Yes, with others. With each other, though, we've had fun. Interesting thing? We are into S&M."

Jenn smiles. She hadn't expected that, from these two, both rather mousy and nondescript. She wonders what horrors they get up to in the wee hours. She wonders who is the Dom.

"I'm Sonja, my partner is Kyler, this is our second time at Aphrodite's. I run the Madison SlutWalk every year. In Wisconsin."

"What's SlutWalk?" asks Mona.

"A protest march. That women, anyone really, but women especially should be allowed to wear whatever they want and not be," she makes air quotes, "'Asking for it.'"

The table agrees with the sentiment.

"I'm Josh, married to that wonderful woman there," he points to Brooke. "We've been on every Xanadu trip since number one. Found Raymond's band of merry misfits accidentally on one of the old lifestyle sites. Followed them here." Josh grins.

"Interesting thing, honey," stage-whispers Brooke.

"Oh, yes," he pokes his lower lip out, an expression that makes him look younger than his fifty or so years.

*Adorable*, thinks Jenn, grinning.

"I have a Prince Albert."

"That's," says Jenn, before she's fully comprehended it, "the cock—"

"Indeed, I have a penile piercing. I'd show you, but that's frowned upon in here." He grins roguishly.

"Mona," waves Mona. "David's wife. I'm his Domme. Some of you might have been lucky enough to see my leather cat-suit it in the brief appearance it made during the masquerade the other night."

Scattered nods around the table, while Jenn loses the rest of Mona's words in a vision of skin-tight black leather, zipper displaying heaving bosom, the same nervous expression on her face.

"I didn't see that," says Josh, "but I'd like to."

"I'm straight," continues Mona. "I'm not saying that to avoid anything. Just that it's unusual. Certainly the minority, I've noticed."

Brooke nods, affecting the distinct *very interested* demeanor of a television interviewer.

"I'm Kyler. Sonja and I don't really label ourselves as swingers. We have people in our lives we fuck, others we love. Mainly we do what we enjoy."

Jenn nods, reminding herself to quit staring at his hair. He's so much more than hair, after all. She wonders what it would be like to run her fingers through it.

"Are you interested if they want to play?" she asked Ryan as he buttoned his shirt before dinner.

"Which they?"

She held up two dresses, a blue one she'd already worn, just not with these people, and a lighter yellow cotton dress. She wiggled the yellow dress a bit, enticing him to pick it.

"Blue," he said.

"I wore this one the other night," she reminded him.

"If someone confronts you on that, you can just take it off."

She smiled at him. "Sonja and Kyler," she said. "If they want to play."

"Yeah, I'm interested." he agreed. "She's cute. Sorta boyish."

"That help?" she asked.

He thought about it. "No, just words."

"She *is* cute and boyish," agreed Jenn, "and Kyler, with that long hair..." She pulled the dress over her head.

The perky woman leading this forced mixer snaps her back to dinner. "I'm Brooke, and I've helped Raymond out with organization and planning on the last several Xanadu trips. I'm a travel agent, so, comes with the territory. On my first visit to Aphrodite's, I discovered I was multi-orgasmic."

"Point me to the spot where you discovered it?" says Mona.

"Can't do it, eh?" asks Sonja.

Mona shakes her head.

Brooke presses her hands to her chest and beams. "I honestly believe everybody can get there, just takes time and practice."

Ryan sits quietly while the rest look at each other. Jenn extends her leg to nudge him with her toe.

"Right," he says.

The table's attention turns to him.

"I'm Ryan. Jenn and I have been swinging for almost two years, if we count the couple rough patches—"

"I count them," says Josh. "It's how we learn."

"Yes," says Ryan, his face blank. He looks to Jenn, panic creeping into the blank. "I, um..."

She streams suggestions through the air to his head. *You had bareback sex for the first time this week! You're bi-curious, they love that stuff! You were topped for the first time yesterday!*

"I told a man I'm interested in guy-on-guy play for the first time this week," he says slowly.

Smiles and nods around the table.

"And what did he say?" asks Sonja.

"Well, he was going on a boat, so rain-check."

"Better get to it," says Brooke. "Back half of the week goes quickly!"

When the introduction game ends, the conversation drifts to hushed chatting between people sitting next to each other. On the end, Jenn is distracted, looking at the couples eating at tables around them in pairs, foursomes, none as ambitious as this lot. Videos play on large flat-screens around the room, burlesques and strip teases. Every time she catches a glimpse of the far door opening, she wonders if it'll be Paige. She yearns for it to happen, with an undercurrent of displeasure. Maybe Paige will explain why she's been so distracted, why she's off away from Bruce, what's going on with Emily. Paige can have her secrets, of course – she doesn't need to share everything – Jenn just wants to know the reasoning. Wants to know if Paige, her girlfriend, her love, the woman she less-than-threes, doesn't trust her.

The video on the screens shows an incredibly pale curvy woman, who looks like a living pin-up, bathing in a giant martini glass. *Dita somebody,* thinks Jenn.

She realizes she's apparently thought the name aloud when David leans over and whispers "Dita Von Teese. Mona and I saw her in Vegas. *Unf!*"

Jenn nods.

Across the table, Brooke has her hand on Ryan's shoulder. He appears to be answering questions quickly and directly, one and two-word answers. Brooke laughs, and at first Jenn thinks the two of them are hitting it off. After hearing the laugh for the third time, though, the same laugh, same duration and pitch, she suspects it's all surface. Not forced, exactly, but done for effect. The TV interviewer, again.

Across the table, Kyler smiles at her before taking a bite of something green and sprouty. Next to him, Mona and Josh have abandoned their meals to make out like high-schoolers. David glances nervously at them from time to time. Jenn wonders if someone should say something. When she was new, nervous and uncertain, she'd often wished someone would've said something comforting. Reassured her. She puts her hand on his, and he turns to her with a smile.

"You look worried," he tells her.

She nods.

"I'm a cuckold. It's better if the men are younger and more attractive than me. I like having that rubbed in my face."

She nods again. Unexpected! *What have we learned, Jennifer? We must stop judging people by their appearance.* "You enjoy that?"

"Very much."

She doesn't understand it, and the showiness of their making out continues to make her uncomfortable. A mantra she's heard in their time as swingers surfaces, *Your kink isn't my kink, and that's okay.*

Before long, Brooke has finished questioning Ryan and is making flirty faces at David across the table. He smiles and awkwardly flirts back. Ryan finishes his dinner.

Brooke and David, Josh and Mona. *That completes a foursome,* she thinks. A fellowship is had. And if two of the four couples are about to pair off, maybe the other two should as well.

When dinner ends, the group stands and moves as a pack toward the doors. As they go, the couples gravitate back toward their partners, the apparent foursome trending toward the back of the group.

"Thank you for the captivating conversation and dinner," Brooke says.

"We're going to," says Josh, laughing as Mona bites his bicep, "head back to our room."

"Nice to meet you," says David to them.

"Thanks for indulging my mixer tendencies," says Brooke. "Hope to see you all in the hot tub later!"

With no more fanfare, the foursome disappears into the night.

Kyler lights a cigarette, leaning against a column down the wall from La Grande Fête's entrance. He holds it up and looks at the Lamberts. "This bother you?"

Jenn shakes her head and waves it off. "No big." She doesn't like the smell or taste of cigarettes and is surprised she hadn't noticed it on him earlier, in the pool. Maybe the chlorine. Oh, but to run her fingers through that lovely hair…

"So," says Ryan, "we were trying to figure out what sort of trouble to get ourselves into."

"Oh, yeah?" asks Sonja.

"Interested in getting into trouble with us?" he continues.

Jenn grins at him. Cheesy, but effective.

"I'm going to say no, thank you." says Sonja.

"Oh," says Jenn.

"Okay," adds Ryan.

"We enjoyed talking to you earlier, and going to dinner. You are awesome people."

"We've got some friends we're meeting in a half hour," says Kyler. "Happy we got a chance to spend some time with you both, though."

Jenn nods. "Well, we'll just have to go exploring." She grins at them tightly, hoping they don't notice.

"I hope you find something naughty," says Sonja, and offers Jenn a hug. Jenn wraps her arms around the woman in the barest of hugs, but Sonja holds her tight, like an old friend. She hugs Ryan too, same tight squeeze. Then the couple with the beautiful hair waves and walks off into the night, leaving Ryan and Jenn alone.

"Well," says Ryan, "didn't expect that response."

Jenn frowns and nods.

"What should we do with the rest of our evening?"

"I'll tell you one thing," says Jenn, sticking her lip out in a pout that she hopes her husband finds endearing, "I want another fucking creme brulee, and I want to eat it in bed with my feet up."

"That sounds like a plan to me." He kisses her, pulls open the door of La Grande Fête, and waves her in. "After you."

Jenn smiles and goes back inside to get another fucking creme brulee.

A glance at the bedside clock tells Ryan that it's just after 10:30. He sighs, looking down at his body with a grimace. Despite all the dieting and exercise, he's still rather doughy, same as always. He doesn't lift weights, and he's not likely to grow visible muscles anytime soon. He pokes his belly, just now supporting an empty creme brulee dish. That's probably it right there, what Sonja wasn't interested in. He looks across the room at his wife, sitting on the small bench cushion, holding her tablet but not looking at it. He tosses the dish aside to get a better look at his body. He takes a special long look at the tiny form of his flaccid penis, small thanks to the cold, to lack of excitement, to growing and not showing.

"Did you enjoy your creme brulee?" asks Ryan.

Distracted, she asks, "Hmm?"

"I'm sorry," he says, "about Sonja and Kyler, I know you wanted to play with them."

She turns and narrows her eyes at him. "I don't understand. Why are you sorry?"

He's not sure how to put it. *I'm sorry I'm not attractive enough? I'm sorry I'm not interesting enough?* "I'm sorry they weren't interested. In me."

Her face changes, going from perplexity to concern. "Oh, honey," she jumps up and drops the tablet, "that wasn't it."

"Looked like they were really into you."

She sits next to him, her hand on his knee. "Maybe, I don't know."

"In the pool, with the flirting."

"Oh," she says, "I mean, they had other plans."

"Yes."

"And it's not like we've never said no before," she says. "Doesn't always have some big important reason behind it."

"Sometimes it's just the length of a drive," says Ryan. He frowns at the thought. "I don't believe in karma."

"Ryan," she says, squeezing his knee, "this has nothing to do with Vince and Kendra."

"Maybe not," Ryan concedes. "But I probably could've been nicer to her."

Jenn nods her head from side to side. "Eh, maybe. But I don't think your sexiness—"

"Or lack thereof."

She swats at him. "Stop. Or karmic revenge had anything to do with it."

"It's a bummer," he says. "The rejection. Whatever the reason."

"Yeah," says Jenn solemnly, "it really is." After a moment's contemplation, she stands abruptly. "I think we should go out!" She pokes his shoulder. "Relax in the hot tub." Her voice has a bit of a manic timbre.

"I'm sure everybody's paired up by this point," Ryan grouses. "Remember how empty it was the other night?"

"I remember hot thunderstorm sex the other night."

Ryan nods. The storm sex had definitely been memorable.

"Are you really going to let one couple's rejection bench you?"

"Are we doing sports references now?" He cocks an eyebrow at his wife. He notices, out of the corner of his eye, that the flaccid thing in his pubic hair has begun to look more like a respectable penis. Not just a penis, a cock!

"C'mon. Let's get espresso martinis and hot tub it up!" She grabs his arm and tugs, slowly tipping him off the bed.

He laughs and acquiesces. "Alright, alright," he grabs their go-bag.

The hot tub crowd is, as expected, rather sparse. The guests at Aphrodite's are finishing their late dinners, dancing at the disco, or off having some post-dinner fun. Ryan and Jenn sit at one side of the empty bar, and before they can even ask, Julio has set two espresso martinis in front of them.

"*¡Muchas gracias, Julio!*" says Jenn.

He grins at her, and she hops up over the bar to give him a kiss on the cheek. He looks bashful for a moment and waves her away, smiling all the while, then heads to the other side of the bar.

Across the bar, on the side facing the patio, sit Debra and James. "Hello, friends!" says Debra, as the couple raises their glasses toward them.

"Are you coming in?" asks Ryan, returning the gesture.

"Letting dinner settle," says James.

Ryan leans against the bar, looking at the few people in the tub. Along the wall are a couple in their late forties who look very eastern European. Way at the other end of the bean, the hot end, are Raymond and Mia. There might be more staff up here now than guests. "We could go talk to—"

Jenn seizes her moment. "I want to give you a blowjob."

He blinks at her. "I, uh..."

She pulls at his hardening cock below the water and presses her lips to his. She strokes him and kisses him, until he's fully hard, then turns to the ledge just above the waterline, backed by plexiglass, looking out over the ocean. She pats the tile ledge.

Ryan looks from Jenn to the ledge to his already much harder cock poking just barely out of the water. "Alright," he says and leaps up on the ledge. He spreads his legs and she slides up between them, running her fingernails up his thighs. She runs her tongue from his balls up the underside of his shaft, making small circles on his frenulum. His head swims, and he exhales slowly. After a few more circles, she follows the line up to his urethra, poking her tongue at it.

Such odd pleasure. He shifts in his seat.

She looks up at him, those hazel eyes, a smile on her face. Then she takes his head into her mouth, puckering around it. Sucking and sucking and sucking. He feels the pressure change inside her, the tension rise. Then she lets him go and gives him another lick, the sides of her mouth a widening grin.

"Woo!" he hears from someone across the hot tub, Raymond, he thinks. A woo of approval from their Bacchus.

He smiles with a twinge of exhibitionist glee and closes his eyes to the world, focusing on the here and now. She takes him deep. He puts one hand behind her head, fingertips finding the short hairs. His other hand grips the side of the ledge, hard. She alternates sucking and licking and sucking and licking, occasionally just resting her nose against his frenulum, breathing. Her hot breath against the evaporating saliva. He shudders. Shouldn't be long now.

"That looks like fun," says a woman nearby.

Ryan opens his eyes and sees Madison, very close to Jenn, crouched so her shoulders are just out of the water. Jenn stops and lets his cock slurp out of her mouth. She turns and smiles at Madison. Without Jenn in front of it, his cock is surprisingly close to the face of this young woman who'd just said that sucking it looked like fun. His erection fortifies, his head throbbing larger.

"It *is* fun," says Jenn.

"Can I help?" Madison asks Jenn. After a moment, both women turn to look at him, Madison wears an expectant grin. His wife wears a similar smile with a touch of surprise.

Ryan feels a pit of worry in his chest and stomach. He searches the hot tub, still seeing only a few people. Raymond and Mia, Debra and James. Two other couples have come to the patio and are fucking on the bed. The Eastern Europeans seem to have moved on. No sign of— "Where's Will?"

Madison scowls. "Not here," she says.

Ryan is cautious. "Do we *want* him here?"

"No," she says, "we do not." She turns toward him, big brown eyes blinking, then cocks her head to the side and waits.

"You, uh," Ryan looks to Jenn for objection and sees none in her smile. She gives him an almost imperceptible nod, and he returns one of his own.

"I would love help," Jenn says, grabbing hold of Ryan's cock and pointing it at their new friend.

"Yummy," says Madison, opening her mouth and surrounding him.

They alternate, licking and sucking. Then they slide their tongues in parallel up and down his shaft. After a while, Jenn moves to the side and Madison takes center stage. She takes him all the way into her throat, lips pressing against his balls. She makes a momentary gagging sound and pulls back, leaving thick ropey saliva behind. She uses it to stroke him while she makes out with Jenn. When she returns to his cock, she squeezes his balls as she sucks, ramping up the intensity more and more. He has to hold the ledge with both hands to keep from rocketing off. Jenn kisses the back of Madison's neck, watching him. She winks when their eyes meet. Then it's building, rising, he's about—

"I'm gonna come," he calls to her.

Madison doesn't change her method, continuing to bob her head, his cock sliding in and out of her mouth faster and faster. He holds on as long as he can, waiting for her to stop, to open her mouth, to move away so he can shoot. She doesn't, and after a moment she opens her eyes and looks at him. "Well?" she asks, garbled by the penis inhibiting her diction. The question seems to hang in space between them, and then he lets go. He imagines he can feel his cum traversing all the way through him and out, firing deep into her mouth. After what seems like an eternity of orgasming, she slowly lets his cock slide out, wiping her mouth and smiling up at him.

"Wow," Jenn says, "that was intense."

"Yes, I," Ryan tries to find better words, but just repeats. "Intense."

"Thank you," Madison says.

"No, really, thank *you!*"

She stands between his legs and wraps her arms around his neck, pulling him toward her. "You tasted good," she tells him, then presses her lips to his. He can taste his cum in her kiss, the bitter saltiness, and he opens his lips and lets her tongue carry the flavor further inside. He wonders if other men taste the same, or different. He lets the thought go for the moment, pushing his mind to focus here, on this sudden surprise experience, kissing Madison, being in the hot tub, feeling Jenn wrap her arms around them both.

Here, at this moment, he's very happy they re-emerged from their room this evening.

# 51

## PAIGE

"I really want this," says Paige.

"Let's make it happen," says Alejandra, reaching out her hand across the table at Rakuen, concern in her eyes as she squeezes Paige's hand. "But are you sure you don't want Bruce there?"

Paige takes a deep breath. "I don't want to think about where his mind is. I want to be present," she says. "Tonight, with this gang bang, I can squeeze every last drop out of this resort at once. Really get to the marrow. Take it by the balls and ride."

Alejandra laughs and nods. "Alright."

"The situation with Bruce is complicated right now," she stirs sugar into her coffee. "I don't want to be in the middle of an authentic experience – because those come along so rarely – and have the emotions about Emily or whatever we're calling what he did."

"Betrayal?" offers Alejandra.

"I think that's too harsh," says Paige. Bruce has been an idiot this week. She's been an idiot with Emily too, before. "What can I say? Emily makes fools of us both."

"You are better at forgiveness than I am."

Paige chokes on her coffee. "Am I? I'm the woman who just spent her twenty-fifth wedding anniversary with another woman instead of her husband. Another woman who, I might add, I just met this week."

"True," agrees Alejandra. "But I am awesome."

"You are that." She smiles. "I hope he had fun today. I hope he did what he needed to. But I also hope he didn't call Emily." These are the conflicting pieces here. Today, she needed to abscond, and found a partner in crime to do it with. What Bruce needed, she isn't sure. But it had been up to him to discover it himself. Maybe he has, and they'll reconnect at the hot tub later, and all will be well. "I don't want to be angry for another day. I want things to..."

"Settle."

"Yeah," says Paige with a nod.

"Me too."

They clink their coffee cups together.

After a quick stop at the room to grab her bag and leave a note for Bruce (**I have something I need to do. I will reconnect with you after. -P**) she swings by Alejandra's. In the small white room, Alejandra tightens the straps on her leather harness. The big purple dong she'd worn earlier juts out in front. Paige snickers.

"What?" asks Alejandra. "I told you I wanted to go first."

Paige grins in response. She holds up an emerald green corset with raised black damask across it. "Will you help me with this?"

"Ooh," says Alejandra, "I love that!"

Putting the corset on before a party has long been a transitional moment for Paige. She hopes it will be tonight as well. She pulls it on and adjusts it. Alejandra begins to tighten the laces on the back, occasionally kissing up and down her neck. Paige can feel herself slipping. Slipping from the world of stress and work and drama, from the reality outside Aphrodite's. She slows her breathing and is present at the tug of each lace, mindful. The corset squeezes in a way that has been both comforting and claustrophobic in the past. Tonight, it holds her. As the boning shapes her body, she feels herself transforming, putting on the costume, the role. Tonight, she will be pleasured and provide pleasure. And she will ignore that distant, quiet ping from Emily, deep inside.

Suddenly the tightening stops, and Alejandra's mouth finds her ear. "You're ready," she whispers.

"I'm ready," confirms Paige.

Rather than go up the long wooden staircase outside, like sneaking in the back door, Alejandra leads Paige through the sliding glass doors into the lobby. Luis gives them a warm smile and a slight uptick of his eyebrow at Alejandra's cock. *Probably that body, too,* thinks Paige. All the gorgeous woman wears are the harness, a bikini top, and high-heeled shoes. They reach a spiral staircase on the opposite side of the lobby, classy white, surrounded by hanging translucent beading. Paige holds for a moment at the bottom step, hand on the rail. She takes a breath.

"Are you—" begins Alejandra.

"I'm good," says Paige, "Let's go."

The playroom is dim and full of bodies gyrating and thrusting and moaning. Blowjobs and hand jobs and cunnilingus. The sex swing is occupied. Paige's quick glance around reveals that none of her people – Jenn, Ryan...Bruce – are here.

(slut)

Emily's ping hits her brain, louder this time.

Paige takes Alejandra's hand, and her companion turns to look at her. This is it, isn't it? The moment where she leaps. *Carpe*s the fucking *diem*. She nods at Alejandra, telling her without words to do the thing we talked about on the boat, and over dinner. Ringlead this thing.

"Ladies and gentlemen," says Alejandra, and Paige can hear the newscaster confidence and importance in her voice. It quickly silences the room. Waiting. Paused thrusting. "This gorgeous woman next to me is looking for something special tonight, and we're hoping there are a few people who can help us out. Tonight, we're looking for a gang bang."

A few scattered whoops and some applause from the crowd. Paige notices Malcolm with a drink off to the side. *I hope he joins,* she thinks.

"Okay, rules," Paige told Alejandra over dinner. "They must wear a condom, they can't hit me or bruise me, and can't come on me." She thought about it more. "And they must be nice. This isn't a humiliation scene."

Alejandra explains those rules to the rapt audience of revelers, adding a few of her own caveats ("polite and orderly"), and already quiet conversations are happening between men and their partners and playmates. These people are negotiating to fuck her. Because they want her. Now. Here. They want her, bad. Paige grins. Sucking the marrow. *Carpe diem.*

"Be a gentleman," finishes Alejandra. "You're being offered a tremendous gift, and you will treat her like the goddess she is."

Paige smirks. *Must've made quite an impression on her,* she thinks.

Across the room, standing naked with his hard cock in his hand, is a man who isn't allowed to play. "Not Will," Paige whispers to Alejandra.

"I'd intended to corral him anyway," Alejandra whispers back.

As Paige lies back on the round cushion in the center of the room, Alejandra kneels between her legs, slathering lube on the massive purple dong. Paige wonders how it's possible that she's come this far, been open this long, and not done a gang bang. A few certain items have remained unchecked on her fuck-it list, but not many. Not many at all.

(slut)

The ping echoes in her mind again, like the warning beep on a dying smoke alarm you can't find, as Alejandra slips Paige's panties down her legs.

"I don't know why that message bothered me so much," she confided in Jenn late last year.

"Something you worry about, maybe?" her girlfriend suggested.

"Maybe. Or societal shame. Misplaced former Catholic guilt."

"I know that one," said Jenn.

"I mean I *like* being a slut," said Paige, frustrated, tense.

Jenn licked her pussy, and all the frustration went away.

Later, heads on pillows, arms and bodies intertwined, Paige's question turned into, "Why do I feel like a slut when I think about her, but not when we're together?"

"Because we love each other?"

Paige kissed her nose and lips. "Yes, true," she said. "You're special."

Jenn pulled her shoulders up and grinned. "I'm special."

"And adorable."

*You should be present, here,* she tells herself in the playroom, feeling Alejandra slide inside her for the second time today. She closes her eyes and holds the sensations, the moments, the feeling of Alejandra's warmth on her thighs, a light caress on her cheeks. The thrusting ebbs and flows and ebbs and flows. Alejandra kisses her nipples and neck and face.

"Is this okay?"

She looks up to see Malcolm, nude and shiny. His uncircumcised cock hangs very near her face. She nods and opens her mouth.

Hands find her breasts, freeing them over the top of her corset, then her stomach, her legs. She looks around the cock in her mouth, seeing some people she knows. There's the bisexual guy in the triad. He's running his fingers through her bush while maintaining a considerate distance from Alejandra's body. Next to Paige, tentatively playing with her left breast is a man she's seen with that woman with all the tattoos. He has a goatee, and his flaccid cock doesn't extend below his balls. She makes eye contact with him in a silent question. He nods, and she takes his cock in hand, feeling it begin to stiffen almost immediately. There's a cock in her other hand, a bold request from a man with flowing brown hair that she finds quite sexy. Behind, arms around him, stands a woman with a magenta mohawk. With her mouth full and her hands full and her pussy full, Paige closes her eyes. She feels movement everywhere. The textures and sensations of friction. The difference between the circumcised cock on her left and the uncircumcised on the right. Her jaw begins to ache from the girth of the cock in her mouth. Even if she gives no other blowjobs at this gang bang, she'll feel it in her jaw tomorrow. He's begun to thrust, and the grunts above her indicate the end is nigh. She opens her eyes and catches his. She nods, tugging his cock as she does it, and she feels the warm blast of salty bitterness hit her tongue and slide down her throat.

Malcolm slides his already receding cock out of her mouth, leaving the smallest trail of cum down her cheek. He produces a hand towel and wipes her off, then kisses her deeply. "Thank you," he whispers to her.

"Thank you," she says. "If you fancy a round below, I would be quite pleased with that."

(slut)

"If it's all the same to you, I think I'd rather take a rain check."

"Of course," says Paige, and he kisses her again. She feels a flutter between her legs, an emptiness, as Alejandra slides out of her. The woman moves up her body and kisses her nose, probably to avoid the taste of cum on her lips.

"I'm still exhausted from our earlier playtime, so I need to rest my thighs," Alejandra says. "But I'm going to sheriff the shit out of this for you."

"You're awesome," Paige says.

The emptiness between her legs yearns to be filled again. Going from four cocks at once to two feels woefully inadequate.

(slut)

"You," she says to the man on her left, taking her hand off his penis.

"Ted," he tells her.

"Would you like to fuck me, Ted?"

He gives a brisk nod.

"Please do," she says, biting her lip.

Alejandra produces a condom from thin air and hands it to him. He fumbles a little when putting it on, his nervousness endearing. Paige wants to tell him that, but in this room, surrounded by men, it may have the opposite effect she wants. When he slides inside her, he's half limp, but her juices are flowing and the lube facilitates. She grabs him with her Kegels, and Ted's eyes widen.

"Can I kiss you?" a soft voice asks.

Paige looks to the spot vacated by Ted and sees a woman who appears incredibly tall from this vantage point. Between her legs hangs a thin cock, curving leftward. Paige's eyes widen, and she nods.

"I'm Mädchen," she says as she lowers her face to kiss Paige.

"Paige. I've just had cum in my mouth."

"That's fucking hot," says Mädchen, kissing her.

Paige's hand finds Mädchen's inner thigh, sliding up to cup her hanging balls. Paige runs her fingers along Mädchen's taint and feels the intensity of their kiss rise and flow, peaking as she circles her fingers around her cock and tugs.

Moments blur into others, Ted giving way to the man with the long brown hair, a few people she doesn't know appearing and disappearing from the sides, most begging off before they come. One shoots unexpectedly along her arm and slinks away.

When Mädchen fucks her, it's as though the woman's cock follows a homing beacon direct for her G-spot. They hold their faces close to each other, and Paige floods the cushion (noticing that Alejandra has, at some point, slid towels under her) and Mädchen's legs. "Oh, wow," says Mädchen with a grin as she strokes herself a few final times, erection subsiding.

"Can I?" asks the podcaster quietly. He has his plaid shorts on. She experiences a moment of discordance, irritated by the personality he's shown so far, and now, in this moment, there's something endearing about his bashfulness. Something so off-brand about it. And after enduring being pissed on by Will... She reaches up her free hand and yanks down his boxers, exposing cock. She takes it into her mouth.

A new cock arrives in her right hand.

She hears Alejandra say, "No," and her right hand is free again.

An older man with a gray beard takes up position between her legs. He slides slowly into her, then slowly out, breathing in time with his gradual thrusts. Must be a meditation guy, or one of those—

He hits her G-spot in exactly the right way, and she arches her back. Eric, or Strom, or whatever...the podcaster's cock slips out of her mouth, and she clutches both of her hands to her chest as she gushes again, and again, and again.

She waves for Alejandra. "Water."

Alejandra nods.

"Sorry," she says, realizing she's apologizing to the group, then looks up and draws the podcaster's penis back into her mouth. He's gone rather soft, and she's determined to suck him back to full strength. Then she drops Eric's cock back out and announces to no one in particular, "I want a cock in my ass too, but I think we have to rearrange for that."

(slut)

She looks up at the podcaster, who at this moment seems younger and more frightened. "You okay?"

He nods.

"Are you interested in the job?" she asks. The cock currently in her pussy, the girthy one belonging to the older gent, would certainly not be ideal for rear entry.

Eric hesitates.

"It's okay if you're not into it," she tells him. "I expect nothing."

They hold each other's eyes for a moment. Paige sees that Eric's are a similar shade to hers.

"I'm interested," he says.

She grins at him. "We need a momentary disengage," she calls. The pop when the bearded man pulls out triggers another wave and squirt. "And more towels." She takes charge, despite a swimmy feeling inside. Things meld and shift. She's high on the sensations and the musk and the sweat and scent of the room. "You, on your back," she tells the bearded man. "And what's your name?"

"Grant," he says.

"Grant, here," she points at the cushion where she'd been. "And grab towels for—"

Grant holds up two rolled white towels and grins. He lies on his back, and she climbs on top of him, entry much faster this time.

She leans down on him, turning toward Eric at the same time. "Whenever you're ready."

Eric nods and disappears behind her.

"Lube please!" she calls out. She sees someone in the dim light rush with a bottle toward her rear.

*My God,* she thinks, *we've even got lube service!*

A cold finger circles her anus before sliding inside. She continues to ride the cock below her, breathing as the fingering intensifies, two, then three.

"How are you doing?" comes the podcaster's voice from behind her.

She nods. "Go for it." She feels the squishy press of his less-than-fully-erect head against her. She hopes he can manage, wondering if he'll recover here if he's unable to penetrate all the way. The sudden fullness causes her to spasm. There's the slightest touch of glorious pain, but it subsides quickly, and she feels them both inside, sliding against each other. Sometimes synchronous, sometimes not.

"Holy fuck," she says and the swimminess intensifies. She looks at the man with the beard— Grant. "This is intense."

He nods. "I agree!"

A cock appears near their faces. Grant moves his mouth up to meet it.

"Oh my God," says Paige, now with wonder instead of intensity. She tilts her head back and sees Terrence. She watches for a moment as the man below her, the one she's riding, sucks his cock. No matter how many times she sees that, it doesn't get old. She opens her mouth and shares Terrence's cock with Grant.

A cock presses against her hand, and she takes it. It's soft, so she tightens her grip, sliding it through her fist.

The intensity of the movement down below is making her light headed. Should she stop? Should she take a moment?

But the sensations are—

But it feels so—

*But I could just—*

She hears grunting, and Eric presses himself against her back. She shudders as he slides out of her ass. She doesn't stop riding Grant, doesn't stop stroking, doesn't stop sucking. She feels wave after wave building inside her, as though her body is readying a major blast-off. An orgasm to top them all. As though every wave, every squirt so far, was merely prelude.

Someone moves between her legs, ready to fill her back up. The sound of the world is muffled, but she catches bits of intense conversation. She wants to ask why anyone would be tense in a place of love. A place like this.

"I told you no!"

"Why am I—"

"Because she said—"

"That's not fucking—"

"Dude, stop."

"If she's gonna be a fucking slut—"

(slut)

Like a slap in the face.

(slut)

Like a thunderclap.

"Stop. Now!" says Alejandra.

"God, this place is full of stuck up sluts with—"

Paige stops. Grant stops. Terrence stops. They disengage. She knows who it is before she sees him. Will's face is beet red, his flaccid cock hanging sadly between his legs.

She hears it in her head.

(slut)

She feels it in her body, as her anus adjusts itself closed again, as the fluid she's expelled begins to evaporate from her legs.

"You're calling me a slut?" she asks, a waver in her voice.

"Yeah," he says and moves toward her.

The podcaster— Eric leaps in front of him. "Get the fuck out of here, man!"

"What is with all of you? Whoring it up and then acting like you're not sluts. Like you're better." Will's fury rises.

Alejandra steps next to Eric. "In about ten seconds," she says, "I'm going to kick your fucking balls into your abdomen."

"Ah, this one," he points to Alejandra, then directly into Paige's face. Eric shoves his finger away.

The come-drunk intensity has already abandoned her. She can't move.

(slut)

"This one's protecting you? When you lie down and invite anyone here to fuck you. To fill all your filthy holes? What do you call that? Are you enlightened? Discriminatory? With those cocks in your ass. Sucking on—"

"Last warning."

Paige sees him shift his eyes to Alejandra, but that accusatory finger stays pointed right at her.

(slut)

"Oh yes, manly lesbian swinger," says Will. "Fucking feminazi ruling the—"

"You pathetic little man," Alejandra replies, stepping in front of his finger, blocking its aim toward Paige. "You don't belong here. You will not take a safe space from us all by—"

He lunges toward her but is caught from behind by Luis and Tomás, each holding one of his arms.

"Time to go, *Señor*," says Luis, his voice calm and measured.

Will's face changes. "What, no? They—" His accusatory finger flails out again. Paige flinches as his eyes meet hers. "Dirty slut," he says, directly to her. There are splotches in her vision. She falls to her butt on the cushion, watching Luis and Tomás drag Will away from the group.

The pinging sounds in her ears with her heartbeat, over and over and over.

(slutslut*slutslut***slutslut**)

The refrain magnifies. In Emily's voice, in Bruce's, in her own, and now Will gets a chorus. Every time heavier and heavier, louder and louder.

How could she do this? Ask for this? Want this? Need this? One last lucid moment, last clear thought, before she gets the fuck out. *How could I have done this without Bruce?*

Paige leaves her corset and shoes and kit behind, hits the swinging door at the side of the room and blasts into the disco. The thumping music picks up the echo in her head, the beat intensifying.

She's got to get out.

Out of here.

Take it back.

Can't

(slut)

take it back.

She hits the back door of the disco and the heat smacks her. She looks at the tops of trees, waving in the warm November night. Below there are people, fellow denizens of this resort. Fellow sluts, but that doesn't make her feel better.

She looks at it all and wonders what now, what next?

She's done this all wrong, hasn't she?

She pulls herself down the stairs, going alone into the night.

Maybe this is exactly what a slut like her deserves.

# 52

# RAYMOND

They'd spent the afternoon together, and it had been lovely. Then dinner at La Grande Fête, and walking along the beach, talking about life. Now, Raymond Horne sits in the hot tub on top of the world next to his colleague and long-time friend Mia Benjamin.

"Told you I'd get you up here," he says.

She elbows him in the side without turning away from the blowjob happening on the ledge next to the bar.

He watches too, taking a voyeuristic thrill from the unbridled enthusiasm on display. "I remember when I threw myself in like that."

"I seem to recall that someone was the center of a group scene in the orgy yesterday," says Mia.

"Does that count?"

"Alright, alright, Raymond, you get the trophy for feeling sorry for yourself," says Mia. She takes a long sip of her drink, which smells more like rum than fruit, then puts an imaginary tiara on his head, humming *Hail to the Chief*.

"Mia," he says.

"What?"

"I think you may be drunk."

She blinks at him, as though assessing her own status, then slowly nods.

"Only took five days," he says.

She continues to nod.

He wonders if she'd let him kiss her. If she'd be interested in other things. She's been cagey about her activities on the resort, aside from the long expanses of time spent on the beach bed with books and tablet.

"Will I have to read your blog to find out what you did here this week?" he asks.

"You'll have to sign up for my newsletter for notifications," she says with a snicker. "Or, you know, you could ask."

He nods. Somehow that idea hadn't crossed his mind. *Video 38: Use Your Words. C'mon, Ray!* Using his words with Mia would be hard, though. She's always been gracious in the twenty years of their friendship, when drinking or other indulgences have brought up the topic of them getting together. Would she continue to be gracious tonight? She did explicitly say she wouldn't fuck him on this trip, after all.

"Mia," he says. What does he want to tell her? That he's attracted to her? She knows that. That he wants to fuck her? Surely, she knows that, too. That he probably won't experience joy or pleasure from the act? She damn sure knows that.

"You're going to do it, aren't you?" she asks.

"What?"

"You're going to make it weird."

He frowns. He knows how well she can read his face after all these years. He looks down at his hands in his lap under the water. He sees the twenty years gone by. His chest is sagging, his chest hair graying.

"You don't have to, though," she tells him, leaning closer.

"Yeah," he says.

"What good would come of it?" She drops her voice down to a whisper, and the shakiness he'd heard in it a few moments ago is gone. "If we got together and fucked it'd make weird what we have now. It'd dredge up all the old shit, Mr. Horowitz. You remember."

He does remember, of course, when he was Ray Horowitz and not the vaulted personality that he nearly abhors now. He remembers how he treated people back then. How he treated her. He nods.

"Besides, you couldn't even find pleasure in a giant group scene at an orgy. How would you find it with me? Wouldn't that be a frightful waste?" She smiles and leans her head on his shoulder, turning her eyes back to the threesome at the opposite side. "If we do again have sex, Raymond, I'd like it if we both enjoyed it. Let's not waste that. Let's not allow anhedonia the casualty."

He follows her gaze. Now the couple is going down on the young woman. Watching in silence, Mia finishes her drink.

"May we join?"

Raymond looks up to see Debra and James. He smiles at them and gestures to the wide-open seating at this end of the hot tub. "Please do."

James stoops and helps Debra in, before following himself. He puts his arm around her immediately when he sits.

"How are you two this evening?" asks Raymond.

"Besides getting winded coming up those stairs, can't complain," says Debra.

"Those three put on an excellent show," James says, gesturing over his shoulder toward the threesome.

"You old perv," says Debra. "Don't admit it!"

"People tend not to do things in public that they don't want to be watched," says Mia.

"See, they like to be watched," laughs James.

"Just like me!" cackles Debra. "How's your day been, honey pie?"

Raymond smiles at her. "Contemplative. Resort asked me if we wanted the same week next year."

"And you told them unquestionably!" says James. He laughs and runs his hand over his shiny bald head.

"I said I'd let them know by the end of the trip. Not feeling so sure," admits Raymond.

"Want to try a different week?" asks Debra.

"May want to try something else entirely." Raymond looks away, feeling Debra's eyes on him.

"I wouldn't ever leave here," says Debra. "If that were an option, of course."

He meets her eyes. They're wistful. He smiles at her, but his heart isn't in it. He feels himself about to spill it all. The depression, the breakup, the anhedonia. Piss in everyone's Cheerios. At the last moment, he swerves. "What is it about this place, Debra?"

"What is it I love?"

"Yeah."

She leans her head back and looks up at the sky. "You've been open for most of your life."

Raymond nods.

"You?" she points at Mia.

"Yeah, actually never been in a monogamous relationship."

"I have," says Debra. "Same with James. I was a teenager before the love generation, remember. The fifties were different. You had to stand up straight, fly right. Certainly couldn't be curious outside your relationship." She looks askance and adds as an aside, "Or about girls."

"I came of age in the sixties," adds James, "and I still just missed the awakening."

"Married Clark in sixty-one. Had the girls. He skedaddled in ninety-six. Probably got randy about a dozen times in those years. Couldn't ask for it, you know. Wasn't my place."

"My wife didn't want sex."

"Clark didn't much care for it either. But I was faithful every damn day." She smiles wickedly. "Thought about gettin' dirty with almost everyone who came to the door, though."

"Oh, and the girls at the office."

"When James and I got together, we thought it'd be different. 'Cuz we both actually like sex."

"And we'd experienced what sexless marriage is like."

"But routine is routine. And after a couple years, I was still thinking about all these men I'd see."

"Yeah," says James.

Raymond pictures Debra the cougar, a couple decades younger, lusting after the bag boy at the local Piggly Wiggly. He smiles at the thought.

"Then we came here," she says.

"And everything changed," James agrees.

"Those things we'd been feeling, the urges. We weren't the only ones."

"Even people who do their spouse daily," says James, "they all want to screw other people."

"Everybody does," says Mia. "The monogamy lie is that our partner is all we need. That lie can feel like oppression if you're not completely on board with it."

"Yes, oppression!" exclaims Debra.

"Of course, some people *are* on board. But they still look at Farrah Fawcett."

"What did Carter say?" she asks her husband.

Raymond laughs. "That he looked at others with lust in his heart."

"That's it," she says with a finger snap. "Lust in our hearts. We do that. People, I mean. Even if we're happy. Then we feel guilty."

"And we feel shame," adds Mia.

"Here, there's no shame," Debra says, and her voice catches just a little. "Or judgment. And we may not be the newest cars off the line like…" She whistles and throws her thumb toward the threesome. "But we've had our fair share."

"Oh, yes," says James.

"This place not only understands the stuff inside you, but says it's okay…"

Raymond nods. "It accepts your truth."

"It accepts our truth," agrees Debra, leaning over, touching his knee. "Why would I ever want to go anywhere else?" She turns to her husband, who smiles at her with such love. Are those tears in his eyes? Raymond watches as they kiss, embrace, then lean back against the side of the tub and look up at the sky. "Our first time here, we were in this tub, I think on this side even," she says, looking at the stars. "And we'd just been invited to dinner by this gorgeous couple. You remember their names—"

"Alan and Georgia."

"Georgia, yes," she agrees. "Thought it was a state. Anyway, I stood up, and there was something stuck to my rear."

"A tile," says Raymond with a smile.

"Have we told you this story?" she asks, looking back at him.

"No," he laughs, "but it doesn't surprise me. The tiles do that. I think I've collected three this trip."

"Ah," she laughs back. "Well, James pulled it off. I figured he threw it in the trash or something. But on our next anniversary, he—" She stops and puts her hand on her face, eyes wet. "He'd made it into this necklace." She holds a gold chain off her neck. At the end of it hangs a pearlescent white square, surrounded by golden edging and swirls.

Raymond stares at it. "It's beautiful," he says. "I can't believe I didn't recognize it."

"Don't spend enough time checking out my rack, probably," Debra says, her voice full of humor again. "I don't take it off. Only in the MRI, and only 'cuz they make you." She holds the necklace in a fist. "We haven't gone anywhere else since we discovered this place. Why would we?"

"Home," says Raymond.

James shakes his head. "This isn't home," he says, after a quiet moment. "When they welcome us home, it's a nice touch, of course. But home is where you pay bills, it's where you collapse after a grueling day at work. It's where you fight with your family. It's where you get unwelcome news." He takes his wife's hand again and kisses it. "This place is better than home. Here, we can be who we want to be. We can be who we can't be at home."

Debra smiles at him, then puckers her lips. When he notices, James smacks her a kiss.

Raymond smiles.

"I think I may be a pumpkin, Jimmy."

James nods.

"See ya in the morning," she says, opening her arms. "Good-night hugs?"

Raymond leans forward to give her a hug. "Goodnight kiss?" he asks.

She plants her lips on his. They kiss, and he feels every moment. *Take in the real, Ray. Anhedonia be damned.*

"Oh, gorry," she says after the kiss, mock fanning herself with her hand. "What're you tryin' to do to me? I'll be up half the night thinking about that."

"She will," says James.

"Happy to give more tomorrow," says Raymond, and the Koonzes head for the stairs.

"They are delightful," says Mia after they're alone again, just the two of them.

"They are indeed," says Raymond. "Sorry I almost made things weird."

"You're you," she says.

"Oh, thanks," he replies.

"Don't take that negatively," says Mia. "You're you." She kisses him on the nose. "I may also be a pumpkin. You?"

"I'm going to stay up here a while longer," he says. "Meteor shower is coming, and there's bound to be some early arrivals tonight."

"If you can enjoy that," she says, "don't let yourself believe that you can't enjoy anything." She puts her hand on his shoulder and squeezes, then pulls on her robe and heads for the stairs.

The threesome opposite him has finished and are enjoying espresso martinis. He raises his glass to them, even though it's long since almost entirely water. They tip theirs back.

*This place is special,* he thinks. *Better than home.*

## 53

---

## BRUCE

Tying his shoelace after coming off the beach, Bruce notices a dark shape in the center of the pool. This whole side of the resort is empty and quiet late at night, with the pool and the restaurants closed. He is only here looking.

Looking for her.

Bruce has made his way across and through Aphrodite's multiple times this evening. Passing through the disco and playroom, around the courtyard bar, into every nook and cranny of the resort, and up and down the beach multiple times. He's found so much sexy, so many brilliant people. But not what he's looking for. He hasn't found her anywhere.

The dark shape in the pool bobs. He moves closer. A gesture, the dark shape reaching up a hand to wipe across its nose, and Bruce knows that it's her. He walks to the edge of the pool.

"Hello, angel," he says.

When Paige looks up at him, he feels her emotion radiating, slamming into his chest. She looks so scared, so sad, so ashamed. Then she looks away and moves away to the opposite side of the pool, further from him. He watches for a moment, wondering if she's still this hurt from yesterday, well two days ago, now, as they've surely crossed into Thursday. That wouldn't explain the shame. That wouldn't—

He looks down at the water and bends to remove his shoe.

*No, fuck that.* He steps forward and drops in. The sensation of being weightless in clothing, surrounded by water, is startling. He moves toward her. "I'm sorry," he says as he closes the distance between them. "I'm so sorry."

She turns to him, her back against the far wall. He stops. Less than five feet separate them, but it still feels like a gulf. He scrambles to explain. "I didn't talk to Emily again, after—"

"I don't care," she whispers, distant.

"You…" He isn't sure where to go from there. He narrows his eyes, trying to read her face. He's about to go back to, "I'm sorry," but decides that it probably won't get him anywhere. Something else is happening in his wife's eyes, on her face. "What's going on, angel?" he asks and waits.

She looks away from him, but doesn't turn so far that he can't see her face. The white twinkle lights in the palm trees reflect off the water into her dark eyes. Her eyes close, and now her face is all shadow, surrounded by wet dark hair. Is she still so upset? She says she doesn't care, but—

"I found the edge tonight," she says, her voice little more than a whisper. "My edge."

He nods, and waits for her to continue.

"I thought it was a safe place. It felt like a safe place."

He waits.

She doesn't go on, just tilts her head toward the water.

"What happened?"

"There was a gang bang, just like I wanted…"

He nods. She's spoken about the phantom allure of a gang bang for years but has never reached out and taken it, even among friends at the bigger parties, where such a thing could easily have been had. But she grabbed it here. He feels a knot in his stomach.

"And that fucking—" she stops, abrupt, and turns away again so he can't see her tears.

"I wasn't there," he says, more to himself than to her. He's not completely sure what he means by it. Is he angry that he wasn't invited? Sad that it happened without him? Or is this simply his acknowledgment that while his wife was doing important things, a huge portion of his mental real estate was being taken up by a selfish woman in— No, that's not fair. That mental real estate was being freely given by a selfish man at Aphrodite's. "I'm sorry I wasn't there."

"You would've made it safe." She looks back. "He was so awful."

What had happened? The knot in his stomach grows larger. "Please, my love, tell me what happened."

"It was incredible, everything I'd hoped. Until *he* wandered over. Will. And..."

Will. Fucking Will. From the moment Bruce first saw him, he knew he was *that* guy at the party. The one who'd be cruel. The one who'd demand. The one who'd feel he deserved. That guy. His blood surges, and he vividly imagines beating the ever-living shit out of that man. Surely someone has a paddle, a cane.

"The things he said. I'm a slut for wanting it all. Wanting to be here. Wanting to feel all of this and touch and be with all of the—"

He puts his arms around her, and she cries into his shoulder. She lets go, eases into the sobs. He doesn't say anything. She needs to let this out before new stuff can come in. After a while, the sobs slow, and she lifts her head off his shoulder.

"You're wearing your clothes."

"I hadn't noticed," he tells her.

She laughs, a choked sound mingling with the sobs.

"You're *not* a slut," he says, hitting the word *not* with all the emphasis he can muster.

"I *am* a slut," she says, but her face is no longer sad. "I can call myself that. He can't call me that. Ever. And Emily can't, either."

The text messages from last year, of course. Emily's farewell stab. Jesus, what was he thinking?

"Want me to beat him up?" asks Bruce, allowing a trace of a smile to reach his lips.

"Yes, but don't. I still want to have the option to come back here in the future. Luis dragged him off."

"Good." A cool breeze blows off the ocean over the deserted pool and they shiver. "Do you think we could make Thursday our anniversary?"

"Yeah," she says, "a do-over."

"A do-over." He shivers again. "Listen, I'm freezing, and I'm wearing a lot more wet clothes than you. Do you have any interest in going up to the hot tub?"

She considers it for a long time, then gives him a slow nod.

He climbs up on the side of the pool, water pouring from his clothes onto the deck. He reaches down and helps his wife out.

They stand for a moment, facing each other. How odd they must look, a soaking wet man in slacks and a button down and a naked woman so pale she'd shimmer if there were moonlight. They take hands and head toward the hot tub, making one quick pit stop as they go.

"I'll be right back," he tells her, giving her a quick kiss. He slides into the alcove, unbuttoning his shirt as he goes. Vaguely, way in the back of his brain, he hears the music of John Williams as Superman unbuttons his shirt. *The door will probably be locked anyway,* he thinks, but the handle turns with a satisfying click, and the door opens to the clean scent of detergent and fabric softener. A cart near the last of the industrial washing machines is loaded with stacks of freshly laundered thick brown Aphrodite's robes.

He snags two.

The hot tub has attracted more people since he peeked up here looking for Paige. The last call before the pizza, after all. As he strips off his wet clothes and hangs them over the rail, he notices Paige sitting on a bed, staring at him.

"I love you so much," she says.

He stops and crouches before her. "I love *you* so much."

"If you need Emily in your life—"

"I don't." He says it without hesitation. "She's a distraction. Because I'm afraid. I'm afraid that I can't take care of you, or that you don't need me to, or that you don't want me to..."

"I do."

"My fears may not be rational." He presses his forehead against hers.

"You can take care of me. You do take care of me. Whether I need it or not, or can admit I need it or not. You, being here with me, is what I choose."

"I'm here," he says.

"Let's go see those two," Paige says, extending a pale hand toward Jenn and Ryan, sitting at the bar. "I think I owe an apology."

Bruce nods and holds her hand as she steps to the floor of the tub. The Lamberts look up as the Shepards make their way over to them. Jenn's expression is cautious.

Bruce sits across from the three. Ryan nods to him, and he nods back. He watches as Paige runs her finger along the back of Jenn's hand. Jenn looks down at it for a moment, then takes

Paige's hand, brings it to her lips and kisses it. Both women close their eyes. When they open them, all are glassy. They say so much without speaking: small smiles, the way they touch their foreheads together.

Then Jenn kisses Paige's cheek. "Hey," she says.

"Hey," Paige responds.

# PART VII

*Thursday*

# 54

# JENN

Sailboats pass on the horizon, and clothed guests from other resorts pass their beach bed. Ryan is sleeping next to Jenn, after scrambling very early this morning to claim this bed, two down from the bar. Jenn sits against a mountain of pillows watching the morning with a plate of bacon. She wishes Paige were here, lying with her. Not as a replacement for her husband, of course, but the two of them still have much to talk about. Their reconnection in the hot tub last night had been so frightfully brief.

"I missed you," she told Paige, holding her girlfriend's hand to her chest.

"I missed you, too," said Paige, leaning her head against Jenn's shoulder.

There they sat in silence for a while, as conversation and music and the bubbling of the hot tub surrounded them. After a while, Paige announced her exhaustion.

"Let's get you to bed," said Bruce.

*Wait!* Jenn thought, but didn't say it. There was so much that needed saying, or at least asking. Why hadn't Paige wanted her around yesterday? Why hadn't she told Jenn she and Bruce were having issues? Why hadn't they talked more about whatever the hell was going on with Emily?

Jenn held Paige's hand as long as possible until Paige stood out of her grasp. Then her girlfriend, the first woman she's ever loved, leaned down and kissed her. "Goodnight, beautiful girl."

"Goodnight," Jenn said, adding, "I love you," loudly and impulsively. She saw Raymond raise an eyebrow across the hot tub. Not judgmentally, she didn't think.

Paige kissed her again, reciprocating the love. Then the Shepards left the hot tub for bed.

"Do you ever worry I love Paige more than you?" she asks sleeping Ryan without taking her eyes off the horizon.

Apparently not fully asleep, Ryan replies with another question. "Do you?"

Jenn looks down at him. His right eye is closed, but his left squints open. She doesn't know what to say.

"I think you love her differently than me," he says.

That makes sense. Jenn nods.

"But you haven't told me how you see it." His left eye is still squinting at her, waiting, unwavering.

That's the question, indeed. How *does* she see it? She looks from Ryan to the water, then back to her husband. She feels her love for him, love she's never doubted. Even before non-monogamy, when their relationship had just barely reached the level of good friends and roommates. Even after the complications of their early time swinging together. When they were both stupid.

"We were stupid together," he insisted as the previous summer turned to fall. "Young and gloriously stupid."

"Is this a toast?" she asked.

He looked at the bottle of hard cider he was holding aloft, chuckled, and put the bottle to his mouth. The flames from the fire pit reflected in his eyes and the bottle. "I think it's like that paradigm shift thing the Shepards talk about. The transition from the earth being the center of the solar system, to the sun."

Jennifer nodded. "The big change."

"It's a complexity thing, then. When you're the center, things are easier, because they're all there to serve you, right?"

She supposed.

"But when that shift happens, and you see the complexity beyond. Like you being in love with Paige..." he held that for a moment, then went on, "or me going out with Kendra. Then there's a lot more moving parts. A constellation of interaction."

She blinked at him, hearing his words, "like you being in love with Paige," echoing. It's something she hadn't considered, really. That wasn't part of the deal. They could have fun and play and fuck and hang out...but... She shook her head. "Constellation, solar system, you're mixing your space-themed metaphors."

"I know your face," he said, a warm smile spreading across his own, "and I know I'm right about the Paige thing."

"No, *you're* in love with Paige." She was defensive suddenly, why?

"How about I just tell you that I'm okay with it, and you can figure it out however you need to?" He held out his cider toward her.

She stared at it, then him, then back at the bottle, before clinking her own against his. As she stared into that fire, she realized he was right. She did love Paige.

The paradigm shifted.

"The paradigms are shifting again, aren't they?" she asks him on the beach. This place holds so much change. She can feel it everywhere.

"I think they are," he says. He stares at her from his squinty eye a moment longer before sitting up and digging in their tote bag for his sunglasses. "I'm okay with that, with shifting. Are you?"

She nods but looks away, back out at the water. "It's just scary."

"All of it is," he says. "Do you see Rory down there?" Ryan points down the beach toward the triad and another couple in the water. Terrence and Rory kiss as Marley chats with the pair.

She nods.

"That scares me."

"What?"

"The idea of actually playing with him," says Ryan, "of taking it from fantasy to reality. Trying something like that."

She nods again and grabs his hand. "I can be there if you—"

"No, that's not it," he says. "It's all big shifts. In our understanding of ourselves. That's what I got from that first night with Bruce and Paige. Things changed. Or actually, *we* changed. Everything else was just different in comparison. When you open yourself up to change like that, who knows what you'll look like on the other side."

"You'll still be you," she says, squeezing his hand. "And I'll still love you."

"I don't worry about what you asked before," he says, "about you loving Paige more than me. Mostly because she and I aren't in competition." He laughs. "And that's a good thing, too, 'cuz she is a *tough competitor*."

"You'd win," says Jenn, not certain if she's reassuring him or herself.

"My hope, my love, is to never get to a point where there's a question of who is more important, more loved. She and I can exist in equilibrium, symbiosis."

Jenn feels tears in her eyes and kisses him. "I wish she'd told me all of it, what's going on with her."

"I know. She will."

Jenn nods. Maybe Paige will tell her today, about what's going on with her and Bruce, and with Emily, and with Alejandra. Maybe they can sit down and have the conversation Jenn needs, and all will be well. "Maybe," she agrees. She looks back at Ryan and asks the question she's been avoiding for days. "Are *we* going to be okay?"

He snaps his gaze back to her. "I'm going to need you to give me some context for that question."

She blurts out, "Everything," then looks down at her lap. "Work. Money."

"We've been through harder," he tells her. "I know it doesn't seem like it, but we have."

"And if our relationship changes?"

"From the paradigm shifts."

She nods.

"We deal with that when it comes up. Like it said in that *Opening Up* book we read, relationships evolve, then the people in them decide how to respond to the evolutions. We did okay moving to swinging."

She cocks an eyebrow at him.

"Well, sure, there were a few distinct issues there, but—"

"No," she interrupts him, "you're right. You're in it with me?"

He nods.

She reaches out and takes his hand again.

"Hey," says Rory, approaching the foot of their bed.

"Hey," Ryan says back.

Jenn waves.

"So, Marley and Terrence have a morning tryst, and I'm going to head over to the courtyard bar for a drink."

Ryan nods. "Okay."

*He's asking you to play, you doof,* she thinks and lightly pokes Ryan in the thigh.

"Just wanted to make sure you knew where to find me if you were interested in doing so," he says. "Finding me. Nice to see you," he tells Jenn, then walks toward the courtyard.

"Do you think he wants—"

Jenn nods, hoping her grin doesn't look too eager.

"You're excited." Ryan laughs.

She nods again, this time more vigorously. "But you shouldn't feel pressured."

"Aha."

She shakes her head. "If you don't like it, that's fine." She reaches out and puts her hand on his thigh. "But honestly, if you do, that'd be the hottest thing ever. You don't have to. I want to say that again. Don't do it for me. Do it for you. I'm talking too much."

"But I shouldn't feel any pressure."

"None at all," she says, then kisses him. "It was a big deal for me. It might be for you. Might not be, of course. Wouldn't it be better to try and know, one way or the other?"

Ryan looks down and nods. "But I don't want to just leave you here all—"

"Nah," she says, waving him off. "I'm fine. You should go."

"I don't think you're being entirely truthful with me," he says, pulling down his sunglasses so he can squint over them at her.

"Maybe not," she says. "But I'll be okay. And I've got a beach to relax on until I am. And there's bacon. How can I be sad in a world that gives me beach bacon?"

He kisses her. "So, I should go do this?"

"Fortune favors the bold. And telling me after *also* favors—" Still too enthusiastic? *Dial it back, spaz!* "If you want to, I mean."

He stands up, next to the bed. "You're okay for now?"

"I am."

"Do I look okay?"

"You're naked in sunglasses, and he just hit on you."

"Good point." He lingers, looking at her a moment longer.

She leans forward and takes both his hands. "Look," she says, "I'm scared about money and the job. I'm jealous of Paige and Alejandra. I'm confused about where we stand with the Shepards in the 'telling the Lamberts important stuff' department. There are only about forty-eight hours left here, maybe less, and there's so much more to do. You have something you want to do. Whether it's scary or not, you should go for it."

He considers it, then nods. "Yes."

"Yes?"

"I'm going to go talk to him."

"You go pick up that hot gay dude."

He leans down and kisses her once, twice, the third runs deep.

She watches him go. There's the compersion. She wonders what makes it different when it's Paige.

# 55

## PAIGE

"Good morning, handsome," Paige whispers into her husband's ear. He stirs only a little. She turns onto her side next to him, and the sheets drop away enough to watch his chest rise and fall. She leans over and kisses him just above his left nipple, holding her mouth there and inhaling his scent. Yesterday's Old Spice, remnants of chlorine from the pool and hot tub, and beneath those, the scent of him. The smell of his sweat, of his body. Her man. She nuzzles her nose in his chest hair, then lays her head there.

Curious, she reaches out and lifts the sheet. Beneath, in the gray-tinged semi-dark, she sees his erection. "Good morning, wood," she whispers and reaches out, encircling it with her fingers. He stirs more but still doesn't wake. Holding him now, grasping him, things feel so much better than they had last night. Safer. She doesn't doubt that there are still issues to come up, fallout to be discovered, but last night the Shepards shook the fucking Etch-a-Sketch. It's blank enough now that they can lie here this morning, her head on his chest, hand on his cock, growing harder as she tugs him from sleep. His heartbeat quickens slightly as she makes a ring out of her thumb and fore-finger just below the ridge of his head. She squeezes, slow and rhythmic, and his heart beats faster. She turns her head to press her left ear against his chest. From this position, she can see him. His eyes remain closed, but his breathing quickens. She tugs and squeezes and tugs and squeezes. Back to her right ear on his chest, listening to every sound his body makes. She throws back the sheet with her other hand and continues to tug and squeeze. His hand, warm, fingers spread wide, finds her back. She turns her head and his eyes are open.

He smiles down at her. "Good morning, angel."

She bites her lip and rolls on top of him, reaching between her legs to guide him inside her. She closes her eyes and takes herself back to the gang bang, last night, before Will, before the shame, before

(slut)

she got lost. When it was good. When it was fun.

"You should've been in me," she tells him. "You should've been the last one."

"I," he says and stops.

She opens her eyes again and shakes her head at his worried expression. "Oh, no," she tells him, feeling him move in and out of her. "No regretting. Not today. The moment is fixed. I'm amending this, today." She runs her fingertips through the hair on his chest, smiling down at him, and the distress in his eyes fades. "It's an edit," she tells him. "You're my final ride, final patron, final lover, final fuck at the gang bang."

Her eyes close and she can see it. The group spreads out. Alejandra smiles from the side. Paige takes Bruce's hand and lays him down on the cushion in the center of the room and climbs on top. Then she rides. She arches her back, and her hands slide down to just below his navel and his upper thigh. Her hair bounces as she tilts her head toward the ceiling. Her eyes are closed here so she can be there. One last time, an end cap, the closing parenthesis. Bruce, where he should've been all along. She hears him grunting beneath her. Exhaling sharply. His hands find her hips, then move up to cup her breasts as she rides. She squeezes him, outside and in. Her legs hold as she milks his cock. He's hers.

"Oh," she says, drawing the word out long. He responds in kind, and soon she feels him thrusting beneath her, filling her up.

Now the gang bang is finished, and she can return to Thursday morning in their suite. The sheer curtains are backlit by brilliant white light from the sun high in the sky, and they've slept in much later than usual.

"You were on fire," he tells her, "that hip action."

She smiles and lifts herself slowly off his softening cock, relishing the moment where his head briefly catches on her labia, then drops out. She feels his semen sliding out, lets it all fall onto him, then licks him clean.

"Man," he says, laughing.

"I don't much feel like going all the way down for breakfast," she says.

"It's probably over," he tells her. "What time is it?"

She shakes her head, not looking at the clock. "I don't care," she says and lifts the phone off the side table.

"*Hola*, this is Marisol."

"*Hola, Marisol,*" Paige says. "*¿Cómo está usted?*"

"*¿Muy bien, y tú?*"

"*¡Muy bien!* This is Paige Shepard in 1111, would you please have Eduardo bring us some fruit and some waffles?"

"And some bacon," adds Bruce with a yawn.

"*Mi esposo* would also like some bacon."

"Of course!"

"*¡Muchas gracias!*" Paige hangs up the phone.

When Eduardo arrives with their food, the two of them have moved to the balcony. He whisks the large domed lid from his silver tray with a flourish, and they applaud the bounty as well as his presentation. Before them are not only waffles, fruit, and bacon, but sausages, potatoes, and grits. Far too much for them to eat.

He bows to them, a broad smile on his face. "*Buen provecho,*" he says and leaves them to it.

"Jenn's mad at me," Paige tells Bruce.

"I don't think she is," he tells her, spreading butter on a waffle.

"Hurt, then." She picks a few grapes off the spread, then takes the whole bunch and leans back in her chair, putting her feet up on the white wicker foot stool. "Hurt that I left with Alejandra and not her. That I didn't go to her when I needed a confidante."

He nods.

"I should tell her about Emily, too."

He looks at her. "You mean Emily and me?"

"Emily and me. How deep the waters go, you know? Not gloss over things. Give her the real picture."

"I think she can handle that," he says.

"I hope so."

He puts his knife down and reaches out to her. "But we're good?"

She turns to look at him. At this moment, in this light – with his hair wild and big and uncombed, and the scruff on his jaw beneath his mustache, and that amazing hairy chest – here she sees the Tom Selleck that everybody always references in him. Beyond it, she sees the warmth and concern on his face.

"Yes," she says. "Clean slate."

"Clean slate." He nods. "What would you like to do with your final two days here?"

She looks out over the water. "Let's do something for our friends on Friday night."

"What did you have in mind?"

She shrugs. "Take over the beds up by the hot tub, invite Ryan and Jenn, and the people they're enjoying, and the people we're enjoying."

"Maybe our neighbors?" he asks.

She smiles at him. "Want another shot at Malcolm and Alexis, do ya?" She makes sure to emphasize playfulness, so he won't think she's needling him.

"Oh yes," he tells her.

"She's into you," says Paige. "I think they'd be up for it."

He smiles.

"And how about you, my love, what would you like to do with the rest of your time here? Note that I did not use the word *final*."

"I did note," he says.

"Because we'll be back." She feels it deeply. Regardless of what happens with life or the company. "No matter how many waitressing jobs or tricks turned it takes, we'll be back here."

"That's the spirit," he says.

"So?"

"Alexis."

"Is on your to-do list?"

He nods. "What I'd like to do is spend time in the sun, and in the ocean, and in that grand hot tub. Preferably with a drink in my hand that sports an umbrella."

"You should talk to Debra," Paige says. "I hear she brings her own umbrellas."

"She does," he says. "Thank you."

"For?"

"For letting me make mistakes." He doesn't look at her, and his mouth is stoic. She knows what his eyes look like beneath his Wayfarers. There's pain there. Regret.

"We both make mistakes," she says.

He nods. "Well," he says, a catch in his voice. "Right now, what I'd like is to enjoy this bounty with my wife. And look, I've got it." He grins at her.

She leans over and kisses him. "Dork."

# 56

## RYAN

"How about we sit down," suggests Rory, gesturing toward the bed.

After looking at it for a moment, Ryan nods and sits. The large suite with the bed as the centerpiece is the mirror image of Bruce and Paige's. Rory sits next to him. He wonders, looking down at Rory's blue and orange board shorts, if he should've put on clothes. "Naked is under-dressed," he tells the room.

Rory chuckles. "Naked is just fine, I don't know who told you otherwise."

Ryan nods, then chides himself for nodding too long. He wonders what to do. What's next?

"I'm going to put my hand on your leg," says Rory.

"Okay," says Ryan, quietly.

Rory does. "Do you have anything specific you'd like to try? Is there something that really intrigues you?"

Is there something that really intrigues him? He's not sure. He's not sure what he's doing here, either. Maybe he should say that. "I'm not really sure what I'm doing here."

"Okay." Rory smiles. "How about I take off my shorts."

"Solidarity in nudity," laughs Ryan, determined to knock off the nodding thing.

Rory stands and drops his shorts. Ryan looks from his shoulders to his feet. *This man is attractive,* thinks Ryan, *objectively so.*

The objectively attractive naked man in front of him smiles. Rory reaches down and tugs twice on his long flaccid penis. It twitches and hardens, but only slightly. Ryan knows that tug, the uncomfortable repositioning tug, that all men do when they're alone. A bit more awkward in front of someone. He looks from Rory's penis to his face. The smile there is genuine, though something about the expression suggests that he knows what Ryan is thinking. Rory knows he's hot.

*If I had those abs, I'd probably feel the same,* thinks Ryan. "Do, um... Is anything off limits for you?"

Rory shakes his head. "Also, tested negative for everything two months ago. You?"

Ryan nods. "Cold sores sometimes."

"That's fine. I use condoms for anal, of course."

"Of course," repeats Ryan, realizing the weight the word has on him. Anal. "Is that on the table?" he asks.

"I generally don't take things off the table if I'm attracted to someone," Rory says.

"I didn't realize I'd asked that out loud," says Ryan, then replays the rest of the sentence. "You're attracted to me?"

Rory laughs. "Do you also doubt it when women say it? Or just the gays?"

"I tend to doubt it when anybody calls me attractive."

"Fair enough," says Rory, sitting down. "You're a good-looking guy. You have a nice body, a nice cock. You look good with a few-day-old beard..."

Ryan reflexively scratches at his face.

"And it's fun to explore, isn't it?"

"Do you ever have sex with Marley?" Ryan asks, then apologizes.

"No need to be sorry," says Rory. "I have. Only when there's been a lot of wine. And only twice. I think..." He looks up at the ceiling. "I like outies more than innies. Like Terrence. Like you." His hand returns to Ryan's thigh, sliding up, then down ever so slightly.

Ryan hardens.

"Well, look at that."

"I'm nervous," says Ryan.

"That's alright," says Rory, smiling. He holds Ryan's gaze for a moment, then lifts his hand up. "You know you don't need to do anything you don't want to."

"I know. I'm okay."

"Okay," says Rory. "What if we just play with ourselves for now." He grabs for the remote and turns on the TV.

On the screen, a pale woman slides the largest cock Ryan has ever seen down her throat. "Whoa," he says, "there's porn on the TVs?"

Rory laughs. "Yeah, four channels of it. You didn't know?"

"We haven't turned on the TV."

"We find it inspirational, though there's a definite dearth of bi men in it," says Rory. "Chalk it up to that bi invisibility thing."

Ryan nods. His cock hardens more as he watches the blowjob on the TV. He notices, out of the side of his eye, as Rory takes his own flaccid cock in hand. He slides it through his fingers, in and out, and it hardens and grows.

*Okay,* Ryan thinks, *I can do that.* It's something that had seemed a possibility once or twice in high school. Once, at a sleepover, his friend Aaron brought out a video that his father taped from the Playboy channel. They'd put it on and both sort of looked at each other. What do we do? What's next? After Ryan had gone to sleep, Aaron took care of himself in his sleeping bag. Ryan awoke, heard the shuffling, saw the movement and the quiet gasp of climax and always wondered how he cleaned up, or if there was a sticky wet spot in there all night.

With Rory, whose cock seems to have reached full mast, which thankfully is only slightly larger than when flaccid, stroking, there's no hiding. And Ryan feels only the mildest sense of perplexity about what comes next. After watching the real-life cock and the one on the TV, Ryan grabs his own and strokes himself hard.

"We could make out," suggests Rory.

The suggestion shouldn't be surprising, but it is all the same. He's kissed Rory before, true, but in all his imaginings of what it might be like to be with another man, kissing has been strangely absent.

He is silent for longer than he meant to be, and Rory answers his own question. "It's okay if you don't want to. A lot of bi guys don't."

Ryan wonders why, what's the hesitation? He looks down, descending into thought.

"Can I suck your cock?" asks Rory, trying another tactic.

The question is straightforward and open, but Ryan doesn't

understand for a moment. He can't find the right words, so he just nods. He watches, as if in a dream as this man reaches his hands out, one cupping Ryan's balls, squeezing them lightly, the other surrounding the base of his cock. Then Rory leans down and warmth envelops Ryan's penis. His first thought is how it feels almost the same as a blowjob from a woman, except the moment Rory brings his lips all the way down. In that moment, he feels the rough beard against his leg and balls. The strangeness doesn't linger long, as he quickly becomes distracted by just how *good* Rory is at this. Moments in and he's already feeling the beginnings of an orgasm.

Ryan slides his fingers against Rory's head, finding little purchase in the man's short hair. "Okay," he says. "Okay, hold on."

Rory stops, holding position.

"If you continue like that, I'm going to come."

"Feel free," says Rory, lifting himself up slightly.

"No, I, uh—" How to put it. "After I come, I..."

Rory sits up next to him. "Lose interest?"

Ryan nods.

"Me too, sometimes. Your body produces a chemical to do that, in fact. Some people get drained. Some just can't do anything."

"I get that feeling, that I never have to have sex again."

"I know that one."

"You do too?"

"Not usually, but it's happened." He smiles. "Then reluctantly, I will stop sucking your cock."

"It was good," says Ryan. "Jesus Christ."

"What?"

"I'm not sure I could be any more awkward about all of this."

"You could," says Rory. "Many have. Oh, and you literally can. It doesn't bother me."

Ryan marvels at how calm and collected Rory seems. He feels a stirring. Maybe it's attraction. Maybe that's how his attraction to a man feels.

"Would you like to give it a try?" asks Rory.

It takes Ryan a moment to understand. He looks down at Rory's cock, thinking about how different that experience would be, how new. His brain raises a glass at him. *To new experiences. Hold your breath and jump.* "Why not?"

"Such enthusiasm," laughs Rory.

"Sorry," says Ryan.

"No more sorries."

Ryan nods. "I'm probably not going to be good at this."

"You know what the difference is between a good blowjob and a bad one?" asks Rory.

Ryan shakes his head.

"Very little. Don't use your teeth."

Rory's cock seems to be pointing right at him. He thinks about the times people have sucked his cock, including just now, what made them similar, or different. What makes for a good one? An exceptional one? What had Rory done just now that got him so close so quickly? What should—

"Try not to overthink it."

Ryan nods and kneels between Rory's blond hair covered thighs. The cock looms in front of him. He reaches up and grips it, noting that despite its girth, it doesn't really feel all that different from his own. He takes one last deep breath and licks the length of Rory's cock, feeling everything vividly. The texture of the large head, the lines and raised areas, the scar line of his frenulum. He traces all of it with his tongue.

"That feels great," says Rory.

As Ryan runs his tongue up that line to the top, he tastes the bitter sweetness, the salt of Rory's pre-cum. He's surprised by the similarity to women he's been with. Not the same, but familiar undertones.

*Let's really give this a try,* thinks Ryan, parting his lips (and teeth!) and sliding his mouth down. He feels the head run along the roof of his mouth as he closes his lips around Rory's shaft. Spongy again, smooth. For a moment, he pushes too far and feels the beginning of a gag. He instinctively begins to pull back, but recalls those best blowjobs, and the slight gag they'd included. He allows for the gag, and when he does pull back, he reaches up and feels the shaft of Rory's cock covered in thick, slick saliva. He strokes it, hovering over the cock, mouth open, taking a minute. It feels like a strange out-of-body situation, stroking a cock that isn't his. Feeling the familiar shape and texture, but not feeling the sensation.

*Of course, this one is much bigger,* he tells himself, then thanks his irritating inner monologue for the reminder. "Was that good?" he asks.

"You did great," Rory replies with a slight laugh. "How was it for you?"

"Different?" He looks up. "I don't know how else to describe it."

"Different bad? Different good?"

"Not bad," says Ryan.

"Good," says Rory.

Ryan looks down at the cock he's still holding. He tries to articulate his thoughts, not meeting Rory's eyes. "I'd like to do more," he says, "but I don't think I could take all of you inside me."

Rory laughs. "Fair enough. Honestly, I'm more of a bottom anyway."

"Heh."

"Listen," Rory says, "if this is something you'd like to do, I'm into it. If not, that's fine too. We can go back to blowjobs. Or we can stroke each other off. Or hell we can just watch more porn and jack off on the far side of the bed from each other."

"I'd...I'd like to try."

Rory nods. "Now? Or—"

"Now," Ryan says. He wraps his hand around his half-erect cock and strokes it back to attention. He doesn't add, *Before I change my mind*.

"Well then," says Rory, grabbing a lube bottle and a condom off the end table. He bites to tear the gold and black foil package, then squirts a shot of lube into the condom and puts it over the head of Ryan's cock.

Ryan watches as his already fading erection gets its rubber. Rory gives it a few good strokes after.

"You okay?" he asks.

Ryan nods.

Rory squirts some lube into his hand and runs his fingers around in it, then flips over onto his knees on the bed. He leans down on one arm, sliding his other hand back between his legs, inserting fingers into his anus.

*This is a new perspective,* thinks Ryan. But he's seen men bent over like this, hasn't he? Usually there's a woman beneath them.

*I wish Jenn was here.* He had been so certain he wanted to chart this course on his own. To do it for himself, not for anyone else. The way she had done with Paige.

The night of their first date with the Shepards, on the stairs in their townhouse, he returned from making up the bedroom and saw his wife in her underwear looking overwhelmed, standing with Paige, also undressed. "Would you like Ryan and Bruce there with us, or maybe just Ryan?" Paige asked.

His wife looked up at him on the staircase, like she hadn't even considered this becoming real.

*Which is how I'm feeling now,* thinks Ryan, looking at the man on the bed in front of him. Legs spread, well-groomed balls hanging between them.

"Maybe," Jennifer said then, the beginning of their grand swinging experiment, "maybe just us for a few minutes."

He asked her about it later, and she told him she'd been worried about fucking up in front of him. "If it didn't go well, they'd go home, and that'd be it."

Here, if this doesn't go well, he'll leave the suite and find Jenn back on the beach bed, and that'll be the end.

"I'm ready when you are," says Rory, stroking himself.

Ryan nods, even though he knows Rory can't see it. The nod is for himself. Because this is about his exploration, his search for that moment, that thing. For a paradigm shift, like Jenn's. Not just the transition from monogamous to not, but something that hits him so hard he changes his name.

He moves behind Rory, stroking himself as he goes. He's not fully erect, but it'll be okay. He could try to get harder, but when has *trying* ever helped? He moves closer and presses the tip of his condom-clad penis against Rory. This part isn't so different, is it? He's had anal sex with Jenn, with Paige, with a couple other very enthusiastic women. The man in front of him isn't that different.

He presses and slides away twice.

"Need any—"

"No," says Ryan, "I'm good."

"Kay."

He strokes, and strokes. Harder now. Trying again. Pressing and pushing, and then in he slides. He hears Rory gasp and wonders how big Terrence's cock is, if he's even making a dent? So foolish, he knows, and he's on the larger side, but—

He slips out. "Sorry."

"Don't worry."

He takes his now more flaccid cock in his hand and strokes. Closer now, closer. He slides back in.

"You feel great," says Rory.

Ryan doesn't respond. His eyes are closed. Moments and feelings all around. When Paige grabbed him internally with her muscles. When Lydia ran her teeth down his cock. The way Jenn felt, now that he didn't have to use a condom with her. He feels himself harden, enough to slide in and out. He leans forward.

*This is okay, this can work.*

He feels himself close to coming and ignores the instinct to make it last. Instead, he squeezes his eyes shut, running through the carousel of images in his mind. Lydia flogging him, Jenn's lips around his cock, the time he fucked Paige so hard in the ass that she came all over the bedspread. Everybody had been surprised by—

"Unh!" grunts Ryan as he comes. He thrusts once, twice, again.

"Yeah," says Rory. "Fuck yeah."

When he finishes, Ryan grips the base of the condom and slides out. He's already completely flaccid. He looks down at himself, the limp penis, the dangle of the condom, tip hanging white and pendulous. He turns away and removes it. He feels his face redden, a rough gnawing in the pit of his stomach.

"Man," says Rory, "thank you."

Ryan smiles but won't meet his eye.

"Mind if I wash off quickly?" asks Rory. "I don't like feeling all slippery back there."

"Oh, uh," says Ryan, "no, go ahead."

Rory stands, wrapping his arm around Ryan's chest. "Hope that was good for you too," he says.

Ryan nods.

Rory disappears into the bathroom and closes the door. Ryan sits on the ledge around the bed. There'd been no paradigm shift. No eye-opening experience. Instead, there's just...whatever this is. He's not sure. He puts his hand to his chest. He looks down at his other hand, holding the used condom. He feels the rush that often accompanies his post-orgasm, the distancing feeling, the "I don't ever need to have sex again" feeling. But looking at the condom turns his stomach. This is more. There's something else riding shotgun on the feeling, something darker.

*It's shame,* Ryan realizes, *and it's growing.*

He chucks the condom into the bedside trashcan and leaves the room before Rory returns from the bathroom.

The shame follows him.

# 57

## CRISTA

"Can we talk now?" asks Crista.

"We can," says Allie.

Silence. After a while, Crista asks, "Will you?"

Allie purses her lips and opens her mouth to say something that Crista is sure will be biting, cold, but instead nods. Crista looks at her, standing at the foot of the bed. She wishes her wife would sit, on her own, without being asked. She probably won't, so Crista pulls back the sheet and pats the bed. With an almost theatrical level of reluctance, Allie sits.

"You got in late last night," says Crista.

"I did," says Allie.

"Did you have a good day yesterday?"

"Yes."

The silence lengthens, and Crista sighs. Maybe there's nothing to be done here. It'll end quietly, with a whimper, and they'll go back home to single people lives. To their separate worlds. To whoever they'd been before that awards ceremony. But no, she isn't giving in to that just yet. "I really think we need to talk."

Silence for a while, then Allie agrees.

"Will you please engage with me?"

Allie turns toward Crista. Her brown eyes give no clues to her emotional state, but they are penetrating. What do they see?

"Before we talk," begins Crista, "I need to know if you've

checked out of this relationship. Because if you have, I should change my talking points."

Allie blinks. Her face softens. "No," she says, "I have not."

"I'm sorry about the overnight," says Crista. "I shouldn't have allowed myself to get caught up like that. And I should've come to find you. I'm sorry my libido is complex and unpredictable. I wish it weren't. I wish I knew myself how it would react to things."

After a moment, Allie nods.

"I missed you. All day, I missed you. I wanted you back here, by me, with me. *With* me. My life changed when I met you, because you—" Her voice catches. She sniffs, trying to stay in control, calm and collected, here at the beginning of the conversation, when it's most important. "Because you told me I didn't have to continue what I was doing. When the trip to Syria— When it was too awful to continue." Deep breaths. "My happiness. The kid's books. The lack of trauma. It's all because you gave me permission to *not* be a journalist." Crista puts her hand on the bed near Allie's leg. Not touching, not quite.

"I didn't give—" Allie begins, then stops. "You shouldn't give me credit for your life choices, for taking care of yourself."

"Maybe not," says Crista, "but I do anyway."

"Okay," says Allie, "so what do we do? I'd like to be in a relationship with someone who wants to be with me. Who wants me. You don't have to want me *all* the time, but some of the time, yes. I despise the trope of *those lesbians who don't have sex,* and will not let that be my life."

"I do want you," says Crista. She knows that she needs to do it now, rip off the band-aid. To say the thing she's been thinking all day. The thing she's been thinking since wondering if Sergey fucked her. Since being a part of that threesome. The scary thing, the big thing. The gigantic question mark atop her sexuality. There's no time like the present. It won't get any easier. Just say it. Just take the breath and blurt it out. "What if I'm not a lesbian?"

Allie is looking at her now, her expression changing, moving from flatness to confusion. Crista can hear her own question still hanging in the silence. "Could you," begins Allie, looking away then back, "could you please clarify that for me?"

"If I wasn't a lesbian, would you still love me?"

The tension in Allie's voice grows. "I need you to say more things."

"It's straightforward, *mi amor*." If Allie would only answer the question, Crista could proceed. "If you said you weren't a lesbian, my only question would be, 'Do you still love me?'"

Allie frowns. "Do you have any idea how difficult it is to be asked a loaded question like that with a specific response in mind. A *surprising* question at—"

"No, you're right," sighs Crista. "That was unfair."

"Look," Allie says. "I love you. Truly. Deeply. I don't know what you're asking, but if you're telling me you're straight after all, I think that will cause a pretty un-traversable rift in our relationship."

"I'm not saying that," says Crista.

"What then?"

Crista looks at the ceiling, seeing herself in the mirror affixed there. Surely that mirror has seen so many better things. Now it's stuck with the two of them, the first lesbians at Aphrodite's. "What if I'm actually bisexual?"

"Are you?"

"The venom in that response was—"

"No venom."

"Sounded like."

"I'm sorry you heard it that way." Allie takes a breath, asks very calmly. "Are you?"

In a moment, all the thought Crista has put into this, all the searching, all the analysis, is gone. "I don't know," she admits, tears in her eyes. "But I know you don't give me that option."

"What does that mean?"

"You lead every encounter with, 'We don't play with men.'"

Allie narrows her eyes. "We don't."

"You don't. You're the gold star lesbian."

"Okay," Allie puts her hand up, "hold on a second."

Crista nods.

"Would you please tell me what you're feeling, because at the moment I feel like I'm being attacked for being a lesbian. Attacked by my, I thought, lesbian wife. So please, take a moment, take a breath, and tell me what in the world is going on."

Crista takes that moment, that breath. "I'm not attacking you for being a lesbian."

"Okay."

"I'm not saying I want to be with men, either."

Allie says nothing, but nods.

"What I'm saying is that I've never felt able to tell you if I did. Like, if I look at a guy and think he's hot, I don't feel I can say that."

"Why not?"

"Because you're a fucking gold star lesbian, and your wife should be a full-throttle lesbian too, even if she's had dick in the past."

"I. Never. Said—"

"No, I know you didn't."

"So, what are you accusing me of?"

Crista sighs. She should be able to do this. She'd been a journalist for fuck's sake. She hadn't turned in the communication skills card when she started writing about rabbit detectives. *Simplify, Crista. Get to the meat of it.* "If I'd told you I wanted to fuck a man. Here at this resort." She holds up her hands to indicate the whole place. "What would you have said?"

"I don't know," says Allie. "But I'd wonder if it's why you don't want to fuck me." There it is. The crux.

"Did you ever doubt your sexuality?" asks Crista. "Wonder if there was something wrong with you?"

"*Mi madre* made it pretty clear there was," says Allie.

Crista tries not to show her frustration with her wife's quippy obtuseness, and her own inability to make her point. "You know what I'm asking."

"No," says Allie, "I never wondered about men or my sexuality."

"Gold star," says Crista.

"I'd really like you to stop throwing that in—"

"Sorry," says Crista, "I know, it's not helpful."

"Feels judgy."

Crista nods in acknowledgment. "I have doubted. At every stage of the game. From the first dick that I sucked to the first time that I tribbed a girl. Every step in between I wondered if this was really me." She tries to blink away the tears in her eyes. "When your sexual urges are so uneven, doubt is everywhere, and you wonder, if *maybe* you just alter what you're looking for, try something different. Maybe..."

"So, you want something different." Allie's voice is flat.

"I want you not to judge me." Crista looks away, not wanting to face that expression. *No, this is important, look at her.* She turns back. "You don't judge our playmates for liking men, why would you judge me for the possibility that I might?"

"I—" Allie shouts, then takes a moment, dials it down almost to a whisper. "I'm not judging you. I'm sorting out what this meandering discussion means for our relationship."

"It doesn't have to mean anything," pleads Crista. "We swing because of the declaration that it is unfair to assume one person can fulfill all our needs."

"Yes."

"So, I'm not necessarily saying I'm bisexual. Or that I want to do anything with men."

"Okay."

"I'm saying I don't want to feel like I can't tell you if something comes up for me. I don't want to worry about you fretting about the end of our relationship if I decide I'd like to suck a cock. And I don't want to feel like I'm less important because I'm not an amazing lesbian like you." Crista looks down at her lap, covered with the white sheet. There's a small speck of something dark on the sheet, she picks at it with her nail.

"Do you, um," Allie starts shakily, then clears her throat and the words sound stronger, "do you feel that I've put you in this box intentionally?"

"No," says Crista.

"Good, because I have not. And not once, not *once*, have I led you to believe that I'm perfect."

Crista nods. "You haven't. But it's a lot of pressure. The lesbian swingers who lead with the disclaimer that we don't play with men. Ever."

"I only do that so—"

"I know why," says Crista, "and I know why it's important. To tell the truth, I don't think we've ever played with a couple where I particularly wanted to do anything with the man."

"Okay."

"I just don't want to feel like I'm stuck in a box anymore. Because we're out-of-the-box people! We're married women! Long-term lesbians! Swingers, jeez. We don't abide by other people's restrictions."

"No," says Allie, "no we don't."

"And I think the pressure merged with my already erratic libido and did...the stuff."

"Let me just outright ask if you're blaming—"

"No, I'm not. I'm recognizing myself, my needs, my eccentricities." Crista touches Allie's leg with the tips of her fingers. After a moment, Allie puts her own hand on top. "I'm in this relationship," says Crista. "But I need to know I can be myself. Whatever that might be. And if it no longer works for us, we can resolve that when it happens. But until then, I'm in." She takes a deep breath, feeling the weight beginning to lift. Only one question left, after all. "Are you?"

Allie looks at their hands. "I am."

"Thank the goddess," says Crista. She kisses Allie's shoulder, and they sit in silence a while, remembering how to be near each other.

# BRUCE

When Paige returns from her run on the beach, Bruce smiles and reveals the massage table in the seating area of their room.

"Oh, and what is this?" his wife asks.

"An anniversary gift," says Bruce. "This is Claudia."

Claudia, clad in a white polo shirt, stands and offers her hand to Paige. Her long black hair is held back in a ponytail. She's older than most of the polo-wearing staff, but fit.

"You bought me a massage, eh?"

Bruce nods.

"Does it come with a happy ending?" Paige asks him flirtatiously.

"*Claro*," says Claudia.

Paige smirks. "Why haven't we been getting massages thus far?"

He laughs. "I don't know. Something about plenty of hands for free."

"Oh, right," smiles Paige. "Claudia, would you mind if I shower quickly?"

"No problem," says Claudia, returning to her seat on the sectional couch to scroll through her phone.

His wife returns from the shower covered by a towel from chest to thigh, another wrapped around her head. He's amused by the sudden apparent modesty. When she reaches the table, covered in what look like even more luxurious white linens than their bedsheets, Paige winks at him and drops the towel to the floor. She stands naked, smiling. It's not a stretch for him to imagine her riding that clamshell across the surf.

"Face down, please." Claudia pats the cushioned O at the head of the massage table.

Paige climbs up, releasing her hair from the towel and lying face down. Claudia snaps a belt around her waist like a soldier, several pump-bottles her ammo of choice. She takes two squirts from the second on her left and rubs her hands together.

"Enjoy," Bruce whispers, then points the sound system remote across the room and presses play. Sounds of a babbling brook, lightly backed by choral sounds, fill the room.

"Seriously?" asks Paige from the hole in the table.

"Two hours of New Age not going to do it for you?"

"Fuck off." She laughs.

Claudia finishes rubbing her hands together and presses them against Paige's freckled upper back. His wife moans, both a sexual sound and a sound of relief. They are, after all, quite similar sounds, aren't they? He presses the remote again, and the opening notes of Massive Attack's *Teardrop* play. He never could divorce the song from the opening titles of the TV series *House*, but this track, and the group, is a favorite of Paige's.

"Cliché still," says Paige, "but lovely. All of it, a beautiful gesture. Thank you, my love."

"Happy anniversary mark II, angel," he says, opening the door to head out to the balcony.

"You no want to help?" asks Claudia.

Bruce stops.

"That sounds fun," says Paige from the cushioned ring.

"I can, absolutely."

"We massage *señorita*," says Claudia, as though that was what he'd signed up for in the first place. *Who knows,* thinks Bruce, *maybe I did*.

"Yes," says Paige, "that. Let's do that."

Bruce smiles and nods, closing the door again and wondering if he's overdressed or underdressed in his shorts and T-shirt. He rubs his hands together to warm them.

"Wash hands, *por favor*," says Claudia, looking from his hands to his face disapprovingly.

He chuckles. "Sure."

When he returns from washing his hands, he finds Claudia tracing full circles around Paige's back. He steps up next to her. She shakes her head and points to the opposite side of his wife. "Sure," he says and stands across from Claudia. When he gets there, he puts his hands on Paige's side.

"No!" says Claudia.

"She could be *your* Domme, I think," giggles Paige.

"Shh!" commands Claudia.

"Sorry," says Paige, sheepishly.

Claudia holds up both of her hands, glistening with massage oil. She crosses her thumbs in a way that makes Bruce recall a hand puppet bird shadow. They remain interlocked at her thumbs as she presses figure eights into Paige's back. "See?"

"That's exquisite," moans Paige.

"Good," says Claudia. "Shush."

"Yes, ma'am."

Bruce nods and interlocks his thumbs. Claudia returns the nod and tilts her head toward the pump bottles on her utility belt. Bruce takes a squirt of oil in each hand, crosses his thumbs again, and meets Claudia's dark eyes. She smirks, just a little, and nods.

They spend a long stretch of time on Paige's shoulders and back, Claudia demonstrating new moves for Bruce to mirror across from her. Occasionally they switch sides, "So she can get all the places I missed," he mutters to Paige.

"Quiet," says Paige.

They move from her back to her legs and work the muscles there. Claudia goes to work on Paige's ass with gusto, kneading and pushing her heart-shaped rear, causing the occasional moan to drift from relief to pure pleasure. Bruce catches the slight smile on Claudia's lips. Claudia holds up her right thumb, then covers it in oil from her left hand. Bruce nods, to show he's indeed paying attention. She presses her thumb between Paige's ass cheeks.

"Oh my," says Paige.

"For tension," says Claudia, then returns her eyes to Bruce. "Circles."

"Circles," Bruce repeats.

"*Sí*, circles," insists Claudia. "Look and see!"

He looks. Claudia separates Paige's cheeks with her left hand, dripping oil. Her right thumb traces small circles around Paige's anus.

"She likes that," says Bruce.

"I do," says Paige.

"Everybody likes that," insists Claudia. "Now you."

"Circles," Bruce repeats, taking Claudia's place.

He hears his wife's breathing quicken and wonders if Claudia has brought a change of covers for the table. Quickening, quickening.

"Not time yet," says Claudia after a moment. "Flip."

"Yes, ma'am," says Paige. She flips over. Her face is red, both from the pressure against the cushioned ring and from pre-orgasmic flush. She grins at Bruce.

"Circles?" he asks.

"Circles," she repeats.

He leans down to kiss her but is interrupted by Claudia's shiny hand. She snaps her fingers. Bruce stands again, giving Claudia his full attention. He hears Paige chuckle.

They work up and down Paige's arms, working out the tension as they find it. Around her breasts and abdomen. Down, then back up her legs.

"Okay," says Claudia.

"Okay," agrees Bruce.

"Okay," says Paige.

"Shush," says Claudia.

"Yes, ma'am," says Paige.

Claudia fills both hands with oil. "Hold out your hands," she tells Bruce.

Bruce nods and does as he's told. Claudia reaches her hands out and takes his, rubbing the oil into his palms, filling them.

"Waterfall," she says, and cascades her fingers down the length of Paige's vulva, first her left hand, then her right, then left again. Continuing and continuing.

Paige's breath quickens again, faster and faster. She's gasping. "Ho, jeez," she says, her grip on the sides of the table tightening as Claudia continues to alternate hands in an endless cascade of touching.

Bruce stands, hands covered in oil, ready and waiting for his moment to shine. "Put me in, coach!" he whispers to himself, smiling.

"Now you," says Claudia, ignoring him. She doesn't stop her own waterfall of fingers.

He reaches his hands out. Still, she doesn't stop. He brings his hands right above Paige's pubic hair. He's ready. He's able.

"Go," Claudia says and removes her hands. Bruce delays only a moment before continuing the waterfall. As he does so, Claudia presses the ball of her hand against the bottom of Paige's vulva, and if his wife's gasp is any indication, one of Claudia's fingers is now making circles.

"Oh, God, oh, God," the repetition from Paige begins quietly and rises, rises, rises. This time she's not shushed by Claudia, and when she comes, she vibrates the table.

Claudia moves from between her legs to Paige's shoulders, massaging lightly as the orgasm moves through her body, Bruce continuing waterfalls all the while.

"Okay," sighs Paige, reaching up from the table for the first time to stop his hand. "Okay," she says again.

"*¿Cómo te sientes?*" asks Claudia.

Paige looks up at her with eyes that seem to move wildly, unfocused. "*¡Bien, muy bien!*"

Claudia smiles, gives each of Paige's shoulders a long squeeze and claps her hands together. She looks at Bruce. "Good," she tells him. "You could get job."

"He has magic hands," says Paige, smiling at her husband. The look on her face calms him, the openness and warmth. It is a face of forgiveness, of the promised clean slate.

Claudia helps her sit up.

Paige smiles at her. "Do you have another appointment right now?"

"No," says Claudia.

"Could we do that for Bruce?"

The masseuse turns to him, giving him an appraising once over. He wonders what she's looking for.

Claudia turns back to Paige with a nod. "*Sí,*" she says. Then, to him, snapping her fingers, "Clothes off."

He does as he's told, lying face down on the table and reaching below to adjust himself. Soon he feels two sets of hands on his shoulders. Strong hands working in circles. He closes his eyes.

In the darkness, his mind swirls. He thinks about Paige's gang bang. Who had been there? What had they done? Did she do

DP? And if so, who got her ass, something he'd done for the first time only a handful of years before. The desire to punch Will in his hateful mouth surfaces and subsides. He wonders about Emily and his credit card at a hotel in Wisconsin. She'd never steal from them, no, but desperation leads to—

*No, stop.*

He focuses on breathing, in through his nose, out through his mouth. He feels the movement of their hands on him, sliding down his back. He feels the bird shapes. The playlist has restarted. He slows his breathing in time to the music. Will he be able to ever let Emily go completely? Will Paige? What if she's always in the margins, at the—

*Stop. Really. Now.*

"Paige," he asks.

"Yes, my love?"

"Could you put on Yo-Yo Ma?"

"Of course."

*Teardrop* stops, and moments later the cellist Yo-Yo Ma begins the *Prelude* from Bach's *Cello Suite No. 1,* his favorite piece of music in the world. In the darkness behind his eyes the swirling slows and stops. He sees his cello between his legs, in a spotlight circle on a darkened stage. On the cello in his mind, he matches Yo-Yo Ma stroke for stroke, and the world, at last, falls away.

He's surprised when he is asked to flip over, sure that much time hadn't passed already. The brightness, even with his eyes closed, interrupts his private recital – the lights on the audience are up. There they sit, those on his mind, Emily front and center, his sons, the phantom participants of the gang bang.

"Would you like it darker?" asks Paige, whispering in his ear. "You're all squinty."

He nods, and moments later feels the smoothness of a silk scarf against his face. The lights on the audience fade. They're all still out there, he knows, obscured by darkness, but their chattering quiets. It's just him and Bach on that stage. And he lets go.

He sees his wife next to him, dressed to the nines in a black dress with folds of white, sharing his spotlight. "You don't need to fix it all," she whispers. "Showing up is what matters."

He nods.

When he's pulled from the darkness this time, it isn't by the faces in the audience, instead, it's the intense variation of the waterfall that four well-oiled hands are performing on his erection.

The speed and intensity are too much to bear, and when he comes, Paige laughs and says "Wow."

Claudia says, "Yes, good."

Lips on his, then on his forehead. Hands on his shoulders.

He drifts back to the dark stage in the dark concert hall. "You've always shown up. And that's always been enough," says Paige in his mind.

"I love you," says Paige in his ear.

He exhales a long slow breath he's held for far too long.

# 59

# RYAN

"How was it?" asks Jenn with a grin almost wider than her face. She crawls down the beach bed seductively as he approaches. Such enthusiasm. He wonders how she'll feel when he tells her. What he did. How he left.

Ryan steps up to the end of the bed. "Need a drink?"

She shakes her head and kisses him. "Celia just brought me one." She waves at Celia in the bar not more than twenty feet away. Celia returns the wave.

"*¡Señor Ryan! ¿Cómo estás?*" asks Celia.

Ryan holds his hand flat and tilts it back and forth. "*Asi asi.*"

"What would you like? Make it better," she asks, her face turning solemn.

"What're you drinking?" he asks Jenn.

"Banana daiquiri," she says.

He points at the daiquiri. "I'll have one of these." He begins to head toward the bar.

"No, no!" Celia says, waving him away. "You sit, I bring!"

Ryan slowly nods and looks back to his wife. The change in her expression says she can tell that his smile isn't genuine. He sees her lose the enthusiasm, feeling like he's taken something from her.

"I had sex with a man," he says, but there's no passion in it. It's not exactly melancholy, but it's clearly not what she'd hoped: an unbridled, enthusiastic, "I fucked a man, and I liked it!"

She nods and pats the bed. "Want to sit down and talk about it?"

He climbs up next to her and looks out at the water. The early afternoon has turned cloudy, and the sky is muddled shades of white and gray, the water dull iron.

"Not the game changer you'd hoped," his wife says, not a question.

He shakes his head.

She rests her own head on his shoulder, putting her arm low on his back. "Will you tell me about it, anyway?"

He nods and wonders where to begin.

His wondering is interrupted by Celia with two daiquiris. "I made you another, *señorita*," she says with a smile.

"*Muchas gracias*, Celia," Ryan says.

"*De nada*." Celia heads back to the bar.

Ryan takes a drink, then another. "It's good."

"It is."

"I left while he was in the bathroom."

"Oh, Ryan," she says, "that's not—"

"It's fucking bad, I know," says Ryan.

Jenn frowns but doesn't say anything.

"I didn't know what I'd say to him when he came back out. He was so nice about everything. Nice, encouraging." He shakes his head. "It was too different."

"What do you mean?"

"Like I didn't know what to do," he says. "I didn't really want to kiss him, and I felt weird about that. Because who doesn't kiss when they're playing?"

"There was that couple we met at—"

"I know," says Ryan, "and remember how weird that was? To not be able to kiss them?"

Jenn nods. "But you could kiss—"

"I know. I could've, and he would've been into it. But I didn't want to. Maybe it's just not—" He looks down at the drink in his hands. He doesn't know how to say this, how to process it. "I don't know. I don't know what was wrong there. It just was something that—"

She reaches over and takes his hand in both of hers.

"I also didn't want to come back here and tell you it wasn't right. I know how excited—"

"Don't give that another thought," she says. "Seriously. This isn't about me. I can watch all the guy-on-guy porn I want. You shouldn't do something just because you think it's what I want."

"I wanted to feel that big moment," he says, "like you did."

She nods.

"We jacked off a little, and that was all right. We gave each other blowjobs…"

"How was that?"

"I was very aware of my teeth," he says.

She snickers. "Sorry."

"No, don't apologize," he says. "It was funny. Penises have a weird texture in your mouth."

She smiles and nods. "They do indeed."

"His is huge," Ryan tells her. He widens his eyes in emphasis.

"I've noticed. Though I've not seen it hard."

"It gets even bigger," he says.

Jenn exhales sharply.

"I wasn't prepared to take that…"

She cocks her head at him, waiting.

"In me."

"Oh!" She shakes her head. "I don't think I could take that in my ass either."

"That's good, 'cuz he's gay," Ryan pokes her.

"Yeah, yeah, okay."

"But I thought, I'm here, I really should go for it. And he said he's usually the bottom."

"So, you actually…"

Ryan nods.

"And?"

"I couldn't stay hard. And that felt terrible. And it was weird, and I was detached. Especially without kissing. And when I finished…" Ryan sighs. "He went to the bathroom, and I just sat there and felt terrible. So, I snuck out." He doesn't look up from his lap, running his fingers over each other, thinking about his exit.

Ryan stood outside Rory's door, debating knocking again. He could say he stepped out for some fresh air and got locked out. But when he heard the bathroom latch, he made his way down the stairs as quickly as he could.

Out to the beach where he could stand in the water.

"I felt shame," he tells Jenn.

"For leaving?" she asks.

"For leaving, yes, but also during. I've never felt shame for doing something, trying something."

"Because you were doing something gay?"

Ryan processes it for a moment. Was that it? His religious days are long past. He doesn't feel negatively about gay people or culture. "Not on the surface, at least. Sometimes it lingers."

"I know how you feel, though," she says. "I had the shame triggers, too. Both early on, and after Paige and I said, 'I love you.'"

Ryan nods. "I also didn't know what I'd say to him if he asked if I had fun. 'Yeah, sorta?' 'Not really?' 'I'm all ashamed?'"

She squeezes his hand. "I'm sorry you didn't find what you were hoping for."

He looks at his wife, who gives him a little smile. "Is it bad for me to yearn for a moment like you've had?"

"Which one?" she asks.

"That's even more to the point," he says. "You've had multiple! Realizing how interested you were in women. Understanding the paradigm shift, that it was more than just interest. Finding real love there. It's all momentous."

"Do you," she starts. "Are you jealous of what I've found? Do you wish I hadn't—"

"No!" he says, wiping his hand down his face. It's a good thing he hadn't stuck around to talk to Rory. He can't seem to articulate much of anything. "Envy," he says, the word coming to him as if from nowhere. "Envy, not jealousy. I don't wish you didn't have it. I just wish I could."

"Maybe this isn't it, your thing, your paradigm," says Jenn. "I know how much you worked yourself up about it and thought that this would be the thing for sure."

"This isn't it."

"But," says Jenn, really emphasizing it, "but also you shouldn't determine that this is your official stance. Like Raymond says, 'Try everything twice in case you did it wrong the first time.'"

Ryan looks at her. "I don't think I'm in a good place to try—"

"Oh, no, hon, not here probably. And probably not with Rory."

"Yeah, I'm sure that ship has sailed, after ditching out like that."

She nods, and her face says, *Duh,* though she doesn't say it aloud. "This isn't a failure." She squeezes his hand. "It's learning.

Maybe you're not going to want to do it again. Or maybe you'll try, and you still won't feel like it's for you. You confronted your sexuality, and that's worth praising. Very few people in the world would ever do that."

He smiles at his wife.

"All that positive stuff said," she narrows her eyes, "you need to apologize to him for leaving while he was in the bathroom."

Ryan agrees, and they sit in silence awhile.

"So, what'd you think about the blowjob? Besides the teeth thing."

"Well, when he was giving me one, it was all scratchy from his beard."

"Yeah," she says, "now you know why I like it when you shave."

Ryan laughs. He remembers the feel of Rory's cock in his mouth, running his tongue over it. The finale of their time together may have caused some dramatic mixed emotions, but he didn't feel the same about the blowjob. "It was interesting giving one. Unique. I'd probably do that again. Maybe I could share a cock with you."

Jenn's eyes open so wide they look like they'll roll right out of her head.

"I take it you like that idea," he says with a laugh.

"I *love* that idea," she replies. Then she centers herself, and looks at him sternly. "Though I'll reiterate that you don't need to do anything for me."

"Thank you," he says.

She leans over and kisses him. "You're okay?"

He nods. From down the beach, he sees Paige walking toward them. He raises his hand in a wave, and she returns it.

"Hey," whispers Jenn, "would you mind me spending some time one-on-one with her?"

"Not at all."

"You're good?"

"I'm good," he assures her. "Take all the time you need."

Jenn kisses him again, then climbs off the bed.

Ryan watches her head down the beach toward Paige. Her girlfriend. The one other person she truly loves.

Not jealous.

Envious.

## 60

# JENN

The two women meet and pause for a moment in front of the bar, then walk in silence down to the very edge of the resort, where the sign warns folks brave enough to traverse Cancún's public beach that *ahead thar be naked folk*. They stand a while there, not crossing the line, pointing their nakedness outward toward the world.

"I want to tell you about my feelings," Jenn says to Paige, "and then you can share whatever you'd like to share."

Paige nods. "I'm listening."

Jenn takes her hand, and they step onto the cobblestone path that winds back through the resort, along manicured grass and palm trees. "I feel like you're holding back," she says, after a long silent stretch.

Paige says nothing.

Jenn appreciates her girlfriend's willingness to just listen, but can't help but yearn for the feedback that usually characterizes their conversations. She pushes through. "It feels like you don't trust me. Or like you think I can't handle knowing some things about you. Bruce told Ryan about some conflict with Emily. I didn't know she was back in the picture." Jenn pointedly looks at Paige, who nods in response. "I know I shouldn't feel jealous, but seeing you on that boat with Alejandra, knowing that you were out somewhere, with someone else... I thought that maybe you didn't want me along."

"That's not the case," says Paige, then she mimes zipping her lips.

Jenn looks at her. "People have said something went down last night. With you. No one has given details, and I didn't push, because you'll either tell me or you won't, and I don't need the gossip." She takes a long, deep breath. "I share most everything with you. Maybe more than I should sometimes. Because I've been scared in our relationship, and I think you should know that. Because we have a relationship, I think, based on trust." She wavers a little. "And it helps to talk to you. When I see you off with someone like...that..." She's unsure herself quite what she means. "Alejandra, I mean, she's gorgeous. And tall, and on TV! And the boobs! And someone said she won a *Pulitzer!* Is that right?"

Paige nods.

"Jesus. Why would you want to be with me? When I don't have things all figured out. And I'm still trying to understand what being in a relationship with you is about. Being in a relationship with a woman. Being poly, I guess."

"Can I—" Paige begins, but stops herself.

Jenn turns and sees tears in Paige's eyes. She nods.

"I want to be with you," Paige says firmly. "I love you. I haven't had a relationship like you before."

"But Emily—"

"Was completely different," she says, "and a shit-show, more often than not." Paige leads her to an alcove with a long cushioned bench. On the wall above the bench is a painting of a woman's nude back. Jenn finds the swooping brush strokes soothing. They sit silently, Paige holding both of Jenn's hands. "It's hard, sometimes, to admit things that make you feel... Less good about yourself."

Jenn nods.

"My interactions with Emily have been... She's not healthy for me, at all. And when she blasts through she always leaves me worse for the wear. I hate that someone can do that to me. And it makes me feel like I make horrible decisions. And why would *you* want to be with someone who makes awful decisions." Paige laughs mirthlessly. "When she spiraled in last year, it wrecked me when she left."

Jenn nods. "I know."

"No," says Paige. "Wrecked."

Jenn frowns. Had Paige downplayed that situation? The one that ended with the nasty texts. **Bad influence. Slut.** Why would she do that? They don't have to share everything with each other, of course, but, "We're supposed to tell each other when things are significant, when they *matter*."

Paige nods. "I know. But I was so embarrassed about the way she made me feel, and so worried you'd think less of me. That I'm not trustworthy because—"

"Keeping important things from me isn't trustworthy," says Jenn. Immediately she feels bad, those were dagger words. She takes a deep breath and tries again. "Maybe the boundaries of our relationship are a little bit ill-defined."

"Maybe."

"We may have grown to a point where—"

"I don't want you to go," Paige blurts out.

Jenn looks at her and frowns.

"What?"

"I don't want you to see me, and then decide that you don't want to—"

"Wait," says Jenn, "do you think I'm leaving you?"

"Emily did. Does again and again, really." Paige wipes her eyes.

"Right."

"I know you're not Emily. When I hold back, it's to..."

"To what?"

"Spare you," says Paige. "You don't need to take on my problems. I know how much stress you have yourself."

"That's not for you to decide," Jenn tells her.

"It is," says Paige, "a little."

"Not if you want me to trust you." Jenn hears the firmness in her own voice. "Not if you want this to be more than casual, like I do. You know I hardly dated at all before Ryan, so I have no road map here." She takes a long breath, hoping to quell the rising pitch, but can't. "You're a lot to live up to!"

"Live— What?"

"Whenever I feel like I'm being jealous, or childish, or whenever I struggle, I wonder if this'll be the last straw. Enough to make you just decide to quit because dealing with the newbie is too hard. Like before." Jenn brings her hand to her face, feeling the wetness on her cheeks. The words had been out before she'd even processed them herself. But that was the beginning, wasn't it? The time that she'd fucked up, and they got cut off. And that was the tough time. The worst time. The newbies, the drama couple. "It happened because I was too intense. Because I couldn't take something that I should've been able to. Because I got jealous—"

"Jenn, please," says Paige.

"What?"

"I'm sorry."

Jenn nods and waits.

"That moment at our house was unlike anything you've ever done in our relationship. It's an outlier. I assure you that I don't see you as causing drama, and I sincerely do not see you as a newbie."

She nods again, wiping her nose. "Well, then, I *need* you to tell me things! Good and bad! Because then I won't feel like I'm the only one. Like you don't feel these things."

"I do," says Paige.

Jenn doesn't believe her.

"Truly, I do. This week. The reason I've been weird? It's because I'm jealous that Bruce is talking to Emily. And because I feel her pull again. And I don't want to because she's toxic. I've been watching you and Ryan acclimating to this place so well. It's amazing. Inspirational to watch. And here I am, just fucking everything up."

"When you fuck up, it reminds me that you're not perfect," Jenn says. "I mean—"

"No, you're right. It's good to see people fail."

"That's not what I was saying."

"No, but it's what I'm saying," says Paige. "Some of the people we know, who seem the most successful, never appear to have any problems. It's disheartening to compare ourselves to them. So, when there's a tidbit of problem, we pounce on it. Because they're human. Like us."

"Well, I'm not pouncing on your problems."

"Thank you."

Jenn takes Paige's hand. "And I'm not going anywhere because of them, either."

"I'm glad," says Paige. "Neither am I."

"But you *need* to stop protecting me."

Paige looks at Jenn, eyes still red, face devoid of makeup. She nods.

"Be honest with me. Tell me what you're feeling and thinking."

Paige nods again.

"Can we spend some significant time together tomorrow? Just the two of us?"

Paige smiles. "I'd love that."

"So would I." Jenn leans over and kisses Paige's cheek, tasting the saltiness of her tears. She presses her forehead to Paige's, wrapping her arms around this woman, her girlfriend, this imperfect slice of perfection.

"Now," says Jenn, "would you please tell me about this gang bang?"

Paige coughs out a laugh. "It was awesome, until it wasn't."

Jenn nods. "Tell me about the awesome part."

The smile spreads across Paige's face. When she looks back at Jenn, she looks the way she did the night they met, the woman who stood out in a crowd, all mythical enthusiasm with a shining glass of pinot gris. That night, at that Christmas party, Jenn knew she wanted something, but had no idea what that might be.

As Paige begins her story with Alejandra, Jenn's initial feelings of jealousy transform to intrigue and lust. She feels herself getting wet.

# 61

# ALEJANDRA

"I've been thinking about what you said," says Alejandra, across the table from her wife at Rakuen, "and I feel I need to respond to some things."

Crista nods.

Alejandra opens her mouth to continue, but is interrupted when their waiter places a plate of quartered egg rolls drizzled in spicy orange mayo. He doesn't have a name tag, but announces himself with a wave of his palm. "Ortiz!"

"Thank you, Ortiz," says Crista with a smile.

"*¡Sí*, Ortiz!" he announces again and disappears back into Rakuen's kitchen.

"He's like Dalí," says Crista. She holds her own hand out and says "Dalí!" Her face asks for a laugh that Alejandra isn't ready to give yet.

Alejandra nods.

"Okay, just tell me," says Crista.

"I understand," Alejandra begins, choosing her words carefully, "that my insistence on the 'lesbian' label and my mentioning of 'gold star' status may have caused you to feel...less than."

"Sometimes, yes," agrees Crista.

"I want you to know that I acknowledge and don't diminish that."

Crista tentatively puts her napkin on the table, looking down slightly, and Alejandra sees more of her forehead than the rest of her.

She feels an urge to put her out of her misery, to let it go. "But I'm also not going to take responsibility for our problems. I'm happy to share them. And work on them. And talk about them. But we need to find our way back to a baseline respect."

Crista nods without looking up.

"I'm not scolding you," says Alejandra. "I'm not the parent, it's not my job."

"I didn't say you—"

"No, sorry, you didn't," says Alejandra, dialing it down. "That was probably more about me than you." She's always the strong one, the confident one, the one in control. She puts partners in boxes without thinking about it, assumes roles, as Terrence, the handsome bisexual center of the threesome, noted when she ran into him at the bar before dinner. He asked a polite and unobtrusive, "How are you doing?" and she responded by spilling an abridged version her last three days all over him, ending with, "And apparently, that's been making my maybe-bisexual partner feel she can't share things with me."

"Maybe-bisexual, eh?" asked Terrence. "And you're...?"

"Gay," she said.

"Thought so. The other outliers." He laughed and sipped his drink. "The weird triad and the lesbians."

"Lesbian, at least," she said, emphasizing the singular.

"Word around the resort is one of you has a gold star," says Terrence with exaggerated interest.

"God, if I never hear that phrase again..." Alejandra sighed. "In college, my friends were so proud of it, the few of us who could call ourselves gold star lesbians. Because we never sullied ourselves with boys." She looked at Terrence, still smiling. "That's not offensive, is it? I feel like my barometer might be broken."

"I'm not *personally* offended," he said, putting his hand to his chest. "I enjoy the transgression of it all. One of the gifts of a Catholic upbringing."

"Hey," said Alejandra, "me too."

"Aye!" he replied and offered his drink to clink. The plastic tumblers clacked together.

"I think we thought there was something inherently purer

about never having had sex with a man," she said, then rolled her eyes. "Purity, another Catholic concept."

"I think many other religions might also stake a claim on that one, but yes. Rory was a gold star when we met," Terrence said, dropping his voice low, "but Marley and I corrupted him." He stared at his glass for a moment. "Nope, too much rum, I shouldn't have shared that."

"I won't tell anyone."

"And you've never been curious?" he asked.

"No!" she said, tense, firm.

"Sorry I asked," said Terrence.

"No," said Alejandra, "no, just...been asked that a lot lately."

She reaches across the table to her wife at Rakuen and rests her hand palm-up next to Crista's plate.

Crista looks from her hand to her face with worry. "I've made you so tense."

"No," Alejandra replies. "I'm just doing a lot of thinking. Talked to Terrence – from the triad – at the bar, before you came out."

"He's the bi one?" Crista asks, some tension in her own voice.

"Yes," she says.

"He asked me if I've ever been curious about men," Alejandra says and waits.

Crista blinks once, twice, then nods.

"Do you remember us talking about that?"

"I think we did when we first started dating, and you went on and on about how repulsive an appendage the penis is."

Alejandra purses her lips. "I couldn't remember if we had."

"Yeah," says Crista. "I didn't bring it up again."

"It would appear that yet again we find me responsible for 'putting you into a box.'"

Crista's eyes narrow. "You didn't put me into a box."

"Isn't that what you were saying back there? That I forced you to be this thing that you're—"

Crista's eyes dart back and forth around the table. Alejandra sees her wife becoming a flight risk. She drops her voice an octave and sands down all the edges. "*Mi amor,*" she says. "Take my hand. And slow deep breaths."

Crista reaches up to the table and puts her hand in Alejandra's. She sits for a while, breathing the air in, breathing the air out, staring at the transected egg roll between them.

Alejandra considers and dismisses various tactics. What's her goal? They're out to dinner, they're talking. Crista is finally speaking to her honestly. Alejandra pauses a moment to scrub the word *finally* from that sentence in her mind. Either the goal is to prolong the argument, to get to a level of "right," or the goal is to improve their relationship, or the goal is to end things, which both of them have stated is not their ideal outcome. Looking across the table at her wife, she knows what she'd like to have happen. "I'd like for us to be okay," she says. "I'd like for us to go out dancing tonight, and then tomorrow enjoy the hell out of our last day here."

"I'd like that too," whispers Crista.

"I'd also like to feel like I'm not causing you to cower in fear of me."

Crista looks up. "I'm not."

"It feels like I've made you afraid."

She looks away, nibbling on her lower lip. "I'm worried about breaking us beyond fixing."

"I can wrap my head around the idea of you as a bisexual woman. I can help you out of the box I crammed you into."

"Yeah?" asks Crista.

"Yeah," says Alejandra. "What I can't do, though, is deal with erratic behavior like you going out and staying out all night with that couple. And I can't deal with you being unsure of what sex you had because you got wasted. And I'm sorry if that feels judgmental."

"No," replies Crista, "no, that's fair." She leans forward. "I got really scared that I couldn't remember."

Alejandra nods.

"And," Crista's eyes drop back to the egg roll. "And I'm sorry. Really. For all of it."

"We can get past this," says Alejandra. "I can. But you can't keep something major, like your maybe bi-ness, from me for so long, ever again. You need to talk to me about this stuff. About all of the stuff."

Crista nods.

"Now we should eat this and order our main course, before they take it away." Alejandra gestures at the egg roll with her chopsticks.

"Psst," Crista says, after they've placed extravagant dinner orders.

"What?"

"Did you see his...thing?"

Alejandra blinks at her wife. "Terrence?"

Crista nods.

"I'll assume that by 'thing' you mean his penis."

Crista nods again. "I hear they're both huge."

"Is this what it'll be like, being married to a bi girl?"

"I don't want to do anything with it," says Crista, her voice meandering. "I just wanted to know if it's as huge as all the ladies have been saying."

Alejandra thinks back to the bar. Her cursory glance downward had been unintentional, but she'd often found her eyes wandering when she met people naked here at Aphrodite's. She looks down at the table, then lifts her chopstick, putting her index finger about two-thirds of the way up. "Like this," she says.

Crista laughs. "Thicker, though."

"Seriously, I can support your curiosity and not be interested in discussing dick, right?"

"Yes," says Crista.

"Then I'll suggest you scope out the penises of the triad yourself before we leave."

Her wife laughs, louder than she's heard in quite a while. The kind of laugh that's unafraid to be heard. The kind that draws the attention of others in the room. The kind that's infectious. The laugh Alejandra has always loved.

She laughs, too.

# 62

# RAYMOND

The bar is crowded as Raymond takes his seat. The half that faces the courtyard is full, with about fourteen people down the line. He knows most of them, can pick out their names from his scattered thoughts. Now, though, he just wants to sit in silence, down here, in the back corner, on the opposite side.

*Hard to be alone in public.* He chides himself for leaving his room.

"Rum punch?" asks Miguel, making a special point to come all the way down instead of staying near the swarm, dancing with Gabriela as she shoves pizzas into the oven for the guests.

Raymond's guests. He led them here.

Does that make him responsible?

"You can absolutely cry," James told Raymond. "I did." The old man put his hand on his face. "Apparently, I still am," he said with a laugh.

"I still am, too," says Raymond at the bar, wiping away tears with his hand.

Miguel cocks an eyebrow at him, tossing a couple extra napkins on the bar. "Tequila?" he offers with a half-smile.

Raymond's about to decline, but instead nods and taps the bar in front of him.

With a nod, Miguel grabs the elegant squat bottle of Don Julio off the shelf behind him and sets down a short tumbler, into which he pours one, two, three fingers. "Look like you need it," says Miguel. "Pizza?"

Raymond shakes his head, lifting the drink from the bar top. "No thank you." He offers a short tip of the glass to Miguel, who answers it with a nod of his head. Then Raymond is alone again. He's not sure why he came out here. If people see him, they might want to talk to him. All of them, any of them. They'll ask what's wrong. They'll ask if something new happened with Colleen.

He'll say no.

Well, what then?

"You heard her last night," said James this morning, sitting next to him on the white lobby couch. "How much this place meant to her. How much you meant."

The lobby was so empty, so quiet. The resort outside it, too. Aphrodite's hadn't yet awoken, no music playing. So early that the morning rain had not yet dried under the heat of the sun. Raymond looked away from James as the tears fell. Unacceptable to put this man, today, in the position of taking care of *his* needs. This man he's known for years.

This man whose wife had just died.

He couldn't hold it in. The tears fell.

He'd been sleeping for real, sleeping soundly, for the first time in a while. The knock on his door had come just before six, and Raymond staggered up and out to find Luis.

"Jesus, man," said Raymond, "are you ever *not* on duty?"

"*Señora* Koonz," said Luis, then paused. Paused long enough that Raymond almost interjected with the story she'd told about the tile the night before. The piece of Aphrodite's that had gone home with her that first time, her first trip. He smiled, thinking about it. Then Luis broke the silence. "She died."

Raymond's smile stayed on his face because the words didn't make sense. He heard them, processed them, understood them, but couldn't turn them into a thing that happened. Not here. How could that be?

"Oh my God," said Mia from the bed.

"I was just with her," Raymond said, as though that could fix it. Clearly if he'd spent time with her recently, she couldn't possibly have died.

"*Señor* Koonz asked me to call you. I didn't want to tell you over the phone."

Raymond scrambled to put clothes on, rejecting the first shirt because it said **Party Naked** in seventies-style bubble lettering. An article of clothing recommending nudity had always amused him. But he couldn't go in that. Go where? "Is there a shuttle I can take to the hospital?" he asked Luis. Taxis needed to be ordered well in advance here, so they could make their way down the sprawling back roads to reach the coast.

"They did not go to the hospital. *Señor* Koonz is in the lobby."

"Where is Deb—" He grabbed onto Luis as his legs got spongy.

The big man had slung his right arm under Raymond's armpits, holding him up effortlessly. "She is in her room. We are waiting for..." Luis frowned, mumbling in Spanish. "*Juez de instrucción.*" He looked back up after a moment and offered, "Coroner?" with a question in his voice.

The word *coroner* pushed it all to the forefront, and Raymond again felt spongy. He steadied himself, though, because this wasn't about him.

"Would you like to come wait with *Señor* Koonz?"

"Yes, I'll be right behind you."

Luis released him, squeezed his shoulder for a moment, then left.

Raymond sat on the edge of the bed to put on his shoes.

"Would you like me to come with?" Mia asked. "I don't know him as well as you do."

He looked at her and shook his head. "It's...I'll let you know if I need your help with anything."

She grabbed his hand as he rose again. "Not just *help* with anything," she said, making him look at her face. "If you *need anything.*"

Raymond gave her a very slight smile and nodded. "I will."

"More tequila?" asks Miguel at the bar.

Raymond looks down at his empty tumbler. "No," he says. Miguel moves away, but Raymond stops him. "But, a pizza would be great," he says. "Smart too. I can't remember if I've eaten today." He laughs humorlessly. Miguel's smile is politely concerned. He must see plenty of lost and bewildered guests, here at the bar at night.

Raymond wonders if Miguel had even heard about Debra. Surely there must be gossip around the resort. Though the coroner came and went through the side entrance and along back paths, all before 7:00 in the morning. Still, he can't believe no one has questioned him about it at all today.

He found James Koonz on the small white couch in the corner of the lobby. The one where guests sit to wait for transportation away from the resort. "I'm so, so sorry, James," he said, standing over him.

James looked up and nodded, wearing ill-fitting khaki shorts and a white undershirt, miles from the happy man who'd sat in the hot tub with him the night before. Mere hours before, they'd sat together and laughed together.

Then Raymond had kissed Debra goodnight.

"I didn't think that kiss would be goodbye," Raymond said.

"Neither did I," said James.

*How selfish of me*, thought Raymond. *This isn't about—*

"Sit," said James, patting the couch next to him.

Raymond sat.

"She may have known," the old man said after a while. "When she said goodnight to me, she gave it flourish. She told me how happy she was to have found me. How happy she was that we found this."

"Was she sick?"

James nodded.

Raymond's mind raced, connecting dots.

("I wouldn't ever leave here. If that were an option, of course.")

"Is that why you canceled back in the summer?"

James expelled air through his nose, an approximation of a laugh. "I thought we should. That it'd just be too much, and there wouldn't be much time. But she said, 'James! If you cancel that trip, I'm divorcing you!'"

Raymond didn't know what to say, how to react.

"You can laugh," said James. He shrugged. "They said up to a year in June. What kind of a thing to say is that? Up to a year. Could be anything. Except, I guess, more than a year. She made five months."

Raymond lightly patted his back, then went back to being not quite sure what to do with his hands.

"This place was important to her. You, too," he said, poking an arthritis-twisted finger into Raymond's shoulder. "'My boyfriend Raymond Horne is throwing another trip, and he personally emailed me to attend.'"

Raymond choked on a sob.

"It's alright," said James. "This was where she wanted to be." He lit up, as though a thought had suddenly occurred to him. "You were there two years ago! When that storm hit on the last night, and everybody ran from the hot tub because the lightning was crashing."

Raymond nodded, remembering the night. The squeals when the chilly rain had hit. Seeing Debra lying back, elbows on the side of the tub, face turned toward the heavens as the rain pelted down. James had told her they ought to go, that the hot tub could get struck by lightning.

"'What a way to go that'd be,'" Raymond said aloud, hearing her say it in his memory.

"Yeah," said James, laughing to himself quietly. "She told me after we got the 'up to a year' garbage that it wouldn't be so bad. But she hoped that year included one more visit. One last time." The words caught in his throat as he turned to look at Raymond. "And she got that." He smiled. "Even got that kiss she wanted from you. This is how she said goodbye."

Luis appeared near them, hands clasped, solemn. Raymond looked past him to the white van in front. When he looked back to James, he knew the old man had seen it, too.

"Thank you for what you did for her, for us," James said, standing.

Raymond didn't know what to say, so he stood with a rote and distant, "You're welcome."

"You're one of the good ones, Raymond. Never let things overshadow what you actually do for people."

His instinct was to deny, to push off, to minimize, but Raymond thought all those things would do a disservice to the man saying them, and to the woman he'd kissed goodbye last night. "Let me know when you get her home safely?" he asked James. Immediately, he felt he shouldn't have said it. Shouldn't have suggested—

"She would've told you that's idiot talk, you know. Not much bad can happen now."

"Yeah." Raymond smiled. "She was a hell of a woman."

"She was. Be happy we got to know her. And that you gave her this place to make her exit in."

"Even while I'm happy for that," asked Raymond, "do you think she'd mind if I cried?" The question took him all the way back to age six, when his grandfather had died.

"You can absolutely cry," James told Raymond. "I did." The old man put his hand on his face. "Apparently, I still am," he said with a laugh, then stuck out his hand. "I probably won't see you again," he said, "lest you get out our way sometime. My way."

"I hope I do," said Raymond, pulling the man into a hug that was for more than just him, for the woman he'd lost. *For the woman we all lost.*

The late-night pizza fills him only a little, as he loses interest after his second slice. He manages to leave the bar with no contact beyond a wave to Paige and Bruce. He walks along the beach. Stopping midway down, with his feet in the rolling surf. He looks straight up. In a moment, he sees a streak across the sky. Then shortly after, another.

"I wish you could've been here one more night," he says.

"Hey," says Mia. "Saw you head down here. How're you holding up?"

"As well as can be expected, I think," he says.

"She really meant something to you." It's not a question.

"She was a fixture here. As unchanging as Luis, or the mariachi band that plays during dinner, or..." He stops, staring out at the water. "I think I understand the stasis, Mia."

"Really?" she prompts. "Tell me more about that."

"When we assume something or someone will always be there..." He turns to her.

She gives him a small smile and nods.

"We don't appreciate it as much." He feels the world tumble out beneath him, and he's sandy in the surf. Water and grit pass through his pockets and his shorts.

"Okay, steady. You've had a day," she says, helping him back to his feet, "and tomorrow is another."

"I need to be strong for them," he says.

"No," she assures him. "They'll understand. You need to be whatever you need to be, Raymond, for you."

Raymond nods. Another ball of fire streaks across the night sky. "I wish we could've watched the shower together. Just one more meteor."

# PART VIII

*Friday*

# 63

# JENN

"Good morning," says Mia Benjamin, climbing onto the beach bed next to Jenn's.

Jenn welcomes her. The morning has been quiet thus far. Their last real morning, probably, since tomorrow will be a mad scramble to get everything back into their suitcases for the trip home.

Sigh. Home.

She kissed Ryan's forehead on the way out the door, leaving him to sleep. Walking along the beach, she took in the tropical birds chirping and cawing, the accompanying undertone of music way off in the distance, bits of Spanish here and there as the cleaning crews moved about. She reached the beach just before 8:00, early enough to claim a bed from Marco.

"You're the first person I've seen that I know this morning," Jenn tells Mia.

"Raymond said that today begins the shift. Some of our guests begin to leave, and non-takeover people show up. The vibe changes."

Jenn frowns. The vibe is perfect, has been perfect all week.

"Has it been a good week?" asks Mia.

Perfect all week? Jenn takes a long deep breath.

"Eventful?" suggests Mia.

Jenn nods. "Eventful indeed."

Mia situates herself and pulls her billowy wrap over her

shoulders, dropping it next to her. Jenn can't help but stare at the woman's toned and well-tanned body. She feels a sense of discord, that she first saw this body, those breasts, on a blog. That she's lusted from afar for so long and now is mere feet away.

"You must like what you see," says Mia.

"I've masturbated to pictures of you," blurts out Jenn. "I have no idea why I told you that."

Mia laughs. "Usually it's the boys telling me that, and offering to show me their cock. Hearing it from someone as lovely as you is unexpected and delightful."

Jenn gives her a half-smile, still feeling the heat in her cheeks, and stares down at her hands.

Mia is now leaning against the large wedge cushion at the back of the bed. Her floppy hat is on her head, her large circular sunglasses on her face. She looks out at the ocean contentedly. "So, you lost your job."

"I did," Jenn says. "Morality clause."

"Morality clause," repeats Mia. "And did you like your work?"

Jenn frowns. "It was customer service at a hotel."

"Let's not be judgmental, some people enjoy the social interaction and the variety of connections that you get from working in customer service. I'd also bet you saw some clandestine shenanigans."

"I did." Jenn laughs. "More than a few. Most were less than clandestine, though." She recalls the night she saw that actor... Shit, he was on the show Ryan liked, played the handsome second fiddle. He'd brought three girls up, then one by one they left adjusting their clothing. Before swinging, Jenn had found things like that terribly intriguing. Fleeting glimpses from afar of a world she'd never know. She wonders what that second fiddle actor would think if he could see her now. Would his foursome in a hotel room seem...*blasé* in comparison? Ahh, yes, her exciting life now. The one that had gotten her fired. "And my own less-than-clandestine shenanigans brought down the hammer of the morality clause."

"You feel shame? Guilt?" asks Mia.

Jenn nods.

"Forgive yourself." She leans toward Jenn, across the gulf between mattresses. "It's not a command, just a suggestion."

"Look where you are," says Mia, holding out her arms. Jenn

glances downward at Mia's pert breasts as they bounce with the gesture, then back up to the dark mirrored eyes of her sunglasses. "Not a minute goes by on this resort without something that would violate that clause. Probably just being here would do it. Announcing on your profile page that you're at Aphrodite's." She affects a silly voice. "'Aphrodite's, what's that?'" She mimes typing. "'Holy jeez!'" She holds up her tablet and shakes it. "We're all connected now, whether we like it or not. I tried to disconnect for a while, when I got outed and during the custody hearings. I couldn't do it. Couldn't leave it. You know why?"

Jenn shakes her head.

"Because it's too magnificent."

Jenn considers that, looking back down at her hands, then out at the water.

"Connection is the missing piece, in most of the world. Lack of connection, lack of touch or interaction, can make people hard and bitter, judgmental. But the vastness of it all can also be a problem. Too many connections to maintain. Too much input, too much of everything. It can make us lose touch."

"And leave dirty pictures of a threesome in the hands of a vindictive person who sends them to your boss."

"Ooh," says Mia, lips drawn downward in a scowl. "Sorry."

Jenn shrugs and nods.

"But let me ask, what does it all mean to *you*?"

"I'm not following."

"Okay, answer this. Do you miss your job?"

"I miss the security," Jenn snaps.

"Okay."

"And the money. That was good for—"

"So, no."

Jenn remembers walking through the Westin's revolving front doors after defiantly striding across the lobby with her box of desk supplies, her plant, her picture. Grace had told her to exit via the back door, wanting her to cower, to slink. Not one day since has she wanted to be back there. "I just miss the things the job provided, not the job."

"Telling, isn't it?"

"Yes," says Jenn.

"Now I want you to close your eyes," says Mia, "and total up what this place, these friends, and this lifestyle mean to you."

Jenn does as she's asked, and lets her eyes close. She understands the point of the exercise as she sits in darkness. If her job meant nothing and this means anything... *Mia fucking Benjamin is helping you out! Do the work!* This lifestyle. She hears herself, back in the living room of their townhouse almost two years ago, say the words that changed things. "Well, there's always swinging." In the dark, she sees her husband and feels her open affection for him, no longer obscured by the things they used to hide from each other, tedious suburban melodrama. She sees Bruce with wine, Paige talking about his magic hands. Then they're all at the Horn Lodge that first night, and she's having a panic spiral that Paige makes better with a kiss, lifting her out of her panic. Later in the evening, Paige saves her again, catching her, as they stand nearly naked in the living room, with the vast potential stretching out in front of them. Mere moments between that and Paige taking her upstairs. Mere moments between panic and orgasms and exploration and experimentation. They came together, she and her husband, with people who showed them everything. And then they came again and again and again.

"That's a lot," says Mia.

"Did I say it out loud?"

"Some, pieces. Enough for me to catch the drift."

"I probably wouldn't still be married without this, swinging, poly, whatever," says Jenn. "This is..."

Mia just nods. "It's why I couldn't give it all up, why I fought my ex harder. This is my life, my lifestyle. How dare they ask me to change back?"

"Yeah," says Jenn in a whisper. "But that still doesn't take care of the money! Or security."

"How secure are we, anyway?" asks Mia. "The economy could fall apart at any minute. You could've been fired for other things. Our world can change in an instant because we walk out of our houses. But still, we go. We must."

"And now we've seen what's out there."

"You didn't choose the hospitality industry, did you?"

"Not really," Jenn shakes her head and tries to suppress an eye roll. "I got a bachelor's in business."

"I dropped out of high school, did the GED," says Mia. "Don't reject your path. What came before doesn't matter if you don't let it. Every day is about evolution. What am I today? What can I be tomorrow?"

"I don't know."

"Nor would I expect you to – you only just heard the questions! But in a week, two, you might have an idea. I encourage you to follow it. And if you don't then, don't worry! It'll come. Think about what you love, what you wanted to do, wanted to be, before you got the job that overtook your ambitions."

Jenn looks back down. "I minored in social work."

"You seem as embarrassed by that as by your business degree."

"I only minored because I refocused. First it was Shakespeare, then social work, then my parents thought I should get a real degree."

"Man, you've been put through the ringer. A major and a minor in money-making fields, education in the arts, embarrassed by all." Mia reaches out and puts her hand on Jenn's knee. "Try not to judge yourself too harshly. Recognize the value of connection and interaction, like we were talking about. That's all over social work."

"But I quit."

"You paused." Mia smiles at her, warm and friendly, and puts Jenn surprisingly at ease.

"I paused."

"You did," says Mia. "The wonderful thing about pausing is that, when you're ready to resume, you can unpause. Life may be hard for a while, with you out of work. I can say from experience that it probably *will* be hard. But would you like to know the best part of not having a job?"

Jenn nods.

"The eight or nine hours a day you've been gifted, time enough to find your focus. Half of every day, at least, should be about you. Finding your passion, your direction. Figuring out how to unpause."

"Thank you for giving me permission to do that," says Jenn.

"It's not permission," says Mia, "it's a prescription. I can write it down if you'd like."

Jenn laughs. Looking for a new job had seemed such an insurmountable task in the weeks before their trip that Jenn did little of it, and even the tiny amount had consumed time and emotional bandwidth. Most of it was spent adjusting her résumé or scanning through ads, and much of the rest spent in fear and loathing.

Mia squeezes her knee. "You know how to reach me after this. I'm easy to find."

"I do."

"I want to hear what you discover about yourself, without you filtering or judging it first, okay?"

"Okay."

"Now," says Mia, "that woman over there..." She points to the surf. "She's been looking over this way a bunch while pretending she's not."

Jenn glances over her shoulder to see Paige, in the water up to her waist. She turns back to Mia. "That's my girlfriend," she says with a grin.

"She's a lucky woman," says Mia.

"So am I," says Jenn.

"No morality clause can change that."

Jenn agrees and hugs Mia, thanking her, before heading out into the surf to her beloved.

# 64

# RYAN

Sleeping until nearly noon on his last full day? Ryan shakes his head at his laziness, stepping onto the balcony in front of their room. He hears the distant calls of the party planners at the pool, feels a rumble in his stomach and knows he should get some food, see what Jenn's up to on the beach. But that would require walking all that way. He laughs at himself. Tomorrow they head back to Chicago and a winter that has arrived early. He isn't looking forward to the cold, the snow, especially while here he can stand naked and warm, even in the shade. He gives his cock a quick tug because he can. He looks out at the small courtyard between buildings lit by the brilliant morning sunlight, taking it all in, the tans of the grass roofs, the greens of the palm trees. A raccoon wanders between buildings. "You're out early," he tells it.

"What?"

Ryan looks down the balcony to an alcove where Crista sits in a plastic wicker patio chair, her feet up. She squints at him.

"Just talking to the raccoon," he says.

"Aha," she replies. "You're talking to the raccoon, and I'm reading," she flips over her magazine, "well, it's still People, but it's People *en español*. And I barely *hablo* it. Sounds like we're both making excellent use of our final hours."

"So it does."

"Pull up a chair if you'd like. I've got edibles." She shakes a tin of mints at him.

He laughs. "I was going to go grab some food." He looks in the direction of the restaurants, across the resort. "But it's so far," he says, mock forlorn.

"You do know about room service, right?"

"Isn't that just for the fancy people on the other side of the resort?"

"They'll deliver anything you want from the grill."

"Tempting," he says, "but I'm rather enjoying the whole free food thing."

"It just costs five dollars for delivery."

"That I did not know," says Ryan.

Twenty minutes later, they are sitting together in the alcove, feet up in front of a spread of fajitas, nachos, and corn fritters, Ryan's favorite resort lunch snack. "I don't know why nobody told us this was an option."

"They did, at check in," she says, "and there's a big menu behind your phone."

"Must've missed that." Ryan grins. "Though there's also something to be said for leaving your room to meet people."

"I'm not really feeling up to that today," says Crista.

"Neither am I."

"To introversion," says Crista, holding up her piña colada.

Ryan returns the gesture. "And avoiding complicated social interactions."

"Oh, are we avoiding someone?"

Ryan nods. "Multiple someones, actually."

"What happened?"

He looks at her, guarded. These avoidances make him look bad, mean spirited, even selfish. But the woman in front of him looks sympathetic to his plight, and it's not like he can ruin his non-existent chances with her. He takes a breath. "There's a couple who came here because of us. They decided we'd be their first full swap experience," he tosses a corn fritter into his mouth, "and informed us of the fact at dinner on our second night here."

"Seems like a recipe for disappointment, or at least drama," says Crista.

"Both, I think. The other is a guy I played with yesterday. I left while he was in the bathroom."

"You ditched?" asks Crista with a surprising amount of enthusiasm. "I ditched!"

"Oh?" Ryan laughs.

"I shouldn't get excited about that, should I?"

"We appear to be kindred spirits."

"Apparently! Yeah, no, the other night I got really drunk with a couple and left in the morning before they woke up."

Ryan looks at her. "Wow. You spent the night?"

Her expression changes, and she leans back in her chair, taking a long deep sip of her drink.

"I'm not judging," says Ryan quickly. "Just didn't even consider that it could happen here."

"Well, it can," she says, voice cautious now, "but it shouldn't have. I shouldn't have." She shakes her head and is quiet for a moment.

Ryan regrets his tone.

"Why did you leave?" she asks, breaking the silence.

He thinks. Why sugar coat it? "It was my first time with a guy, and I felt ashamed."

"Ashamed that a guy fucked you?"

"I fucked him..." Ryan corrects, though he's not sure why that's important.

"Po-tay-to, po-tah-to."

"I felt a lot of feelings without a lot of context, and I figured if I didn't understand why I was feeling that, I couldn't really explain it to him."

She nods and tips her glass toward him again, understanding replacing caution on her face. "Sexuality is complicated for those who don't reside firmly on the outside edges of the spectrum," she says as though making a proclamation.

"Don't you reside there?" he asks. "I mean, you're lesbians."

"And you're straight," she snaps.

"I didn't mean it like—"

"That's why it's complicated, though," she says. "We make assumptions. About the people around us, about the ones we play with, sometimes about ourselves."

"I mean, you told us you're lesbians," he insists.

"I'm not talking about you, dammit," she says with a tight smile.

"Oh."

"Allie makes assumptions about me. The rest of the world

makes assumptions about me." She sighs. "And I make assumptions about me."

"What did you assume?"

"That I was straight for a while, then bi for a while, but now I'm a lesbian," she says.

"But you're not?"

She shrugs. "I honestly have no idea."

Ryan nods, sliding thoughts around in his head. *What do I want? Who do I want?* "I don't know if I'm straight, either."

"What made you want to play with that guy?" she asks, then drops her voice conspiratorially, "and will you tell me who it is?"

"Rory, from the triad."

"Does he have a big dick?"

Ryan laughs. "Yes." The memory of its girth still makes him clench up at the idea of their positions having been reversed.

"Sorry," says Crista.

"No, don't be," he says with a smile. "I wanted to play with him because he's attractive. And not just objectively, but, like, *I* find him attractive, too."

"You don't generally find men attractive?"

Ryan shakes his head.

"What is it about men, then?"

"They have cocks," says Ryan.

"Women can have cocks too," says Crista, poking her finger at him.

"True."

"And they can strap one on if they don't."

"Also, yes." Ryan thinks about it for a moment. "For a while, when I was younger, I worried I was gay. Because when I'd look at porn, I wasn't just looking at the women."

"Honestly the only porn Allie and I watch is gay men..."

"That's..." Ryan's not sure how to process that. The discordance of it is too much. "I'd like to come back to that later."

"Sure," says Crista, grinning. "What made you worried? Would it be so bad?"

"If I were gay?"

Crista nods.

He remembers his early teens, watching porn with his friends and wondering if he was different. Watching porn alone and wondering if he was different. He didn't recoil when a penis showed up, like his buddies did.

"Their recoiling was probably so *you* wouldn't think *they* were gay," suggests Crista.

He agrees. "Being gay wouldn't have been bad. I just figured I was straight. Not just in the default societal expectations way, but very attracted to girls. Looked forward to dating, once I got out of my own socially awkward and anxious way."

"And you never thought bi?"

"I didn't know bi was a thing. I can't even tell you when I first encountered the concept." He frowns, trying to remember when he'd become aware of bisexuality. Surely it had to be after high school.

"See, I was straight. Because society. And then there was some trauma. I didn't switch to girls because of the trauma, I just spent a lot more time with the girls than the guys after. And when I spent time with them, I realized I liked them. Went to prom with a boy, fucked a girl at the after-party. Dated both for a while, but then I tapered off, fewer and fewer men. Then I just wasn't attracted to them anymore. I figured, I guess this has been my long journey to realizing my true self."

"Yes!" Ryan exclaims.

"What?"

"I've thought that! That was why I was worried I was gay. Because that would mean I never quite understood myself."

"Do you feel like you know yourself now?"

Ryan blinks, suddenly dejected. "Maybe not."

"Understanding oneself is overrated." She smiles and pops another of the tiny yellow candies from the tin into her mouth. She offers one to him.

He shakes his head. "Last day, and no idea how that'd affect me."

"They're very mellow," she says. "But I'm not trying to talk you into them."

"Good, I've never been good at withstanding peer pressure."

"After it all, I stopped dating because I was traveling so much. And when Allie and I hooked up," her face turns wistful and she looks down the path between the buildings. "Well, when she asked, I said lesbian because that's what I understood."

"But now..."

"But now," she agrees.

"Is that something that's okay in your relationship? She

seemed pretty firm on—" He regrets the question. "Is that too personal?"

"Nah," she says, waving it off. "I hope it's okay. I think it might be. Besides, I couldn't tell you where I identify now. Only that I'm probably not a six on old Kinsey, not 100% homosexual."

"Do you think it's okay not to know where you fall?"

"I think you have to come to a place where you're okay not knowing," she says. "That allows for experimentation, exploration. The rest is up to your partner."

"At least this lifestyle allows for exploration," he says, "though swingers don't tend to like bi guys, according to their profiles."

"They certainly don't seem to. Like your school friends, desperation to appear *not* gay causes the pendulum to swing wildly. Lesbian stigma is a thing, too, but it's more like, 'When we get into the bedroom you'll still suck my cock, right?'"

"That sucks."

She shrugs again. "It just means we have to be very selective with our playmates. Find people who understand and accept us. It's a high bar to clear. Quality control. Some people pass it. Like you guys."

He feels warmth within from the compliment and smiles at her.

"You and...shit. Tom Selleck."

"Bruce."

"Yes! Why can't I remember that? It's such a classic swinger name."

Ryan laughs. "And the shark in *Jaws*."

"The shark had a name?"

"The puppet had a name," says Ryan.

"That makes more sense," says Crista. "You and Bruce were perfect. Ideal, even. Never pushed boundaries; shared your amazing women with us." She laughs, looking off somewhere. "Your wife, man. She's something."

Ryan smiles. "She is."

"It's been awhile since I've done any fisting, and Allie has a small vagina." She snorts and covers her mouth. "Maybe TMI?"

"Is anything, anymore?" he asks with a laugh.

"I'm sure I could find something."

"Probably," he agrees. "I'm glad you had a fun time. I know she did, too."

"Maybe we could find more," says Crista.

"Time is short," Ryan tells her.

"It is. Why waste it on worry?"

He nods and contemplates ordering more fritters.

# 65

# PAIGE

"We're throwing an orgy," Paige exclaims as Jenn strides through the shallows to meet her in the water.

"You are?" Jenn asks.

Paige smiles, feeling the excitement overtaking her. "*We* are."

When Jenn reaches her, they stand submerged past their belly buttons in the salty Caribbean Sea. Paige opens her arms wide and envelops this lovely woman as much as one person can envelop another.

"Squeeze," says Jenn, elongating it to a point where she sounds like she might pop.

"Sorry," says Paige.

"I love the way you squeeze."

Paige smiles at her.

"So, we're throwing an orgy?"

"Yes!" Paige scans the beach, looking for people who might participate. "I feel like there's a lot of connecting that can happen, but it has to happen fast."

"Open invitation?" asks Jenn, sounding a bit nervous.

Paige considers it, but reasserts what she said to Bruce yesterday. "I want this to be for our friends, and their lovers, and their friends. Not private, really, but I want to make sure certain people know."

Jenn nods. "Will we, um..."

Paige turns to her and kisses her cheek, then neck, then nibbles a little just where neck becomes shoulder, tasting the salt of the surf. "I'd love to play with you at the orgy." The deep exhale from Jenn tells Paige all she needs to know. "Who would you like to invite?"

Jenn considers it for a moment. "Crista and Alejandra."

"Absolutely," agrees Paige, spending a moment on thoughts of her tryst with Allie on the catamaran.

"We should invite Vince and Kendra," she says.

"Should? Or want to?" Paige doesn't have strong feelings either way. While Vince and Kendra are nice, neither are especially her type.

"I want to," says Jenn, "but not to play with them. I just want them to feel included."

Paige nods.

"Lydia, and her husband, for Ryan," says Jenn. "I think he really likes her."

"*Likes her* likes her?"

Jenn considers it, then smiles and nods. "Yeah. Not sure if he realizes how much."

"Sometimes we don't realize things like that without someone pointing it out," says Paige, recalling their own history.

"Maybe we could invite Raymond, and Mia," suggests Jenn, looking back toward the beach.

Paige looks up and sees that the beach bed next to the bar is now occupied by two people instead of one. She squints and sees Raymond there. "Let's check in with him."

They make their way out of the water, heading with purpose toward the bed.

"*¡Hola!*" calls Celia from the bar.

"*¡Hola!*" Paige calls back with a wave.

"You ladies are a vision coming out of the surf," says Raymond. His eyes are hidden behind sunglasses, and he wears a Xanadu 5 baseball cap from before he'd switched to Roman numerals.

"Thank you," says Jenn with a grin.

"We were wondering if you would mind if we put together an orgy up at the hot tub beds tonight. A farewell fling."

"Do you want to make it an official event? I can post it on the board."

"No," Paige says, "just don't want to step on your toes. People can participate if they ask, but I don't want people just coming up and feeling they have some sort of right to be there." She pauses, hearing the tension in her voice. She smooths a smile across her face.

"Yeah," says Raymond, "about that..."

Her smile falters.

"I'm sorry I wasn't there to take care of Will. Actually, I'm sorry I didn't take care of him earlier." Raymond removes his sunglasses, and she sees weariness that she hadn't expected. "I'd gotten a couple complaints, but nothing..." he waves his hand around, looking for the right word.

"Actionable," offers Mia.

"Yeah," he says.

"Don't worry about it," says Paige. She takes a breath. *We're not thinking about that. We've rewritten it.* Slowly, she releases the breath.

"So, you took care of Will?" asks Jenn

"No, uh," Raymond looks down, then over at Mia. "He. Well, as of this morning, it would seem that he's unable to leave his washroom."

"What happened?"

"Traveler's diarrhea," says Mia, without looking up from her tablet.

"Yep, Montezuma's Revenge," says Raymond. "I don't know how it happened. Luis has assured me that all the taps are filtered, and all the food is washed in filtered water. So, I sincerely doubt that we will be seeing him again today. Hopefully not this trip at all. If you throw your orgy up by the hot tub, I plan to spend much of the night there myself for the meteor shower. I will ensure that he goes nowhere near it."

"Thank you, Raymond," says Paige. "But we actually came over because we wanted to officially invite you to the orgy."

He smiles and cocks his head. "Really?"

"Yeah. You've worked really hard and deserve some relaxation."

"Well, thank you," he says. "I'll say maybe for now."

"Mia?" asks Jenn.

Paige smiles at the look on her girlfriend's face. Expectant, hopeful.

"Yes?" asks Mia, looking up from her tablet.

"Would you come to our orgy?"

Mia smiles. "I'd love to."

The relief and excitement on Jenn's face is lovely. Paige throws her arm around Jenn's neck and kisses her head.

"What?" asks Jenn, after Paige grins at her for a little too long.

"You're astonishing," says Paige.

Jenn grins back.

They walk toward the pool, hoping to catch the rest of their invitees either having lunch or staking their claims on the pool chairs.

"You're okay?" asks Jenn as they walk. She reaches out and takes Paige's hand. "About the Will—"

"I'm okay," says Paige. At this moment, walking through the warm shade in paradise, it's easy to say. She can push everything else away. When she returns home, hopefully she'll never think of Will again. There's some lingering

(slut)

stuff, sure, but maybe that just means it's time to start seeing her therapist again. Good to have someone objective to talk to. Maybe she can help the work thing make more sense, too.

Or maybe just ease the transition.

"Hold on a second!" says Jenn. She rushes over to the courtyard bar. Paige squints in the sunlight and sees Madison. The petite young woman sits at the bar, playing on her phone. Jenn greets her with a hug and a showy kiss, the kind of kiss that young women sometimes do to demonstrate—

"Whoa!" says Paige to herself, "let's dial it back now."

Jenn returns, a big grin on her face. "Madison's interested in the orgy. Don't worry, she's not even talking to Will at the moment."

"I trust you," says Paige. Before leading them off again, she stops and puts her arms around Jenn.

"What?"

"Just want to kiss you," says Paige.

Her girlfriend grins. "Okay!"

They kiss long enough that they're interrupted by a somewhat curt, "Excuse me." They separate, and Paige smiles as the couple goes by, clothed and trailing a luggage cart. First day on the resort. So lucky.

"Shall we go in search of more?" Paige asks.
"Maybe also in search of lunch?" Jenn suggests.
"I'm a yes for that," says Paige.
They head for the grill.

# 66

## BRUCE

lexis's eyes have met his more than once, and each time she's offered just the slightest of smiles, a twitch of the eyelids, one cocked eyebrow. She's playfully withholding, but the dance has begun. Bruce has little doubt that it's on at this point, and all he must do to reach the destination is *not* be absent thanks to text messages from home. His phone is still dead in the safe, and the private "vanilla" line at the front desk hasn't rang for him again, so he sees no barrier to this entry. Alexis winks at him, putting the daintiest portion of beef Wellington into her mouth. He returns the small smile, smooths his mustache with his index finger, and winks back. The delicious woman shudders in a way that tells him she feels tingles up and down her body. Her dress gives way to glorious cleavage, and he looks forward to kissing every inch of it.

As enticing as Alexis is across the table (and Good Lord is she!) Bruce moves his attention toward his wife, standing at the end of their long table, a glass of champagne raised in the air. She's lit from above by a very well placed hanging light, and her hair is fire and sparkle, thanks to glitter in her shampoo. Her shoulders shimmer with glitter, too, all the way down to the freckled expanse of her cleavage. Tonight, she wears a black corset and skirt, that combined look every inch a ball gown. The riding crop leaning against her chair breaks the illusion, and it becomes apparent that the corset and skirt are leather. He loves this outfit.

"I look around this table and see such deliciously raw sensual energy," says Paige. "Such women, such men. I find it difficult to even remain standing."

He smiles at her. Tonight's do-over dinner with Malcolm and Alexis is larger than expected, but he welcomes the inclusion of Ryan and Jenn, Crista and Alejandra. As Paige stands before the group, Bruce knows that some of her confidence and enthusiasm may be the "fake it 'til you make it" sort, but he still watches in awe as his wife commands the room with gusto. Even beyond the confines of their own table.

"I know all of us have things," she continues, then looks up at the ceiling. "Things here, things at home. Things." She crinkles her nose. "Everybody knows what I mean, here, right? Things? The bad gunky."

He smiles at the phrase, something her mother used to say, something he hasn't heard from her in quite a while. He's heard the boys say it from time to time. The bad gunky had been the tether to home, now that tether has snapped.

The rest of the table seems to grasp her meaning, and they nod.

She catches Bruce's eye and gives him a warm smile. "But there is no time but now. No night but tonight, right?"

"Yes!" the table calls.

"Or is that from *Rent?* No matter." She stops a moment, looking down at the table, moving her eyes from him to Jenn, and back. She winks. "The final day at Aphrodite's is often a scramble, everybody trying to make that last connection, and I'm so happy to be here with people I have made a connection with already, some I've been lucky enough to make a connection with *here*." She takes another moment to acknowledge everyone with a look and a smile, then lifts her glass higher. Everyone around the table follows suit. "No matter when we depart tomorrow, or what bad gunky we might go home to, tonight is ours. *Carpe noctem.*"

Bruce grins as his fellow diners, including those at the neighboring tables, call their own boisterous, "*carpe noctem,*" in return. An invocation in Latin, followed by a response from the gallery. He is relieved that he doesn't have to participate in that final scramble. Not this year. After all the conflict and tension of the last several days, this final day has been a wonderful low-key affair. They'd begun the day with dinner plans. He spent much of it on their beach bed with a drink and his e-reader, moving to the swim-up bar in the pool when he saw his wife and her girlfriend head in that direction. As they ate lunch, he watched his fellow travelers, feeling the sense of urgency wafting off them in every word and gesture. The patterns of the game were becoming increasingly visible: couples connecting with other couples, disconnecting, then reconfiguring, as though the entire resort was a living, breathing organism desperate to assemble itself into something resembling order. Scrambling to avoid the dreaded panic. What if we don't connect? What do you mean our time is almost up?

He turns to Jenn, sitting next to him at dinner, and smiles at her. She returns the smile, then puts her hand on his thigh, giving it the slightest squeeze. He reaches up and puts his arm on the back of her chair. Her back is bare, darker than usual after her time in the tropical sun. He runs his finger just below the nape of her neck, and she shivers and bites her lip.

Paige retakes her seat to his left. He reaches out his hand. She lifts it from the table, inserts his index finger into her mouth and sucks at the end, just for a moment, then bites. When he retrieves his hand, the grin on her face is electric, and he returns it. After all this week, all this stress, he's elated to see her so amped, so fired up. Something would have to be done about that, wouldn't it?

He tosses his head in the direction of the entry to the restaurant. She narrows her eyes, not understanding. He drops his napkin to the table; his plate empty save a broken roll. "Excuse me for just a moment," he says and stands.

She looks up at him, eyes still narrowed.

He again tilts his head toward the door. "Mrs. Shepard, would you accompany me for a moment?"

Paige laughs and blinks at him, then nods and stands.

He takes her hand and leads her outside, the two of them moving more quickly as they pass through the glass doors of the restaurant, around the corner to the dark pool patio. Around another corner, just secluded.

"What's—"

He interrupts her with his kiss that returns the bite. She responds in kind and drags her fingers across his back, nails out.

"Hello, Mr. Shepard," she says with a grin.

"Want to get fucked?" he asks, already reaching under her skirt.

"Mmmhmm," she says hungrily. She turns around and bends over, reaching back to lift her skirt.

He slides his hand up her thigh, aiming for the wetness in-between, feeling the warmth as he nears it. He fumbles with his belt buckle. Impatiently she reaches her free hands back, stroking him through his pants with one, and with the other she deftly unbuckles, unbuttons, and unzips. He gasps as her cold fingers find his cock.

She looks over her shoulder at him, icy blue eyes penetrating. "Fuck me, my love," she tells him.

He's inside her in a heartbeat. The day's build up, even in his relaxed state, comes to a head, and a handful of thrusts is all he needs before admitting, "I'm close!"

"Fill me!" she tells him, backing into him harder than he can thrust forward. Her ass hitting his thighs creates the distinct rhythmic slapping, anyone who can hear it would know. A glance back toward the restaurants shows a couple grinning into the darkness toward them. If those two can't quite see him and Paige, they can certainly hear them. The request to fill her, accompanied by her enthusiastic motion, is more than he can bear, and he gasps and grunts, unloading himself inside her. She moans with him, taking it, letting out a long and satisfied, "Mmmm."

He stumbles back into a stray chair. His cock goes into decline while pumping out the last drops of cum into the hair that surrounds his balls. "Would you," he pants, "like me to—"

"No, no." She turns to him, dropping her skirt back down. "I am going to go to the restroom, and then I will meet you back inside."

"But are—" he tries to protest.

She lifts a cloth napkin off a stack and tosses it into his lap. "My love, clean yourself up! We have dinner guests!" Paige, his wife, his friend, his lover, bends down to kiss him on the lips. "*Carpe noctem,*" she whispers.

He does as bidden, cleaning himself so that he can rejoin their dinner party. "*Carpe noctem,* indeed."

# 67

# JENN

"This is the last time we're going to climb these stairs," says Ryan, sighing, as they make their way up the second flight of stairs toward the rooftop patio next to the hot tub, where Paige's orgy is to be held.

Jenn holds his hand and rests her head against his robe-clad shoulder. "Let's not give into melancholy, hon," she suggests. "We've still got several more hours before we have to catch a shuttle." He looks down at her, such sadness on his face that she can't help but laugh. She stops him on the landing just before the final flight of stairs. She can see the lights at the top, the flickering shimmer of the water, and the music of the evening echoes indiscriminate beats into the night. She steps up on her toes to kiss him, and he smiles at her. "We're seizing the night, right?" she asks him, tells him.

He nods.

"Part of that is not thinking about tomorrow morning."

"I know, there's just...packing, and organizing, and, Jesus, we need to find the passports, and..."

"That's for Saturday Ryan and Jenn to worry about," she tells him, her smile wide. "Look up! The sky is falling, Ryan. We are here! And I personally invited Lydia and her husband to the orgy! The night is primed for us to seize." She bounces excitedly. "Will you grab hold with me?"

He smiles down at her and tucks the long hot pink lock of hair behind her ear. "I love you."

She beams back at her husband, this man who held her hand and plunged into the deep end with her, where nothing would ever be the same. They couldn't have put the genie back in the bottle if they'd tried. "I love you too," she says. She lifts his hand to her lips and kisses his fingers. "To the fun?"

"To the fun," he agrees.

When they crest the stairs, they see that the orgy has already begun. Three of the bed frames on the patio have been shoved together, and in the center, like gods in some Bacchanal, are Bruce and Paige. With them are Malcolm and Alexis, that gorgeous couple from dinner. The swap is full, and the pleasure is loud.

Alejandra and Crista wave from the dry side of the bar. Jenn waves back and looks at Ryan, but his thoughts and attention are elsewhere. She follows his gaze to a bed off to the side where she's not sure exactly what's happening, but mussed brown hair and a tattooed back tell her that it involves Lydia. She breathes a quiet sigh of relief, knowing that Lydia's presence on this last night is important.

In the hot tub, among couples and singles and another blowjob buffet, are Raymond and Mia. She wonders if either will journey to the opposite side of the patio and join the fun. She hopes Mia will. In any case, the night and the orgy are still young.

Paige's screaming orgasm pierces the night, the showy one that comes out at parties, in group situations, the one that she doesn't feel the need to perform any longer when it's just the two of them. *She can be genuine with me,* thinks Jenn. *She can be herself.*

"Hey," says Ryan, "would you mind if I went..." He gestures toward the bed on the end.

Jenn glances over again. Lydia's back is flexing. All at once the rest of the group fades away. She wants to know what's going on there. "Can I join you?"

He smiles and nods. "That'd be awesome."

Lydia stands at the foot of the bed, her husband on his back in front of her. She has an ankle in each hand and is thrusting into him. Her face displays concentration and intensity, and Ted's own face is tense and tight, his mouth open, his breathing heavy. One of his hands grips the sheer hanging curtain, the other is behind his head. He arches his back, shaking.

"Wow," says Jenn.

"Yeah," says Ryan.

"That looks intense."

Ryan's eyes are fixed on the couple. She knows that expression of quiet awe, of intrigue, and it's not just the girl, it's the act. It intrigues Jenn as well. "What do you think?" she asks him, watching his reaction closely.

"What do you mean?" He glances at her, then back.

"Of that," she asks, pointing.

"It's hot."

She smiles. "It *is* hot." She waits, hoping for more, but none comes. "You haven't done that, have you?"

He looks down at her, perplexed. "With who?"

She shrugs, "I don't know! Kendra?"

"I think that would count as full swap," he says, returning his gaze to Lydia and Ted.

"Do you have any interest?"

"In what?"

"Ryan!" she snaps her fingers in front of his face. "Let's go over there in a second, but before we do, I'm curious if you might be interested in doing that with me."

Now she has his attention. "Really?"

She nods with a smile. "I'd be totally into that."

He looks over. "It might take some...getting started."

"Of course." She reaches her hand out to him and draws him across the patio.

When Lydia sees them, she lights up, pausing long enough to say, "Greetings and salutations!"

Ted opens one of his eyes and nods at them. "Hi, there—" He seems as though he might say more, but jitters all over and closes his eyes again. "Sorry, I get—"

"No need to apologize!" insists Ryan.

"Shush, my darling," says Lydia.

Ted nods.

"Can I sit here?" asks Jenn.

The couple agrees, and Jenn sits next to Ted. She meets Lydia's eyes, and the woman smiles back at her. The vast pale canvas of her body shines in the dim light. Her face scrunches again, and she speeds up, slapping into him. Jenn looks down

Lydia's body, past her breasts, noting an *Alice's Adventures in Wonderland* tattoo with a smile. Around her waist, Lydia is wearing a white leather harness with red trim and a large red cross on the front. Jenn almost exclaims about how amazing it would be for nurse/patient scenes, but recognizes that she and Ryan have already been disruptive enough. Besides, Lydia almost certainly must have bought it with that in mind. The cock sprouting from it is long and crimson.

Lydia slows her thrusting, elongating the moves. Leaning forward Jenn watches the dildo slide in and out of him. His balls have crawled up close to his body, the sack tense. His cock hangs limp against his stomach, a long trail of clear pre-cum tracing around his belly and pubic hair.

"Fuck, yes!" he exclaims. "Okay, okay, okay!" His words crescendo and he holds a hand up, palm toward Lydia. She ceases her movement immediately, staying still, silent.

Jenn looks over at Ryan, still standing, staring at the scene on the bed. The awed, confused, intrigued look mixes with the other thing, the thing she's already seen: his interest in Lydia. He'd told Jenn about his evening with her, the Domme/sub play they'd done, how she intrigues him. Like the revelation about Jenn's interest in women, she thinks he probably doesn't quite realize the extent of his interest in Lydia. She may have to nudge him.

"Okay, yes," says Ted, eyes still closed. "Ready to disengage."

Lydia loosens her grip on his ankles and brings his legs down, while at the same time sliding backward. He gasps, and she pauses. "Hold?"

"You're all right."

She nods and continues to slide backward.

Jenn leans down again to watch the dildo emerge. *It keeps going!*

Ted gasps one final time just before the head pops out. He breathes slow, deliberate breaths. "Never had an audience for that before," he admits, without opening his eyes. His wife leans down and kisses him tenderly.

"Amazing," says Ryan, in a breathless way that nearly makes Jenn giggle, though she holds it in.

"So happy you enjoyed," says Lydia, giving Ryan a quick peck. "Will you keep my lovely man company while I clean this up?" She points to the massive red cock hanging between her legs.

"Yeah, of course." Ryan sits on the bed. "What does it feel like?"

"It's intense, filling. Sometimes she thrusts with vigor, other times she doesn't. When she's in a thrusting mood, we use the longer and thinner dildo; when she's tired, or if we just want to cuddle with her inside me, then we use the big guns." He gestures absently to the doctor's bag above his head.

Jenn can't see much inside but does see the coronal ridge of a colossal dildo.

"Do you come from it?" asks Ryan, in his *tell me everything* voice.

"Yeah, but not always, and it's different," says Ted. "Like I don't shoot, I just get really drippy. 'Cuz she's milking my prostate." He wipes at his abdomen, trailing tendrils from his fingers.

Lydia returns from the restroom nude, holding the harness in one hand and the dildo in the other. "How're we doing?"

Ted sits up suddenly, and claps his hands to his thighs. "I am parched."

"You worked really hard," says Lydia with another kiss. "And if you're going to the bar anyway, you may notice that Sergey and Polina just arrived."

"Are you trying to get rid of me?" Ted winks.

"Never," she says, "but time keeps on slippin', and you have a plan."

"It's now or never. I've got this," he says, the end of the sentence rising slightly.

"You've got this," she insists. "You're hot as hell, and you just got ass fucked in public. You're a maniac."

"So true," says Ted. "Would you two mind terribly if I vanished?"

Jenn sees the conflict on Ryan's face, the look he has when he's trying to please everybody. She sees him trying to work out how to not appear selfish while hoping for time with Lydia. Jenn wonders when she should tap out, too. There are, after all, so many things left to do. So much more *noctem* to *carpe*.

"As long as you're not doing it because we showed up," says Ryan.

"Absolutely not," assures Ted, "I've been circling her all week, and time is short." He points toward a striking Eastern European woman climbing into the hot tub. He stands and gives Lydia a soulful kiss, then saunters off in the woman's direction.

Lydia plops on the bed between Ryan and Jenn.

"If you two would like alone time, I can go over—"

Ryan cuts Jenn off. "What?"

She smiles at him. "I don't mind."

His eyes widen as he looks between the two women.

*He thought he was being subtle,* thinks Jenn, smiling.

"Would, uh, would you teach us how to do that?" he asks Lydia.

"The pegging?"

He nods.

Her eyes light up with enthusiasm. "Sure!"

Jenn meets Ryan's eyes. "You really want me to stay?" she asks him.

"If you don't, how will you learn to fuck me like that?"

She smiles, reaching for their go bag and the harness inside.

# 68

# CRISTA

"Have you felt this thing for a while?" asks Allie, out of nowhere, as she transfers another drink from Julio the bartender to Crista.

Crista exhales sharply, not anxious to wander into a trap. "Felt—"

"The bisexuality thing."

"We're having a good time," says Crista pleadingly. The hot tub patio has begun to fill up, and they've been invited to an orgy.

"We are," agrees Allie.

She searches her wife's face for intent, but can't find any warning signs, no narrowing of Allie's eyes, no sharp downturn of the mouth. "So, why would we want to—"

"I'm not starting shit with you," says Allie firmly.

Crista waits, still finding no answers in her wife's face. She takes a long deep breath. "Yes," she admits, "but it was never in the foreground. Rarely even had a form I could understand."

Allie nods and sips her drink.

"And I'll assure you again that I'm not suddenly a three on Kinsey. At most I'm a five. And I think you could probably still round up to six."

Allie puts her hand on Crista's. "I want to understand. I will keep my own prejudices as in check as I possibly can."

The word "prejudices" pings Crista. As much as she has felt

boxed in and categorized by her wife's expectations, she's not felt prejudice from her. "I think it may be more baggage, than prejudice," she suggests.

"I withdraw the word," says Allie. "*Baggage* might serve nicely. I have not, traditionally, had good luck or experiences with people who consider themselves bisexual. In a relationship way, I mean. I've had great fun, obviously."

"Nor have I," admits Crista. "In a relationship way." The time she'd spent identifying as bisexual was confusing no matter which direction she pointed, and dating other bisexuals seemed to increase the drama quotient exponentially. *No wonder people don't think we have it figured out*, she thought at the time.

"Do you think you'd want to have a relationship with a man?" Her wife asks the question flatly, without any malice, but it still causes crawling panic in Crista's chest.

"What?"

"I'm asking, because I feel like I've been on the outside of your thought process—"

The panic takes the wheel. "I don't know myself! I don't share stuff before I've figured it out."

Allie's hand moves to her shoulder. "*Mi amor*," she says, her voice calm and quiet, soothing. "We can talk about that later. Right now, I'm just trying to process with you."

"I," begins Crista. She stops and looks at her drink. "I need to feel like sharing is a safe space."

"I understand."

"And I'm not putting this all on you. My lack of sharing has made space unsafe for you."

Allie gives a slight nod and a long blink as a reply.

Crista feels a wave of guilt climb atop the anxiety in her chest. Of course, she's made space unsafe for her wife, with this thing building inside her, informing her behavior for as long as it's been growing. Those confused yearnings had defined their environment, their relationship. All of it built on foundations which may not have been as sturdy as they both thought. "I will try to be better at sharing," she says between breaths.

"I will try to be better at hearing," says Allie. Her hand is warm on Crista's shoulder. A slight squeeze helps reduce the crawling anxiety.

Crista reaches up and puts her hand atop her wife's. She considers the question. Her last relationship with a man seems so distant now, and Michael had definitely not understood her sexuality. No major surprise, that so many of her relationship issues have come down to that same question. Can she say she's ever really understood it herself?

"I don't want another relationship," says Crista. "I want you."

"I want you, too," says Allie. "For all of it. The reason I ask questions like that is because you can tell me what you like, what turns you on. Even if I can't do it for you, it's still educational. Don't forget the reason we opened up. Why we wanted to fuck other people. Because we realize we can't meet all of each other's needs."

Crista nods. "Right."

"Having a bio-cock is definitely something I can't do."

The pressure in her chest resumes, and she knows her voice is defensive. "I'm not saying that's what—"

"*Mi amor.*" The squeeze on her shoulder tightens again for a moment, and Allie has her attention back. "I get turned on by you being turned on. How will I know if it'll work with guys unless I ask you questions?"

"Right," says Crista, feeling the pressure subside ever so slightly again.

"I'm trying, right now," says Allie, her voice tighter than before. "I'm working hard to be okay and understanding, and I'd very much like it if you made that leap with me."

Crista looks into her wife's eyes. There's still hurt in them, isn't there? Guilt overwhelms the anxiety. "I know you are," she assures Allie. "And I know I'm not helping."

"Will you come with me?"

"Where?

"Let's go watch the orgy, and you can tell me what turns you on..."

"Oh, I—" says Crista, feeling the powder keg in front of her.

"If you do this with me, I promise that I will take everything in and will not make you feel sorry for a single thing you tell me."

Crista breathes. If it sounds like a trap and it feels like a trap, then it must be a trap, right? This isn't a new one, either.

"Tell me what you want to do with a woman," more than one boyfriend had said before then turning it into, "Threesome or nothing."

People haven't been kind when she's really opened up. With Allie, it's been mostly smooth, so many of their turn-ons are mutual. This one, though, dick that isn't made of silicone, seems like—

"This will show me you're trying," says Allie in a whisper, "and will show you that I am, too."

"Could be bad, though," says Crista.

"Couldn't everything?"

"Well, that logic is sort of—"

"Could also be good," Allie says. Her smile is weary, and Crista feels her own weariness respond. "At some point, we have to take risks. Like swinging. Like flagrantly getting gay married."

"Okay," says Crista, louder than she intended. "But you can't accuse me of lying if I don't get turned on by dick over there."

A man across the bar glances up, his hands full of espresso martinis. He cocks his head.

Allie smiles. "That may be one of the strangest things you've ever shouted at me at a bar. C'mon." She stands and reaches out her hand.

Crista allows herself to be drawn toward the orgy. As they near the beds, the splendid sounds rise. Moans, kisses, slapping of thighs on thighs. She looks across the panorama, stopping on Paige and her husband, writhing in rhythm with Malcolm and Alexis.

"The strawberry-blonde," says Allie in her ear, "turned out to be both of our types, didn't she?"

Crista nods. She feels Allie's arms encircling her from behind. As she watches the foursome, her wife begins to play with her nipples. The left one pops up immediately, unlike its shyer counterpart. "Alexis," she says over the sound of an ecstatic exhalation, "is also very sexy."

"I wholeheartedly agree."

Knowing the experimental nature of this game, Crista turns her attention to the men in the foursome. "The men," she begins, then thinks a while. She looks from one to the others, from Bruce, to Malcolm, to Ryan off to the side. She scrunches her lips in frustration. "It's not the men."

"What do you mean?"

"I like that," she says, pointing to Paige riding Malcolm. As Paige lifts her body into the air, Crista sees the bit that makes her quiver. "Look at the point where his dick is like a tether, holding them together."

It is especially apparent with this pairing, the man's dark dick sliding in and out of Paige's milky pale body, pink vulva velveted with red curls. Her red curls meeting his course black waves. Crista feels the lust and yearning deep inside, the wetness between her legs.

"Okay," says Allie, "I can understand that."

"Yeah?"

"Yeah," she says, "I get a similar feeling seeing a dildo slide inside."

Crista turns toward her wife and wraps her arms around her, lying her head on Allie's shoulder. Allie's arms encircle her.

"Do you want to do it?" asks Allie.

"Do what?"

"Look down and see that dick, or any dick, slide into you? See that tether closer than as a third-party participant."

Crista forces herself to really consider it. Maybe Bruce, who she likes; or Ryan? She's seen both of their dicks and has been able to appreciate them. They're both attractive men in different ways. Does she want that? Them on top of her, her on top of them, that umbilical connection. "No," she says after a long moment. "No, I don't think I do."

"Okay," says Allie.

"I might in the future," Crista says, holding tight, not wanting to see her wife's face yet.

"I know," says Allie. "Just...tell me, okay?"

Crista nods into her neck, smelling the faintest whiff of perfume. She kisses her neck, then her ear, then her cheek. Then her lips.

"Want to go play?" Allie asks her.

She nods.

"Ourselves? Or with the group?"

"What would you like?" asks Crista.

"Why don't we play with the group," says Allie. "I can fuck you at home."

Crista's jaw drops, and she pulls back. The smile on her wife's face is devilish, and Allie chases it with a wink. Crista feels the warmth and wetness between her legs build and she gives her own wicked smile. "Well, what if I want to fuck you right now *in front of* the group?"

"I'm a yes for that." Allie pokes her. "And I brought your dick." She reaches down into the bag beneath her, pulling out Crista's favorite dildo. It's shorter than most of theirs, stout and wrapped in a rainbow pattern, a Pride gift from a couple years back.

"Will you suck it?" asks Crista.

"Strap it on, *mi amor,* and you can put it anywhere you'd like."

Crista obliges with glee.

# 69

# RYAN

"How do you feel about rimming?" asks Lydia.

"I feel good," replies Jenn.

Both women look at Ryan from their position between his legs at the end of the bed. He nods and smiles his feelings about rimming toward them.

"Then let's start there," says Lydia.

His wife's tongue circles his anus. His eyelids flutter. In the haze, he looks from the top of his wife's head, partially obscured by his growing cock, up to Lydia. Their eyes connect and she winks. Ryan feels heat within him. From his position on his back, he can see the broad expanse of stars above him. In the periphery, bodies undulate on the clustered beds. The heat in his chest and stomach is amplified as a spasm rocks its way through his abdomen, a wild shake thanks to an exceptionally dexterous swoop of Jenn's tongue. "Wow," he says.

"Yeah?" she asks from between his legs, without looking up.

His cock grows ever more turgid.

"We're looking good up here," says Lydia to her protege, noting the growing erection.

The tattooed woman kneels on the mattress next to him and leans over his face. "We're going to have some fun," she tells him.

He nods and feels the warmth again, unconnected to the rim job below. He follows Lydia as she lays on her stomach next to him, her head near his thighs and Jenn, her feet up past his face.

She props up her chin on her folded arms, leaning over to peer between his legs.

"Shall we try fingers?" asks Lydia in a sing-song tone.

The rimming stops and his wife laughs. She pokes up between his legs like a prairie dog. He nods.

"It's all about eye contact at the beginning," says Lydia, pointing from Jenn's eyes with her two fingers to Ryan's. "This way, you can see if it's too fast, or too hard, or just watch him go mental."

Jenn's grin widens, and for a moment the women lock eyes, smiling broadly at each other. Looking down at them, Ryan's warmth intensifies. He's not sure quite what he's feeling. Seeing Lydia and Jenn together makes him feel good, certainly, but ever since he'd seen Lydia holding court the other day, he's felt a tug.

"Can I touch you?" Lydia asks, and Ryan is about to reply when he realizes the question was for Jenn. When Jenn realizes it, a blush crawls across her nose and cheeks as she nods.

Lydia puts her hand on Jenn's shoulder and begins to talk his wife through hand motions and lube selection. Jenn nods studiously, playing the role of the novice well. They've done ass play before. Rimming before. Some fingers before, too, but mostly Ryan doing the inserting into Jenn. He wonders if he should be paying closer attention to this lesson, and hones his focus.

"And remember, the prostate is our goal here," says Lydia. "This isn't about arbitrarily pounding. Well, it may be about arbitrarily pounding for *us*, but not for him. So, I guess you have to decide if this is a for-him night or a for-you night. The prostate is just barely inside, and feels pretty much the exact same as the G-spot, which is sorta—"

"Like a squishy walnut," says the student. "I'm familiar."

"Yes!" exclaims Lydia. "Oh my God! Squishy walnut." She presses the back of her hand to her mouth to stifle a laugh.

"I've got hours of G-spot time," says Jenn with gesture toward Paige across the patio. She turns and winks at Ryan, then places a very light kiss on his still squishy erection. He laughs at the mixture of sweetness and naughtiness.

"Primo! She's a lucky girl!"

Jenn blushes again, looks down, then shakes it off. "What's next?"

Lydia cups one of his butt cheeks, pulling it to the side. "Slow and steady."

Jenn nods and vanishes below. She traces her tongue around a final time before swapping for a finger, which traces its own circles once, twice, and then presses at the doorway. Ryan feels the pressure build until her slippery finger slides slowly inside.

His body tenses and then releases as he expels a gasp.

"Too quick?" she asks, popping up between his legs again.

Ryan looks down the length of his body at her and smiles reassuringly. "All good," he tells her. He breathes in through his nose, out through his mouth, as his body begins to relax. Lydia puts her hand on his pubic bone, sliding her fingers around in the hair, adding light pressure.

"Good for more?"

He nods, breathing, as his wife inserts a second finger. He feels the pressure in his belly and below. A third finger joins, and the pressure builds. "I feel like I need to pee," he says without thinking, then rolls his eyes. "Sorry."

"No need for sorry," says Lydia. "That means it's working! Carry on!" she tells Jenn.

"Oh," he says, "good." He closes his eyes and lets himself feel it all. The pressure, the sensation, the need to pee. He wraps it all together as his wife's fingers slide, not really in and out, but back and forth ever so slightly. He wonders if he'll be able to take the whole dildo, the one Jenn usually uses with new playmates. It's not very thick and is longer than many they have. It's the girth that matters here, right? Time dilates, and slowly the pressure reduces as fingers slide back out. He opens his eyes again to see Jenn kneeling between his legs. Lydia has craned her head around to watch the fingering. Jenn's eyes are fixed on him. When they connect, she smiles. He smiles back.

*How are you?* she mouths.

*Good,* he mouths back. "Great," he corrects himself, aloud.

"You ready for the next phase, Ryan?" asks Lydia.

Is he? The sensation is intense. The fullness, the pressure, the need to pee. Will it become too much when that orange dildo slides inside him? What if she can't get all the way in? What if it hurts? What if— "Yes," he says. "Ready."

"Can I help you...equip?" asks Lydia giddily.

"Sure!" says Jenn with a grin.

Ryan watches as Lydia helps Jenn into her black nylon

harness, tightening the straps, tugging at it. Jenn produces the orange dildo, and the two women manipulate it through the O-ring until it pokes out, nearly ready. Lydia holds up a finger, then pulls a condom out of her small shaving kit bag, opening it with a flourish. Then she pops the tan circle into her mouth before sliding down onto Jenn's dildo.

"Oh!" says Jenn, looking back at Ryan, wide-eyed.

He watches this intense woman fellate his wife's cock in preparation for him. In preparation to fuck him. An anticipatory shiver runs through him.

Lydia pulls back, the cock exiting her mouth with a surprisingly loud pop. She keeps her attention on it while reaching blindly for the lube. Ryan nudges the clear bottle toward her hand. Two squirts of the thick gel lube, and she begins to stroke the dildo. Slowly, twisting first one, then both hands together and opposite.

Jenn titters wildly, her arousal clearly peaking. "You're great at that."

"Yeah?" asks Lydia. "Do you mind if I assist here, too?" She moves one of her hands to hover above Ryan's half-erect cock.

"Yes." He nods. "You can, I mean."

Lydia doesn't hesitate and grabs his cock. He feels a spasm and an immediate hardening as she strokes without loosening her grip. It's the hardest he's ever been stroked, and he can't believe how good it feels.

"Are you ready?" Jenn asks, squeezing his knee. Their eyes meet again, hers filled with enthusiasm. He nods. She looks down between her legs and grips the orange dildo. Then he can't see it anymore, but he feels it, cold and wet against him.

*Here we go,* he thinks. Is it pain, or just intensity? The pressure grows and grows. He holds his breath, bears down and, suddenly, the external pressure vanishes, and he feels his insides fill.

"Fuck, that's hot!" says Lydia. She looks back up the bed at him. "How do you feel?"

The intensity ebbs and flows. His eyes are wide, taking in his surroundings in hazy glimpses. The stars trail and he's uncertain if that's the meteor shower, or if he's lost his ability to hold objects steady in his vision. His body swirls with intense pressure and a dull tugging in his abdomen. He feels stretched and full. He could let go, from either end, at any moment. "I'm not sure how I feel," he says to no one in particular, forgetting who asked the question.

"Ted says it's a feeling like no other."

*Like no other. That fits perfectly, and not at all.*

"Is it bad?" worries Jenn. "Your face—"

"No," he says, shaking his head. "No," he repeats. He tries to figure out what to tell her, considers asking what she feels from anal sex. "No," he says instead.

"Good," says Jenn.

Lydia whispers something to her, and her face goes from apprehensive to neutral. She nods and looks down between their legs, at the orange silicone connecting them. She begins to move in and out, just an inch back and forth. The pressure that's building rises and falls with the motion. Lydia squeezes his cock, following Jenn's rhythm.

*Am I fucking myself?* he wonders for an absurd moment. He laughs at his foolishness and covers his face, finding it wet. "Is it raining?"

"You're crying," says Jenn. "Please reassure me it doesn't hurt."

"It's...completely unlike everything," he says. *Crying?* He wonders. *Why would I be—* "And awesome."

"Okay."

Lydia sits up and rotates on the bed. She keeps her grip on him, but can now kiss his cheek. He wonders how Jenn feels about this closeness, how Jenn feels about Lydia in general. He looks to her for some indication.

She mouths *Okay?* again. He gives her a thumbs up. Her worry breaks and she snickers. "Alright then." She smiles warmly at him.

*I love you*, he mouths.

*Ditto*, she responds.

"Can I ride you?" Lydia whispers to him.

"But you don't—"

"I don't *often*."

"If it's okay with—"

"I'm happy to ask her, too."

"Then, yes. Yes, that'd be...awesome."

"Jenn, I'd really like to make out with you and ride his cock while you fuck him."

"I, uh." Jenn blinks at her, then smiles. "Yes."

Lydia produces another condom as if from nowhere and repeats her blowjob trick, sliding it all the way down until he hears the gag. "We're going to use a lot of lube," she tells no one in particular, then squirts him three times. She turns away and swings her leg over. "You guys are so cool," he hears her say to his wife. Then her hand is on him, squeezing him, then warmth and wetness. He hears her sigh the entire way down.

He exhales a long, slow breath. For a moment, the three of them are still. He sees Lydia's pale art-covered back, as she leans forward toward his wife. Jenn looks over her shoulder, then kisses Lydia's shoulder, neck, and ear.

The women kiss, and the machine resumes.

Lydia's riding style is entirely different from his wife's, less vertical bouncing, more rhythmic grinding back and forth. He slides within her, slow, and intense, but doesn't move very far in and out. He watches her tattooed back undulate, and her ass rubs intensely against his thighs.

Jenn ramps back up to speed, using the new excitement as an excuse to thrust harder. The three of them move together and separately, in sync and not. The pressure in his abdomen builds and builds and builds as he holds back. *Don't come too quickly, not this first time!*

"I'm sorry," says Jenn. "My legs— I need to take a break!"

"It's okay," says Ryan. "Really!"

"Dismount slowly," cautions Lydia, slowing her own movements.

He feels the dildo slide from his ass, sending a shudder down his spine as it slips past his prostate, renewing the feeling of needing to pee. Then it pops out, the fullness replaced by a pleasant vacancy. The sudden change sends shudders through his body.

"Holy shit," he says.

"Was it good?" his wife asks, making her way to the side of the bed, orange cock flopping as she walks.

"Yes!"

Lydia takes the momentary lull in the action to rotate halfway while still connected. Ryan's eyes roll at the twisting sensation.

He turns his head toward his wife, standing beside him in her black harness, orange dildo hanging between her legs. She looks uncertain. He knows that look, he's felt it himself. "Worried about intruding?"

She nods, glance at Lydia.

"Want to sit on my face?" he asks, dangling one of her favorite things before her.

"Well, yes, but with all this excitement I might drown you," she tells him as she removes her harness.

"Ooh! Are you a gusher?" asks Lydia

She nods.

"That's so fucking hot!" Lydia grins at Jenn, then at Ryan.

He winks at her as Jenn climbs onto his face, slowly lowering herself down onto his outstretched tongue. He loves the way she tastes. He licks and prods and slides his tongue deep inside her.

Lydia, again facing toward Jenn, resumes her ride, and he knows he won't last long. He grabs both of Jenn's thighs and puts all his effort toward tonguing in the most effective patterns he ever has. First up and down, then circles, then around the interior, then the exterior. Then sucking on that one lip, the one that makes her self-conscious because it sticks out like a tongue, but the one that also, so often—

"Close!" says Jenn, then amends in a panic, "like really close!"

He feels his own build up, and then he's coming, thrusting his thighs off the bed, pushing into Lydia. He feels her elevate herself slightly, controlling the depth of his wild thrusts. He continues his oral efforts, hearing his wife's moans, feeling her thighs clench on either side of his head.

Here she comes.

"I'm coming!" she shouts above him. He tucks his chin to point his nose down and away. The slight adjustment keeps him from drowning as her ejaculation cascades over his face, down his hair, over his shoulders, to the towels covering the mattress below.

He distantly hears Lydia exclaiming, but everything has become detached and hazy as he finishes thrusting.

"Well," says Lydia, after they've collapsed to the bed together, "I can honestly say that I've never done *that* threesome before."

"Thank you!" says Jenn.

"Who're you thanking, gorgeous?" asks Lydia.

"You! For teaching— Well, both of you, of course. Thank you, too, Ryan. But Lydia, for teaching me that!"

"All I did was offer—"

"Don't downplay it," says Jenn.

Lydia nods. "You're welcome."

"I don't mind being an also-ran here," gasps Ryan, still trying to regain control of his breath. "That was one of the most intense things I've ever done. So," he coughs and wipes his face, "so, yeah, awesome. Kudos all around." He kisses his wife. Then Lydia. Then pulls them both together for the always awkward, but excellent nonetheless, three-way-kiss.

"Indeed, intense and amazing," says Lydia. "And as I told you, I generally don't do the whole PIV thing..."

"PI—" Jenn begins.

"Penis in—"

"Vagina, got it."

"Yep," says Lydia. "So, thank you both. Now, if you'll excuse me, I could use some form of liquid replenishment, and I'd like to get eyes on my husband. Can I get either of you anything?"

"I'm good," says Jenn.

"I'm better," says Ryan with a laugh.

"Don't brag," says Jenn, socking him in the arm.

"Then I'll take my leave," says Lydia, first leaning over Ryan to kiss Jenn, then giving him a tender kiss. "But I expect to see both of you again tonight at some point. If not for play or pizza, just to let me know all is well."

"All is," he says.

"We will," says Jenn.

Lydia, the tattooed lady, stands, stretching in the dim light of the patio, colors deep against her skin. She waves and turns on her heels to head toward the bar.

Jenn and Ryan lay arm-in-arm.

"Can we do that more in the future?" asks Ryan

"Me fucking you?"

"Yeah, that was incredible."

She kisses him. "Absolutely!"

"Good," he says, and they both roll on their back to look up at the sky. After a few moments a meteor blazes overhead, streaking yellow behind it, then vanishing into a pinprick.

He squeezes her tight.

# 70

# PAIGE

"The shuttle comes at six," says Alexis, sticking her beautiful lower lip out in a pout.

Paige can't resist and leans forward to kiss it. She kisses both Alexis and Malcolm goodnight, they wave, then the couple shakes Raymond's hand over the hot tub steps and descends the stairs to their room.

"That was worth the wait," says Bruce, his arm slipping around Paige's waist.

"Told you," says Paige. She smiles at her husband and kisses him. "Mind if I have some girl time? When she's done with her current fun, of course." Paige, grinning, points across the patio to Jenn, standing between Ryan's knees in the black nylon harness Paige picked out for her on a whim. She gazes up the petite body to the top, where Jenn is making out with a lovely woman covered in tattoos.

Bruce follows her eyes and smiles, then tilts his head, recognizing the activity. "Is that Ryan?"

Paige nods and bites her lower lip.

"Wow," says Bruce with a laugh. "Didn't know he was into that. When did they arrive up here?"

"You were busy with Miss Alexis."

"That I was," he says. "I'm always happy to give you girl time and space, angel. And as I've been fucked silly—"

"I can vouch for that being the case," she says, squeezing his hanging penis.

"Yes, well, I was thinking of stepping away for a bit anyway. You know, to keep the throngs at bay."

"There are throngs," says Paige, "I've talked to a few of them."

He narrows his eyes at her.

Her expression gives him nothing. What fun would that be? But indeed, several women have asked about her husband throughout the week, and she's overheard, "How about Tom Selleck over there?" more than once.

"Well, throngs or no, I'd like to grab a drink and bask in the evening."

"Bask away, handsome."

A kiss and she returns to the now-empty bed in the center. To her left, Alejandra is riding Crista cowgirl style. Tossing the damp towels aside, Paige puts a new set down and sprawls across the middle bed, lying at an angle so she can look up at the woman doing the riding.

"Hi," says Alejandra.

"Hi," replies Paige with a smile.

"You were fun to watch," says Crista.

"So are you." Paige pulls herself up to her elbows and leans between them. "Kisses?"

They both nod. She kisses Crista below and Alejandra above, then returns to her back on the bed. As she looks up toward the starry sky above her, she focuses on being extra mindful of the world around her. The *umph-umph* music is so quiet it's little more than a vibration. She hears the surf in the distance, waves shushing against the shore. The night birds chatter. All of it intermingling with the moans of ecstasy, the slapping of flesh against flesh, the glorious slurping sounds that accompany so many extraordinary acts of carnality. The sounds of one last evening in paradise.

As she listens, she catches a first streak across a quarter of the sky, then a second. Raymond was right, tonight must be quite the shower. She watches the meteors crisscross the heavens and is content.

"Hey," a voice murmurs.

Paige looks down to her girlfriend at the foot of the bed, leaning against one of the corner posts. The transition between her pale skin and the dark night define the curves of her breasts and hip wonderfully. Her head rests against the beam. She smiles.

Paige returns the smile. "That was hot."

"You saw?"

"I made a point to watch," Paige replies. She lies back on the bed, opening her arms to Jenn, who comes to her embrace. On their backs, Paige turns her gaze back to the sky. Two streaks in quick succession, an exclamation from the hot tub. "The meteor shower is really something."

"It is," agrees Jenn. "And that was a wild experience, over there."

"I'm sure it was," says Paige. "I've only pegged the once. Bruce isn't a big fan."

Jenn turns to her and smiles. "I'm sure Ryan would be up for you doing it with him."

Paige laughs. "I'll have to ask him."

"Are you taking a break?" asks Jenn.

"I was waiting for you."

Jenn's shoulders go up, bashful. "Stop." A wave of embarrassment dusts her cheeks with red. She looks away.

"God, I love you," says Paige.

The blush intensifies.

"How long do you think I could keep you collapsing with embarrassment until you just turn into a tiny ball."

"You could keep me all night," Jenn says with a twisted grin. The smile fades momentarily. "You could keep me forever."

"So," Paige says, leaning her head against Jenn's shoulder, "what would you like to do tonight?"

Jenn smiles slyly. "I dunno."

"See, you say that, but your face tells me an entirely different story."

Jenn begins to kiss Paige's shoulder.

"This is lovely, but just a distraction."

The kiss trails down her breast, and Jenn takes Paige's nipple into her mouth.

"Again," says Paige, "not complaining, but you seem to have something on your mind, and I'd like you to share it with me."

Jenn stops, nipple in mouth, turning her eyes upward toward Paige. Those hungry green eyes, full of, *I want all of you.*

"Fuck," says Paige. "Whatever you want, darling, it's yours."

"I know I said I wanted time with just you..."

"Yes."

"And I do want that," Jenn's voice takes on a reassuring tone.

"Honey, you don't have to convince me of anything," says Paige.

"I kinda just want to be mellow for a little while. Cuddle with you."

"Well," Paige pauses a moment, taking that in, "of course we can cuddle. Be mellow. It doesn't have to be just a non-stop orgy."

The bashfulness returns. "You sure? A cuddle pile isn't lame?"

"I'm certain. Shall we invite other lovely people?"

Jenn flicks her eyes toward the women on the next bed over. Paige turns to look as well. Alejandra has collapsed atop Crista, and both women lie cheek to cheek, looking at them. Their eyes widen as they're caught.

"We weren't eavesdropping," insists Crista.

"Join us?" asks Jenn, grinning.

Alejandra and Crista lock eyes for a moment. A series of facial expressions, minute changes in their eyes and smiles. Then Alejandra disengages and rolls onto the middle mattress. Crista follows.

Paige finds herself in the center, flat on her back, with Jenn on one side, and Alejandra on the other, Crista rounding out the group on the end. Arms and legs meet in the center of the cluster, feet and toes, hands and fingers, entwined. Paige lets the moment elongate, gazing at the sky.

"This is nice," says Jenn.

"It is," Paige admits. To have people in her arms, and not be thinking about what might happen next, who is going to put on the harness, or who gets the top position in the sixty-nine.

They lay together and listen to the night.

They lay together and watch the sky.

"Ooh! There!" shouts Crista, her arm entering their field of view.

From somewhere in the darkness, not so far away, comes the voice of their host, "As we get closer to midnight they'll become even more frequent. The peak is after 1:00."

"Well," says Mia, a very sheer scarf wrapped around her curvy frame, "and here I thought there was an orgy happening."

"My girl wanted to cuddle," says Paige with a smile.

"Well, I'd planned to just stop over and say hi to an orgy, but a cuddle is a different story." Mia smiles back.

"Would you like to spoon me?" asks Jenn.

"I very much would." Mia climbs onto the bed next to them, and the foursome becomes a fivesome. The warmth radiating from their bodies counteracts the chilly evening breeze.

Paige feels content as their breathing seems to synchronize. There is safety, security. When this place hadn't offer her its usual level of safety, she'd become adrift, hadn't she? Scrambling to find something resembling that security, or if not, at least distraction from its absence.

*This is beyond distraction, though,* she thinks. *This is connection.* She turns her head and kisses Jenn's forehead. She holds her lips there and inhales deeply, smelling the scent of Jenn's hair, and the scent of Jenn herself. The sweat of her exertion with Ryan and Lydia, the musky sex, and below it all, the scent of Jenn, her love.

Their cuddle pile grows as Kendra, Madison, and Mädchen join them.

Paige thinks about how lovely it might be to engage with all these women, to drink deeply from their fonts. Time marches on, doesn't it? The hour grows late. But she can't bring herself to disengage. Not now, not yet.

Instead, with her lover, her girlfriend, in her arms, Paige looks up into the sky and watches it fall.

# 71

# ALEJANDRA

lejandra isn't sure how long they all spend cuddling, spooning, watching the sky on the hot tub patio bed. Tucked below Paige's arm, with Crista spooned up behind her, she feels herself fill up with a profound sense of warmth and comfort, maybe even safety.

When she hears the first kiss, somewhere up and to the left of her, she knows the cuddle pile is about to evolve. Time and the real-world tug at her. Their airport shuttle will arrive just before lunch tomorrow to whisk them from this place to the airport, to the plane, to their home, where they'll return to their lives.

Things between Crista and her aren't settled, are they? For now, they've mellowed. When they return home and the harsh city lights of Cincinnati are upon them, what will they make of bi-curious Crista, their relationship? Alejandra hopes she can continue to be supportive, the way she'd want to be supported.

The way she wishes her mother had been.

It's all that, isn't it? Just sliding up or down a scale, a continuum, a Möbius strip, where the end is the beginning is the end is the beginning, all sides being one. All sides being equal.

Alejandra laughs. *It's fucking late.*

"What's funny?" asks Crista, a whisper in her ear.

"Pondering myself into a quagmire," she tells her wife.

"Well," says Crista, "don't do that."

"I'll try not to."

Alejandra glances above her head and sees that the kissing is spreading. To let go, to be drawn into this mass of bodies, could be glorious. Her exhaustion, both mental and physical, has begun to catch up, though, and she excuses herself to the restroom, sliding down the mattress from the group. Crista holds her hand as she slides until the tether cannot be sustained any longer.

She looks at her reflection in the mirror. Her skin tone has deepened this week, nicely browning thanks to her heritage, while her poor wife's skin has begun to lobster. Her hair, which had been flouncy curls just a week ago, is straight.

*This is the end of the party,* she thinks. *We don't have to go home, but we can't stay here.*

She drifts out of the restroom to the bar, leaning against the dry side.

"*¡Hola! ¿Qué puedo traerte de beber?*" asks Julio.

"Tequila," says Alejandra. She sees that the cuddle pile has transformed into an undulating mass of bodies. Just making out for now, but soon the orgy will resume. Alejandra wonders if Crista will be sad if she leaves, if her wife will feel pressured to leave as well. She knocks back the shot of tequila and looks across the bar. The hot tub is hopping, and she sees people she's encountered or just missed all week. A few wave at her. She smiles, noticing Raymond silent in the corner, his head back on the side of the tub, staring at the sky with a broad smile on his face.

"Hey."

She turns to see her wife, elbow on the bar. Beyond her, the orgy has begun in earnest, fingers disappearing, the kissing drifting beyond head and neck. A tug inside tries to convince her to ignore the exhaustion, to stick around, explore this.

"You okay?"

She nods to Crista, feeling the haze of fatigue descending. "Yeah," she tells her, "just tired."

"Can I get you anything?" Crista asks.

"No, *mi amor*," says Alejandra. "But I think I may need to tap out tonight, as much fun as that looks." She points with her glass.

Crista looks back over her shoulder, nods, and then turns back. "C'mon, Allie," she says.

"No, I really am too tired."

"I know," her wife says. "Let's go back to the room."

Alejandra searches Crista's face for warning signs that this will lead to conflict. All she can see in those pale eyes is calm and content. "Are you sure?"

"Yeah," says Crista. She walks away toward the cubbies against the wall and returns with their robes. She hangs one over a nearby wicker chair, and holds the other out, open. Alejandra slips her arms in, and Crista pulls it over her shoulders, smoothing it with her hands, then planting a light kiss on the back of Alejandra's neck.

She turns to face her wife, looking deep into Crista's face, still seeing only calm. "I really don't want to pull you away from all this, if this is what you want," Alejandra says.

"Will you stop?" asks Crista. "I want to go with you. If you're tired, I want to take you home. Though I may stop and get a pizza on the way."

"That sounds fantastic," says Alejandra. Her stomach rumbles. She looks around at the people on the bed, in the hot tub. Almost everybody she knows is leaving this place tomorrow. So many of them are here right now. She feels the pressure of it welling up. "I don't want to say goodbye."

"To this place?"

"To all of it."

"I know," says Crista. "We'll see a lot of them tomorrow, I'm sure. Mornings are longer than they seem."

"I worry tomorrow's will seem frightfully short. But if I start to say goodbye..." Emotion swells in Alejandra, as she watches Paige and Jenn kiss tenderly in the sea of lust.

"I know," says Crista. "Tonight, let's ghost."

Alejandra frowns. "Really?"

"Wave as we go by," she says, grabbing Alejandra's hand.

They do wave as they pass, to the beds on the left and the hot tub on the right. Most in the orgy are too occupied to notice, but Paige extends a hand and a smile. From the hot tub waves the young redhead with the pixie cut, and Bruce stops as he climbs down the ladder into the water to blow them a kiss. Then they're on the stairs, heading down.

"So empty," says Crista, as they walk the paths between buildings.

"People are packing, or fucking, or sleeping," says Alejandra. Crista nods.

The courtyard bar is also sparsely attended. Alejandra recognizes only one couple, Zoë and Kohl. They exchange waves across the bar.

While they wait for their pizza, Alejandra and Crista sit on the wicker furniture in the center of the courtyard. Abstract Aphrodite looms over them, back-lit by pink and purple floodlights on either end of the lobby's roof.

"It was hot, fucking you in front of everybody," says Crista.

"It was," agrees Alejandra. "Thank you for offering."

"I do want it, you know," says Crista. "Sex with you."

Alejandra looks at her and sees that Crista's placid expression has faltered. "I know," she says.

"The impulse is just small. Not with you, with everybody. Like a very faint radio signal. It's easy to drown out, to be distracted from it."

Alejandra nods.

"A sexy time, like one of our swing dates, or a play party, or this place...puts an amplifier on it. It's harder to be distracted from it. Like a beacon."

Watching Crista looking around the courtyard, looking anywhere but back at her, Alejandra feels the smallest bit of understanding. "I imagine you want to hold onto that feeling when it happens, not let it get waylaid by another conflict."

Without looking back, Crista tilts her head from side to side, then nods.

"I'm sorry if I've made you feel you can't be yourself. It's never been my intention."

"I'm sorry if I've made you feel undesired, or somehow un...considered."

They smile at each other, the exhausted but loving smiles of a long-term relationship. Alejandra reaches across the expanse between the chairs and takes her wife's hand.

"I'll try," says Crista.

"So will I," says Alejandra.

"*¡Señoritas!*" calls Gabriella from the bar, holding up their fresh pizza.

In their room, in their bed, with Mexican sugar cane Coke from their fridge, the pizza tastes like heaven.

# 72

# RAYMOND

"I can offer a cigar or company, if you're interested in either," says Bruce, sidling up to the end of the bean-shaped hot tub where Raymond is relaxing, head upturned to the heavens. Bruce waggles a cigar.

Raymond laughs and nods. "I'll take both, in fact. But we should move to the smoking area posthaste." He points to two empty lounge chairs in the far corner of the patio.

"Indeed," says Bruce. "You make the move, I'll get drinks. What's your pleasure?"

"Ask Julio for something with banana in it, and tell him it's for me."

"Something with banana." Bruce heads off toward the bar.

The crowd in the tub has grown sparser. Raymond dips to his shoulders below the waterline before climbing out. He shuffles into his plush brown robe and picks the lounge chair closest to the thick plexiglass barrier at the edge of the roof, overlooking the pool and restaurants below. From here he can see nearly the entire sky, from the forests and jungle to the east, all the way out to the ocean. Aphrodite's has been very accommodating of his meteor shower hopes, dimming the lights across the resort ever so slightly and turning off the blinding LED rope lighting around the hot tub. All the lights can't be turned off, of course, that'd be unsafe. But this gentle muffling of the resort's light pollution has made for a truly spectacular evening show.

Bruce returns in his own robe with two tumblers.

"What've we got?"

"Rum runner," says Bruce.

"That'll do," says Raymond. He takes one of the two cigars from Bruce's outstretched hand, then runs it under his nose, enjoying the sweet scent of tobacco, mixed with undertones of something. Whiskey? Scotch? He looks at the end and sees Bruce has pre-cut it. He smiles. "Looks like you thought of everything."

"I try," says Bruce.

Raymond pops the cigar into his mouth and leans into Bruce's lighter. He takes a long pull, tasting the tobacco. It's no cheapo, which he supposes shouldn't surprise him from Bruce, but he hadn't anticipated the sheer complexity of it. "Thank you," he says, lifting the rum runner toward Bruce, who clacks it with his own. "Have you had an enjoyable time?" he asks after the two men lounge in silence for a while.

"I have," says Bruce, "despite certain..."

"Foolishness," suggests Raymond.

Bruce nods.

Two blazing lights cross the sky above them, and Raymond takes another puff of the cigar.

"You've been scarce," says Bruce, "these last couple days."

"Lots to do," says Raymond. He's not sure why he's keeping it so close to the vest. Maybe he just doesn't want to ruin anyone's last night. He coughs and holds his hand out toward the tub. "We've arrived at the point of exhaustion, haven't we? So few people up here, and it's not even 1:00 yet."

"This is the end," Bruce says and chuckles to himself. "Beautiful friend,"

Raymond chuckles back. "The end."

"Time to collapse."

"Indeed," says Raymond. "The ritual espresso martinis at breakfast to counteract the four or fewer hours of sleep thanks to espresso martinis the night prior, accompanied by all the vigorous emotional and physical activity. It's unsustainable."

"I'll crash at home," says Bruce. "Seems a shame to waste time here." He pauses and takes a long drag on his cigar. "Think I've wasted enough of this trip."

Raymond shrugs and tilts his head this way and that. "I believe I've done the same," he says. He stares at the sky a while, thinking about how much he wishes Debra were here tonight. On all trips previous, she always managed to outlast everybody on the final night. One year she made it to dawn. "Debra," he says.

Bruce looks over.

"Debra died, the other night."

Bruce holds his gaze, face filling with empathy. "That's a damned shame. She was an awesome woman. I know how much she meant to you."

All Raymond can do is nod to keep the tears from falling anew.

"To Debra," Bruce says, again offering his tumbler.

Clacks for Debra. His nodding doesn't stop. Clacks for Debra. Nods for Debra. She should be here.

"I'm thinking of shoving two of these in my suitcase," says Bruce, examining the lapel of his robe, "in case it takes us a while to get back here."

Raymond coughs a laugh. "Yeah?"

"How nice it'd be to wear as I march around the house."

"It is," says Raymond. "I've snuck five out myself."

Bruce's grin widens, enhanced by his mustache, until it seems to outstretch his face. "Five," he says.

"Over the years. Multiple girlfriends. Don't want to leave anyone out. You know how it is."

"I do," says Bruce. "Paige has absconded with a full set of the cappuccino dishes."

"Well, aren't we the most obnoxious petty criminals?"

"It would seem we are," says Bruce. "Is James okay?"

Raymond nods. "I'm sure he was putting on a brave face, as he's gotta get home and... Jesus, customs. But honestly, he seemed to take it better than I did. She was sick. She wanted to be here."

"Boy, do I understand that."

"This place really isn't like anywhere else, is it?" Raymond turns to Bruce, the seriousness of the question on his face. "I mean I tell people endlessly about the magic you feel when you step onto this resort. That it's transformative. That it's...*other*. Some of that's hype, right? 'Cuz I'm running a trip. But the rest..."

"I've never been anywhere like it," says Bruce. "Hedonism, Caliente, Couple's Retreat. I've been to them, and they can be fun. But, nothing like this. It's the only place in the world that I think about going back to while I'm on the plane ride home. Not a hint of vacation fatigue."

"None," agrees Raymond.

"So, yeah," says Bruce, "I think *transformative* is pretty apt."

Raymond smiles. He feels his heart lurch as a fireball meteor shoots across the horizon. "Holy shit!"

There is a lull of silence on the patio, then a burst of chatter. "Whoa." "Didja see that?"

"Big one," says Bruce. "Did you find this week transformative?" he asks after a while.

"I think so," says Raymond. "I tend to just do the same thing over and over. Projects, talks, trips, girlfriends. I need to actively work against that habit."

"No Xanadu XI?" asks Bruce, pronouncing the numerals as letters.

Raymond shrugs. "I don't know. Luis and I planned to sit down this week to hash out the details. After Debra died, I just couldn't."

"Well, just so you know, Paige and I have continued to join you on this trip every time because it is, and always has been, transformative for us. And if you do it again next year, we'll be here if it is within our power."

"Thanks, man. That means a lot."

Bruce nods and puffs his cigar.

"I may need a reboot," says Raymond. "Press the button, black the screen, start fresh."

"There's no shame in that," says Bruce. "You're in the unfortunate position of living your life very publicly. I imagine it's easy to continue down an ever-narrowing path."

Raymond nods, thinking about the times where his calendar has filled with speaking gigs, coaching sessions, and these trips. Since Colleen left, he's taken no clients, scheduled no gigs. For the first time in years, maybe a decade or more, his January and February aren't already booked in November.

"You're a good man," says Bruce, "no matter how see yourself. We know it. Debra knew it."

The apple returns to Raymond's throat and his cheeks grow damp. "Thanks," he says. He takes a deep breath and clears his throat. "You sort out your stuff?"

Bruce nods. "As much as can be sorted without talking to her.

She hasn't called the resort again. My phone is dead in the safe. I can tell you I don't look forward to powering it back up tomorrow."

"Never forget what people meant to you when they were at their best, when your relationship is at its worst."

"Good advice," he says.

"Oh, it's not advice. I was quoting someone. Don't remember who," Raymond says with a laugh. "There are people we have in our lives because we need them here," he holds his hand to his chest. "Some we keep because we desire them here, others are here by default, like our obnoxious family members. And then there are some who have worn out their welcome, but inertia keeps them here. Fear of letting go keeps them here. Stasis. It's always admirable to attempt to put others' feelings first. Sometimes, though, we need to take care of ourselves, and our loves, the ones we keep because we desire them in our lives. As for the ones who have long since worn out their welcome..." he trails off, then shrugs toward Bruce. "Some choices are easy, some aren't."

Bruce nods and turns his eyes back to the sky.

"Thanks for the cigar," Raymond says with a smile.

"My pleasure," says Bruce.

One final clack for Debra, for Xanadu, for the whole damned thing.

# PART IX

*Saturday*

# 73

# ALEJANDRA

Tingles. Softness. Warmth.

Alejandra stirs in the darkness, then lets the sensations envelop her.

Warmth. Wetness.

From her.

From another.

A shudder. A moan. From somewhere. From her. Alejandra realizes that the moan came from within her. Another shudder. Tingles.

Softness. Warmth.

A dream? One of those that sometimes cause her to wake with the sheets around her drenched in sweat and sex? No, in the dark room it continues.

Is she still asleep?

Her left-hand hits the pillow next to her, finding it empty.

"Fuuuck..." escapes her lips as a spasm courses through her.

The warmth, the wetness.

She reaches and finds her wife. Crista's face is buried between her legs. Now Alejandra can discern details, the motion of her wife's tongue as it slides between and around the folds of her vulva.

*This is new*, she thinks.

Her hazy memory cannot recall a single time when this has happened, despite her hints and vague suggestion throughout their years together. But it's unfair to think of that now, here, today, with Crista munching like her life depends on—

Crista's tongue slides deep into her, and she feels the G-spot rumble, a sleeping behemoth awakening. After tracing several circles inside, the tongue moves back out, duplicating the circling around her clit.

She feels her wife's chin on her pubic bone and looks down. There, in the dim light, Crista smiles up at her. "Good morning," she says.

Alejandra can't help but laugh as she repeats the salutation.

"I hope this is okay," says Crista, a momentary flash of worry.

"Holy shit, my love," says Alejandra, losing her train of thought as her wife's hot breath blows through her trim pubic hair and up onto her belly. "*Mi amor*," she murmurs.

"I'm going to take that as a good thing," says Crista.

"Good. Yes."

"Would you like me to continue?"

Alejandra lies her head back on the pillow, nodding as she bites her lip in anticipation. "Use your fingers, too?"

"*Sí, Señora.*"

She hears her wife sucking on her own fingers, and the faintest of gags. She's about to ask if Crista is okay when she feels those two fingers plunge inside her. It's nearly enough by itself to bring her to climax, but she holds the lid down, hoping to ride this one a little bit longer. She feels a turn, and her wife gestures "come here" with her hand, directly against the roof of her vagina, as her G-spot comes fully online. "Jesus."

Then Crista is sucking on her clit and running circles with her tongue, from sucking to circles to sucking to circles, all while index and middle fingers press against her G-spot. Rubbing, pressing, in and out, sucking and circles.

"Coming!" announces Alejandra. She grabs at Crista's head, struggling to find purchase in her hair, trying to be conscious about not grinding her pelvis into her lovely face. She bucks and Crista doesn't stop sucking and circling, fingering, in and out, rubbing and pressing and sucking and circles.

Bucking and coming and bucking and coming until the tension leaves her body all at once, and she collapses in a heap on the bed, feeling as though she's soaked the sheets through. Sweat on her forehead, momentary loss of focus – she might not be able to come in a train like some of the other women here, one after another after another, but her orgasms are shock and awe. She giggles at the comparison of her orgasm to flag-waving chest-beating nonsense.

"I hope the laughing is good."

"It is excellent, I promise." Alejandra covers her mouth to stifle the last of the laughter, then reaches out her arms toward her wife, still kneeling between her legs. "Come to me."

Crista leaps into Alejandra's embrace. For a moment, as their nipples touch and dance together, a final shudder of orgasm rocks through Alejandra's body, and then it's finished. She kisses her wife's forehead, then her cheek, tasting herself only a little until she moves to her lips. Then the musky, salty sweetness is there and all around. She licks Crista's lips clean.

"That was," says Alejandra, struggling to form words, "unexpected."

"And good?" asks Crista, again with a touch of concern.

"Amazing," says Alejandra. "Amazing and wonderful and orgasmic, of course."

"Good."

"What brought that on?"

"I woke up and you looked delicious." Crista smiles.

The straight-forward flat delivery of the words amuses Alejandra. "Well, I'm quite happy you helped yourself to me. Can I do anything for you?"

"I'm good," says Crista, resting her head on Alejandra's chest, nuzzling against her breast. They lie there, breathing together for a while. "I don't want to go home, Allie." She can hear the pout in her wife's voice.

Home. Where problems live. Where life lives. Work. Alejandra sighs. "I don't want to either."

"You're still a citizen, right?"

"I was never a Mexican citizen." Alejandra laughs. "Don't be racist."

"We could pretend," says Crista, looking up at her with the wide, child-like eyes. "We could pretend and stay. Work on the beach."

"If only we could," she says. "But, you know, we could come back."

"Yeah," says Crista. "That'd also be good."

They lie in silence, drifting, ebbing and flowing through sleep, until the light of the day begins to brighten the room.

When they drag themselves from the bed to assemble the scattered contents of their personal belongings, it's a slog that they honor by behaving like drones.

"Packing is awful," says Alejandra.

"Let's just leave it all here," says Crista.

"Even your dick?" Alejandra points at Crista's favorite dildo.

"Well, no."

"How about we go to breakfast, then do the rest of this with a full stomach."

Crista nods, with endearing enthusiasm.

At breakfast, Alejandra watches her wife eat, hardly touching her own food. She sees everything in Crista here, everything that triggered her first attraction. The imperfections and awkwardness, the mousy outward presentation. All the things that Crista sees as liabilities. She should tell her, shouldn't she? Let her know that they're not? How do you say, "I'm attracted to your awkward," when the person you're saying it to is intensely self-conscious about her awkwardness?

"What?" asks Crista.

"Nothing," says Alejandra. "Just looking at you."

Crista laughs nervously. "Okay."

"Did I ever tell you I was attracted to you before you came up to me?"

The fork hangs in the air before Crista's mouth. Big green eyes blink. "No," she says, imbuing the syllable with intense incredulity.

"When you accepted your award," Alejandra says, recalling the moment she first laid eyes on her wife, standing at the podium, in that too-large banquet room for a too-small throng of reporters and journalists and honored guests.

Crista stood at the podium in a dress that clearly was far more elegant than anything she'd ever worn before. She didn't know how to hold herself in that dress, to stand in those heels. At that moment, Alejandra knew she was a zip-up hoodie woman, who'd throw the hood up over her head to vanish within it. She probably would've happily traded the bra-induced cleavage framed by the scoop neck of that dress for an over-washed t-shirt. Her thank-you speech was all stammering, pauses, scanning the room with big eyes. The content of it, though, took Alejandra's breath away.

"You said such beautiful things, and didn't seem comfortable being the one to say them."

"I'm not a speaker," says Crista, finally finishing the mouthful of waffle on her fork.

"You weren't like the rest of them. Or the pretty men who always flank me, demanding the attention they think they deserve. Or the pretty women who can't bring themselves to ask the question. You took a deep breath, knocked back several drinks, mustered up your courage, and approached me and just asked."

Crista exhales sharply, and a smile appears.

"People almost never actually ask. Even in all your glorious, tragic, beautiful, incredible awkwardness, you did the thing." Alejandra's eyelids flutter as she recalls the rest of the evening, feeling a twinge between her legs again. "And you munched like a champ."

A flash of redness crosses Crista's pale cheeks. "Well, thank you. Happy I'm still able to live up to that first time."

"Live up? Oh, no, *mi amor*, this morning you exceeded." Alejandra leans over and kisses the flush as another mouthful of waffle vanishes. "And I want you to know, those things that you worry about the most, the ones you think will make me stop loving you?"

Crista's eyes glisten and she stops chewing.

Alejandra knows her wife is running through her list of catastrophic flaws. She reaches out and holds Crista's hand on the table. "Those things I love even more."

Crista swallows.

"If you need to explore with men..." Alejandra begins, hesitating. "Please just tell me. Don't sneak around and do it behind my back until you announce you're no longer interested in being a lesb— Interested in me, and moving back to monogamy and heteronormativity."

"Neither of those things are in my wheelhouse."

"Nor mine," says Alejandra.

"I will talk," promises Crista.

"I will listen," promises Alejandra.

# 74

# JENN

"You're up," says Jenn, when Ryan rounds the corner to sit on the beach bed next to her. The waves lap calmly at the beach.

"I am," he says with a smile.

"I didn't want to wake you," she tells him.

"Eh," he says, "I couldn't sleep."

"Me neither." Jenn turns her face back to the water. She sits on the edge of the bed on a towel, feet dangling over the sand. The Cancún sun makes her skin glisten.

"Not lying down?" he asks.

"Not our bed anymore," she says. "I don't want the rightful owners to get upset that I'm using it."

Ryan nods and looks down at his feet. "Nice to be naked just a little bit longer, though."

"It is," she says. "I think I'm going to wander around the house naked more often when we get home."

"Heating bill be damned," he says with a laugh. "Can I join you?"

"Of course," she says and slides to one side of the white towel.

Ryan hops up next to her. "Apprehensive?" he asks after a long silence.

She nods. "Apprehensive doesn't begin to cover it."

"We'll do what we need to," he says.

She nods again. They've always done what they need to; their finances have never been as secure as those of their friends. "What if I can't get another job?"

"Of course you'll get another job," he says, waving the suggestion away as if it were an errant gnat. "The Westin can't morality clause you out of all future employment."

She nods, thinking of the photo, the paper atop it to protect Lenny's sensibilities, to prevent his embarrassment. Grace may as well have just had it blown up on a poster board. **Exhibit A: Naked pictures from a swinging website.**

"Someone else could find the photos," she says.

"Let's not tell Beck about your next job," he says. "And maybe make sure she's blocked on social media."

"Yeah." She looks down at her feet. Her red-painted toenails have chipped and lost their luster, as Paige had warned they would in the hot tub. They'd almost survived the week. "And if I want to try something different?"

"Work-wise?" he asks.

"Life-wise."

Ryan looks out at the water. "Hoping I get to be a part of it."

"Of course," she says with a smile. "I mean life, profession, purpose-wise."

"Ah."

The line of tasks in front of her seems so vast. First, get a new job. Then save some money back up to replace what they've been using. Then figure out her life. How can that be a step? *Figure out what to do with my life.* Jesus. "And, if I decide to go back to school, where would the money come from?"

Ryan reaches over to take her hand. "It might not be easy. But we've been through hard. We probably shouldn't look all the way down the list of to-dos, though, because that's when it gets stressful."

"It's stressful already!"

"Well, yes," he concedes, "but that's where it gets 'we're all going to die' stressful."

She laughs despite herself.

"Remember that thing Dr. Petrillo told us?"

She looks at him. That thing? Their couple's therapist had told them so many things, including the barely functional mantra, "Today is the day we change our lives," that had brought them to swinging in the first place. "What thing?"

"Action items," he says. "When life can be boiled down to action items, it's less stressful. You can't get a job, or go back to school, or anything like that here, right?"

She stares at him, feeling the pressure in her chest.

"I mean, first, you're naked."

The pressure lessens as she laughs, covering her mouth.

"So, it's not helpful to worry about it. Because it's literally almost impossible to do anything about that right now."

"Right."

"And while I know the stress is making your throat close up when I tell you that, because mine closes up when I try this, we need to focus on our next action items."

"It is closing up," she agrees with him, then holds her hand in a choking gesture over her throat. "But I get it. You're right."

"I think our next action item is probably: finish packing."

She slumps with a sigh. Packing leads to leaving. "When I was little and went on family vacations, I'd refuse to pack at the end. That way we didn't have to go home."

"Did it ever work?"

"That's beside the point."

"Hey, Lamberts."

They look up and see Vince and Kendra coming across the beach.

"You're wearing clothes," says Jenn, finding it hard to hide her distaste for the concept.

"Our shuttle's coming in fifteen," says Vince.

"Man," says Ryan.

They stand around for a moment, saying nothing. Jenn wonders what there is to say. *You guys are cool and all, but you shouldn't have come with expectations that we didn't talk about in advance, and we're sorry if that ruined your vacation but it's not our fault?* She says nothing.

"Sorry, we didn't..." Ryan begins and trails off, squinting.

"Nah," says Vince, waving it away.

Kendra nods and smiles. "While I'll say it might have been nice if you'd just told us you weren't interested—"

"I didn't—" Ryan tries.

"We were grumpy for a while," she says, "then went to the bar and met Beth and Andy."

Jenn remembers the couple from speed dating, and from a few moments around the resort. She nods.

"They seemed cool," says Ryan.

"They *are* cool," says Vince, just the mildest edge of defensiveness in his voice.

"And we had our first full swap," says Kendra, her smile untinged with resentment or defensiveness.

Jenn doesn't see a, *So there*, or *Your loss*, in it, either. She smiles. "How was it?"

"Pretty great," says Vince. "And they're local-ish. They live in Valparaiso."

"Indiana," says Kendra.

"That's awesome, guys," Ryan says, his voice much calmer and smoother.

"So, are we all cool?" asks Kendra.

"Yeah," says Ryan. "We are. You?"

She nods. "Maybe we could do dinner in a couple weeks."

"Let us know," says Jenn.

"Well, anyway," says Vince. "Time to head through the doors."

After wishing Vince and Kendra de Martolos safe travels, and exchanging hugs and kisses (notably on cheeks instead of lips), Jenn and Ryan sit alone again on the bed.

"I'm glad things worked out for them," she says.

"Yeah, I was worried I ruined their trip," he replies. "And also self-conscious that thinking that made me really vain."

She laughs. "It's possible we overthink things," she tells her husband.

"It's certainly possible."

They hold hands.

"If we hurry through packing we can still go to the grill and get fajitas one last time," Ryan suggests.

"And drinks."

"Well, of course, drinks." He smiles at her, then leans over and kisses her.

The light kiss lingers and deepens, involving tongues, then hands. She feels her pulse quicken, her legs trembling, a steady throb between her legs. "I want to fuck you," she whispers to him.

He looks at her for a moment, his expression hanging like a loading screen on a laptop, then spits in his hand and wakes up his cock.

"We won't need much," she says, "because the juices are flowing." She swings around and climbs into his lap, reaching between them and feeling his cock still hardening. She presses it toward her (no, too far left), then again (need more lube for *that*), and then one last time, sliding down onto him.

His lips part with a gasp. She grins.

"You know we're not supposed to be doing this," he says.

"What're they going to do," she asks, "kick us out?"

"Well, that or call the *federales*."

"Then we'll have to be quick," she tells him and begins to bounce. She bounces faster than she ever has, reaching out to him the way Paige taught her, that little squeeze that can stop her pee, feeling it latch around his cock as she goes. Not more than a couple minutes before his breath quickens in that way she knows so well. "Uh huh! Don't be a hero. Let it go."

He laughs. "Stop being encouraging! I'll come when I'm good and—" and there it is, he spasms, "Ugnhn!" and their arms tighten around each other.

She feels it inside, hitting the walls and then beginning to dribble out. "There we go," she says, putting her chin on his shoulder and running her nails down the nape of his neck. "One for the road." She leans back and kisses him. "Thank you."

"My pleasure," he pants.

*"¡Traviesos!"*

Jenn looks to the bar and sees Celia leaning on the wooden side beam, chin on her folded arms, grin on her face. "Naughty, naughty!"

"Sorry!" Jenn says, hiding her face.

*"No problema,"* says Celia.

Jenn and Ryan giggle into each other's shoulders.

"Time to pack, I think," says Ryan after the giggle-fit subsides.

"I think so," Jenn reluctantly agrees.

They slowly separate and head for their room.

# 75

# CRISTA

"It's like the last day of camp," Crista tells Allie, wiping away a tear and planting a quick kiss on her wife's cheek. "I think I need to do a few laps."

"I get it," says Allie.

The few minutes they've been at the courtyard bar have already yielded an overwhelming stream of goodbye hugs and kisses, dramatically amplifying her anxiety.

"Don't run away," says Allie with a wink.

"I won't."

Crista heads back in the direction of their room, so she can make the winding loop around. As she reaches the break in the trees and finds the cobblestone path, she passes Tomás in his khaki uniform, pushing a gold-toned luggage cart. There on the cart are her bags and Allie's. She watches them pass wistfully with a quiet, "*Hola,*" to Tomás in exchange for his.

They'd finished their packing efficiently and quickly, with some time to spare. Their shuttle isn't the next one but the one after, and should be arriving within the next forty minutes or so. She stops in the shade of the trees to wipe the sweat from her brow.

*It's because of these long sleeves, long pants. You're wearing clothes, Crista!*

She nods and pulls off her shirt, then kicks off her shoes and drops her jeans. She takes a moment to feel the breeze now, chilly from her evaporating sweat, perfect. She looks back down at her simple mismatched panties and bra, function over form. She hadn't meant them for general consumption when she grabbed them off the packing pile twenty minutes before.

Unclasped and dropped.

Somehow this feels so much better, so much more *right* to stand here naked, even in shoes. Has it only been a week since she held that door handle, afraid to let go and be naked outside. A week since she wrapped her sarong around her waist so as not to be so exposed. Exposed now, she folds the jeans and slides them into the shirt, cramming the panties and bra in as well, then tucks the package under her arm. Soon she'll need them again.

But not yet. Not yet.

She reaches the tall wooden fence marking the end of the resort property and heads toward the sound of the waves. Soon her feet hit sand. "Shoes off now," she says, wishing she'd brought her Xanadu tote bag along. She removes the purple Chucks and lets her toes play in the sand a final time.

The beds are mostly deserted. Turnover probably doesn't really get started around here until afternoon.

She stops at Celia's bar.

"You leave today?" asks Celia.

"Soon," says Crista.

"Oh, sad. But you come back soon."

"I hope so." Crista smiles, wondering how she'd do on the beach, day after day, surrounded by naked people. "Does it ever get boring?" she asks.

"Boring?"

"The naked people, the drinks?"

"Oh, no. I love it," says Celia. "I bartend down the beach before. Everybody was always angry. Yelling at their *niños*...children. Here, people are happy."

"Yeah," says Crista.

"Here people talk to each other. And to me."

She thinks about all the vacations she's had in her life. How often did she ever talk to anyone she wasn't traveling with? As a journalist, she spoke with the locals on assignment, but when traveling for leisure, even if she didn't specifically want to get away from people, she still defaulted to isolation. Her parents had, too. The insular family.

"Vanilla people don't talk to each other," agrees Crista.

"No reason," says Celia. "Here, there's reason."

"Sex."

"Connection," says Celia.

Crista smiles and nods. Most people don't seek connection on vacation. They're leaving all but their most vital connections at home, after all. "Thank you for a wonderful week," she tells Celia, slipping her a twenty from the pocket of her folded jeans.

"*¡Hasta luego!*" says Celia.

Crista walks on, waving as she leaves. At the end of the beach, she stops with her feet in the water. She faces the ocean and breathes the salty air, taking in every bit of it. A handsome man in a white polo wipes down the catamaran. He waves at her. She waves back.

"Goodbye, ocean," she says and turns back toward the resort. She steps up the stairs to the pool deck and puts her shoes back on.

"Beautiful Creesta!" calls a voice with an Eastern European lilt. She turns and sees Sergey and Polina in all their naked glory on two lounge chairs.

Crista waves and makes her way over, winding and meandering between chairs.

"Sit," offers Sergey, as they both sit up in their chairs to provide space.

Crista sits on the end of Polina's chair.

"We're so happy you came by!" Polina says.

"Sorry I haven't been more around since our night," says Crista, feeling a weight lifting as she says it, acknowledging that she's avoided them, whatever the reason.

"It's okay," says Polina, touching Crista's leg. "We know you're popular."

A laugh escapes Crista's mouth, one that speaks volumes about the way she feels about herself. She doesn't think these two particularly notice, though. "Well," she says, and isn't sure how to finish it.

"You were the highlight of our trip," says Sergey.

"Really?" asks Crista, then cautions herself to tone down the deprecation, or they might think she hadn't had fun with them. And that wasn't why she'd been avoiding them.

"Oh, yes," says Polina, "I enjoyed very much."

"You were first woman Polina used her dick with," says Sergey.

Crista blinks surprise. "Really?"

"I bought it just before trip. To hopefully use with beautiful woman." Polina grins, then looks away bashfully.

"You didn't seem like a first-timer!"

"No?" asks Polina.

"No," confirms Crista, "you rocked that cock."

Polina blushes fiercely. Crista leans forward and plants a kiss on her beautiful face. The blush intensifies.

"I have to get back," says Crista. "Allie will be wondering what's keeping me."

"Of course," says Sergey, "thank you."

She nods. "It was my pleasure." She stands to walk away, then stops and turns. She needs to settle the nagging doubt, and who knows if she'll ever see these two again. "Sergey?"

"Yes."

"You and I didn't..."

He waits, listening intently.

"Have sex?"

His expression changes to bewilderment in a flash so quickly it surprises her. "No," he says, almost stammering. "You say you only play with women. I enjoy watching you and Polina."

She feels her entire body unclench in palpable relief. "Good," she says, "that's something I would've wanted to remember." She throws Sergey and Polina what she hopes is a mischievous wink and walks away.

Returning to the courtyard, she thinks about that glib sentence, meant to smooth things over with Sergey. But it's true, if she does play with another dick, she wants to remember it. Her tension wasn't so much that she was afraid she'd had sex with a man, it was more the panic of having done something she absolutely couldn't remember. A full blackout.

"Your clothes fall off?" asks Allie when she returns to the bar.

"Until the last minute," she tells her wife. "Every. Last. Minute."

Allie laughs and kisses her.

"You could join me," says Crista. "Be topless until they call us."

"They already did. I'm supposed to bring you in to check out when you return." Allie smirks, then sadly points toward the sliding glass lobby doors.

"Bummer," says Crista.

"But I do like to look at you naked," says Allie.

Crista smiles, opting to take the compliment rather than question it. "When we go home..." she says, feeling the need to make a declaration here, something profound, to make up for the week, for the stuff with Sergey and Polina, to somehow walk some of it back.

"Yeah?"

"I'm going to really try," she says, but that doesn't feel like enough.

"I know," says Allie. "You've said. I've said. We're both going to work on it all."

"Yeah," says Crista. "I know. I just." She looks around the courtyard, where people are still saying teary goodbyes, hugs and kisses and varying levels of nudity.

*Say something profound, something worthwhile.*

"I don't want to say goodbye to you," says Crista. "I'm not certain about a lot. Clearly, my sexuality is one of those uncertain things."

"Clearly," says Allie. She winks.

"But I'm certain about you. I'm certain that I never want to be giving you a last hug. Or a final goodbye."

"We all have to give a final goodbye," says Allie.

"Really?" Crista shakes her head at her wife. "I'm being sincere, and you're going morbid?"

"I'm the pundit, I deal in dark realities. You're the bunny gal."

Crista laughs. "Bunny *mysteries*! It's not all sunshine and carrots!"

Allie opens her arms, enveloping Crista. Crista feels her breasts beneath the softness of her shirt and an unexpected, but very welcome, stirring rumbles through her.

"I don't want to say goodbye to you either," says Allie, "and I'll do everything I can to not have to."

They kiss, a long one, the kind of kiss that occasionally makes them nervous in public in the "real world." Out there, you never really know what type of people are near. You never really know the climate of hate. Here, though, they can give themselves over.

"I should probably put my clothes back on," says Crista with a sigh.

"Unfortunately, you probably should," agrees Allie.

Crista looks down at her makeshift clothes carrier, pulls out the bra and panties, and begins the transformation of herself back into a woman ready for some of what awaits them back in the real world.

She feels a bit readier for the roughness outside.

# 76

# PAIGE

"I usually ghost," Paige tells Alejandra at the courtyard bar.

"Me too," says Alejandra.

"Hence your escape last night?" Paige presses her finger teasingly to Alejandra's breastbone through her Cincinnati Zoo t-shirt.

"Hence our escape."

"Ugh," says Paige, after scanning the courtyard. "I can't take the weeping masses."

"You don't weep?" asks Alejandra slyly.

"I do, but dignified, and at home. In bed." Paige traces a line down her own cheek with her finger. "Single tear."

"I see it." Alejandra sips her brown drink, making whiskey face.

Paige must admit that she'll miss that face. And that body. "Where is your lovely?" she asks.

"Crista's taking a final walk around," says Alejandra.

"Yeah," says Paige. "I know that walk. Bruce and I used to book the earliest flight out in the morning. Home in time to see our boys, spend some catch-up time with them. And we don't—" *Oh fuck, here it comes.* She puts her hand to her cheek and laughs when it comes away wet.

Alejandra offers a napkin, and Paige snatches it with a grimace. "Listen," says Alejandra.

"You're going to make it worse," Paige says. She knows something is coming, something profound. Hadn't she come down here, looking for Alejandra, to say something profound herself?

"I just want to say our boating day..."

Paige nods.

"Meant a lot." Alejandra reaches out and puts her hand on Paige's knee.

Paige looks at it for a moment, then covers it with her own. "To me, too," she says, "and after. Your help, the gang—" Her words catch. "Will."

"Yeah." Alejandra nods. "Now we can resume being superficial, to keep the feels at bay."

Paige smiles. She sniffs deeply, pulling it all back. "Tequila."

"Tequila?"

Paige waves over Andres, the afternoon bartender. "*Quatro tequilas, por favor.*"

"*Sí.*"

"Excellent accent," says Alejandra.

"We're each going to do a shot for the time we spent together, and a shot for the time we'll spend in the future." Paige smiles and wipes her nose with the back of her hand.

"Sounds excellent," says Alejandra. "Chicago isn't that far from Cincinnati, after all."

"Not far at all," agrees Paige.

Andres sets four small plastic glasses down, each with a finger of golden liquid.

"*Muchas gracias,*" says Alejandra.

Paige lifts her glass and Alejandra mirrors her. "To the past," says Paige with a drink.

"*Y al futuro,*" says Alejandra as they knock back the second.

"A last kiss?" asks Paige, leaning forward.

"Are you sure you're not a romantic?"

Paige shrugs.

Alejandra leans forward and presses her lips against Paige's, running her nails over Paige's shoulders and down her back, sending shivers through her. The kiss expands and consumes the courtyard, blocking out the sobbing, kissing, hugging throngs. When the kiss ends, the vacuum it leaves is audible.

Paige stands. "Before Niagara Falls, I'll away."

Alejandra nods, narrowing her eyes.

"Please tell beautiful Crista that it was a pleasure to meet her, and that I and Jenn, and Ryan and Bruce of course—"

"Of course."

"Await your visit to our fair city."

"You have my number," says Alejandra.

"You have mine," says Paige.

They share another last kiss, and Paige ghosts from the courtyard. She stops at a cross path and puts her hand on her face. *This is silly,* she thinks. "Maybe this is what getting older looks like," she tells one of the raccoons as it skitters through the foliage. "Falling to pieces over someone you just met."

"The coatis don't talk back, which make them good listeners." Paige turns and sees Luis, walkie talkie in one hand, clipboard in the other. He smiles at her. *"Buenas dias, Señorita* Paige."

*"Buenos dias,* Luis." She beams at him, wanting to strangle him in a squeezing hug. He'd been doing his job, of course, the night he grabbed Will and pulled him out of the room. That didn't change the fact that he did it. "Thank you," she says. His face grows solemn, and she can see that he recognizes that she is thanking him for more than the usual. Still, she feels she should clarify, let him understand why she feels so strongly. "For the other night," she says. "Upstairs."

"Of course," he tells her, holding up his hand, palm toward her. He smiles and says, *"Cabrón,"* under his breath. "He will not be welcome here again. My promise to you." He presses a fist to his chest.

"Can I give you a hug?" she asks. "A huge one."

He opens his big arms and surrounds her. The fresh scent of his uniform linens is comforting. "You and your husband...all is well?"

She nods. *"Sí."*

*"Muy bien."*

She gives Luis one more hug and waves goodbye as he shuffles off down the path. She takes the opposite crossroad, heading back toward the beach, toward the pool, toward their room and their balcony, where they can wait out the goodbyes.

"Paige!"

She turns to see a luggage cart flanked by a skinny young woman in yoga pants and a PINK shirt. It takes her a moment to resolve the figure. "Madison," she says, walking toward the young woman. "It's hard to recognize people with clothes on."

"You're not leaving today?"

"Today, yes," says Paige, "but later."

"Thank you for including me last night," says Madison.

"My pleasure," Paige insists.

"It's been strange, this week. A lot of people assumed I was like that asshole because I came here with him." Madison looks down, picking at her index fingernail with her thumbnail.

"Luis just called him a *cabrón*," says Paige with a half-smile. When Madison looks blank, she clarifies. "Motherfucker."

"Yeah, well. You and your friends were the only ones who didn't lump me in with him and treated me like a person, not just the hot-piece-of-snatch unicorn."

"You are a lovely young woman," says Paige, putting her hand on Madison's arm. "Without causing you to look at me like a motherly figure, can I just tell you that you deserve to be treated so much better?"

"Oh," says Madison, "I know. At least he stayed down after the water."

Paige cocks her head at the comment.

When Madison notices, she grows antsy. "They don't filter the hose water," she says, "and he's not an observant man."

"Wait," says Paige.

"I'm running so late! I need to catch my shuttle! Thank you, again. Truly!" Madison plants a kiss on Paige's cheek and bounds off after Tomás and her luggage cart.

"I think Madison poisoned Will," Paige tells Bruce when she returns to the chair next to him on their balcony.

He drops his tablet from his face and turns to her, one eyebrow raised, mouth drawn back in a smirk. "Do go on."

Paige smiles and shrugs. "Maybe not."

Bruce stares for a moment longer, then returns to his ebook. "Good thing she did," he says. "*If* she did, of course."

"It's only an alleged poisoning," clarifies Paige.

"Yes, alleged." He sets his tablet on the table.

Paige finds her gaze drawn to his lap, where his dormant penis pokes out of his coarse pubic hair. "Mr. Shepard, would you like a blowjob?"

His eyebrow goes up again as Paige moves toward him. "I'd rather eat your beautiful cunt."

The word sends its own shivers through Paige, and she feels a trickle down her leg. "*Unf!* How about both?"

Bruce wraps his arms around her and lifts her to his shoulder, throwing her over. She squeals as he turns her.

"Oh, Jesus," says Paige, feeling disconnected from gravity. She reaches her hand out and grabs the rail of the balcony. Now she's upside down, and her husband dives into her with a surprising ferocity. She wavers but holds the rail. She reaches up to grab another bar, and when she feels steady, turns her attention to the rising cock before her. She runs her tongue over the hole at the tip and feels him shake. The cock lurches and bounces. "You'd better hold steady," she calls up to him.

His response is lost in her cunt as he increases his intensity. She moans, she gasps, she leans forward and takes him until her lips meet his balls.

Beyond the rails, the ocean laps at the shore.

# 77

# RYAN

Tomás leads the procession, carting their hastily packed bags, with Ryan and Jenn following behind hand-in-hand. Ryan plods, making each step count, taking his time. He tugs at his shirt and the belt on his jeans. His clothing feels odd on him.

Jenn gives him a weak smile. He throws his arm around her and pulls her close. "Paige said they'll be on their patio," she tells him. "She doesn't like goodbyes."

"We're seeing them next week, right?" he asks.

"Yeah," she says, "but still." Her eyes are glassy.

"Go on over," he tells her. "I'll make sure all is good with the luggage."

She looks at him for a moment. In it, he still sees the barest fragment of the woman he knew years ago, the one called Jennifer, the one afraid, restrained and quiet. He pulls her back in and kisses the top of her head.

"It's all going to be okay," he whispers. "Go sit with them. I'll be there soon."

She nods. "Okay." He can't discern whether the shake in her voice is from preparing to leave or the prospect of what awaits them at home.

Jenn peels off when the paths diverge; he heads toward the courtyard, and she toward the beach.

He pulls his phone out of his pocket and checks their departure time again. He's done it three times already: turn on the phone, open the email, check their flight. The text notification at the top is new, though.

**Now you have my number -Lydia.**

He smiles and saves her to his phone.

The night before, after their play time, he'd handed her a napkin from the bar, his name and phone number hastily scrawled.

"What's this?" she asked without looking, but her smile told him she knew.

"My number."

"In case I want to text you after school?"

"For whatever use you see fit."

He holds up the phone and types out his response. **Finally, a place to send all my unsolicited dick pics.** His thumb hovers over the send button. Too much? He takes the gamble.

Her response: **Why would you think I wouldn't solicit them?** Then: **Have you left yet?**

**Bringing my luggage to the lobby,** he says and stumbles as the path becomes a bridge over a tiny trickle of water in search of the ocean. He looks around, but the only person nearby is Tomás, and he's well ahead with the luggage cart.

**What a coincidence, I'll be there soon.**

Ryan smiles. Last night he tried very hard not to be needy, not to overwhelm or lurk. After the cuddle pile formed, he saw Lydia at the bar. They stood next to each other and shared a silence for a while.

"I really enjoyed our time this week," he told her.

"Hell, yeah," she said, giving him a kiss. She ran both hands through her hair, shaking it out and increasing its volume. "Usually when my hair turns into a Muppet, I call it a night."

He nodded. He could ask her to stay just a little bit longer, stay to have another drink, or stay to make out, or stay to talk, or stay to watch the meteor shower. But he didn't.

After a few moments, she nodded and stood. "You're an awesome guy," she told him, leaning forward. She kissed him again, and bit his lower lip, lightly at first, then just enough to make him wince. "I had an exceptional time with you."

The foliage breaks, and he follows Tomás and the luggage into the sunny courtyard, full of more people in more clothing than he's seen all week. He sees people he's chatted with briefly, people he's had more extensive conversations with, or spent sexy time with. A scan of the crowd doesn't reveal Lydia or her husband, and his shoulders droop.

"I will bring these to the front," says Tomás. He checks his watch. "Your shuttle should be in *treinta minutos*."

Ryan nods.

"You will need your wife to check out."

"We'll be there," he says, handing Tomás the last few loose dollars in his possession. The man and their luggage disappear through the sliding glass doors of the lobby.

He drinks it in, hoping to etch this place firmly into his mind. The mirrored windows of the lobby itself. The grass roof on the building, and over the bar. The bizarre shapes of the sculpture in the middle of the courtyard. All these people.

And there, at the end of the bar, is one of those people he ought to talk to. Rory faces away from him, leaning on the bar top, a beer in one hand, his phone in the other. He's dressed simply, in shorts and a polo shirt. Ryan tries to remember where the triad is from, that getting off a plane in November wearing shorts won't be such a big deal.

"Hey," he says.

Rory glances over his shoulder, and his face hardens slightly. "Hi," he says, his voice clipped.

"Can I?" Ryan asks, pointing to the empty seat next to him.

Rory shrugs and nods. "Terrence will be back," he says, turning his attention to the TV in the apex of the bar's roof. There's a weather report playing, featuring a buxom brunette.

"Not really your type," says Ryan with a laugh.

"Vanishing like that isn't cool, man," Rory says.

"I know."

"It's why I probably shouldn't play with guys who haven't done anything before."

Ryan doesn't know how to answer.

"Sometimes the self-loathing is too much."

That he understands. He nods. "It brought up a lot of stuff," says Ryan, "and I didn't really know how to deal with it."

"Could've told me that is all I'm saying," says Rory. "Instead of leaving me to come out of the washroom and find the room empty."

Another nod.

"People don't need to be reminded of their own self-loathing, their shame," says Rory. "When you ditch someone, they wonder what they've done, if they've hurt you. They blame themselves."

"I'm sorry. It was all my stuff. Not you."

Rory purses his lips. "Did you have any fun, at all?"

"I did," says Ryan.

"Just wrapped up in stuff?"

"Lots of stuff." Ryan stares at his fingers on the bar top.

"Look," says Rory, "about being bi. A lot of guys who are cool with everything, who want to feel positive and progressive, try to push themselves into bisexual. Because sexuality is a spectrum and all that. But it's also okay to be straight." He smiles and claps Ryan on the shoulder.

"That can't come up often," says Ryan, laughing softly.

"You'd be surprised how often it *should* come up."

"I wanted to experience something like my wife did," he says, still talking to the bar top.

"When she explored her sexuality?"

"Yeah."

"Wanting it will not make you bi," Rory says. "However, I will give you the caveat that maybe you and I just didn't mesh. It happens. As amazing as I am..." He grins. "It's possible."

Ryan nods and gives him a little smile.

"If you don't want to play with another guy, that's totally cool. And if you do... give yourself permission. Try everything twice, in case you massively fucked up the first time."

"I know," says Ryan. Massively fucked up. "Thank you."

"Don't ever vanish again, though. It's thoroughly, totally, amazingly shitty."

He'd done that, made someone feel thoroughly, totally, amazingly shitty thanks to his selfish actions. "Sorry," he says again, quietly.

Rory purses his lips for a moment. "Accepted."

"Hug and kiss goodbye?" he asks.

"I'll take a hug," says Rory.

They embrace. It's short, with the clap on the back Ryan knows from his vanilla friends at home. They exchange perfunctory pleasantries about safe flights, and then separate. There's little doubt in Ryan's mind that he's unlikely to encounter this man again, and that Rory won't mourn that.

He still doesn't see Lydia in the courtyard, and he feels desperation, now. He looks at his phone. Their shuttle should be here in fifteen minutes. His searching grows more frantic. He takes a deep breath. He'll go get Jenn, and then hopefully Lydia will be here. Yes, that sounds like a plan. He walks at a brisk pace through the winding paths, making a point to take in the sounds, the smells, the distant *umph-umph* of the music.

Climbing the stairs to Bruce and Paige's balcony, he hears talking and laughing. Bruce and Paige are still nude. He smiles to find Jenn has removed her t-shirt and bra.

"Hey, you," says Paige.

"We have to go?" asks Jenn, noticing Ryan's frazzled expression.

"The shuttle will be here very soon, and we still need to check out."

Jenn nods and puts her bra back on.

"Aw," says Paige. "Such a shame to put those away."

"You'll see them Tuesday," says Jenn.

"It's a date," says Paige.

Bruce stands and opens his arms to hug Ryan. Paige steps up next, running her nails up and down the sides of his arms as she kisses him. "Safe trip," she says. "See you at home."

"You, too. See you at home."

He watches as Jenn does the same – kisses, hugs, the lingering kiss with Paige – then pulls her shirt back on as she follows him down the stairs.

"Did you get to say goodbye to Lydia?" asks Jenn.

Ryan frowns. "No," he says. Their pace quickens.

"Do you want to go find her?" Jenn asks.

He sighs. "I don't think there's time." He pulls out his phone, the last message still reads, **I'll be there soon.**

In the courtyard, the sense of loss grows. She's nowhere to be seen, and the clock has run out. He thumbs out one more quick text, thankful for auto-correct. **Checking out. Not enough time.**

At the touch screen on the desk, Marisol puts her hand on Jenn's. "This isn't goodbye. You'll be back before you know it."

They surrender their bracelets. Two snips and they fall to the glass desk, then Marisol sweeps them away before Ryan can think what a great souvenir they would be.

He checks his phone as they step outside, surrounded by luggage and vans. **I'll be there soon.** They identify their bags, watch them get loaded into the van, then climb in themselves.

Ryan's stomach lurches when he sees her. In the back row sits Lydia, head on her husband's shoulder, her hair covered in a baseball cap, tattoos mostly covered by a shirt for a band Ryan doesn't recognize. Jenn pokes at Ryan's back, then peeks around him.

"Why don't you sit next to her," she suggests in a whisper. She pats his back.

He looks back at his wife, smiling a tired smile at him. "You sure?"

"I'm going to put on my headphones and sail away," she says, holding up her noise cancelers. "You should have a few more minutes."

"Thank you," he says, giving his wife a deep kiss.

"I love you," she says.

"I love you," he replies.

He climbs all the way in, seeing a delight in Lydia's eyes when she finds him. "I'm sorry! My phone died! It's off and charging."

"Can I sit here?" he asks.

"Please do," she says.

Jenn puts on her headphones as she sits directly in front of him. He leans forward and plants a kiss on the back of her head. He hears Jenn's "cheer up" playlist – Madonna, Katy Perry, Florence + The Machine – drifting barely audible from her headphones. She reaches her hand back and touches his cheek briefly.

Ryan sits back next to Lydia, this woman who has drawn him in a way he can't explain. She puts her hand on his leg, palm up, fingers slightly curved. He looks at it a moment, then takes her hand.

"I'm happy we met," he says.

"Me too," she says.

The driver shuts the van door and climbs into the front seat. After a moment, they pull forward and away from Aphrodite's Resort and Spa.

*Adiós*, thinks Ryan.

# 78

## BRUCE

**B**ags packed. Clothed. Checked out. Waiting.

The courtyard outside the tinted windows of the lobby still swarms with throngs of people, but the tenor of the crowd has changed. Bruce watches through the window as people rush up to each other, strip off clothing, raise shots to the air, and begin their party. He sits at the tail-end of the exodus, waiting on the small white couch in the lobby, feeling the burst of heat in the air-conditioned chill whenever someone passes through the doors. By now, more people passing out than passing in.

The doors slide open, and in comes his wife, holding two glasses of champagne. "I just took them off his tray. They don't need to know that we're not arriving."

"I think they'd give them to you anyway."

She sits next to him, pressing her body against his, and holds up her glass. "To Aphrodite's."

"I'll drink to that," he says.

He takes a sip of the dry champagne they serve *en masse*, in an entirely different ballpark from the bottles that show up to their suite daily. Quaffable, but far from transcendent. He chuckles at his own stolen pretentiousness.

"Did you look?"

"Hmm?" he asks.

She points at his phone, face-down on the glass-topped table in front of them.

"Oh," he says, "no. But there were a lot of notifications."

The phone came out of the safe this morning, and remained off. It charged while they packed, and remained off. They spent their day on the balcony and ate at the grill for the last time, and the phone sat, face-down, and remained off.

"I thought about just packing it," he told Paige as they watched the luggage be loaded onto the cart.

"You could if you wanted to," she said.

He nodded.

"I know you want to know," she tells him as she finishes her champagne in the lobby. "I do, too. And I'd rather know now, before we're on a plane, before we leave this place...I'd like to leave as much of this situation here as we can."

He agrees and lifts his phone.

"How many?" she asks.

He squints at the notifications. "Looks like fifteen messages. One from our new friends Malcolm and Alexis..."

"Oh, good, I'm glad you exchanged numbers."

"Three from Ryan." He presses the notification, and the messages pop up.

**Safely at the airport.**
**Safely through security.**
**Safely on the plane.**

Bruce laughs. "Sometimes I wonder if he treats his dad like this."

"Aw," says Paige, punching him playfully on the shoulder, "he loves you. And looks up to you!"

Bruce nods. He wonders if he deserves such reverence. Ryan had cut through all the bullshit the other day, after all. "Do you think the two of them got to wring every drop from this trip?"

Paige nods. "And then some."

"Good," he says. He turns back to the phone.

"Are the rest from her?"

He nods and presses the last notification. The screen scrolls, and the cascade of messages from Emily arrives. The first bubble has three.

**Thank you again for the hotel. You saved me!**
**I'm settled and warm. Don't have any of my things,**

**but that's okay. Had to order room service, hope you don't mind.**

**Goodnight, you wonderful man.**

The second bubble

**I don't know what to do. I feel like it's all falling apart.**

**I just jilled, feel better, thought of you.**

**He's calling now. I can't answer.**

**Please text me back.**

**I don't know if I can handle this!**

"If she really needs help," says Paige, reading over his shoulder, trailing off in a way that tells Bruce she's not sure what she's about to say.

He turns to his wife. "We can't," he says. "We're too much on the hook."

Paige nods. They both lean into the phone to read the last set of messages.

**He apologized.**

**Said he only wants me.**

**Headed home.**

"The last message was sent on Thursday," he says.

"Seriously?" asks Paige, an edge of anger in her voice.

Bruce shakes his head and shrugs. "I guess the drama wasn't so—"

"I don't know why I'm surprised," says Paige. "You and I, we're the fools here."

He looks down and swipes to hide the messages. He does feel like a fool. "Such a minor domestic spat that could have its resolution described in three text messages..." He shakes his head.

Paige takes a long, angry breath, staring out of the lobby into the sunshine. "Let's just stay," she tells him, finishing her glass. "Just put it all on a card, stay the extra week. Put it on a cash back card. That's almost worth it, right?"

"We'll be back," he says. "I promise you."

She nods and turns back to him.

"Are we good?" he asks.

She looks from the phone to his eyes and nods. "How about you?" she asks.

"I was never angry at you," he says.

"About her. Are you okay? Are you good?" She looks away, scratching the back of her left hand with her right. "I know how she does it, gets inside, stakes her claim." She turns back, her expression trading anger for worry. "Are you okay?"

He kisses her. "Yes. It was iffy. But yes."

He looks down at his phone and knows that what he needs to do is mostly symbolic, but it's worth doing. He clicks his contacts app and finds Emily, holds his finger on her name in a long press. The options menu pops up.

**Rename - Delete - Block.**

He holds his thumb over the last option. Moments flash through his mind like 8mm film on a screen. "I want to have a relationship with you both," in their kitchen. When they were three. Their kisses. Their sex. Their spats. Watching Paige last year. Watching the wreckage. "A tornado barely notices the farm," he says.

"You don't have to," Paige tells him. "I really do get it."

"Yes, I do. For me." He kisses his wife and taps the screen. When he looks back, there isn't even an empty space where she'd been.

Luis gives them hugs as they walk through the lobby. "See you both very soon," he insists.

"Well, we'll have to, since you decreed it," says Bruce.

"It's beyond us," says Paige.

"I wish you a safe flight."

The second set of sliding doors part to reveal a single shuttle, their bags on the driveway next to it.

They hold hands.

*We are whole.*

Time to go home.

# 79

# RAYMOND

Raymond and Mia sit across the checkout desk from Marisol, where they'd sat just eight days before. Raymond defers to Mia for the guest survey, and she taps the screen, answering questions, quietly reusing the word "Excellent" over and over.

"Tequila?" asks Luis, appearing with a small bottle of Don Julio.

"None for me," says Mia.

"Definitely," says Raymond. He stands to clasp hands with this man he's known for years, since that first moment, on that first trip.

"*Buen trabajo,*" says Luis, handing him a small Aphrodite's-branded shot glass.

"I didn't know they made these," says Raymond, turning it to see the Aphrodite logo. "Thank you."

"They don't," Luis says. "I make them." He taps his calloused finger on the tiny glass. "Laser etching."

"You do laser etching?"

"In my garage," he says with a grin. "Is a hobby. These are for you." Luis holds his glass up, the evening light making the etched logo glimmer against the pale liquid. "There's two more in here," he sets a small shopping bag on Raymond's chair. "Is my gift, to you." He bows slightly. "Will we be talking about next November?" asks Luis.

Raymond nods. Up until this morning, he'd still hesitated, wondering if doing this again, doing Xanadu again, would only be perpetuating the stasis.

At the bar in the courtyard, he waited for his guests to begin coming down for their exits. As difficult as he found goodbyes, he knew the value of them, knew that it was his charge to both welcome and dismiss. On the bar in front of him, his Moleskine notebook sat open, a smattering of scribbles on the page. His attempt to remember the week, write it down before it was gone. Time at Aphrodite's was so ephemeral. He found that so little could be retained without notes, and so, on trips past, he'd ended each day by scribbling in this book. A quick flip through would reveal the time he and Colleen had stumbled into an orgy, the oral sex on the beach at night with the sand fleas, the year that strep throat had spread like wildfire, and of course, the final day of year one when he and Colleen had stayed up until dawn. It had seemed so important to experience the sun rising, flaming light cutting through the fog on the plains of Quintana Roo, casting long shadows on the trees, and bathing them in the warmest of good mornings.

They'd made love against the rail, taking the sun, taking each other.

"Different times," sighs Raymond, flipping between the two pages written so far on this trip. The word Colleen is in this week's notes far too much. Far too much for someone at home. Far too much for an ex. He tore the new pages out of the book and crumpled them, tossing them over the bar into the trashcan. Andres looked up but said nothing.

The new page was blank. On it, he printed, as legibly as he could, **Debra Koonz died, and I already miss her terribly.** He nodded at that, unable to think of anything else as important. If that was all he wrote, though, he wouldn't remember the point. Beneath, he added **Life is for the living.** After a moment, he attributed it. **– Langston Hughes**

"If you listen to this morning's release, you'll be pleased to hear that Xanadu X got great marks from us," said the podcaster, Strom, Eric, sliding into a seat at the bar. Raymond looked down, noting that the young man had left two seats between them.

"In case you want to take a swing at me," Strom said with a feeble grin.

"Why would I take a swing at you?" asked Raymond.

"'Cuz I was a huge ass to you," said Strom.

Raymond laughed. "Isn't that your shtick? Your M.O.?"

"We do get more downloads when we complain," he admitted.

"'I did it all for the ratings, man,'" Raymond said, affecting a voice.

"I've never seen escalation like the other night."

"Oh?"

"At the playroom. The gang bang."

Raymond nodded, feeling another pang of regret he hadn't been there to stop it. "It was that bad?"

Strom shrugged. "I haven't seen much conflict at all, in the lifestyle. None really that isn't…stupid teenager stuff."

"You're lucky," said Raymond.

"I know," said Strom. "Slut shaming usually comes from the outside. Like the Catholics, I mean."

"Well," said Raymond, "I don't think he was one of us anyway. He was a tourist in our world, but not really 'open.'"

Strom seemed to chew over the idea. He knocked on the bar top and turned to leave. "You should listen to this one, though," he said. "Kitten raves. I say good things. Both about the trip, and about you. You're a good host. You're a good man. And you've influenced more people than you think." He knocked once more on the bar top and turned to leave.

Raymond frowned. "Eric," he said.

Eric returned.

"It's obnoxious when someone alters your perfectly fine negative opinion of them."

Eric smirked. "I know."

"Thanks," said Raymond, offering his hand.

"Our pleasure," said Eric. "Do it again next year?"

Raymond had avoided the question for days, putting Luis off with a mention of "considering all angles," corporate and meaningless. Now here it was, and Raymond was amazed that the moment hadn't come sooner. "Yeah," he said. "Xanadu Eleven."

"We'll be here," Eric gave Raymond a wave, and walked away.

In the lobby, Raymond repeats his intent to return next November. Luis smiles wide. "Wonderful," he says. "The staff is so happy to see your group, to host it."

"They're special people," says Raymond.

"Now we drink," says Luis. *"Arriba,"* he holds his glass high.

"*Abajo*," he drops it down low. "*Al centro*," he holds it in front of his chest. "*Pa' dentro*," says Luis and sends the shot down the hatch.

Raymond does likewise.

Luis pulls him into a side hug, clapping his back. "You bring many wonderful people. They're friendly, they're respectful—"

"With certain exceptions," acknowledges Raymond.

Luis nods, growling, "*Cabrón*," under his breath.

"Indeed," says Raymond.

"The assholes of the world do not overshadow the great. And little hills, no matter how steep, cannot overshadow the mountains. Aphrodite's is a mountain. Your wonderful guests are mountains. *You* are a mountain." He taps Raymond's chest and nods.

Raymond nods back, feeling himself well up. Not now. There'll be time enough for crying later.

"*Adiós, mi amigo*," says Luis, "*nos vemos pronto*."

"*Nos vemos pronto*," repeats Raymond.

Luis heads through the back exit of the lobby, clipboard in hand. So much to do, so many new guests.

Raymond returns to the seat next to Mia, who is examining the shot glasses. "These are great," she says.

"So," he begins, clearing his throat to prevent another crack in his voice, "how're we doing here? What's next?"

"Just that," Marisol says, pointing at his wrist.

Raymond looks at it, the cord and faux wood logo of the Aphrodite's bracelet. He'd forgotten he was wearing it, but to lose it now... He nods and holds out his hand.

She smiles at him. "I'm sorry!"

"Can I keep it?" he asks.

"Of course!" she tells him, "I just need to cut."

He feels Mia's hand on his shoulder as he offers his wrist. There's a snip, and the bracelet falls into Marisol's open palm. She hands it over, dangling it between her thumb and index finger.

"Thank you," says Raymond.

He looks back toward the courtyard, at the sliding glass doors that open into paradise. The arrival, the cold lobby after the heat of the shuttle, is all apprehension, anticipation, fear, excitement. Then you step forward and the doors part with a *whoosh*, and you're home.

This place.

Then the doors loom ominously for a week, parting if you get too close. He's always noticed that his guests make a wide berth, as though worried they might get too close, and the doors would swallow them up and take them away.

They are the threshold, the gateway. They are a conduit between two worlds.

For now, he's on this side.

("Did you remember to dress?")

In time he'll be back, be welcomed home to pass through those doors again. When that happens, he hopes he'll feel more mobile. There is already an inkling of it inside. Movement in the right direction. His hope turns to determination. It will happen. "Stasis no more," he tells Mia, who squeezes his hand.

His heart is full of joy.

# ABOUT THE AUTHOR

Cooper S. Beckett is the author of A Life Less Monogamous the first book of *The Swingularity*, and his memoir, My Life on the Swingset: Adventures in Swinging & Polyamory. He co-founded *Life on the Swingset* and hosts its swinging & polyamory podcast. He speaks, coaches, and teaches classes on swinging, polyamory, pegging, play parties, and non-monogamy. He has been a guest expert on Dan Savage's *Savage Lovecast*, and is the announcer for Tristan Taormino's radio show *Sex Out Loud,* is a graphic and web designer, photographer, and voice over artist. He is currently developing a supernatural fiction series.

He lives in Chicago with his wife, constant, and binary star, Ophilia Tesla.

Want short stories, erotica, and essays in your email? Sign up for Cooper's email newsletter today at CooperSBeckett.com/list

*Contact Cooper:*

CooperSBeckett.com
me@coopersbeckett.com

# ALSO BY COOPER S. BECKETT

*Fiction*
A Life Less Monogamous

*Memoir*
My Life on the Swingset:
Adventures in Swinging & Polyamory